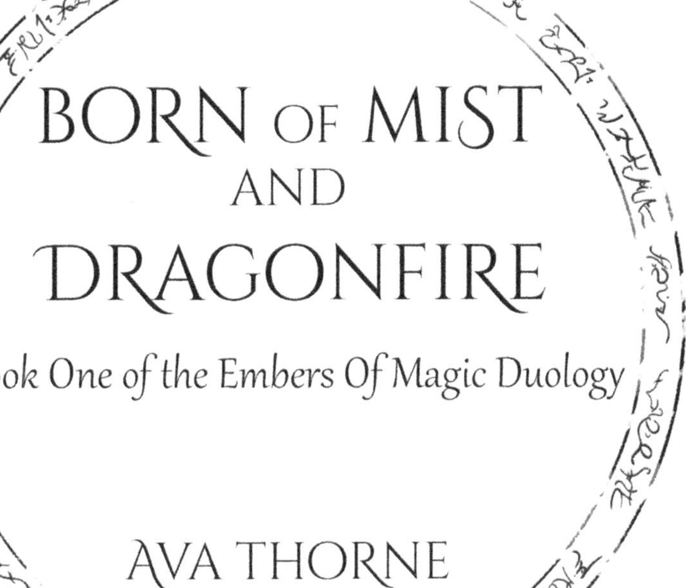

BORN OF MIST AND DRAGONFIRE

Book One of the Embers Of Magic Duology

AVA THORNE

Author: Ava Thorne

Editor: Samantha Swart

Cover Design: Ava Thorne

To all the ladies who fell in love with the brooding, white-haired anime antagonist. This one is for you.

Trigger Warnings

This book contains themes and elements that some may find difficult. These include blood, gore, violence, on-page descriptions of death and killing, torture, cursing, sex with explicit descriptions, and attempted sexual assault. Please read at your own discretion.

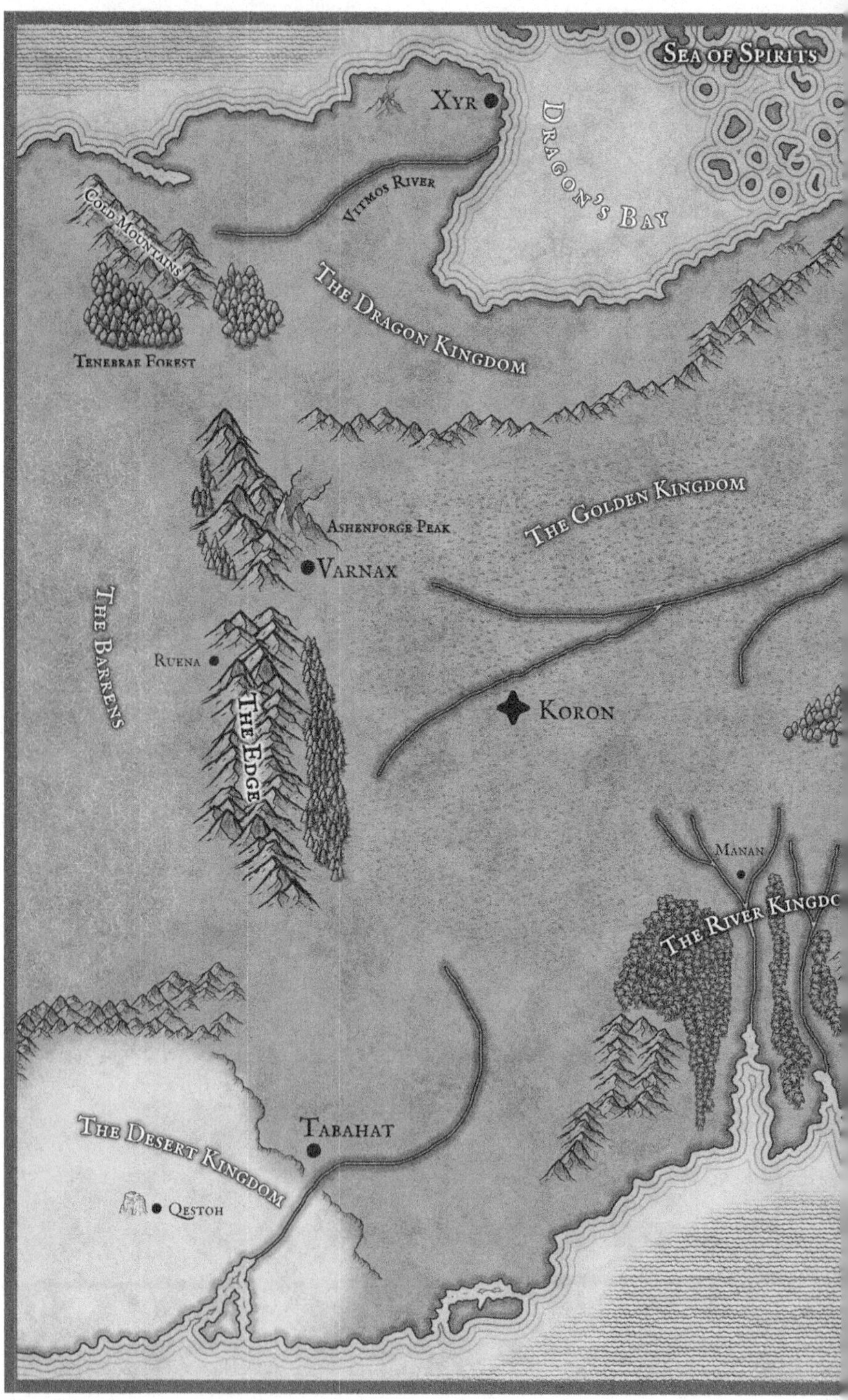

Sea of Spirits
Xyr
Dragon's Bay
Vitmos River
Cold Mountains
Tenebrae Forest
The Dragon Kingdom
The Golden Kingdom
Ashenforge Peak
Varnax
The Barrens
Ruena
The Edge
Koron
Manan
The River Kingdo
The Desert Kingdom
Tabahat
Qestoh

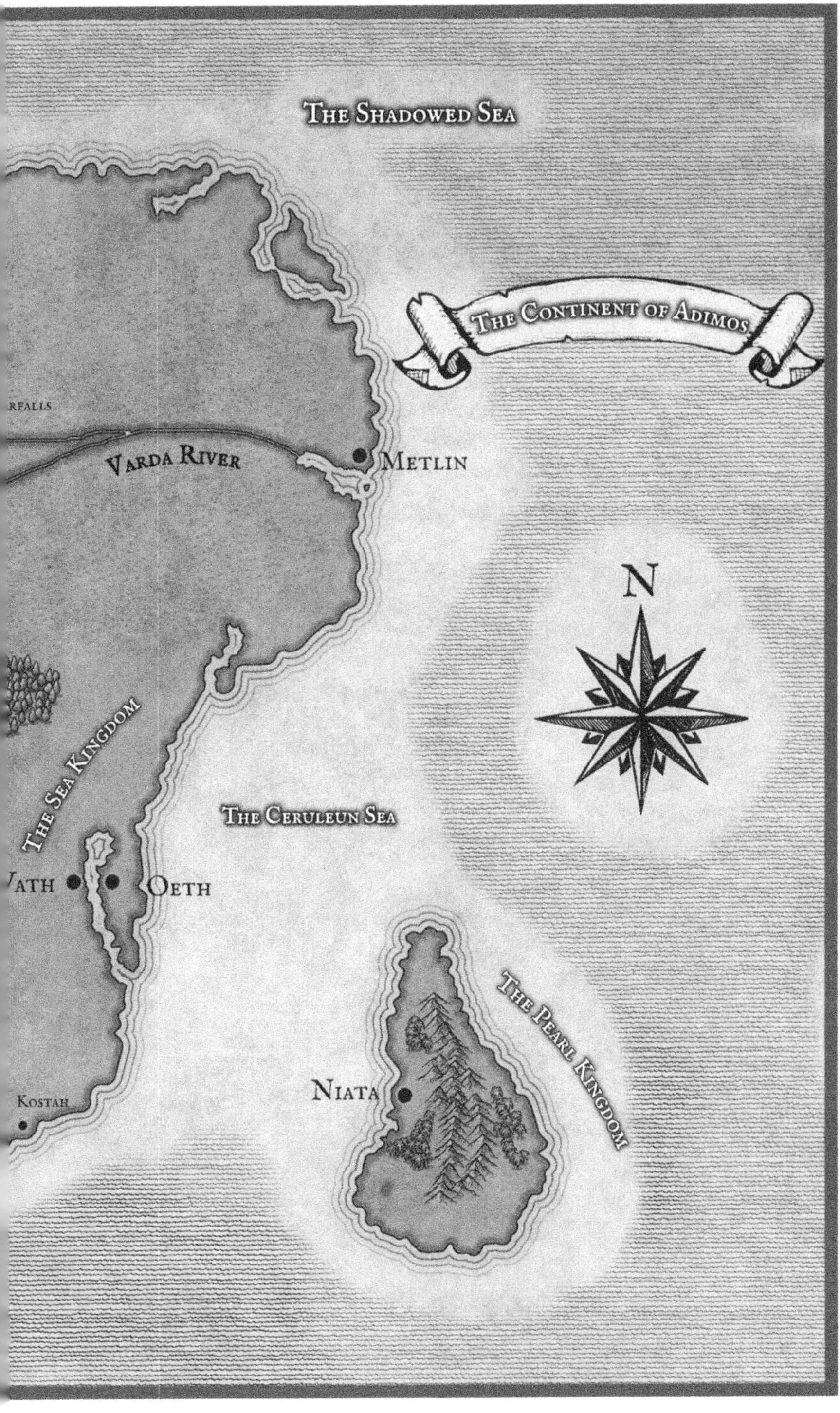

The Shadowed Sea

The Continent of Adimos

rfalls

Varda River

Metlin

N

The Sea Kingdom

The Ceruleun Sea

Vath

Oeth

The Pearl Kingdom

Niata

Kostah

Part 1

The Great Prophecy of the Third Age

In dragonfire is born the World Breaker,
Whose power shall shake the earth and skies.
With magic in its fiery wake, it will take
The life from all that's born to die.

A curse upon the world it brings,
As sorcery and enchantments fade.
The land shall mourn the loss of its mystical things,
As the World Breaker's wrath is laid.

The creatures of magic shall meet their end,
Their spirits shattered, their bodies rent.
No more will they rise or fly,
As the World Breaker's flames touch the sky.

For the world can be saved,
When the World Breaker's power is laid to rest.
But the cost is great, the hero's heart must be brave,
As magic fades from the world's crest.

In dragonfire is born the World Breaker,
Whose power shall bring an end to magic's reign.
But in the hero's hand lies the power to make,
A new world, free from the World Breaker's pain.

Chapter 1

Tori

The sky was shrouded in mist. It was the most I could remember seeing in over two hundred years.

I walked through the palace courtyard, filled with fruit trees and climbing vines that threatened to overcome the white marble walls. It was only due to the arduous work of a small army of gardeners that they were held back. Unlike many other parts of the Pearl Kingdom, where drought and famine seemed to be growing more common, the plants of the palace always seemed to thrive.

My twin brother, Jun, walked with me, unusually silent. He could normally be heard singing. His song varied depending on his mood, but it was always beautiful, like the first sound of rain after a long dry season. I always joked with him that the leaves themselves would turn to listen, but he never seemed to find that very funny.

His silence today spoke more to me than any words could.

"What's wrong?" I asked him. Jun never did well with polite, indirect questions.

He turned to me, and still said nothing. But his eyes were

puffy with harsh circles, and his gaze pained, containing a worry greater than any I could remember. I reached out and grasped his shoulder gently, "Jun, what's wrong?"

He shook his head, "I cannot say sister, but the day feels... wrong. Perhaps it's just the weather?" The mist had been unusual, but I hadn't given it much thought. Jun always gave these things too much attention.

"Are you worried about the petitions today? I can go in your place." He finally broke into a smile then.

"Don't act like you are doing me some big favor, sister. I know you love holding court, and you know I hate it. If I have an excuse to be gone, Father won't be able to find a reason to deny you."

He was right, of course. Although I don't know why I bothered anymore. While I loved the opportunity to knock some of these petty lords around, it seemed court always ended with me upsetting my father. I had once dreamed of proving to him I could be the heir to the Pearl Kingdom, but that dream had long since died. Luckily, I had Jun, who had saved me all those years ago. But a daughter's craving for her father's approval would always linger.

Jun absolutely despised his title as heir. He would much rather be left alone to his music. Recently, it seemed the only person he enjoyed being around was me. I smiled sweetly back at him.

"Me? Take advantage of your hatred of court? Never. Just like it was always in your best interest to let me copy your work with our tutors growing up." I knew my smile was wicked, stretching between my long, pointed ears, but I saw some of the worry fade from his eyes and it made my heart glow. In truth, Jun was the only person in this whole damn court I really enjoyed being around, too.

Though we were brother and sister, we almost looked identical. We both had tan skin from the Niatan sun. We both had the dark hair of our mother and father, although he grew his out long as was traditional, whereas I had cut mine short in a small act of defiance in my youth. We both shared the dark grey eyes that mimicked the sky on this misty day. We walked together without saying a word, but I stared into the face that was almost a mirror to mine, so similar that it was almost funny the gods had decided to make us brother and sister. Almost.

We meandered through the gardens until we came upon an ancient cherry tree. It had always been my favorite to climb as a youngling, the branches the perfect distance apart. Jun would often sit under the tree as I climbed, singing or reading me a story.

I thought back to another misty day. It was nearly two centuries ago when the tree was young, and so were we.

Jun was reading quietly under the tree, while I made a ruckus in the branches. That was until a few of the noble boys approached, swinging their wooden swords.

"I'm going to be Hadeon; you be Abraxas." The boy's name was Kalim, the son of one of the fae nobles.

"You always get to be Hadeon! I want to be the hero. You can be Abraxas," said Sano, another noble's son.

"No way, besides, Abraxas is the better swordsman, you should be excited."

"No way, Hadeon slayed at least five dragons, he's obviously the better fighter. You just don't want to be the bad guy."

They continued to bicker as they approached the shade of the tree, and then they spotted Jun.

"Look, Jun can be Abraxas!" Sano sounded quite pleased with his idea.

The first boy gave a sinister laugh that would have fit the dark King Abraxas very well. "No way, Jun's way too much of a pussy to be a fighter. Better for him to play Malech."

Jun didn't even look up, rooted to his book. Kalim struck Jun on the arm and he dropped his book with a wince, "Better run, dragon."

I saw red. I dropped from the tree between Jun and his attackers, "Leave him alone!"

For a moment, both boy's eyes widened, then Kalim laughed again, "Get out of the way, Princess, we're having fun."

I spread my arms wide, "I said leave him alone." The boy gritted his teeth and raised his wooden sword to my chest.

"Move out of the way. I don't want anyone to get hurt." Even at that young age, I had heard the lie in his statement, his heart-beat racing. Suddenly the bruises I had seen on Jun's arms recently made a lot more sense.

I balled up my fists, "Make me."

Kalim gave me that ugly smirk again and raised his sword, but before he could swing it, I punched him straight in the face. I hadn't known what I was doing, so I heard my thumb snap, as I'd had it wrapped inside my other fingers. I yelped at the pain, but Kalim's nose bled, and I couldn't help but smile as whimpers fled his lips.

I saw Sano dash away, and I stood up shaking my hand, but Kalim recovered quickly, "You bitch!" He slammed his sword into my shin, and I crumpled under the pain. Next thing I knew, we were rolling on the ground and his hand connected with my face while the other pulled my long hair. I scratched at him and heard him yelp again. His knee collided with my stomach, and I curled up as his feet started hitting my side. Tears poured from me then, as the pain took over my mind and I wasn't able to think, let alone fight back.

"*Tori!*" My mother's voice rang across the garden, and the immediate pain stopped, even as the lingering soreness from Kalim's strikes remained. My mother's bodyguard pulled me off the ground, his grip firm, but gentle as was befitting the handling of a princess.

"What were you thinking, getting into a fight like that? And in front of Jun? What sort of example are you setting?" I didn't respond, it never mattered what I said anyway. Everything was always my fault. "To your room, now!" The guard gently pulled me out of the garden. I looked back to see my mother cradling Jun in her arms, not a scratch on him. Kalim's nose still ran with blood, and his face was covered in the scratches from my nails. That was the day I decided I wouldn't lose a fight again.

"Where did you go, Tori?" Jun's voice snapped me back to the present.

"You know me, head always in the clouds." He frowned again. I hated to see him so glum.

He reached out for the tree, "I always loved this tree, but it seems it might be at the end of its life." He was right. The once beautiful tree was now gnarled and rarely bloomed in the spring. It, like so much else in our kingdom, seemed to be dying a slow, painful death. But as his hand touched the bark, I could almost imagine a few of the leaves reaching back to him. But his face was still clouded in sadness.

"Now, remember what Mother told us, Jun? Walk around

with that darkness showing on your face, and it will summon King Abraxas straight here."

Jun screwed up his face in annoyance, but I saw the smile hiding underneath again, "Don't you think I'm a bit old to believe those children's tales?"

"Perhaps. But not too old to try and avoid your responsibilities. Come on, let's find a reason for you to be gone today." We walked a bit further, arm in arm, and I heard a sweet tune slip from his lips.

That was until my mother rounded the corner. She saw Jun and I together and her face dropped to the expression of someone who had seen a child running around with a sharp knife.

"Jun, Tori, what are you doing?" Jun stopped singing, and we unlinked arms quickly, shuffling away from each other as we had been coached for the last two centuries.

"Jun wasn't feeling well, Mother. I was just walking him back to his room." Jun managed to raise an eyebrow at me, acknowledging our shared deviance. He was a terrible liar, but I more than made up for that.

"Oh, my darling! What is wrong? Your father will be so disappointed not to have you at the petitions today!" I worried for a moment that Jun might not be able to hold up this charade, but he didn't really need to with how much Mother was doting on him. She took his arm and led him away, only at the last minute calling out, "Tori, dear, please join your father in Jun's stead." Sometimes it was too easy.

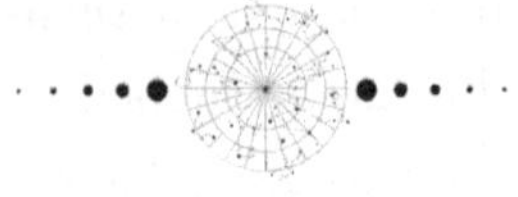

I SAT ON THE THRONE TO THE LEFT OF MY FATHER. THE SEAT that was meant for Jun. My father, Fae King Rahul Khato of the

Pearl Kingdom, was being petitioned by his lords. I had sat through a dozen already, keeping a royal smile plastered to my face as was expected. I greeted each lord and then remained silent—as was also expected. So far, they had all been quite boring disputes, and I wondered if Jun had gotten the better end of this arrangement.

But then the throne was approached by Lord Diam and one of his vassals. It had been quite some time since I had seen a vassal bring a petition against their Lord, so I was intrigued. Unfortunately, Lord Diam had fought with my father in the last war, so I didn't have much hope for his unbiased judgment.

"You see, Your Majesty, Ayame has not been able to meet her quota from the fruit harvest. I have been lenient these last few seasons, but enough is enough. I have ordered her to harvest the timber from the forest instead to make up for the deficit, but she refuses." Lord Diam spoke as if the matter were already closed. I turned my attention to Ayame. She was an older woman, half-fae by the look of softly pointed ears. The only one in the room besides my bodyguard. Her skin was dark and freckled with numerous sunspots from years spent exposed to the elements working the land. She almost looked human with the amount of wear on her body, but she held her back straight and didn't flinch at Diam's pointed stare, or that of my father. I liked her already.

She lifted a finger to point at Lord Diam in accusation, her fingernails lined with dirt.

"I have told you countless times that harvesting the timber from the forest is a fool's game. It would guarantee that we would never see a fruitful harvest again."

"We are going to be cutting down the lumber trees, not the fruit trees." Diam's voice dripped with disdain.

"You think that cutting down one tree doesn't affect another? These trees have lived together for generations. We cannot remove them." Ayame stomped her foot, her indication that the point was closed.

"You see, Your Highness, how she speaks? I've had nothing but trouble from her since her husband died." He spoke about her as if she weren't standing right beside him, and my stomach roiled in disgust.

My father turned his gaze to Ayame, "It seems you owe your Lord a debt, and he has come up with a very reasonable solution. You will cut down the trees."

Ayame's face dropped, and I couldn't help myself as I spoke, "I wonder, Lord Diam, when was the last time you harvested fruit in the forests of your lands?" Both Lord Diam and my father turned their heads to me. Lord Diam looked at me, dumbfounded. I didn't wait for him to answer. I didn't need to turn to my father to know the look he gave me. But I never had been good at holding myself back.

"And, Ayame, how many years has your family worked the land of these forests?"

"We have been vassals to these lands for nearly two centuries, Princess."

I turned back to Diam, "It seems it would be prudent to take the advice of the people who have actually lived and worked in the forest you are looking to decimate."

Lord Diam turned a very satisfying shade of red, but before he could respond, my father surprised me, "That is enough, Princess Tori." He spoke more forcefully than I had heard him in quite some time, his anger seeping through. My father always prided himself on the stoic control of his emotions, so my head spun to see the ugliness of rage mar his expression. "There must be a harvest and a tithe paid to Lord Diam. Ayame, you will harvest the lumber to repay your debt, and I will hear no more of it."

"Thank Hadeon for that," I heard Diam mumble.

My father stood, and both Lord Diam and Ayame bowed, but I jumped to my feet. "Father, you cannot–"

"I said that is *enough*!" I could not remember the last time my father had shouted at me, at least not in front of the nobility. I saw my mother shift in her seat, but she remained silent at my father's side, as she always did. She rose, her long elegant robes dancing over the marble floor of the throne room, as she came to my father's side. She looped her arm through his, and guided him out, leaving me with one last glance that seemed to say, *Not today, Tori.*

I turned and stormed past both Lord Diam and Ayame, my bodyguard, Lyle, rushing to keep up with me. I pushed out of the throne room, but not before I saw a grin pasted across Lyle's face. I was pissed, and he knew what always came next when I was in a mood like this.

We had hardly reached my room before I was ripping at Lyle's trousers. He didn't even try to hide that masculine smile as I pushed him down onto my bed, not even bothering to pull off my formal robe before straddling him. His hands came up, sliding underneath the top of my robe, pinching my nipples through the fabric of my underslip. I hissed at the harsh sensation but relished in the pain as it drove my thoughts of the throne room away. I had just about unlaced his pants, my hand reaching inside when I heard a great crash in the distance. I froze, and Lyle let out a disappointed groan as I withdrew my hand, but I slapped it across his mouth, "Quiet."

I held him there for a moment and heard nothing. He started to push his hips into me, no longer willing to wait. I was just about to resume when my whole tower shook, and we were both thrown from the bed. "What the hell was that?" Lyle scrambled up, grabbing his sword and tossing me the dagger I always kept at my bedside. It was the only weapon I was allowed to keep inside the palace. I pulled my robe back into place after I strapped it to my thigh, and ran towards my window, yanking back the long curtains.

I was greeted with the view of the Cerulean Sea that I had risen to every morning for the last two centuries. But today the normally placid and calm ocean was filled with ships. Not just any ships—warships, an armada's worth. As I stood at my window stunned, a great trebuchet on the closest vessel hurled a purple flaming projectile straight at me. I strained every muscle in my body to throw myself away from the window, just before the outer wall collapsed.

My head buzzed, and I felt a tug at my arm that seemed far away. Lyle was shouting my name, pulling me out of the rubble, as I tried to orient myself. Dust and debris littered my entire room, and Lyle was still hauling me across the floor. I snapped back to the present, and we ran.

Every few seconds a deafening crash would pound into my head as the floor beneath me swayed like the deck of a ship. Dust flew from the cracks between the white rocks of the palace as more and more pieces of the ceiling fell as we dashed down the hallway.

"Lyle, we have to get Jun out. If we can–" Another deafening crash overhead, and the hallway around us collapsed. Lyle gave me a great shove, and I flung forward as rubble came crashing down over him. "Lyle? *Lyle*!" I grabbed at the bricks and beams that had covered him, but a great, empty pit opened in my stomach, and I knew the truth. Lyle was dead, not even a fae like me could have survived that. But still, I clawed at the rubble, hoping to reach him, when another great crash sounded, and more of the ceiling collapsed. No, I had to keep going, I had to get out.

I ran. I kept running and running, my lungs burning like the ceiling above me. The dagger strapped to my thigh feeling useless against an enemy too large for me to fight. I ran past the bank of doors that opened into our main courtyard at the center of the palace grounds. They were beautiful, fragile things made of light wood and paper that had been hand-painted to show a mural of our kingdom, taking artisans hundreds of hours to complete. All of the doors either lay destroyed or burned now, my view to the courtyard unobstructed.

Chaos and destruction lay in all directions. My feet stopped moving, as I was overcome by the sight. The bodies of warriors and servants lay strewn across the courtyard. Some were burned beyond recognition, others bleeding slowly from wounds caused by the falling debris. Our castle had been beautiful, the base built on the large boulders moved up from the coast, the white marble and stone above reaching up into peaked gold tile roofs. The main hall had stood five stories tall, with the golden spires reaching straight up to the sky. Now those spires lay smoldering as one whole wall had collapsed. The wound on the building lay charred with ash, but a thrumming power pulsed like a heartbeat through the flames. Purple lightning flashed and spread like a spider's web, poison to fuel the flames.

Another projectile flew over the outer wall and I saw it, that purple lightning lacing throughout the flames of that meteor, burning up my home with its unnatural magic. But if this truly was magic—oh gods. We had to get out. I needed to find Jun, I had to protect him.

Another fireball slammed into the courtyard, too close for me to stay. I ran again before my mind caught up.

Sweat beaded on my forehead, plastering my short black hair to my face. I dashed for the tower that held Jun's quarters.

Servants fled as the outside wall collapsed. I ran into Jun's bedroom.

"Jun? *Jun!*" I screamed for him, but no answer came. I turned over his bed and wardrobe, in case he had been trapped, but nothing. My lungs heaved, but I willed myself to calm. I took several deep breaths and stilled my quaking mind. I listened, and through the shouting and crashing of walls, it was as if I could hear Jun's voice. *The tunnel.*

Yes, the tunnel hidden in the kitchen. Jun and I had used it to sneak out as younglings. That's where he would have gone. Where I had to go.

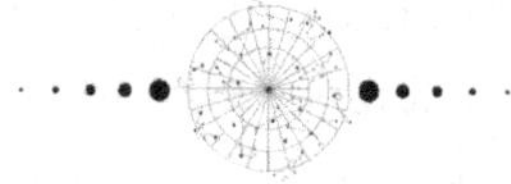

I FINALLY REACHED THE BUILDING CONTAINING THE kitchen when I heard the stomping of hundreds of boots in unison, the clashing metal plate armor as they moved. An army was coming, but I had a feeling it wasn't my father's. I climbed through the wreckage of the splintered and burned front door, careful not to touch any of the magic that lingered. I heard fighting inside, the clashing of swords and the moans of the wounded.

I rounded a corner to see the backs of one of my father's cohorts in their pale silver mail fighting a horde of soldiers in black plate armor, their huge swords and maces pounding against the shields of our guards. They held the line, but I could see their shields splintering and their knees giving out over the repeated blows. I longed to join them, to take my place among the ranks and defend our home. But I had no weapon and knew I would only be a liability.

Then a tall warrior in dark armor stepped forward. He was

like a starless night, the metal of his armor absorbing all the light that touched it. He moved with an unnatural speed and slammed his way through the front of their phalanx, his great sword cleaving through everyone who crossed his path. I couldn't help but watch as he moved, his motions so controlled and swift, almost like a dancer's. But his was a dance of death as soldier after soldier fell before him. He had cleared an opening when his head snapped up. His helmet had been forged to resemble the head of a dragon, its gaping maw obscuring his face with fangs. I couldn't see them, but I knew that his eyes were locked on mine. Before he could clear his way, I sprinted in the opposite direction.

Around the corner I pulled up a panel on the wall that concealed a servant's path, knowing it would put me out near the kitchen, but I was surprised to find several sets of small eyes staring at me.

"Princess Tori, what are you—"

"Hush!" The speaker was Tom, a young human boy of about ten, there with his mother Brianna, who was shushing him. As my eyes adjusted to the dark passage, I saw Brianna's two other young children, as well as several of the other kitchen servants. I looked at the faces around me—human faces. Fear clung to them like a stench. The two younger children had tracks on their faces where tears had cleaned away dust. Their mother held them tight, and I raised my fingers to my lips to silence them.

I motioned for the group to follow me and pushed past to head down the passage. Brianna, who I knew best due to her delicious cream tarts and adorable youngsters, had lingered near the back, so I grabbed the shoulder of the gentleman closest to me. Closer inspection revealed him to be Blaine, a middle-aged man who worked our gardens. "I'm taking you all to the tunnel in the kitchen," I explained. "It will lead us out to the beach, where we can regroup. If anyone gets separated, just keep moving down the tunnel. It's straightforward, you can't get lost."

A deafening crash from overhead shook the roof of our passage, but the walls held. The littlest babe started to cry again, and Brianna did her best to soothe her. I turned to Tom, who looked only moments away from tears. "Tom, I need your help," I said, placing a hand on his shoulder. "We need to be quick and quiet. Can you hold your little brother like that?" I asked, gesturing to his mother and he nodded. "Good. You're going to lead us down the tunnel, okay? It'll be dark, but I know you can be brave."

Tom's eyes shone with tears, and confusion flashed across his face. "You're scared?" he whispered.

"Yes, I'm scared," I admitted. "But I believe we can get through this together. Will you help me?"

Tom nodded seriously, and his brother gave a small, determined nod as well. When we reached the panel at the other end, I opened it just enough to peek out. The hallway was clear, but I could hear fighting just around the corner. We needed to hurry. Visions of the dark warrior caused my heart to slam against my ribs. I motioned for everyone to move, and we slipped into the kitchen with Blaine leading the way. Once Brianna had passed, I closed the door as quietly as I could manage.

Inside the kitchen the oven's fire still burned, the preparations for lunch left strewn about the wood table in the center. The smell of roast chicken smothered in herbs that would have been my lunch floated to me. If I couldn't have heard the fighting outside—and smelled the fear—I might have thought it was just a normal day of me sneaking into the kitchen to grab extra dessert.

I ripped aside a stack of barrels filled with flour and apples in the corner, probably less quietly than I should have. "Help me," I whispered, gesturing to the hutch filled with pots and pans. We didn't have time to empty it and it was made of ancient oak and filled with cast iron. But luckily, with a fae on one side and three of the servant men on the other, we were able to push it to where the barrels had been and revealed the small door in the wall behind. I pulled on the handle, but it seemed to have rusted shut. How many decades had this gone unused? I braced my foot on the wall and gave a great heave. The whole door came loose along with some of the rock wall revealing a tunnel that sank down below the foundation of the castle.

Blaine hesitated, so I shoved him in, unwilling to waste any more time. I thought of Lyle and all the other bodies I had seen scattered on the way here; tears burned my eyes. I'd be damned if I let one more of them be hurt. I herded the other servants towards the tunnel using the door I still held in my hand. Brianna carried her babe, and as she ducked through the small door, I heard another deafening crash from above. *Shit.* I felt the wall shaking so I grabbed Tom and his brother by the back of Tom's shirt and threw them unceremoniously into the tunnel. As the wall started to crumble, I threw the door back in place to try and shield them while launching myself backwards. The roof of the kitchen partially collapsed, bricks raining down, followed by the wood beams of the ceiling, and fine dust covering everything after that.

My leg had been pinned in the fall, but I was able to free myself before wiping the dust from my face A small voice called to me from behind the rubble, "Princess Tori, Princess Tori, are you alright?" Tom's voice. I breathed a small sigh of relief, he sounded unhurt.

"Tom, I need you to lead them out of the tunnel. Go now. Don't wait. I'll dig my way through and join you alright? Go!"

"You said we would go together!"

"Tom, be brave for me. I'll be right behind."

I heard some shuffling, behind the door, and his voice faded as he called, "Alright, see you soon."

I started shifting the rubble in front of the door, pulling bricks and beams away, but every few bits I moved would cause more to fall in their place. A moan of frustration passed my lips as I considered other ways out, when I was yanked back by an incredible force that flung me across the kitchen and smashed me into the stone floor, knocking the wind from my lungs. As I regained my breath, I rolled to the side, using one hand to push up, looking for my assailant when I heard the remainder of the roof and wall over the tunnel collapse. Had I been there moments longer, I surely would have been crushed. I pushed up with my other hand, my head still spinning. Perhaps I had hit it as well. Then a deep voice called to me from the door of the kitchen.

"There you are, Princess. I have been waiting for you." The light from the hall obstructed my view of his face, but I knew it was the warrior I had seen before. I was still on the floor but reached down for the dagger strapped to my thigh. If this was to be my end, he would go down with me.

Before we could engage, a loud crunch sounded above me as the main beam of the building above me snapped. The rest went black.

Chapter 2

Tori

I awoke to my face pressed against the cold marble of my father's throne room. Every inch of me ached like a building had been thrown at me. And in all reality, that's precisely what had happened. The coppery tang of blood lingered in my mouth, and I could barely move. Instead of trying to see, I listened. Angry voices came from the direction I thought would be the dais with my father's ivory throne perched on top. The metallic slide of a sword sounded to my right, and I could hear a woman weeping. The sound slid into the deep cracks of my memory, and I knew it was my mother, though I could not recall the last time I had heard her weep.

My head was turned towards her, so I allowed my eyes to open ever so slightly. One did, but the other was swollen shut. Through the lashes of my good eye, I could see my mother and father kneeling, swords pressed to their throats. My father looked dusty and battered, while a dribble of blood flowed from my mother's mouth. Her cheek was swollen pink where she had been struck. Her long dark hair had fallen out of the elaborate updo she wore daily. Normally, each hair was perfectly brushed and pinned, loops of hair trailing on each side of her face with a topknot held in place by ivory and gold combs on her crown. But today it fell in front of her almond-shaped eyes and was twisted like a bird's nest while tears streamed down her cheeks.

On the floor next to her I saw a body approximately the size of my brother. I couldn't see his face; I couldn't even tell if he was alive. Around us, I saw several of the nobles who had been in attendance today, all kneeling, heads bowed.

"Ah, it seems the princess has deemed us worthy of her presence." A deep, cold voice called to me from the dais. Before I could move, a rough hand grabbed the hair at the crown of my head and lifted me to my knees. Pain shot down my scalp and neck, radiating to the rest of my aching body. A sword came to lay at my throat, just as it did for my mother and father—the King and Queen.

My eyes fell upon our attacker. Above him fluttered the red herald of our kingdom, emblazoned with the white peacock that represented the royal family of Niata with his tail unfurled. But the flag had been burned and slashed, decapitating the image of the peacock. He sat in my father's white and gold throne, below the desecrated flag. The skies seemed to grow darker as he sat there, one foot propped on the opposite knee. He leaned back in the throne, all arrogance, as I stared at him.

Long, platinum silver hair spilled out as he removed his helmet. It was paired with dark eyebrows that framed his viridian green eyes and an aristocratic nose. His lips drew into a wicked smirk, and I was surprised to see the faintest hint of age there.

The fae aged at the same rate as humans until they reached twenty-five, and then their aging drastically slowed. Some humans still whispered that we were immortal, our lifespan so much longer than their own. But the truth was we did age, it was just uncommon to see a fae much older than eight hundred, especially since the War of Flames. My father, the oldest fae in the Pearl Kingdom had just passed six centuries, and my mother barely over three. This fae had just begun to lose that appearance of immortality. The creases around his eyes deeper, and the glow of youth faded from his face. But it only seemed to add to the authoritative look of him. He was truly striking, but demons were always beautiful. By my guess, he must have lived for over a millennium.

At first, I thought he wore the black armor of the other soldiers, but I saw now that his was much finer, made with exquisite craftsmanship. The plates were much smaller, almost mimicking scales that moved with his body easily. He was tall, and while most fae males tended towards a lithe figure, his was clearly broader and more muscled.

He stared down at me, that sneer growing. I couldn't do anything, held as I was, so I did my utmost to skewer him with my stare.

He held my gaze one more moment, then finally returned his attention to my father. "King Rahul, now that most of your family is conscious, I suppose we can continue our discussion." I had a feeling this discussion was very one-sided. "Did you truly think you could get away with cheating the Emperor on the Tithe?"

My eyes shot to my father. My father was many things, but a fool he was not. He would never have done something so stupid as try to cheat the emperor of his payments of food and gold, especially after the great losses we had suffered rebelling at the end of the War of Flames.

"Your Highness," my father's face grimaced in pain as he spoke, maybe he was more hurt than I had judged, "there have been droughts and famine throughout the kingdom. The amount we have collected already taxes our people to the brink of starvation. I gave what was owed of what we could collect—" His words were cut off as the soldier beside him kicked into his stomach, and he collapsed.

"Father!" I scrambled to try and reach him, but the soldier behind me held my hair tight. I could feel the small slice of pain where the sharp edge of the blade at my neck cut my skin.

My father pushed up on his hands, "Your Highness, it is the truth." It was. The earth beneath our feet seemed to be sick and growing more so by the year. We had all taken to rationing food, our household partaking in simple meals and reducing portions. But I had never gone hungry, not once. To know my father had kept the hunger of our people a secret roiled rage inside me along with the sickness I felt seeing him hunched over on the floor. I now understood the rage I had seen peeking through his expression this morning.

"Silence." The word wasn't spoken loudly, but the command in it rippled through the hall unnaturally, every sound seeming to obey, even those beyond the walls of the throne room. "He is owed what he is owed, Rahul, and the state of your sorry kingdom is no concern of his—or mine. I would have thought you would remember what happened the last time I came here."

I felt my father quaking beside me, his breath labored with panic. I'd only ever seen him like this the few times I had asked about his time in the war, and I realized who this man must be. King Abraxas Corignus, the emperor's most trusted general.

After the defeat of the World Breaker, all the kings of Adimos had bent the knee, save for my grandfather. He claimed the Pearl Kingdom should remain independent from the continent as it had been for millennia. So, the Dragon King had come here with his fleet and decimated our home. My grandfather had been killed in the fighting, and my father was named king after he bent the knee.

King Abraxas was ruthless. He had murdered his own father to become the King of the Dragon Kingdom at the end of the war.

That he had come here only spoke to how lost our city truly was. This wasn't just some raid over lost Tithe, but a true military conquest.

The Dragon King continued, "What would happen, do you think, if every king who couldn't properly manage his agriculture skimped on the Tithe?" The question was very obviously rhetorical. "No, no. There must be some retribution for this insult." I looked at our castle that was crumbling to the ground around me and thought of the countless bodies I had already seen strewn lifeless on the ground. *Was this not retribution enough?*

He stood and walked down from the dais, approaching my father. He reached down and grasped my father around his throat, lifting him completely off the floor, "You have threatened the Emperor's peace, Rahul. And such a thing cannot be forgiven." My father clawed at the king's hands, but it had no effect. The Dragon King flicked his other hand, and soldiers clad in black approached every noble in the room, swords drawn. I heard their whimpering along with my father's, and my vision went red. The soldier behind me still held me tight, but my hand was free. I reached for the dagger hidden under my robe, when the King's eyes snapped to me, "Careful now, Princess."

But then the great double doors of the throne room flung open, and the Dragon King dropped my father to the floor.

"Now, now, Abraxas, no need for such violence." He strode in, the very vision of the Great Hero. Emperor Hadeon Aurelius overtook the room, his golden armor glowing, his long mahogany hair flowing behind him. His crown of golden flames and dazzling purple gems glinted in the sunlight as he opened his arms to the room.

"What sort of treatment is this for our nobility? I do apologize, fine ladies and gentleman. The Dragon King can get quite carried away sometimes. I'll make sure your every need is met." He stood tall and smiled with kind violet eyes. He was incredibly handsome, with a strong jaw and high cheekbones, and a long, elegant nose all paired with dark tan skin. Truly, our Divine Emperor.

He walked to the throne and swept his eyes across the room. "Have your men escort them somewhere more comfortable, yes?" The nobles around the room rose to their feet, released by the soldiers.

They quickly shuffled out of the room, not one of them looking back to me and my family. *Cowards.* My soldier had released me as well, and I tried to walk after them, but found I was held by an invisible force. Its grip raised the hairs on my arms, like the sensation just before a lightning strike.

As the last nobles fled the room, the Dragon King's soldiers were replaced by guards in shimmering armor that bore the flaming crown of the Emperor. Hadeon had one leg thrown over the arm of the throne, draping himself casually over it, a look of boredom plain on his face.

He was the only fae still able to truly wield magic. Even now, as he lay across my father's throne, he played with a ball of purple lightning, letting it roll over the back of his hand and back into his palm. Clearly, that was more interesting than the royals he held before him.

But a spark of hope alighted in my chest. This was our Divine Emperor, our savior from The Breaking. The Dragon King was his right hand, but surely he saw the madness in this. He would put a stop to this cruelty. But then why did he hold us here?

The moments stretched on in silence. Hadeon ignored us, and the Dragon King continued to hold me in his gaze. I couldn't bear it any longer and tried to speak, but my voice was restrained as much as I was. I felt that buzzing in my throat, and it made me nauseous.

I kept my eyes on the emperor, and as soon as the throne

room doors closed, his eyes hardened. That smile dropped along with his shoulders, and he turned to my father.

"Rahul, I allowed you to live all those years ago so that you could obey." My father was shaking even more now, but the emperor's eyes slid to me again as a merciless grin crossed his face, "Perhaps you need a reminder of the consequences?"

He shot his hand out straight before him, and I felt a great pressure all over my body, as if I were being crushed in every direction. I felt my body start to lift off the ground, the pressure increasing.

I heard my mother whimpering beside me, "No, no." But I locked my gaze with the emperor and locked my lips. I don't know what was worse, the pain or the shock, but I wouldn't give him the satisfaction. Even as the pressure on my head felt like it would rend my eyes from their sockets, I managed, "Fuck...you..."

He chuckled, "Oh, this one is *ferocious*."

But then I heard a moan, distinctly masculine beyond my father, as my brother heaved a breath and tried to move. The emperor's eyes snapped over to my brother and my body crashed back to the ground with a sickening thud.

"Ah, the prince awakens." Immediately, my brother's body lifted into the air, the emperor's magic now fixed on him. "Why play with the spare, when I can have the heir." My brother let out a blood-curdling scream as lightning shot into and surrounded him.

"No, please, no!" My mother screamed in earnest now.

My father, on his knees, begged, "Your Eminence, please, my son—please..." Something deep inside me broke. Not only to see my father, the most rigid man I had ever known, beg on his knees, but also at the thought that he had stayed silent for me. I shoved that thought down.

My brother's screams still ripped through the hall. His eyes managed to lock with mine, and I saw him mouth my name, a plea. I fixed my gaze on the emperor, my hand sliding to my thigh. This was a very stupid idea, but it was the only move I had. I scrambled to launch myself at him when a cruel hand grabbed my throat. The guard's gold armor creaked as he lifted me to standing, and then had his sword pressed into my gut.

"Oh, I don't think so, Princess." The Emperor's guard crushed me against his body, holding me in place by my throat, his disgusting breath floating over my ear. He had locked my hand at my side, just above my dagger. If I could just get it out, I could stab this prick. "Keep rubbing me with your ass like that. Gives me ideas for later." I froze as I felt the sick wet heat of his tongue trace along the point of my ear, and dread filled my stomach matching the pressure he increased with the point of his sword. I felt the cloth of my outer robe give way as the sword pushed through, now pressed directly against my skin.

But then my brother let out one last weak scream, and the emperor dropped him. His magic receded. Hadeon's chest heaved with exertion, and my brother's body crashed into the marble floor, his head landing with an awful crack. I saw my mother crawl to him, running her soft hands over the gash in his forehead, pulling his long dark hair back.

"Your Eminence, if I may?" The Dragon King approached the emperor quite brazenly and leaned to whisper in his ear as Hadeon fought to regain his breath. Their conversation was hidden from even my fae hearing, but I had no doubt I wouldn't like the outcome.

The Dragon King seemed to finish, and the emperor locked eyes with him before cracking a smile that held zero warmth.

"It seems that perhaps a compromise can be struck." He locked his gaze on my father. *A compromise? What sort of game was he playing?* "I see no need to install a new ruler here if I can assure your loyalty."

My father blinked in surprise before saying, "Of course, Your Eminence, I have always been—" The emperor strode forward and struck him across the face, adding to the swing with a sting of lightning, crumpling my father to the floor.

"Empty words from one I already know to be a liar. But it is easy to instill loyalty in someone as pathetic as you." He snatched my brother's arm then, dragging him across the floor, eliciting a few weak moans from him, my only signal that he was still alive. My mother clawed and reached for him, trying to hold on, but the emperor pushed her away as she wept.

He deposited my brother roughly on the stairs of the dais before retaking his seat. "Your son shall join me as a ward in my court." He slid his hand through my brother's hair softly, a devious grin crossing his face. "And should you behave well, your son will be *very* well taken care of." He flicked his thumb over my brother's lips before letting his head drop to the floor again. I heard my father emit a small growl, but there was no weight behind it.

"And your daughter," he flicked his hand to me without looking, as if I were less important than the rubble gathered around him, "will be going to the Dragon Kingdom, where hopefully they can teach her some better uses for her dirty mouth." The pit in the bottom of my stomach completely dropped out, but before I had a chance to react, I was being dragged away by my guard. It took all of my coordination to keep my feet from sliding across the floor.

I saw my mother crawl across the floor, reaching for my brother. She pulled on the hem of the Emperor's cape, and I heard her beg, "Please, Your Eminence, please..." Hadeon looked at her like a bug that needed to be squashed. "You're pathetic, don't touch me." But she reached for him again, and I saw anything reasonable leave Hadeon as he held out his hand and sent a lightning bolt straight through my mother's heart.

"Let that be a reminder, should you forget my generosity again."

I could smell the sizzle of burnt flesh as my mother's blood pooled around her on the white marble floor. The only sound I could hear was my own screaming as I was pulled from the room.

Chapter 3

Tori

I was dragged down into my own dungeon, my voice hoarse as I screamed, my nails bloody as I scratched at the face of the guard carrying me. Another had joined him in an attempt to contain me.

"Damn hellcat." He tossed me roughly onto the stone floor of a cell, my arm and cheek abraded against the rough tiles. The guard's eyes were filled with malice as he stared down at me. The second guard stepped out from behind him, and the air in the cell seemed to grow thick and choke me.

"Have you ever had a princess before?" The second asked, licking his lips in a way that drove bile to rise in my throat.

"No, I bet she tastes expensive. Better get my piece of that pussy now before the whole Dragon Kingdom has its way with her."

"Who says you get to go first?"

They continued to bicker while I tried to plan my escape. I saw the first shift to unlace his trousers with one hand, still holding his sword out towards me. He was larger than me and full fae, so I had no strength advantage. He was also fully armored, aside from the piece he now let fall away in front of his crotch. The second was the same. I was no fool, there was no way I could take on two armed fae in a fair fight—or even an unfair one—with only my dagger. But I would be damned if I didn't try.

"Oh, there will be no need for that," I said pushing the tip of his sword down with two of my fingers. "There is no reason that we can't all enjoy this." I moved my hands to my chest, slowly sliding my hands under the formal robes I still wore. I allowed them to fall off, revealing the thin silk slip I wore underneath. I repeated the mantra I had used my whole life, *always let them underestimate you.*

"Filthy slut, who said you get to enjoy this?" he groaned as he dropped his sword behind him and bore down on me. I let him close the distance between us, one hand reaching and groping my breast, while the other crushed against my windpipe. I heard his companion complain about leaving something for him, but he sealed his mouth down on my shoulder, and bit down so hard I knew there would be blood. I couldn't help the small yelp that escaped me, and it spurred him on to crush me more violently against the wall. But removing my robe had given me easier access to the garter on my thigh and I pulled my dagger free before I rammed it into the side of his neck.

A faint gurgling escaped him as blood sprayed across my face and chest, the metallic taste of it hitting my mouth and nose. But he released his grip, both hands clawing at the dagger, and I could breathe again.

"You bitch!" The second soldier ran at me, his sword aimed straight at my head. His companions' blood continued to spray thick in the air, as I had struck his artery, each flux matching the increased rate of his heart. He fell to his knees, and I wrenched the dagger from his neck. I held it up, knowing I had little chance against a full broadsword. I readied myself to try and block the strong overhead swing already headed at me when the guard froze. I heard a small squelching noise and a breath escape him as the sword clattered down from his hands.

He too fell to his knees, but when he did, it revealed a third man standing behind him. His black armor was coated in a skin of the fae's blood. He held his right hand outstretched, displaying his grisly prize. The crimson heart he held was still beating, each contraction sending more thick blood cascading over the cage of his fingers, running in rivulets down his arm. He must have ripped out of the fae back, straight through his golden armor and rib cage.

"Well, this is quite a mess you've made," the Dragon King commented with no humor. I raised my dagger and lunged at him. I willed my hands to not shake and failed. I wasn't as well trained with a dagger as I was with other weapons, and it showed. With one hand he easily snagged the dagger from my grasp. "Now, Princess, there will be no need for that."

The king stashed my dagger into his belt and glared at me. His long silver hair was speckled with blood, and that strong, handsome face was twisted into a grimace. He looked at the heart he still held with disgust, as if it were an overripe autumn plum leaking all over his fine armor. He snapped his fingers, and two more soldiers clad in black appeared in the doorway.

"Search the princess to see if she has any other hidden secrets." One of the soldiers stepped forward, and I took a step back but was immediately pressed against the wall again. I thought about trying to run, but my legs barely held me, and I would never get past them all.

The frenzy that had been carrying me since the morning seemed to have finally subsided. I crashed to my knees, wheezing, but it felt like there was no air in the room at all, only blood. I had trained for this, but the reality was always different. I raised my hands to defend myself, but the soldier quickly knocked them aside. The soldier's hands ran over the parts of my body covered by my slip. The touch was firm, but not aggressive, although highly invasive considering what my slip covered. They traced over my front and turned me to trace over my back.

"Nothing else, sir," said the soldier in a voice higher pitched than I expected. I looked at the Dragon King, and his eyes were locked on mine, his expression hard. I saw his eyes drop to my shoulders and chest where I was covered in the soldier's blood, and his expression changed to one of rage. I wondered what sort of punishment I had earned for killing this man. But then his expression calmed to a distant cold look.

He turned and tossed the heart into the corner of the cell like an old apple core and strode out, his soldiers following him. I was prepared for him to slam the cell closed, when he turned back to me, "Well, are you coming? Or would you prefer to remain here with...that?" He motioned to the dead bodies on the floor. My brain wasn't registering what I should do—not working at all really. But my body seemed to have a primordial need to leave the scene of my crime, so I followed him out the door, his soldiers taking up position behind me.

"We will get you cleaned up and into some new clothes. Unfortunately, you will need to remain here until the ship is ready, but I will leave my soldiers with you as escorts, so you won't need to fear any further incidents." He emphasized the last word, menace flowing through him. He turned to me one last time, a smirk crossing his lips as he let his eyes rove over my whole body. I knew I was still covered in blood, but my slip didn't cover much, and I felt the need to cross my arms and cover myself.

That haughty smile only grew, "I certainly do have my hands full with you, don't I?" He turned and strode away as his soldiers escorted me into the nearest cell.

In my new cell, I was provided a bowl of warm water and cloth, along with a new set of clothes. It was a simple ensemble, likely taken from a servant, but I didn't care because they were blood-free. My two *escorts* stood in front of the bars of my cell, but with their backs to me, I assumed to give me some semblance of privacy. For a brief moment, I thought about sneaking up behind one of them and strangling them through the bars. I released a sigh and dropped the thought, as it would likely not accomplish anything but piss them off.

I took off my blood-soaked slip, the sanguineous fluid now faded to deep wine red and brown. I took the cloth and scrubbed my body, the water in the bowl turning pink. I scrubbed my neck and shoulders and winced as I passed over where the soldier had bitten me, the wound still open. I scrubbed it harder, the pain driving away the memories of his hot breath on my throat and his hands gripping me all over. After I was sure my body and hands were clean, I dressed and moved to my face.

My fae blood had already almost completely healed my eye and the scratches on my face, but the new skin was tender and I could feel a cut that still stung on my left temple. Despite my best efforts, some of the blood-tainted water still slid into my mouth, the fresh metallic taste taking me back to the moment I had stabbed the soldier, his blood filling the air. I thought of the second soldier's heart, held aloft in the king's hand. The legends of his strength were not exaggerated, being able to simply punch through plate armor, not to mention the other fae's ribs. I shivered, thinking of the blood as it dripped off his arm onto the floor.

Then, it was the blood of my mother spilled all over the floor as the life faded from her eyes. Tears rolled down my cheeks as I realized that had only been a few minutes ago. She was likely still lying there. Soldiers filled our palace, stepping over her body carelessly, kicking her lifeless form, removing her final dignity.

The tears flowed freely now, although I refused to emit any audible sobs for my guards to hear. I scrubbed harder at my sensitive face, trying to control my thoughts, but they just kept spinning more wildly. My father's screams mixed with the emperor's words, *Why play with the spare, when I can have the heir?* Did he know how closely his words mimicked the ones I'd heard my entire life? To have a male heir in a royal family was a great honor, with fae children being so rare as it was. When my mother had been pregnant, the news of twins had spread like wildfire and great celebrations had been held across the Pearl Kingdom.

Only seven sets of identical twins had ever been recorded in any fae lineage, and with them, great magical power had always arrived. It was believed that the soul needed to be split in two in order to support the weight of the magic. The last pair had been born back when magic still freely flowed, over six hundred years ago. All were now dead, killed in the War of Flames. The healers had predicted two healthy young boys for my mother, unheard of in a royal line. My brother had been born to great celebration. But I had been born next, a daughter, and had been disappointing everyone ever since.

There had only ever been one other set of fae fraternal twins born in written memory, nearly two millennia ago. But they were infamous, for they had started another Great War to allow their incestuous marriage and their tainted offspring to rule their Eternal Kingdom, as they called it. They had been defeated, all their children murdered, and their kingdom dissolved. But fraternal twins were ordained to be an ill omen.

Of course, when my brother and I were born, much of this was hushed, but I could still hear it spoken of behind closed doors. The whispers had been louder ever since famine and drought had settled on the Pearl Kingdom a few decades back. My mother and father had done everything in their power to keep me and my brother separated. Different tutors, different hobbies, even living on different sides of the palace.

But despite their attempts at separation, Jun and I had always been drawn back together. We had become very proficient at sneaking out of our rooms at night, meeting in the gardens to talk together and play games of our own creation. I had always felt the most free under the warm starry sky with my brother at my side.

But our daily separation still had its consequences. My brother and I had developed into very different fae. Jun was always quiet, studious, with a love of music and the most beautiful singing voice. I, on the other hand, had been getting into trouble since the moment I could crawl.

I remembered my mother's strained face, muttering about me forcing her into an early old age. I had been climbing our sea cliffs again, and two guards had injured themselves attempting to retrieve me. I had tried to explain that they should have just let me come down on my own and I was *fiiiine,* but such behavior was not fit for the daughter of the queen. The thought of my mother's face, twisted as she scolded me, but with a mischievous light dancing in her eyes caused my shoulders to heave uncontrollably. I would never see that face again.

I collapsed to my knees and hit the bowl of water with my elbow as I did. Bloody water sprayed all over the floor, and the bowl clattered about with a series of loud clangs.

"Everything alright, Your Highness?" The soldier with the high voice asked. They had turned around, watching me. "Yes... just...fine." I had to speak slowly to prevent my sobs from sneaking through and I hoped the darkness of the cell hid the tears still staining my face. The soldier gave a nod and turned back around, as I lifted the bowl back up onto the bed. I scrubbed my face one final time with the towel and tossed it aside. I had to control my racing mind. I imagined, as I always did, the Cerulean Sea stretched out before me. While my father and I were rarely civil, this was the one practice he had given me that we had shared in peace. I couldn't take my body through the smooth controlled motions that the practice normally entailed, but I imagined them and controlled my breathing.

I went through the routine I had been doing for over a hundred years, the repetition stilling my mind and my racing heart. Any errant thoughts that drifted back up, I visualized as stones that I tossed into the slowly curling waves of the ocean of my home. Each sank below the surface to a collection of rocks being worn away bit by bit in the ocean's grasp.

I threw away my nausea at killing a man. I threw away the grief for my mother, for Lyle, and all the other dead around me, as well as any images that lingered in my thoughts. I threw away the apprehension of what would happen to me in the grasp of the Dragon King, the heart-stealing general.

King Abraxas, his name had been whispered like a dark prayer among the young soldiers. He was a great warrior, and of his strengths, I now had no doubts. But his name was also a curse. Perhaps it would be your village he burned next, your family he would claim with a swift strike of his sword. I was now his prisoner.

When I had finally dropped all my thoughts away, I heard my guards moving. They turned and unlatched the bars to my cell, careful not to touch the iron with their bare hands.

"It's time to go, Princess." I marched out once again, holding my head high, tears cleared from my eyes. As I passed the door, each grabbed one of my upper arms, again with a firm but not aggressive grasp. They lead me out of the tunnels of my home, tunnels I would have known in the pitch black, and out towards the docks.

Mt breath stole away as we emerged into the daylight. I could feel the ocean of my mind growing turbulent as if a storm approached the shore. The palace I had known my whole life lay in ruins. Only a few of the taller towers remained, and ash and that miasmic purple lightning could be seen everywhere. Bodies still lay strewn about, but many had been stacked in mass graves to be burned. I saw one pyre already lit; dozens of bodies nearly charred to nothing. The wind shifted and the smoke of the pyre floated over us, the smell of burning flesh overwhelming, and I dry heaved, doubling over in my captor's arms.

"Ugh, gods..." the taller soldier said, using their other hand to remove their helmet. I was stunned by the beauty of the face revealed underneath.

They had dark brown skin, the color of the richest earth in a healthy garden, and long dark hair that had been twisted into dozens of small braids close to their scalp. Each of these braids was ornamented with copper beads, and they were all pulled back into one larger braid at the back of their head. Their eyes were a soft, honey brown so at odds with the sharp angles of the rest of their face. Long pointed ears emerged from their braided hair, marking them as fully fae.

They caught me staring, and gave a mischievous smile, before continuing to pull me along, "Quite pretty for a brute, eh, Your Highness?" I averted my gaze, but the slight pause allowed me to regain my composure.

"Where are we going? There is no way the ships are ready to leave. What of the fighting?" If I could just buy some time, perhaps I could slip away.

They hit me with a look that was too close to pity for my liking, "The Pearl Kingdom army has been...subdued." I had a feeling that was a very nice way of putting the slaughter that had occurred. "A small contingent will stay behind, but the rest are departing." They walked me towards the docks, and as we rounded the final outer wall, I was greeted by the armada of ships bearing both the flags of the Dragon Kingdom and the Court of Flames.

While Niata had been unprepared for a battle, how had an entire fleet of ships approached our shores unnoticed? No warning had been given when the volley had begun. But then I thought back to the unseasonable fog that had rolled in this morning. The enemy had used it to their advantage, heavily.

At the end of the dock stood a massive ship that was obviously the head of the Dragon King's fleet. The sails were black, emblazoned with the green dragon of the king. He snarled down at me, beady eyes locked on its prey. As a youngling, Jun and I had played dragon hunters, running through the woods on an epic quest to hunt down the final dragon, The World Breaker, even though he had been brought down by Emperor Hadeon long before our time. Regardless, we had fancied ourselves the warriors of old, taking on those fierce enemies with our stick swords and leaf shields. Now, with this one staring down at me as I was taken from my home, I wished I could shove a sword straight through its heart.

Cohorts of soldiers boarded the boat, but they parted with military precision to let my escorts and I climb the gangplank. Once on the ship, I was led to the upper decks and inside quickly. From the main cabin, I expected to be taken down into the belly of the boat, to the brig or other imprisonment, but instead I was deposited into a small room. By my judgment, it was right next to the king's quarters. The room wasn't much, barely enough room for a small dresser and the bed, but it certainly wasn't a prison cell.

My guard gently pushed me into the room, "My name is Avlyn, and if you need anything, Princess, I shall be available to you." A thousand snarky replies died on my lips, and I simply remained silent. "We shall be departing soon," they said and shut the door behind them, before the loud scraping of a key entering the lock sounded from the other side.

I turned quickly and jumped on the bed, ripping at the small porthole window above it. It was sealed shut and didn't budge an inch. I ripped the sheets off the bed and wrapped my hand, before landing a solid punch on the glass. All this achieved was sending a reverberating shockwave of pain through my hand and up my arm. I continued to smash my fist into it until my knuckles bled into the sheets wrapped over them. Avlyn's voice called through the door, "It is reinforced. You won't be able to break it." They did not elaborate, but my knuckles agreed with them.

A frustrated hiss slipped from my lips, even knowing that Avlyn would hear it as they stood watch outside my door. I flopped onto the small bed, relishing in the pain of my arm, focusing on it to drive away my feeling of helplessness. But shortly after, I felt the boat surge beneath me. I scrambled to look out the window as the land I had called home for my entire life seemed to float away from me. I couldn't tear my eyes away—not until the Pearl Kingdom, with her swaying palm trees and rocky shores, disappeared into the horizon of the Cerulean Sea.

Chapter 4

Tori

It took us three days to cross the Cerulean Sea to the shores of the continent, the wind seeming to favor our journey. After Niata was out of sight, and it seemed beyond the distance that any sane person would attempt to swim back, Avlyn let me out of my room to walk the deck and stretch my legs. Unfortunately for them, I was not really a sane person.

I dashed for the edge and immediately threw myself over, diving into the water. The Cerulean Sea was not cold, but it still sent a shock through me as I scrambled to catch my breath. I resurfaced and began pumping my arms and legs rapidly. My outer robe became imbued with water, slowing me significantly. I tore at the tie around my waist and shrugged it off as quickly as I could. I heard shouting from the deck but didn't dare look back. The small voice inside my head nagged me about swimming without any land in sight, and barely any sense of direction other than the setting sun, but I swam harder, nonetheless.

That was until I was suddenly pushed under by a great weight, and felt arms wrap around my torso. They dragged me back to the surface, but I thrashed.

"You'll drown us both, you idiot," Avlyn yelled at me between breaths of air and being dunked back underwater by my weight. But then two more sets of hands grabbed at my shoulders and hauled me out of the water onto a small boat. I heard a sword pulled from its sheath; its tip laid at my throat. The soldiers on the boat watched me intently as I panted and coughed up sea water, while another helped Avlyn climb aboard. It seemed they had removed some of their plate armor before jumping in after me, but how they had managed to catch up with me with so much still on, I couldn't know.

They laid back in the boat, letting the warm sun hit their face in a most appealing way. "I would *not* like to do that again." They turned their face to me, "This will make it much harder to get permission to allow you to roam freely." A stern look, like a teacher scolding a naughty student for speaking out of turn. I shot back daggers with my eyes but said nothing.

Avlyn let out a harsh laugh, "Gods, I'm not paid enough for this." The other soldiers in the boat jostled them and joined in laughing.

"That's what you get for being the king's favorite, ass-kisser," another soldier teased. Avlyn kicked them with their booted foot, but it was more of a playful gesture.

"That's Commander Ass-kisser to you, Lieutenant." More chuckles and playful slaps all around.

Somehow, seeing their camaraderie made me feel more empty. This didn't seem like the army of mindless killers I had heard about. Just a group of soldiers like the ones I had trained with back home. The small boat docked next to the larger one and a ladder was rolled down to us. Avlyn pushed me to go first.

Despite the situation, I could still feel heat rise to my cheeks in embarrassment. I had shed my outer robe, so I was once again in nothing but a short slip that was soaking wet and very see-through. I didn't like to think about the view the soldiers would get as I climbed the ladder in front of them.

Avlyn saw my blush, "Should have thought of that before you decided to go for an evening swim, Princess." No pity there, but definitely a bit of teasing. I made a rude gesture with my hands, and Avlyn laughed again, "Up you get, Princess," rudely grabbing and hoisting me up the ladder. I tried to climb as quickly as possible, rolling myself over the edge of the ship awkwardly. I very unceremoniously flopped onto the deck when a pair of fine shoes entered my line of sight.

"I'm used to women ripping their clothes off for me, but you seem to be making it a habit." I coughed as I looked up at the king. My hair was plastered to my face with salt water, and I probably had the appearance of a drowned cat. He, on the other hand, looked impeccable. It was like he hadn't just spent the day invading a foreign land and ripping hearts from people's chests. He wore all black leather pants that clung to his strong thighs but had exchanged his armor for a black linen shirt that was more appropriate for sailing, the sleeves rolled above his elbows. His long silvery hair was loose and blowing in the wind but still managed to never look disheveled, and his hands bore several silver and gold rings. He stared down at me like I was something disgusting he had found on the bottom of his shoe.

I jumped up. He was slightly taller than me, but it forced him to meet my gaze, that was until he let it lazily trace down my body again. That same smirk crossed his face, "If you wanted to seduce me, Princess, there are easier ways than trying to drown yourself."

"Funny that you think a woman trying to get as far away from you as possible is a seduction technique. I hate to think what your lovers must go through." A cold wind whipped around my wet body, and I felt my nipples go hard from the cold. I hated the sensation of them against the wet fabric, but I latched on to how his eyes lingered there. An opportunity.

But he looked up and raised a single eyebrow at me, "I haven't had any complaints yet. In fact, quite the opposite."

"Oh?" I moved towards him then, and I heard the armor of the soldiers around me shift as they placed their hands on their weapons. But none moved, so I leaned in close to the king, so our bodies were merely a hairsbreadth apart, and I could hear his pulse beneath the smooth skin of his neck. I whispered in my softest voice, "Then how would you like me to seduce you?" He almost didn't react, but I heard his heart rate increase and saw the slightest dilation of his pupils, which gave him away.

But he locked a cold look on his face. "Now, I can *clearly* see that you are disarmed, but I don't intend to give you the same opportunity that those fools in the dungeon did." It was my turn to freeze, as I worked with all my might to keep the taste of blood from rising back into my mouth.

He stepped towards me then. I stepped back to avoid him but smacked right into the armor of one of the soldiers who had climbed up the ladder after me. "So, Princess, are you going to stop trying to kill yourself, or are you going to force me to lock you up?" Something lingered there behind his gaze, something I couldn't decipher.

I raised my wrists to him, trying to call his bluff, and his eyebrows shot up, "Best to lock me up, *Your Majesty*, my tutors always told me that I had a hard time following directions." It almost looked like he was about to laugh, but instead, his sneer locked back into place.

"As you wish." He motioned to the soldier next to me, who, to my surprise, pulled a pair of shackles out and clamped them around my wrists. I was grateful they weren't iron, but my arms sagged under their weight, and I was sure that they would chafe.

And so, I spent the next three days locked in my room, shackled. They did start to rub away at the skin, bright red welts forming that could never really heal as they kept being ripped at. Avlyn would let me out of my cabin twice a day, but I was chained to their side now, and not allowed near the railing of the ship. I didn't see the king again, but I was more than happy about that.

I shifted on my bed, and the shackles ripped a new welt in my skin. *Probably shouldn't have asked to be locked up,* said the little voice inside my head. They were right, as per usual. It had always been hard for me not to push, not to fight back with any weapon I had at my disposal, but it did seem to get me in deeper trouble more often than not. It had certainly ruined my relationship with my father. But I looked out my porthole window again, focusing on the turquoise ocean, and imagined my thoughts disappearing below the surface. I let all my grief hide away until my mind was as calm as the lazy ocean outside.

We were headed for the Dragon Kingdom, a place almost as isolated as the Pearl Kingdom. The only thing that ever left there was this army. The army I was currently trapped on a boat with, in the middle of the ocean. All I could do was observe my captors and wait for my next chance to escape.

Chapter 5

Tori

Our ship came into port at the coastal city of Metlin, where the great river Varda met the sea. This river was the very lifeblood of the Golden Kingdom, and it fed thousands of fields of ambrosia flowers. And Metlin was its beating heart, the continent's largest port.

I could hear the whole ship rumbling with the steps of the soldiers as they moved, loading supplies and performing other shiply duties I knew little about. I had always enjoyed swimming in the ocean but traveling by boat had always been something I disliked. Besides, my father never allowed me to leave our kingdom.

I had been content to read of the continent and experience it through others, especially when so many of the stories were of war and famine, where slavery was not only allowed, but openly practiced on the so-called lower races, especially humans. I had wanted nothing to do with a place that would allow such monstrosities.

But now, as the ship swayed gently in the dock, I couldn't help but look out the window. I mostly saw the great dock that stretched along the bay and the delta of the Varda river, wooden decks and gangplanks lined with derelict shacks, each faded from the sea salt spray that had coated them year after year. People of every race bustled about. I saw a crew of small, winged pixies holding one end of a long, heavy trunk, the other end held up by a single orc, his moss-green skin gleaming with sweat and ocean spray. They loaded ships like many of the other porters then disappeared into the shacks that seemed to be taverns of some kind. A human male, clearly very drunk despite the early hour, was held up by his ear by a matronly woman who viciously kicked him out of her establishment. He landed face-first on the filthy boardwalk, with other citizens simply stepping over him as if he were just another piece of flotsam.

I couldn't help but smile at the humanity of it, the similarity to the docks back home. Niata was much smaller than Metlin, its dock stretching as far as I could see from my small vantage point, but somehow it felt familiar.

A knock sounded at my door, and I turned to see Avlyn open it wide. I moved to join them before the Dragon King stepped into my view. I froze as his tall frame completely filled the door, that haughty look piercing me. Dressed in his formal armor, he certainly cut an intimidating figure. My wrists chafed under his stare.

"Now, Princess, while I have enjoyed having you locked up, I think it's time we try again." He removed a key from his belt and leaned toward me. I couldn't help but flinch, shrinking away from him. *Weak.* I lifted my chin and did my best to face him, pushing my shoulders back to stand as tall as was possible.

"And what exactly are we trying?" He placed the key in the shackles, and they popped open. I couldn't help but sigh my relief and rub my wrists as they were finally able to begin healing themselves.

"I would like you to accompany me into the city. Lord Bolon

is an old business partner, and I'm sure he would be pleased to meet the fabled Princess of the Pearl Kingdom."

"Fabled Princess? What, have I been locked in a tower guarded by a dragon?"

"No, you are just a twin who has been kept on a distant island kingdom your entire life, away from the prying eyes of all of Adimos." His face was deadly serious. I had not really thought about the opinion of me in other kingdoms, as we had so limited contact with them. And the opinion of me at home was suspect, at best.

My father had claimed our isolation was so we wouldn't become tangled in the fae's senseless wars, but the era we lived in now was called the Long Peace. After Emperor Hadeon had defeated the last dragon and every last king bent the knee, there had been the longest period of peace ever recorded. I had pointed this out to him, and he had snapped, saying I had been born too late to understand, that I had lived a sheltered life. I'd snapped back, *Whose fault is that?* I'd earned myself a month of kitchen cleaning duties for that. More painfully, two months without my weapons training.

I looked at the king, wondering what his motive was. But I could hear the hustle and bustle of the city outside calling to me.

He seemed to follow my thoughts, "The city awaits, Princess, if you would give me your word to not embarrass me by say, throwing yourself into the river." He smiled now, "Although, that might be punishment in and of itself, as the river is absolutely disgusting here."

"And why should I trust you?"

"Trust me? Princess, no, we are determining if *I* can trust *you*." He held out his hand, my ticket out of this cabin. Perhaps I could play nice, just for now. I reached out, slipping my fingers into his palm, which was rough with callouses.

"We will see."

Chapter 6

Abraxas

The carriage lurched and swayed over the cobblestone roads of Metlin, as we traveled away from the noise of the docks and up the hills of the city to where Lord Bolon's estate lay.

The princess sat across from me and kept her eyes glued to her window the entire ride, unwilling to look at me. Occasionally, she would run her hands over her wrists, where her freshly healed skin was still visible, slightly pinker than the rest.

I had not intended to keep her in chains, but she had challenged me, and I couldn't let that stand. She was much too valuable for me to allow her to come to harm, especially of her own making. And she was sure to harm herself, she was much too impulsive. No, she would become the crown jewel of my collection, and as such, I would keep her safe.

I thought back to her sultry words on the boat deck and couldn't help but relish in the way they had set my skin ablaze. It had been a very long time since someone had challenged me so openly, so brazenly, like that. To see that fierce defiance burning in her eyes—how I longed to see her succumb.

The thought of her on her knees before me, her pink tongue darting over her warm lips in anticipation had me too bothered. I needed a distraction.

"You know, Princess, I think you will enjoy the view inside the carriage much more."

She turned to me; her face neutral. She scanned me from head to toe, lingering in ways that I couldn't help the smirk that crossed my lips.

"I suppose it's true what they say about you?"

"Oh, and what is that?" I said, quirking an eyebrow.

"That your ego is larger than your army." Her bobbed black hair swung around her as she turned back to the window. *Spoiled brat.* She was being no fun at all.

"Are you planning your escape route through the city?" I saw her flinch, an almost imperceptible twitch of her lips, that told me I had guessed right. But she turned to me again, and if looks could kill, hers would have.

"I have been locked away my whole life, remember? I have never been outside my island before. I was simply...observing." No lie there. What a great waste that King Rahul had kept this jewel all to himself for so long.

I pulled back the curtain on my window, "In the distance, you will see the Alderi Spiral, or what remains of it. It is thought that Metlin, or the city that was formerly here was much larger several millennia ago, but Alderi power concentrated in Koron during the Second Age."

She blinked at me like I was some sort of slimy toad who had emerged from a pond to ruin her summer picnic. "King, general, and tour guide? A man of many talents, I see."

"I think you will find that my *talents* lie in many areas, Princess." I let my voice lower, and I loved the way her nose twitched in distaste at my words. She showed every one of her emotions on her face, and I so enjoyed it.

"I'll add arrogant asshole to the list as well." Gods, when was the last time someone had said something like that to me? This woman. I pulled out of my relaxed posture, raising myself to my full height, letting myself fill the carriage. She shrunk back from me but kept that defiant chin held high, and I could see her clamping her nails into the palms of her hands to keep them from shaking. But I could smell the fear coming off of her in acrid waves like vinegar and the darkness of a moonless winter night. *Good.*

I reached out for her, and she truly shrunk from me now, as my finger slid around her neck. I didn't squeeze, not yet. "You best be careful with that mouth, Princess, or I really will find better uses for it." I saw the whites of her eyes expand, her breath coming in shallow pulses that matched the rapid pulse I felt under my fingertips. "Commanding the largest army on the continent requires a great deal of discipline, and I have become very effective at administering it. I think you could use a few lessons in obedience." I squeezed down ever so slightly on her neck, just straining her pulse. She still trembled beneath me, but I saw embers of anger burning in her eyes.

"I will never *fucking* obey you." Her words were quiet but dripped over my skin like oil set ablaze.

"Oh, Princess, by the time I'm done, you will beg for me."

She moved as if she were going to strike me, but I placed my other hand on her chest, the tips of my fingers just pressing in over her heart. She froze, and I could practically see her memory of what I had done to that soldier. For a moment we stayed there, locked in stasis, until the carriage lurched to a halt, and I heard Avlyn announce us from the roof of the carriage.

I pulled away from her then, relishing my handprint that slowly faded from her neck. "Shall we?"

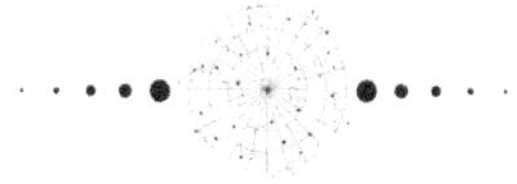

Lord Bolon Tutulis was the same boisterous idiot he had always been. He came out wearing his wine-stained light blue robes, and was clearly drunk, despite the early hour, as he stumbled forward. He was one of the few fae I knew who could be called rotund. As one of the High Lords of the Golden Kingdom, and the lord of the largest port on the continent, he certainly wanted for nothing, and had appetites to match.

His current human wife accompanied him, fresh as a spring flower in a matching bluebell dress. I couldn't recall how many wives I'd seen Bolon go through at this point, but this one was a pretty little thing with pale skin and dark hair. She held a small babe to her breast, who still carried the sweet scent of a newborn.

"Your Highness, we are honored by your visit." He bowed deeply, and his small wife nearly collapsed trying to do the same with her babe. "And we are honored to host you as well, Princess Tori Khato of the Pearl Kingdom." Bolon's eyes shone greedily then, and I knew bringing the princess along would serve me well.

I almost didn't recognize the creature that stepped out of the carriage behind me. A stunning smile revealed dazzling teeth between her flushed lips. She held herself aloft gracefully as she descended from the carriage, her posture tall and elegant. No sign of the ferocious beast I had come to know.

"Please, My Lord, the pleasure is all mine." She cut him another dazzling smile that had me clenching my teeth before she turned to the human woman, and I saw that smile reach her eyes. "And a pleasure to meet you as well Lady ...?"

"Just Livia, ma'am—or I mean Princess, Your Grace—I'm

sorry..." I almost felt bad for the poor thing, shaking as she was. Tori stepped towards the girl, and she swooned. Tori quickly grabbed her and supported her under the arm holding the baby.

"No apologies needed, Lady Livia. If I'm not mistaken, you should be in bed recovering, this babe can't be more than a few weeks old." She shot a look at Bolon then that carried all the menace I knew her for, but I think the man was too dull to notice. He simply shrugged his shoulders and snapped his fingers. A small nymph slave came forward and tried to hold the girl aloft, but it seemed she was a bit heavy, so Tori kept her arm around her. "I shall accompany her," she declared.

"Before returning to join us for luncheon," I said.

She shot me another look that was all daggers, but added, "Yes, of course." She then swiftly turned but made sure to keep her arm supporting the babe in his mother's arms. She held out her other hand and a tiny fist came out from the wrappings to clench around her finger. She made a series of soft coos, and I saw the human girl smile as they entered the manse. I waved to a few of my guards to follow her.

"Should I be concerned that your long bachelorhood is finally coming to an end, Abraxas?" Bolon slurred his words, and I didn't dignify his worthless musings with a response. Unfortunately, this only seemed to spur him on. "I've always told you; married life isn't so bad. In fact, if you don't intend to have her, once I'm done with this one, I wouldn't mind finding out what the Princess of Niata has between those long legs."

"Such vulgar talk is unbecoming, Bolon." My words were calm, but I'd dropped my voice and allowed every shred of malice flow through it as I turned towards the drunk, envisioning his head leaving his shoulders with one swift flash of my blade. I enjoyed watching the blood drain from his face.

"Of course, Your Majesty, my apologies." He wiped the

sweat from his brow and then onto his already disgusting robe. "Shall we head inside to discuss—"

"Yes, I'd rather have this whole business concluded quickly." I strode past the man into his own house as he bumbled behind me.

"Your Majesty, the prisoner hasn't revealed anything. Perhaps—" It was my turn to shoot him a withering look. This time he was smart enough to shut up. Bolon would have been completely worthless if his long tenure as the Lord of Metlin hadn't set him up with spies and contacts in every part of the continent. As such, he was a necessary cretin. I couldn't help but bring my fingers to the bridge of my nose and sigh heavily.

"Avlyn, head down and see if you can't help him remember the information we need." Avlyn gave a curt nod and was off as I pushed into Lord Bolon's dining hall, taking the seat at the head of the table. At least he hadn't invited half the nobles of Metlin like the last time I had passed through, but the table was set with a feast far more plentiful than what the three of us would need.

We hardly had our first glass of ambrosia poured when the princess rejoined us. She sat at my left hand, opposite Bolon. She lifted her glass, thanked the slave who filled it, and then took a few comically large sips before plastering her courtly smile back on.

"Your wife is a lovely woman, Lord Bolon, and quite an adept mother. I would not have guessed this was her first child."

"Her first perhaps, but not Bolon's. How many children do you have now?"

He pondered for a moment, taking his own large sip of ambrosia, "Honestly? I've lost count at this point. I have an accountant who takes care of my payments for them. Damn good accountant too. Even keeps track of which ones try to murder the others in the hopes they'll inherit my holdings. Bloody fools, don't they know I'll outlive them all?"

I could hear Tori's teeth grinding, but as I glanced at her, I could see her smile still held in place. Her fingers, however, gripped her dinner knife so hard I was surprised she hadn't bent it. Since I didn't feel like dealing with the murder of the Lord of Metlin today, I interjected, "What news of the Golden Kingdom?"

"Nothing you haven't heard before. Crop failures have been increasing, and the Varda also flooded so badly this year we nearly lost Haverfalls. The population there was mostly Sidhe slaves, so not too great a loss. But still, it greatly disrupted the ambrosia harvest. Luckily, Emperor Hadeon sent in relief efforts which got us through the Harvest. Took extra Tithe for it, but we just had to extract that from those poor sods having their town rebuilt."

I could see that this line of conversation was only bringing Bolon's premature death by Tori's knife on quicker, but for once the moron saved himself. "But this is basic news, it's been happening for years. Just a shift of the age, in a few more human lifetimes we will be back to normal. I'd much rather hear from our mysterious princess."

Tori's jaw relaxed a bit. "There isn't much to tell. What would you like to know?"

"Everything, everything! How fares the kingdom, why have you decided to leave now?" To her credit, Tori kept her face extremely neutral as she slid her eyes over to me.

I quickly explained, "The princess has become a ward in my kingdom, to help improve relationships between the Pearl Kingdom and the emperor." Her lips thinned, but she did not say anything more.

Bolon let out a jovial laugh. "Well about time, I say! King Rahul has been so isolated for so long, I'm happy to see him improving relationships. Why, he's almost as much of an isolationist as you, Abraxas. One of these days I'll get you to let me inside the borders of the Dragon Kingdom," I said nothing in response, but Bolon lumbered on, turning back to Tori, "Perhaps you could speak to your father on my behalf as trades open up?"

"I will certainly be telling my father exactly the type of man you are, Lord Bolon." Her tone was flirtatious, but her eyes were burning pits.

"Wonderful! You know, back before the last war I traveled to Niata once. Beautiful place. The ocean there was like nothing I had ever seen before." Tori's face softened, if only ever so slightly, the fire in her eyes replaced with melancholy. But she continued to converse with Lord Bolon, as he droned on and on and on about his travels. But she soon had her courtly mask back on, batting her lashes and laughing at all Bolon's inane jokes. The sound was light and filled the room. I found myself seething each time he managed to extract another of the lovely sounds from her. I was ready to stab the man myself when Avlyn entered the room, shaking their head.

"Well, it seems I may have to extend my stay, Lord Bolon, but I think it's time for the princess to return to my ship." My tone left no place for exceptions. "Would you give us a moment alone?" Bolon nodded and stood, bowing to me. He then turned and placed a swift kiss on Tori's cheek—the closest he had come to death during our entire time together—and quickly exited the room.

Tori immediately dropped her mask, her sour expression returning. "I've been at court with lords and ladies my entire life, and that was by far the worst man I have ever met." She paused, "Besides you, of course."

"With magic fading from this world, the currency of power has been transferred to coin, which Bolon has in excess. Yes, the world would certainly not be any worse off if he were gone." I decided to ignore her insult this time. She seemed surprised at my answer, and for a few moments, we simply shared the space in silence.

"You seem quite comfortable with babies. Not a common trait amongst fae royalty."

She bit her lip in thought, causing the skin there to blanch and then come back even redder for a moment. I had to force myself not to imagine what other things might cause the same reaction.

"I've known many generations of humans. My favorite cook, I knew her great-grandmother, I saw each generation grow from babe to crone. Each one of those lives was a blessing to me." She seemed deep in thought, then shrugged her shoulders, "Babies are easy when you're not the one feeding them. I find that when they get older, that's when they are much more trouble." A soft smile lit up her face at a memory I wasn't privy to, but she quickly wiped it from her face. "What does it matter?"

"Just interesting to see that you can be cordial and well-behaved. It seems I am the exception to the rule."

"What can I say? You bring out the best in me." She sank back into her chair, rubbing her eyes.

"Luckily, Avlyn will escort you back to the ship. As I said, I have unfinished business here."

"What sort of unfinished business?"

"That is none of your concern."

"I have a feeling it very much is."

I raised my fingers to the bridge of my nose again. This day was truly turning into a terrible headache. I waved at Avlyn, and they came over to escort Tori out. She faced them and looped her arm through theirs, "I'm surprised the Domineering King over here can stand to have me out of his sight. Hope you don't get in too much trouble when I escape again."

Avlyn was wise and released Tori before I slammed into her,

pushing her up against one of the windows of the dining hall, grabbing her wrists and pinning them above her head.

"Know this, Princess," I pushed my whole weight into her, and felt the breath squeeze out of her lungs as well as the swell of her chest and grind of her hips into my own, "If I should hear that you attempt to escape, and I say attempt because I do not doubt that Avlyn would catch you—again. You shall remain shackled for the remainder of our long journey home. You've gotten comfortable in your quarters. Perhaps a few days roiling in the brig below deck will remind you how to behave."

"Let me go!" She struggled to get free, but all she really did was grind her hips into mine, but she immediately stopped when the resulting friction had a small groan passing my lips.

Her eyes widened, and I leaned in, "Trying to persuade me otherwise? I suppose I could be convinced." I brushed my nose against her cheek and took a deep inhale of her scent, a mixture of evergreen forests and jasmine, now laced with fear—and just the tiniest hint of something much more sinister, much more lascivious.

I pressed my lips to her ear, and in barely a whisper "Would you prefer to be in my chambers, chained to my bed?" She wasn't breathing, but her heart raced, and I could see the color rising in her cheeks.

She couldn't fight me physically, so she spat out, "Fuck you!"

"Try and escape again, little bird, and you'll get your wish," I laughed and then spun her into Avlyn's arms and strode out the door. My feet knew the path to the dungeon, and after the day that I'd had, I was ready for blood.

Chapter 7

Tori

Every cobblestone we passed over on the ride home seemed to taunt me. Each bump sent the carriage handle jiggling, daring me to grab it and fling myself out. Avlyn had very obviously not bothered to lock it when they joined me in the carriage. Now they sat across from me, their eyes laughing. They extended their hand towards the door, as if in invitation, mirth printed all over their face.

But I couldn't stop my mind from running the scenario. Me, jumping from the carriage and making it about four steps before Avlyn would catch me, flinging me over their broad shoulders, hand gripping my ass as they carted me back. They would take me to the king's chamber, but instead of chains, their strong hands would hold my forearms pinned to the king's bed. Abraxas would return with that same dark look from the dining room earlier. I'd fight Avlyn, but it would be of no use as he approached, slowly, dropping pieces of his clothing as he did. His weight would cause the bed to buckle, sliding me toward him as his hand traced up the inside of my thigh, higher and higher, Avlyn joining in to trace my breasts.

I groaned in frustration, rubbing my hands over my face, pulling the skin taught, trying to get it together. I hated that Avlyn obviously knew the direction of my thoughts. I hated that I was having these thoughts about the people who had kidnapped me. I hated how much I was enjoying them.

I pushed it all away. While meditation *could* be effective whenever my thoughts ran wild before, I found that rough hands and the crashing together of naked bodies was a much more enjoyable method of silencing them. Well, my mind had been in disarray for days, no wonder I was seeking out the best solution.

As if thinking of it had summoned them, all my grief came flooding back. Images of Niata burning, my mother wailing and then her dead eyes, the sharp rake of teeth on my neck, blood—blood absolutely everywhere. I felt as if a boulder had crashed into my chest, each breath coming shorter and shorter. My fingers and toes went numb as I felt the blood rushing from my limbs inward. Black clouds began to fill my vision, so I threw my head between my knees, gasping for air.

"Princess, are you alright?"

"Yes, fine. Don't touch me," I gritted out. I heard the movement of Avlyn's armor freeze as if they had been reaching out and stopped.

"We are almost back to the docks; we will be back on the ship soon." Oh gods, the ship. Back in that little room. Chained, imprisoned. My breathing was audibly labored now, and even bent over the edges of my vision were still painted black.

Two gentle hands cupped my face and pulled me up to those glowing amber eyes.

"Breathe, Tori, breathe. In," a whoosh passed Avlyn's lips, "and out. With me now." They held my stare and breathed slowly, their soft breath passing over my face, guiding me to control my own.

After a few moments, my vision cleared, and my breathing

regulated. But Avlyn still held my cheeks, their lips pulled tight in concern. I didn't pull away, something in me craved the gentleness, the softness of their touch. But the comfort of it had me drowning again, the water rushing up to my eyes, threatening to escape. So, I pulled away.

"I'm fine." They nodded and pulled back into their seat, increasing the distance between us. We sat that way until our carriage rolled to a halt. Avlyn guided me back to the ship and into my quarters. I laid down on my bed and placed my hands on my chest. I tried to think of nothing, nothing but the steady in and out of my breath until sleep could claim me.

Chapter 8

Abraxas

The room stunk of piss and blood, the aftereffects of everything that had already happened to the Huldu held in the dungeon. Bolon's men and Avlyn had done their work well. I could see that several of the fae's nails were missing and numerous cuts lined the more sensitive parts of him. His green blood flooded down his blue skin, and I could see the strain in each of his tight muscles beneath his lithe form. But he had held up to days of torture at this point. I had to give the bastard credit for that.

His head hung to his chest; his arms strung up in irons against the stone wall. I could see the burn marks from the iron shackles on his wrists and neck. But as he heard me enter the room, he raised his head to me.

"Seems that they have finally sent someone important to see me. Guess I should feel honored." So, he knew who I was. Good.

"You know you won't leave this room alive, so why make it more difficult on yourself? I can end this now, or I can end this in a few weeks. Your choice."

"My secrets die with me." A tough bastard, that was for sure.

But everyone had a weakness. I approached him, and even he couldn't hide his flinch as I picked up an iron knife from the floor, already covered in his blood. I drew it slowly across his bare chest, and he ground his teeth as the iron burned the surface, slowing his healing. I imagined it was Bolon's chest, as Tori's laughter spilled over him.

Once, this would have sickened me, causing pain to achieve my ends. But I had killed off that part of me a long time ago. He had been consumed by the beast that had fed on my rage these past centuries, and now all that was left was the monster. And he was willing to do anything for his revenge.

"You know what I want. Just tell me how to get to it, and this can all be over."

Hadeon had to have something on this man, to keep him this tight-lipped. He had nothing to fear from the emperor now, unless...

"You are from the River Kingdom, near Manan, correct?" Bolon's men had gotten that much information from him, at least. "It would be an awful shame if my soldiers were to visit there, and visit your original laboratory," his heart rate increased and I knew I was close, "perhaps to find that lovely wife of yours, and the children." His eyes widened, and I knew I had played this correctly.

"Please, please you can't—" I slashed the blade across his face, my rings colliding with his cheek first. "I can, and I will. But give me the information I need, and I can keep them safe, away from the emperor."

His eyes met mine then, "Why should I trust you any more than him? You will just leave them to die."

"I may be your enemy, but I'm a man of my word."

"Tell your father that." Anger roiled in me, and I almost sent the knife through the Huldu's heart. But I needed this more than I needed to unleash my anger. "Then choose, who would you rather have visit that lovely wife of yours, me or him?" As always, my reputation preceded me, and centuries of handling Hadeon's dirty work served in my favor.

"You can't get to it. The enchantment is too strong. Hadeon himself couldn't break it. The only thing that could..." He trailed off, but I knew I had it now. I didn't need the knife for this.

"The Diadem of Soraya, it was said to break any enchantment." Wonderful, another fucking quest. But I saw the Huldu's shoulders slump then, his breath leaving him. I knew he didn't have anything else, nothing left to give. But still, he lifted his eyes to mine, "Please, spare them...save them."

"I will, I give you my word." And I drew the blade across his throat.

Chapter 9

Tori

I could feel the ship moving as the low morning sun showed through my portal. It seemed sleep had found me after all. I looked out the window to see the coast floating by at a leisurely pace as we made our way north. I stretched out as best I could in the small space, starting my morning exercises when a knock came at my door. The bolt scraped open as Avlyn's face peered around the door.

"Time for my morning relief then, is it?"

"Yes, but I thought we might try something different today."

"Um, well I've been doing it the same way my whole life, don't think much can be improved upon." They rolled their eyes.

"It's too early for this snark, Princess. Just come with me, you brat." I walked towards them, trying not to seem too eager to leave the confines of my room.

As we returned from our usual morning journey, Avlyn steered me towards the deck. As we exited the ship's cabin, I couldn't help but rejoice at the sunlight hitting my skin, and the crisp sea breeze whipping at my hair. I allowed myself a moment to just soak in the warmth creeping across me, closing my eyes, before following after them. We walked down the deck until we encountered a small cohort of soldiers who had come out for some exercises. Most were male, many of them shirtless, going through a warmup routine not too different from the ones I had done back home.

Avlyn turned to me and placed their hands on their hips, "Alright, Princess, here's the deal. It's a long journey from here to Xyr, and I'd rather not waste my time guarding you when I don't have to. I'd rather that you spend your day up here with me and the other soldiers, so I can do my actual fucking job." I pursed my lips, waiting for the other shoe to drop. "And don't get any ideas about flinging yourself overboard again. I'll have you know my ancestor was a mermaid, so I'll always catch you."

I couldn't help it as my jaw dropped. "A mermaid? The lost fae race? Surely such a thing would be known? How have you—oh." Avlyn's face was pure delight. "You're teasing me, aren't you?" They laughed, a full-bellied laugh that soothed the burn of my embarrassment.

"I would never dream of it, Princess. Now, do we have a deal?" I tilted my face back to the sun, closing my eyes again. I paused as if contemplating my answer, when really the answer was obvious.

"Deal. And you can call me Tori."

"Not a chance, Princess. Here, put these on," they flung a pair of leather leggings and a loose shirt at me. I looked back at the door to the cabins, wondering where I would change.

"Suddenly so shy, when we've all seen it before?" They practically waggled their eyebrows at me, but the nature of the teasing and the setting reminded me of my time back with the soldiers of the Pearl Army. I couldn't help but feel like I was slipping back into a routine that suited me like a well-worn glove.

I pulled off my outer robe, and a few whistles emerged from somewhere in the crowd of soldiers, most of whom were watching me and Avlyn now. I ignored it, and I slipped the leggings and shirt on without revealing too much under my slip.

"Good, try this out." They tossed me a wooden practice sword, made to mimic the size and weight of a traditional longsword. While I had trained in that style, I had always preferred wielding two lighter and shorter blades, working better at close range. But I wasn't about to complain, too much.

"Got anything made for adults?"

"Not for you, I don't. Now fall in at the end of the line and try to keep up." Avlyn led the soldiers through the rest of the warmup and into a series of fighting exercises. The moves were a bit different, but after a short while, the feel of the sword in my hand felt more and more natural, and I let my body guide me. It remembered the way to move, decades of practice guiding me without conscious thought, and my mind cleared to a beautiful blank. For the first time since I had been taken, I felt like myself again, not an animal in a cage.

The time passed quickly, and soon the sun was directly overhead, and all of us were covered in sweat. Barrels of fresh water were pulled out, and tin cups clinked as tired hands dipped them into the sloshing liquid. I greedily sipped at my cup, letting the cool water spill down my face and body in my haste. It ran and pooled with my sweat and felt absolutely divine. On my tongue, it was sweeter than any ambrosia.

A strong hand collided with my shoulder in a bracing slap, and I choked, sputtering water everywhere. "Looks like the princess here has had some sword training." A soldier whose skin gleamed in the noonday sun smiled down at me. He had his chestnut hair pulled back into a bun and a wide, winning grin, but I barely noticed those, as my eyes slid to the utterly ridiculous display of defined muscles that danced all over his chest and back. I realized he had left his hand on my shoulder where he had slapped me, adding additional warmth to my skin.

"Yeah, she's already better than you, Kaleos." Avlyn maneuvered themselves between us, forcing his hand off my shoulder. But Kaleos didn't seem perturbed in the slightest, a good-natured laugh escaping him. "You think so? Maybe we should duel to settle the matter." He winked at me, and I was glad my skin was already flushed from my exertion, hiding my blush.

"Absolutely not."

"I don't see why not?" I held Kaleos' gaze, "Perhaps I could learn something new?" I let him see me lick my lips. I saw the heat rise in his stare then. Avlyn raised their eyes to the heavens, as if pleading with the gods to spare them, muttering something about *giving an inch.*

"For all the complaining you did, Commander, it doesn't seem like you are working the troops very hard." The king's voice cut through the crowd. All the soldiers around straightened up then, falling out of their relaxed stances. "Just a quick water break, My King, then back at it."

"Indeed." His gaze dropped to me, that face icy. "And you, Princess? Enjoying yourself?"

"Quite a bit, yes." I was so high on sunshine and sweat that I couldn't even come up with anything snarky to say.

"Well, see you don't overexert yourself. I'd hate for you to have to spend tomorrow recovering." Unsure if that was a threat, I gave him a sarcastic salute, but noticed that Kaleos was nowhere to be seen. He stalked off and Avlyn called us back into our lines. We continued through much of the afternoon, but I found myself unable to focus as I felt the king's gaze lingering over me the entire time.

Chapter 10

Tori

I had overexerted myself. The next day every single muscle in my body ached. I moaned as I stretched into it, relishing the soreness. I stood up and found that a few sets of leggings and linen tops had been left for me. I hadn't noticed them before collapsing into bed the night before. I dressed quickly, and perched on the edge of my bed, tapping my toes and waiting for Avlyn's arrival. Minutes ticked by. I checked the position of the sun from my window, and knew it was much past when they would normally collect me.

I rose and knocked on my door. Nothing. I gave the handle a jiggle to find that the door easily popped open. I stuck my head out and saw that there was no guard in sight. My brain rushed with thoughts; plans I had let slip away trying to file themself into place. But as my brain worked on figuring out what it wanted, my feet walked me out onto the deck of the ship.

"Rise and shine, Princess. Look who decided to sleep in," Avlyn called to me from across the deck. Some jeers rose from the cohort, but they all seemed a bit more subdued than the day before. I walked over, Avlyn tossed me my practice sword, and I fell into the ranks. As we warmed up, I kept on the lookout for Kaleos, but he was nowhere to be found. My sore muscles complained at every minuscule movement, so I didn't have much willpower to think about it.

When we finally took our first water break, I grabbed my cup and cut through the crowd, looking for him. The soldiers might have had some sort of rotation on who trained each day, but I recognized most of the men from yesterday, so it seemed odd. After a few minutes of searching, I saw him pressed behind some other soldiers. He looked quite a bit paler than when I had last seen him, and when his eyes locked with mine, he immediately stood and bolted the other way. I sighed, I wasn't *that* desperate, so I didn't follow him.

Luckily, Avlyn called us back to our lines soon after. The soldiers spent much of the afternoon sparing each other while Avlyn had me watch from the sidelines. They narrated the techniques and counter-techniques to me, making it as if they were teaching me something while making it abundantly clear that I would not be participating.

Despite that, the days passed quickly, and I found most nights I barely had time to shove dinner in my face before collapsing into bed. I rarely saw the king, mostly when he would stand on the upper deck and observe the comings and goings of the ship, but occasionally in my dreams. They were the kind of dreams that I mostly tried to forget in the morning, except for a select few that I tucked away, saving those for nights when sleep didn't claim me, and I had to bring my hands between my legs to help get me there. I always felt disgusting after, but it seemed the clear skies and salty breeze wiped me clear of my sins every morning.

I had found great peace in the simple routine of our voyage, and even though I had found my door unlocked every morning, I hadn't moved to take advantage of it. But the sea and sky grew colder as we traveled north, and I knew that this respite wouldn't last much longer. I knew our voyage was drawing to a close when the seas grew so rough and choppy that it became too difficult for us to easily stand on the deck, let alone train.

After two days of this, and more trips to the ship's railing to expel the contents of my stomach than I cared to count, I remembered why I hated sailing. But on the third day, while Avlyn gently held my hair back as I heaved my breakfast to the fish, they whispered, "Look, Princess."

The sea around us was shrouded in mist, and I could barely see one hundred feet beyond the railing of the ship. But there, rising out of the ocean like a great leviathan of legend, a shape emerged from the mist. As we drew closer, I could see it was a giant rock. Its face dark grey like the waters below, cut away by years of dancing with the ocean. But this island wasn't soft and rounded like the boulder back home. Here, they were at war, the ocean taking everything it could while the rock dug itself in. Even as we sailed by, I heard a great lightning-like crack as a huge slab broke loose and crashed into the sea below.

More and more of the rocks and islands rose up from the sea, towering higher than the mast of our ship. We stayed a cautionary distance away, but I could still see the wreckage of enough ships for an age strewn about their bases.

"The Sea of Spirits," Avlyn whispered it almost like a prayer.

"More like the Sea of Pissed Off Motherfucking Ghosts," one of the soldiers nearby glibbed, soft chuckling all around. The Sea of Spirits was the last piece of the ocean we needed to cross before reaching the Dragon Kingdom and was the most treacherous. The entire ocean was littered with small islands and rocks like we were seeing now, many hidden beneath the waves. Only one narrow passage existed that allowed any to travel to the Bay of Dragons and the capital city of Xyr. The passage was only navigable to the most skilled sailors, and it made the Dragon Kingdom nearly impossible to breach.

The islands seemed to be closing in around us when I heard a soft gasp behind me. Looking up, I saw him looming out at us. A great statue beyond proportion. The figure was of a man in ancient garb, holding a dragon's egg out before him, forever frozen in granite stone. He stuck out from the seafloor at an acute angle and leaned against one of the islands. Half of his head and face were missing, and the lower portion of him was covered in barnacles, clinging to him like corrupted jewels. The outstretched hand holding the egg aloft was so high that our entire ship passed underneath it.

"The Gate of King Beher," Avlyn made the sign against evil with their hands, "we enter Apollyon's Pass now." I lifted my eyes to follow the dragon's egg as it passed over the ship, turning my body to follow its path. As it faded into the mist behind the stern of the ship, my eyes shifted to the upper deck, where the king stood, his eyes still trailing off after the statue.

I slowly climbed the stairs to the upper deck, joining him at the back railing of the ship. "He was your ancestor?"

He didn't look at me, but answered, "Yes, my great-great grandfather, actually."

"Did you know him?"

"No, even the fae are not immortal and he had faded from this world before my time." Even to me, the time scale of which the Coringus family had ruled was beyond imagining, ruling since the beginning of the first age. In fact, Abraxas' father, Amaros, had ruled over fifteen hundred years before, well before Abraxas had killed him. *Maybe bringing up family history wasn't the best idea.*

Seeming ready to change the subject, he said, "These islands were once a great land, the first true fae kingdom, but their hubris brought about their destruction." He chuckled then, "Well that, and the massive volcanic eruption that destroyed it all."

"Ah, I see King Tour Guide has made a reappearance." He pinched his nose bridge with his thumb and forefinger, an expression of exasperation I was really coming to enjoy.

"You have labeled yourself as a poor student. I was merely sharing some of my scholarship in history with you, trying to fill in the gaps in your education."

"I don't think it counts as scholarship if you were there to live through it." I flashed him my most winning smile. I saw laughter dancing behind his viridian eyes, and that brought me more pleasure than I cared to examine.

"Careful, young one, these waters are treacherous, and it would be all too easy for you to accidentally fall in here." There was no threat in his voice, and I saw his trademark smirk start to spread, when suddenly the boat rocked antagonistically. I felt my feet leave the floorboards as the boat dropped out from under me. Suddenly, the king had one arm beneath mine, and another behind my back, preventing me from dropping over the railing. When the boat steadied, our bodies were pressed together in a way that was all too similar to our encounter at Lord Bolon's mansion. I shoved out of his arms.

"I didn't think you were going to make good on your threat so quickly."

His face hardened again, "You should go below deck, it seems the seas are riled today."

"Is that an order?" Before he could answer, another wave crashed into the side of the boat, slamming me over to my side, and assaulting me with seawater. My stomach heaved urgently. "Never mind, I'll go."

I clung to the stair railing as I made my way back to the main deck and inside. I closed the cabin door, and pressed my back into it, sliding down to the floor. I could just hear the shouting of the soldiers and sailors over the crashing of the waves. I dropped my head between my knees, willing my stomach to cling to whatever remained of my breakfast. But just as soon as it had started, it was over and the boat stopped rolling.

I remained there for a few more moments. But the silence of the empty cabins pressed in upon me. Dark thoughts crept out of the recesses of my mind, thoughts of a great pressure squeezing the life from me, of my brother laid across the feet of Emperor Hadeon, of blood— blood that stained my hands and my heart.

But then the ship jolted again, and it felt much more...solid. Not like a crashing wave, but as if we had hit something else. Another great crash, followed by more erratic shouts from the deck, then a distinctive scream. I rose up, unsteady on my feet, but I leaned against the door frame and pulled the cabin door open.

I couldn't make sense of what I saw. Soldiers and sailors gathered around what looked like a collapsed mast, slashing it with swords and spears. But then the mast rolled of its own volition, and I saw the underside was covered in massive disks, each accompanied by a vicious hook larger than my arm. No, not disks, but suckers. And not a mast, but a giant writhing tentacle. As I watched, a smaller tentacle reached over the side of the ship and grabbed a soldier around his waist. He screamed as he was pulled overboard, into the depths below.

I saw Kaleos, sword raised, land a solid blow on the main arm, and a great howl echoed within the water below the ship. From the opposite side, another tentacle reached up and slammed itself down, crushing his legs beneath it. Without thinking, I ran out onto the deck. Kaleos was half trapped under the tentacle, trying to free himself, still hacking at the creature. He didn't see the other tentacle about to slam down on his head. I ran and kicked it away with all my strength.

Then I reached out my hand and planted my feet in the crack

between two boards. I grasped his forearm and heaved, but he barely moved. Then, the creature seemed to sense my interference, as another, smaller tentacle snaked over the deck, and wrapped itself around my leg.

I lost my grip on the deck and slid into Kaleos. But as the tentacle on my leg began to pull me away, Kaleos raised his sword to cut it.

"Wait!" I let it pull on me but gripped onto Kaleos even harder. I saw my plan dawn on him, and he gave me the smallest nod and gripped down on me with his fingers. It felt like my leg was going to be pulled out of its socket, but I saw Kaleos begin to slide out from under the beast. I gripped into his arm tighter, but we slipped, so only our fingers held. He reached for his sword to free me, but it was too late, as our fingers released. But instead of sailing overboard, I flopped to the deck.

I turned, and the king stood behind me, where his sword had cut my leg free. I kicked off the tentacle that still clung to me, and sick, circular welts decorated my leg. Kaleos had freed himself and jumped up to re-engage. I jumped to do the same, not thinking too hard about how I intended to fight a creature I could barely comprehend. But then, an arm crashed around my chest.

"Get back in the cabins now." My feet were swinging wildly, as the king pulled me back.

"Is it really any safer in there?" I asked. As I said it, another great tentacle swept over the deck, crashing into the walls, ripping pieces off. "What is this thing?" The king threw us back, dodging another swing, and we landed against a pile of barrels on the deck.

In a soft voice I barely heard over the roar of the ocean, "Leviathan." One hadn't been seen in centuries; it had been thought they might all be extinct. It was unimaginable. The king's eyes landed on mine, "I wonder what has drawn this one out," he said as he held my gaze in a way that made me turn away, before he leapt up again as another great arm crashed towards us. He lifted his sword and cut straight through it as if it were nothing.

Another great howl from below the waves, and I saw the beast release our ship, its arms writhing and spinning as they tried to slip off the deck. But this gave the crew the moment they needed, and they leapt. Spears flew at the arms from every direction, and I saw a pair of sailors run up and uncover something at the bow of the boat. A great harpoon mounted on a crossbow so large it needed both men to maneuver it. I saw them swing it around and aim down at the ocean. As they swung, I saw that the back was attached to a massive rope, thicker than my arm around.

"What are you going to do?"

The king turned to me, with that cold look in his eye, "What we have been doing through the ages. Capture it and kill it." My stomach plummeted, but it might have just been the boat shaking violently again as I felt the beast crash into us. The tentacles I could see had changed from a deep ocean grey to a bright red, and another ghostly howl pierced my ears. The harpoon flew.

It must have found its target as the boat lurched, and everyone on board was pulled down as the beast tried to get away. I rolled to the railing and looked over the edge while clinging to the guide ropes. He was massive, far longer than our ship, and now his whole body was pinned up against the side of it. He seemed to be flashing, his flesh changing from white to red in erratic waves. Tentacles trailed up below a long body, covered in heavy armor and spikes. I could see the huge suckers near his head had hooks larger than my whole body, and as he thrashed to get away. I could see his great maw held rows and rows of teeth, each smaller than the next. They led down into a great gullet, deeper than the pits of hell.

He spun his body, trying to free himself, but it only wound the rope around him tighter, tying him to us. As I leaned over, one great eye turned to me. The eye was bigger than my torso, and a demonic yellow iris with a square pupil bore into me. But as I looked at him, I didn't see rage, but the whites of his eyes around the sulfuric iris, as a long low bellow left him. He held me in his gaze, and I made a very stupid decision.

I bolted from my place at the railing and ran across the deck. Swords and spears had fallen everywhere in the chaos, and I grabbed one and ran to the harpoon. Sailors were shouting as they tried to pull the great wheel that would retract the Leviathan. I leapt to where the rope was pulled taught near the edge of the railing and swung my sword down. Only a few of the fibers came free, but I swung again, and again. I heard shouts behind me, calling for me to stop, but I swung, and I swung, until the boat jolted, only a few strands remaining. I propped my leg up on the railing and swung one last time.

The tension finally released, the creature lurched away, and the boat flew in the opposite direction. Unfortunately, I stayed where I was, which was now out over the open sea, and I tumbled down into the water.

The ice-cold water of the Sea of Spirits engulfed me, and a great rushing of waves and bubbles spun me round and around, my body completely lost for direction. I threw my arms out, slowing my spinning, and when I finally came to a stop, I nearly released the breath that kept me alive.

That great eye sat before me, I could have reached out and touched it. My reflection glared back at me over that black square pupil. I waited for tentacles to snake up around my legs, to drag me down into the abyss with it, but he just held me there in his gaze. Then I heard more spears and harpoons breaching the surface above me. The Leviathan took one last look and slowly sank down, never taking his eye off me until the darkness consumed him.

I beat my legs for the surface and breached to a great breath and the yelling of my name. I looked back toward the ship to see a rope being tossed to me. I grabbed on and was yanked back to the ship. When I reached its side, I placed my feet against the wet boards and walked up the side as the rope was retracted. Once I reached the railing, several sets of hands deposited me back on the deck.

Once again, I lay soaking wet, looking up at the entire crew. But a deadly silence lay over the scene as every single pair of eyes locked on me. I considered throwing myself back to the Leviathan, for he seemed more friendly. Then the king stormed towards me, his anger so palpable he seemed to burn with it. He grabbed me and hauled me back to the cabins. I was in for it now.

Chapter 11

Tori

The king's quarters were fine, a rich mahogany desk set with several golden instruments I recognized for navigation filled the center of the space. Maps and charts filled every inch of the nearby wall, and huge windows opened to the stern of the ship as the ocean seemed to trail away from us. I kept my eyes very purposefully averted from the four-poster bed that lay on the side of the room.

The king had his back to me, his hands on his hips, looking out at the sea. I searched for any weapon in reach, but it seemed the only one available was the dagger at his hip. I once again wondered if I would have fared better staying in the sea with the beast.

"I tolerated your stupidity when it came to your own life, but today you put my entire crew at risk in your attempt to escape." He turned to me then, his face colder than I had ever seen it. "I cannot allow that."

He stepped towards me. "I wasn't trying to escape," I murmured.

He paused then, "Well then, do tell me, what the hell you were thinking?" His gaze bore into me.

How to explain? How do you say that you saw the same feeling in the eye of an eldritch horror that you felt every night? A deep, unending helplessness.

"He seemed frightened."

The king's face went completely blank, then took on a look I knew all too well. The look of a teacher who just couldn't deal with my antics anymore. "The Leviathan, who attacked us—tried to destroy my ship, almost killed you, and did kill several members of my crew—looked frightened?" He looked at me like I was the biggest imbecile he had ever seen.

I was used to that, had used it to my advantage my whole life. Just another vapid princess who couldn't be bothered to pay attention in her lessons. Tutor after tutor had abandoned me, much preferring to work with my quiet and attentive brother. All the better for me, who had preferred to read about what I liked in manic chunks and learn the rest from my interactions in court. And learn I had, becoming very apt at reading people and their internal desires, at filling my mind with subject after subject from my father's library.

But I could still see my father's face, a mask of control over his disappointment. *Control yourself, Tori.* His voice still rang in my head all these years later. *All you ever do is embarrass me.* Seeing that same look on the king's face, it opened that pit in my stomach I feared more than anything. That place where I had shoved away all my shame and guilt. His rage and anger I could handle, but not this.

"It seems an awful waste to kill him if he was potentially the last of his kind." This tact seemed to work better, as the king's lips thinned as if contemplating.

He turned away from me again, and in a voice that was almost too low to hear, "If he was the last of his kind, it would have been a kindness to free him from this world." He turned to me and saw my confusion. "To be alone... it breeds an anger that is worse than the deadliest poison. It festers in the soul, a corruption killing any goodness that remains. Better to go out in a blaze of rage and fight than the slow death of all you were."

"How is rage any different from anger?"

His eyes flicked to me, full of that wicked laughter. "Oh, Princess, rage will set you free."

"Sounds like you have a lot in common with the beast."

I wanted to hurt him, but he just smirked, "I haven't been alone in a very long time, Princess."

He rounded his desk then, and my hands shook as he approached, "Nothing like warm bodies to keep the demons away," I knew that all too well. His smile only grew more feral, and I stepped back, trying to keep some space between us and failing. I couldn't help it as my eyes darted to the bed, and I knew he saw it. I backed up more, my eyes never leaving him, and ran into the door of his cabin. He propped his hand up on the doorframe above me, his body enveloping mine.

"I know you remember what I said would happen if you disobeyed again. So, are you ready for your punishment, Princess?" His face was an inch from mine, and almost every part of me screamed to look away, look away from those eyes that burned with emerald fire. But the part of me that was always screaming, always hurting, the part of me that freed a deadly mythical beast, said *Fight.* And I always listened.

"Is this how you get everyone to your bed? Through fear?" He chuckled, and the sound sent heat flowing through me in a way that I hated, as the warmth from his body enveloped me. Flashes of my dreams came to me unbidden, and the heat curled deeper.

"Princess, not once in my long life have I had anyone who

wasn't willing, *begging*, for me. Besides, you don't smell like you are afraid. So, I will ask you again, are you ready?"

I snaked my hands around his waist, and I saw the smallest hint of surprise in his eyes, "And if I said yes, what would you do?" I ran one hand up his broad chest, and he was solid beneath my fingers. I traced my other hand around his waist and over his back, the muscles there tense from leaning over me, corded and ready to release. My arm brushed the handle of his dagger, but I ran my hand firmly down the curve of his ass, to hide the sensation. I pulled him so his hips collided with mine, and I could feel the hardness of him press into my stomach.

I heard him emit a small growl then, and I knew he was losing control. He leaned down further so his words tickled the sensitive skin beneath my ear, "I would do everything you have been dreaming about at night when you bring those long fingers between your legs." I hesitated then, revealed bare. I looked up and his smile was wicked, and I hated him more than anything else.

"You're right, Your Majesty, I have been dreaming of this since I met you." I swept my arm back, grabbing the hilt of his dagger. I slid it up as I went. Our bodies were too close together for me to apply lethal pressure, but I felt the dagger cut through his shirt and flesh, the warmth of his blood flooding onto me. I tried to raise it to his neck, his chest, his heart, anywhere. But he was too fast, and he slammed my wrist into the door next to my head, and the dagger clattered to the floor. He pushed himself back from me and looked down. I saw the blood welling onto his torn shirt, but his skin underneath was already knitting back together.

"Clever minx." He leaned into me again, and I was crushed between the door and his weight. My heart beat faster than my body could handle, and I felt his teeth wrap around the flesh at the base of my neck, "If it's pain you wanted, you should have just asked." I felt his teeth break my skin and couldn't help the hiss that escaped me.

But then a loud knock sounded on the wood we were pressed against, and he released me as an aggravated huff escaped him, "What?!"

"Your Majesty, the port bow is taking on water, and we need —" He spun me away from the door and wrenched it open. The soldier at the door looked down at the blood on his shirt, and on me as well, and I saw his eyes open in fear, realizing what he might have interrupted.

But the king stormed passed and called, "Get the princess back to her quarters, and make sure she stays there." The soldier swept in and led me off, but I couldn't help but take one last look at the dagger that still lay on the floor, covered in the king's blood.

Chapter 12

Abraxas

The repairs to the ship were simple, and it only filled me with greater rage that the princess and I had been interrupted. Avlyn sidled up to me as the last of the patch was put in place. "Get me the name of that sailor who came to fetch me."

Avlyn raised an eyebrow at me, "I will do no such thing."

I turned to them, "And why the fuck not?"

Avlyn's eyes locked on my torn bloody shirt, "I sent them to fetch you, I won't have them taking the brunt of your rage."

"And why the fuck did you do that?" I was at the edge of my control now, Avlyn could see that.

"You know why," they said and gave me a disapproving look. I turned away from them, trying to regain my composure before I did something I would regret. Avlyn and I had been together for centuries, and I hated how well they knew me sometimes. I took a deep breath that shook, but after a few more, I uncurled my fists.

I looked down at the bloody tear in my shirt, thinking of Tori's face as she had pulled my own dagger on me. Fierce and unafraid. Deadly, if ineffective. I had let her distract me too much and fallen right into her trap. Her hands on me had been intoxicating, but really, I had already been halfway gone when she had hit me with that perfect smile on deck earlier. I should have known it wouldn't be easy with her. She wanted a fight, and I would give it to her.

I shook my head to clear my thoughts, thoughts of my bite directly over where that scum had bitten her before, marking her. I turned back to Avlyn, that annoyed look still plastered on their face. "You've been sloppy with her. You want to let me in on why?"

"No." Avlyn rolled their eyes, something only they could get away with.

"It's too bad about the beast. The injection of magic from its death could have really helped with this season's crops." But their face grew more serious. "The men are talking about her. It's no small thing to fall into the sea with a Leviathan and survive." They raised their eyebrow at me again, "It's no small thing to enter a room with you that pissed off and survive."

I huffed a laugh. "It's your job to keep them under control. Besides, we will be back in Xyr by morning, and then they won't have to be around her."

"So, you would keep her from training then?" So, Avlyn had seen it too. The way Tori's face lit when she worked with the sword. The only time I had seen that darkness hanging over her chased away.

"No, but we will have to keep the situation under control, keep everyone in line."

Avlyn let out a hearty laugh, "I do not doubt that the princess can take care of herself." I had no doubt either.

Chapter 13

Tori

I spent the night running my hand over my neck, tracing the lines of the king's bite as it healed. He couldn't have known, but it was in the same spot that guard had bitten me in the dungeon. His bite had been shallower, but my freshly healed skin stung all the same. It had taken longer than I had expected for it to heal, but maybe it had been the repeated injury. Still, I couldn't help but run my fingers over it again and again, relishing the discomfort of it.

I had killed that man in the dungeon with no hesitation and would have killed the other. My rage and hatred had served me well then. Why had it abandoned me with the king? I felt that same anger, that same burning hatred, but it was tainted. Mixed with something I didn't dare look at too closely, lest it distract me, causing me to hesitate when I shouldn't. *You've already hesitated.* I replayed the man in the dungeon again, willing myself to feel that same way, but my mind always snagged on the king's face as he ripped the heart from the soldier when he had saved my life. He had saved my life again, today on deck, when he cut me free.

I didn't understand his intentions, not in the slightest. He obviously desired me, but that was a simple thing. What was going on between us was anything but simple. I thought back to his comments on my status as a twin. Perhaps he thought I would wield some great magic or hold some great power.

Jokes on you, Your Majesty. The only great power I held was the ability to ruin a good thing. I thought of the soldiers' faces today when I crawled back on the deck. I had put them in grave danger, and worse, I hadn't even thought about it before acting. There was no way I would be able to show my face at training again if I was even allowed to.

Dread filled me, thinking of not being able to train, to not spend my days in the sun. I hadn't even been considering it, but training with them also gave me much better options for planning my escape. My chest tightened, and I felt tears rising to my eyes, and with them, even darker thoughts. No, I needed a distraction.

I let my mind wander back to the king's cabin. To the sensation of his body crushing me against his door, the way he had groaned as I ran my hand over his firm ass. Only now, I reached for his dagger and brought it to his neck. "I think it's your turn to obey, Your Majesty."

I slid my fingers underneath my leggings, finding the wetness already pooled between my thighs. As I imagined him falling to his knees, I slid my fingers inside myself, pulsing in and out, the heel of my hand pressing down on the flesh at the apex of my thighs. But it was his mouth, his tongue, his lips as my climax came closer and closer. My leg hooked over his shoulder, using my knee and calf to pull him tighter, deeper as I found my release.

The new flesh of my neck ached as my pulse returned to normal, and my breath stabilized. I ran my fingers over it one last time before the boat rocked me gently to sleep.

Chapter 14

Tori

I awoke to more shouts, and for a moment I thought we might be under attack again, but the tone of the yelling was much more excited. I rose to exit my room only to find that my door was locked again. I pulled my hand back from the latch as if it were made of iron. I supposed that was to be expected.

I dressed myself in clean clothes and peered out my small window. Mist shrouded everything, but as I squinted, I could just see the outline of the shore approaching, grey and moody in the early morning light.

The handle on my door jiggled, and Avlyn opened it. "Up and at 'em, Princess, we are here." They led me out onto the deck, and the mist continued to burn off. The shore drew closer, and the city of Xyr appeared before me.

The beach that touched the sea was a deep, charcoal grey composed of volcanic rock that had been worn down over the ages. This led to rolling grassy hills that lay up against the edge of the city. Buildings made from wood and stone sprawled across the land, nestled up together like colored eggs in a nest. The city rose into a great volcanic cliff, the rocks there taking on the most interesting formation. The cliffs rose like monoliths from the sea, each column a perfect dark hexagon shape. The basalt rock formed huge crystals frozen in time. From these dramatic cliffs, a dark castle had been carved that loomed over the entire city, The Obsidian Keep. Fires from within lit the windows, as if it were a sleeping beast keeping watch over Xyr. Or was it more like a predator, waiting for a chance to strike?

"Home, sweet home." Avlyn left me at the railing, shouting commands and preparing the ship to dock. I wrapped my hands around the railing, my knuckles turning white. *Home.* What did that word even mean to me now? With my brother taken and mother gone, was Niata still my home? I remembered little Tom carrying around his baby sister, and pulling on Brianna's apron as she swatted my hand away from the cookies she had made, the baby's pudgy little cheeks jiggling as Tom nearly dropped her. I remember my days on the beach, training with my favorite cohort, our bodies shining with sweat in the summer heat as we would duel and test each other.

I remembered running through the deep jungle with Jun when we were younglings, evading our guards and giggling while hidden in the roots of trees. Once the guards had passed, Jun and I would lie back and watch the sun dance through the leaves above us. He'd had a beautiful voice even then, and I remembered how he would sing silly folk songs that seemed to still the air of the forest, as if every bug and leaf wanted to listen. Butterflies would gather on the branches around us, and songbirds would harmonize with him, and then he would giggle, and they would all flit away as our laughter chased after them.

Then Jun's face shifted, he was older, but I could barely see him. His eyes were filled with fear, and his voice sounded so far away, "Tori, wake up, wake up! You can't leave me here alone!"

The railing under my hands snapped, splintered wood falling into the waves below. I willed my breath to still, eyes peering out at the ocean. It was calmer today, and I let my mind mimic it. I shifted my hips and swung my arms, not caring if my motions looked foolish to those on deck. *Control yourself,* my father's voice. I pushed every thought away and synced my breath with my body.

"Interesting dance moves." I turned to see Kaleos striding towards me. He wore that stupid grin I had seen on him before, and I was happy to see he didn't look any worse for wear after the encounter with the Leviathan. I dropped my hands.

"I'm surprised you want to be seen talking to me." He ran his hand through his wavy dark hair, which he had left loose today.

"Yeah, the others are a bit pissed, huh? I don't really know why you let that thing go, but I do know I wouldn't be here to chat with you about it if you hadn't freed me," he said and extended his hand to me. "So I wanted to say thank you." I didn't move, but the warmth in his grin only grew, "Look, I know that normally it's supposed to be the princess who needs saving, but I'm a big enough man to admit I don't mind it the other way."

His hand was still extended, and I slowly placed my fingers in his. He slid his hand up to grip my forearm, and I did the same to him—the same gesture I'd seen many of the soldiers do after a duel. He smiled again and pulled me in to slap me on the back. It was friendly, but it still sent the air from my chest.

"Don't worry about the others. As soon as they get their feet back on dry land, they'll forget the whole thing. Tell you what? I'll convince Avlyn to let us duel, and when you kick my ass, you'll be back in their good graces." He winked at me again, but it didn't feel like before. This felt more— well it felt different. I finally returned his smile.

"Well, I have been doing this longer than you have been alive, Kaleos. I promise not to hurt you too badly," I said with a grin.

"I'm glad only my pride will suffer, Princess." And he released me, returning to his duties.

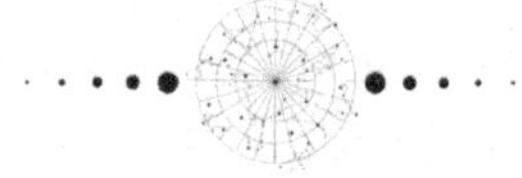

I MILLED AROUND THE SHIP, NOT ABLE TO HELP BUT TRYING to not look too useless. Apparently, this didn't work as Avlyn waved me over and had me coiling a massive rope onto the deck as we pulled into the dock. Even for me, as a fae, the water-logged thing was burdensome, and my muscles were burning by the time I felt the slight jostle of the ship as we collided softly with the dock.

Immediately, Avlyn was at my side, but they didn't place their hands on me as we walked off the ship, merely staying close behind. We were some of the first to disembark, but the soldiers were frenzied to get off the boat, and a great wave of them pushed me further down the dock. Avlyn gently placed their hand on my shoulder and steered me toward an awaiting carriage. A crowd had gathered near the end of the dock, and I saw soldiers sweeping up spouses and children into their arms, tears being shed for safe return. I thought then of those who had died in the Leviathan's grip, and the tears of grief that would be shed for them. My stomach turned as guilt rose inside me. I didn't think any men had died after I had freed it, but I doubt that would make much difference to the bereaved.

As I entered the carriage, I saw more ships docking and soldiers unloading until we were swept away up the street. We made our way through the city using what seemed to be the main road, which was wide and took a direct path to the castle. We passed a plaza large enough to fit two of the boats I had traveled on, the edges lined by three and four-story buildings. A great statue of a Dragon lay in the center, its wings spread wide to the sky.

"I'm surprised that you still have statues of the old gods here, after all that's happened."

Avlyn looked out the window, their lips twisted. "This land belonged to the Dragons for much longer than fae have existed. This was their sacred breeding ground, and the people here lived in harmony with them until... well, until the end. The old faiths are as alive here today as they always were, that's not about to change." I didn't ask more. I knew that the great Dragon Malech —the World Breaker himself—had been defeated by Emperor Hadeon just outside this city, and Xyr suffered terribly during the fighting. Some accounts had called it destroyed. But looking out at it now, that was hard to imagine.

The kings of this land had been the fae's ambassadors to the dragons until the War of Flames which had destroyed them all. Now, there were no dragons, and Abraxas had pledged his loyalty to Hadeon, just like all the rest.

I thought of Hadeon and the deranged wickedness he displayed when he sent his magic straight through my mother's heart. And Abraxas was his right hand. My nails bit into my palms and I pushed those thoughts away, leaving me with only the lingering palpitations of my heart.

Avlyn stared at me. "What?" I asked, incredulously.

"Do you know much about the Dragon Kingdom's history?"

"Not much before the king murdered his own father to claim his throne." I threw the words with the intention to wound, and it seemed they found their mark. They flattened their lips, and I saw anger burning in their eyes.

"So eager to see us as the villains, Princess."

"Oh, I'm sorry. I thought that you had kidnapped me, maybe that's what gave me that impression? Or maybe it was the torture in the basement of Metlin that had me confused," Avlyn's face changed to shock, and I barreled on, "Or maybe it was the murder of my people that convinced me."

Avlyn stared at me, and for a moment I thought they were going to strike me. I itched for it, wanting that altercation. But instead, they calmed, "Your hands aren't clean either, Princess. You were the one I found covered in blood."

"That was different, that was self-defense."

"Yes, but that wasn't the first time you'd killed, was it?"

They were right. I remembered the face of the first man I had killed like it was yesterday, not over a century ago. I had forced my way onto a patrol of the towns outside Niata, and we had come across bandits raiding a small farm. One man had been closing in on a few of the farmer's children, and I had run my sword straight through him. I could still feel the moment his heart stopped and the life fled from his eyes. I'd been sick for a week after, emptying my stomach endlessly, and scrubbing my hands until the skin bled, trying to wipe away that stain.

Since then I had killed again, and each one had been easier. Now, I couldn't even say I felt much about that male in the dungeon. But they had all been justified, to protect someone weaker than myself. I said as much to Avlyn.

The corners of their mouth twitched upward.

"I'm not judging you, Princess. I know I don't have a leg to stand on. But still, you sit here judging me and my people. Tell me, Princess, what would you do to protect those you cared for? To protect your people?"

I straightened my back, "Anything."

They nodded, "Exactly, so perhaps you can understand us as well."

"I didn't realize that the Pearl Kingdom posed a threat to you. How was that, exactly?"

Avlyn's face went dark again, "Everything outside these borders is a threat to us."

I didn't understand, but it seemed our conversation was over. Avlyn leaned back and closed their eyes, "I'll get you a history book on it. Try not to fall out of the carriage while I get some shut-eye."

I was stunned, but Avlyn really did seem to close their eyes and fall asleep, despite the jostling of the carriage. I thought about bolting, but where would I go? I was in a city controlled by my captors. Instead, I turned to the window and did my best to memorize all the streets and buildings I could.

THE CASTLE WAS SURROUNDED BY A GREAT DARK WALL THAT connected to the cliff on either side. A lumbering gate lay open, and our carriage passed through while I observed the guards stationed at the top. More notable were the large dragons carved into the dark stone of the gate. Each beast snarled down at me as we passed underneath, jaws extended revealing a tongue that snaked out, tasting the air. Their spiked backs led up and over the wall.

Inside lay a courtyard that seemed to be full of vendors for a market. Makeshift tents and stalls lined the walls and people milled about everywhere. The air was filled with the smell of bread and herbs, and the sounds of laughter and bartering. From a distance, the castle cut an intimidating figure, not unlike the king who ruled here. Dark and sharp, carved from the ancient rock, and laced with menace as the ocean mists twirled up its tall parapets. But now inside, it felt so...alive. Not some ancient relic, but the heart of the city.

As we entered the cobblestone courtyard, Avlyn shot awake and I again wondered if they had been feigning sleep the entire time. The carriage pulled to the great double doors that led inside the castle. They were taller than three fae and carved from deep, rich ebony. Each door held another great dragon. They reared back on their hind legs, claws and wings outstretched, their tongues lashing the sky above.

Avlyn hopped out of the carriage before it stopped and strolled up to the great doors. The carriage finally halted, and I peeked my head out the still-open door. More sounds and smells hit me, and a chicken ran right past my path, chased by two rowdy youngsters.

"Coming, Princess?" Avlyn waved to me. I stepped down and made my way up the few steps to the doors. Avlyn nodded to the two guards who stood on either side and pushed our way in.

The entry was a grand hall, towering even taller than the doors outside. A great iron chandelier hung over the entire space, tall wax candles twinkling. I saw it too bore the dragon motif; the iron wrought into twisting versions of the beasts.

"Interesting aesthetic," I mumbled.

Avlyn shrugged their shoulders, "What did you expect, the skulls of our enemies?" Across from us, another set of double doors opened into the throne room. It was long, but at the far end, I could see the Dragon King's seat. The far wall had been left raw, the hexagonal basalt columns seen on the coast left bare, and the king's throne had been carved directly from the rock.

But a pair of feet running towards us at high speed had me turning, my body automatically going into a defensive stance. But I was greeted by a kind, round face and golden eyes. A lovely half-fae woman rushed towards us, her dress held up in the front so that she didn't trip. Her ears were pointed, but not as long as my own, and they popped out between the waves of her caramel-brown hair, which was pulled back into a low bun.

"Commander Avlyn, I didn't think you would return so soon. I haven't finished preparing the room."

Avlyn gave the woman a warm smile, "Ciara, you are looking even more lovely than I remember. Such a welcome sight to these fae eyes after such a long, very dangerous journey." They lifted Ciara's hand and placed a light kiss on Ciara's knuckles. *Shameless flirt.* I saw color rise to Ciara's cheeks, but she controlled it quickly and turned to me with a deep, well-practiced curtsy.

"Your Highness, my name is Ciara, and will be your handmaiden during your stay at the castle." I was taken aback. I'd had a few women to tend to me in Niata, but I hadn't expected that treatment here. *What did you expect?* I suppose it wouldn't have been very good optics to keep the visiting princess locked up in the dungeon. So, I supposed we would be going with the charade that I was an invited guest.

"A pleasure to meet you, Lady Ciara." I gave her a slight bow of my head, as was appropriate. She beamed at me, "It's just Ciara, Your Highness. If you would give me just a bit longer, I will have your room prepared."

"No need for that, Ciara, the princess here will certainly help you finish the preparations."

Her eyebrows shot up, "Oh, no. I couldn't possibly–"

"I would be delighted to join you." I motioned for her to lead the way. Her eyebrows stayed raised, but she turned and led me up a side flight of stairs.

"I expect you to behave, Princess," Avlyn called after me.

"Anything for you, Commander," I threw back, blowing them a kiss. I swore I saw Avlyn's eyes reach the back of their head. They motioned for two guards to follow us. So, the charade began.

Ciara led me through the halls, her soft voice chatting about a few of the tapestries and other things, but I wasn't listening. I was memorizing our path, looking down halls and out windows to keep my bearings. We seemed to be heading to the eastern wing of the castle, we had reached the third floor when Ciara opened a door into a fine room.

It was actually larger than my room back home in Niata, with windows that looked out over the sea and the city. No balcony, as I was sure a deliberate choice, and I would have wagered a great sum that my windows wouldn't open. But a large bed lined in cream and tan linens faced the windows, and a small vanity sat off to the side. While the bed was freshly made, I could see that many of the pillows had been pulled off the couches in the seating area, and the armoire was wide open. Several crates lay on the floor near it.

Ciara quickly started fluffing the pillows and replacing them on the couches, and I opened up the nearest crate. None of my things had been brought from Niata, not the number one priority when one was being taken from their home. However, I had expected to find the traditional heavily patterned wide-sleeved robes and decorative belts of home. That is not what I found.

The crates were overflowing with fine silks and other light fabrics, each gleaming like precious jewels turned liquid. I lifted the top one out. It was full-length with long sleeves, made of beautiful silk that transitioned between white and silver like a pearl as I held it to the light that streamed through the windows. But it was also very obvious the light passed directly through it, and I had no doubt that effect would hold while worn. A quick look told me all the other dresses were the same. Ciara had come over to me, her eyes caught on the lovely dress.

"This color will suit you beautifully, Your Highness," she reached out as if she meant to run her fingers along the fabric, then thought better of it. "Perhaps this one for the gala tonight?"

My heart stuttered. A gala? Tonight? Ciara motioned to the open armoire, pulling the dress from me and hanging it so that the fabric could release any wrinkles, "Would you choose your underlayer?" Despite my anxiety about that evening, I released a sigh of relief. Yes of course there would be another layer under the sheer gown.

I turned to the armoire, and my anxiety ratcheted back up. There were no slips or underlayers I could see. Only sets and sets of underwear, each seeming to be tinier than the next. They were all beautifully made, with layers of fine laces and some even lined with jewels and pearls, or intricate patterns of straps, but their loveliness only set my mind racing.

Of course, I had seen garments like this before. In my misguided youth, I had traveled to the midnight sectors of our city with the young soldiers, trying to prove that I was not some simpering princess. I groaned at my younger self, and the things she thought would impress others. The women there who sold their bodies wore outfits like this on the street, luring the gaze of men and women alike, and oftentimes much more. In my youth, those visits had always made me feel so uncomfortable, pitying the women in those situations, assuming they knew no better. Luckily, I had come to learn much in my time since then. Mostly that these situations were never so black and white. While some women were coerced into these situations, many of them chose it, and they held great power over themselves and the people they undressed for.

In fact, as I had started to be more involved in our court itself, I had learned that many of our best spies were these denizens of Midnight Street, seducing secrets from clients without leaving any marks, unlike the less subtle methods of the soldiers. I found myself studying these methods and after some practice, and the company of several willing participants, had gotten quite good at it myself. If I was being honest, I had quite enjoyed it.

"Everything alright, Your Highness?" I must have been standing there for quite a while, lost in my thoughts, for Ciara had sidled up to me without my notice.

"I'm just not used to the fashion here." She gave me a kind smile and turned to the wardrobe.

"The king made sure you had the finest and newest fashions

available." The thought of the king helping in the selection of these salacious gowns had my stomach in knots. She reached in and pulled out a set made of white lace and lined with pearls that shone just like the fabric of the dress. I was grateful, because by comparison, they were modest. I looked at her well-worn linen dress and apron with envy, but I knew the power embracing this would give me. Modesty was just another cage placed on women by men who feared they might realize that power. It was time to put all that practice to good use.

Chapter 15

Tori

Ciara and I had finished putting everything away, and she had drawn me a bath, which after weeks on a boat with nothing but sweaty soldiers sounded divine. I was about to pull off my filthy leather leggings when a knock sounded at my door. I opened it to find Avlyn as they dumped an armload of books on me.

"Some light reading for you."

I staggered as I tried to right the unbalanced stack, "Light indeed." I managed to dump them all on my bed before they fell to the floor. I turned and saw Avlyn eyeing the dress that Ciara had laid out for me.

"So, Ciara told you about tonight?"

"I know there is a gala, that's about it."

"Well, that's really all there is to it. I'm sure you've been to one before. Besides, you promised me you would be on best behavior." They blew me a kiss, and I scowled. They chuckled and headed out the door, "Make sure you scrub good in that bath. You smell awful," and they locked the door behind them. I scowled again, even though they couldn't see. But they were right. I was rank. I gave Ciara credit for staying with me as long as she had.

The bath was calling, but I looked at the pile of books on my bed, and it hurt my heart to see them so disheveled. I picked a few up and took them over and lined them up on the windowsill next to my vanity. Not a great place for them; I would have to ask for a bookshelf. But they looked much happier, stacked and neat. The very last book I picked up was small with a worn, dark leather cover. The embossed title had started to wear away, but I could make out, The History of the Dragons. It seemed Avlyn had delivered on their promise.

I brought the book with me and set it on the table next to the bath. I pulled off my leggings, sighing in relief as my legs were freed from the tight leather. I stepped into the warm bath and a groan more sensual than I had anticipated left me. The warm water caressed every sore muscle in my body, and I felt the tension in my shoulders fade away. The water quickly turned murky with the sweat, salt and grime. I used a small bar of fine-smelling soap all over me, and then a lovely rosemary-scented potion on my hair. The water was practically black after all this, so I drained the tub.

But I wasn't quite ready to get out, so after the last of the evidence of my long voyage circled the drain, I filled the tub again with fresh water, and added some floral bubbles as well. The water from the tap was boiling hot, coming from the geothermal pits below, Ciara had explained. It was accompanied by a faint sulfur smell, but I was unbothered. I let my skin turn red and ran my fingers over the circular scabs where the Leviathan had grabbed me. They hadn't healed yet, which implied the creature had some sort of poison, or maybe it was just the nature of an ancient beast to leave a mark. I let the hot water from the tap flow over my calf, and turning the scabs bright red.

I leaned back in the tub and pulled the book over as the water continued to fill. The first chapter was about the Great Prophecy of the Third Age, as so many history books were, but the last line caught my eye.

But it is this humble scholar's belief that with the extinction of the Dragons, it is our responsibility to capture their history, so that it is not lost to the ages, such as the knowledge of so many of the other great creatures of Adimos.

I flipped through the pages until my eyes fell upon a diagram that looked like a tree. It was, in fact, a family tree, and I saw it was a great map of almost all the known dragons throughout history, showing all their relationships. A long footnote accompanied the chart.

**The lineage of dragons can be easily tracked as dragons are notoriously monogamous creatures. In fact, some of the few dragon tablets that have been translated reference "fated mates" that can be detected as soon as eggs hatch.*

I ran my fingers over the page, tracing down until I found the very last pair. The dragon Malech and his mate, Tezca. She had been the very first Dragon slain when the War of Magic broke out, nearly seven hundred years ago. And Malech, the World Breaker had been the last. I thought of the great statue I had seen in the plaza, and my heart twinged. What a waste. Magic had not returned to this world after his death, despite what the Great Prophecy foretold. And now, this great race was gone.

I thought about that great yellow eye watching me from the deep, and sighed. Despite the crew's anger, I couldn't feel guilty that at least one last Leviathan survived.

The water had filled the tub, so I set the book down and turned off the tap. With the tub so full, I couldn't resist the temptation to dunk my head under and submerge myself. The world around me disappeared into that strange echoing warmth. I let bubbles escape my mouth and giggled. I thought of how Jun and I would challenge each other to see who could remain submerged under the ocean waves the longest. I let the warmth of the water drive the darkness away and just stayed under until my lungs burned. I closed my eyes. I let myself float, weightless for just a moment. Until I was sharply pulled out of the water.

I sputtered. Coughs raked me, as I had swallowed water in my surprise.

I leaned over the side of the tub, and realized someone was shouting, "What the hell were you doing?" It was the king. Suddenly, I was very aware of how naked I was, even if the bubbles covered most of it, and wrapped my arms around my breasts, and tucked in my legs.

"What am I doing? Taking a bath! What are you doing?!"

He had pulled back from me, one of his arms soaking wet from where he had pulled me out of the tub.

"I knocked at the door and there was no answer so I—" he trailed off. I couldn't have been under the water for more than a minute. He obviously hadn't waited very long.

"What, you thought I was going to drown myself?"

"Yes." His look was stern.

"Please, Your Majesty, I would much rather stay and be a thorn in your side. No fun in giving you the easy way out." I flicked water at him and enjoyed the way his face scrunched up. "Now get out, so I can finish with my bath." I leaned back in the tub, stretching out and relaxing, my cue for him to leave. He rose but didn't leave.

"No."

"What?"

"Princess, if there is something I have learned about you, it's that you certainly can't be trusted with your own safety. I'll have to remain here until you are done." He crossed his arms, and that wicked grin rose to his lips. "Please, continue." He couldn't be serious. *He was.*

"Well, I was just about done anyway." He reached over and grabbed a towel from the rack and held it out to me, that stupid grin only getting wider. I tried to give him my dirtiest look and reached for the towel. But just as my fingers brushed it, he dropped it to the floor. I swear to the gods I didn't think a person could look more smug. I cursed myself for not setting a towel out closer to myself. Fine, he wanted to play like this, let's play.

I rose up then, letting the water slide off my body, bubbles running down, not covering anything. I wish I could have captured the dumbfounded look on his face, and how long it stuck before he was able to regain his cold mask. But by that point, I had gotten out, picked up the towel, and wrapped it around myself. I walked right past him back into my room. I threw the bedroom door open, startling the guard outside, and motioned for him to leave. He walked out of my washroom, and straight through the door. However, as I went to close it, his hand slammed into it, preventing me from doing so.

"The gala begins at sundown; I'll send Ciara up to help you dress." He ran his gaze up and down me, and even with the towel on I felt more exposed than before as he leaned into me. "Although, if you wanted to show up in nothing but soap again, I certainly wouldn't complain."

I slammed the door in his face.

Chapter 16

Abraxas

Gods, she was a distraction. I'd been away from my kingdom for weeks, but I hadn't heard a word during the debrief with my officers. Instead, my mind lingered on the way the water had caressed her hard pink nipples and that beautiful sex between her legs. Lingered on how they both might taste.

"Your Majesty? Abraxas, *Abraxas*!" Avlyn shouted at me.

"What?"

They rubbed their forehead, "I said, what are we going to do about the diadem?"

"Lord Plagis will be here tonight, if anyone has information about it, it's that musty old scholar."

Avlyn moved to rubbing their chin, "So what's the plan, ply him with ambrosia, and dangle a few young human maids in front of him to get him talking?" they gagged, "The old lech."

"I had a certain maid in mind who I think can certainly defend herself."

Avlyn raised a brow, "The princess? You think she would comply?"

"Avlyn, you know anyone can behave if given the right incentive. Do you think the cohort would have her back?"

Avlyn shrugged, "Convince a bunch of young warriors to have a beautiful woman amongst them every day? I'm surprised a few of them are even still holding a grudge, to be honest."

I placed my fingertips together at my lips, "Good, and she will be allowed to duel as well." Avlyn shot me a look that clearly told me how they felt about that, but they were a good commander and simply nodded.

"Good, now if that's all, I have a gala to prepare for."

I RETURNED TO THE PRINCESS'S ROOM AND KNOCKED, BEFORE Ciara quickly called out, "Enter."

She had Tori in front of the vanity, trying to add a few pins to her hair and failing, "I told you; my hair just won't be held by things like this. That's why I cut it short." Our eyes met in her mirror, and she frowned. "I suppose this will have to be good enough for tonight. Thank you, Ciara." She stood, and it was certainly good enough.

Without the pins, her straight dark hair fell below her chin, accentuating the strong line of her jaw, and Ciara had done something to also highlight her slate-colored eyes. Her long neck was accentuated by the wide neckline of the gown, her skin glowed, and I could just barely see her pulse accelerate under my stare.

The gown truly made her gleam, although it was disappointingly covering, especially compared to earlier today. "No one would mistake you for anything but the Princess of the Pearl Kingdom tonight. Time to go." I held out my hand to her. She strode towards me, but something was off. I had seen her hold herself with a fine posture multiple times and move beautifully when training with the cohort. But now she slouched and held one arm crossed over herself.

"And if I should refuse?" She looked anxious. This was not a good start. Where was the beast who had stabbed me with my own dagger?

"Well, you are welcome to remain in your room. But I had hoped to make you an offer, if you were inclined to listen?"

She pulled on a sour look, and I couldn't help but grin at how her face twisted, "I'm sure you do."

Ciara scuttled out of the room as I laughed, "It's not like that, Princess. Do you truly think so little of me?" The look she gave me clearly said *yes*, but I shook my head and extended my arm again. "Walk with me and hear me out. Should you refuse, I will walk you straight back here as any gentleman would." I could see the machinations of her mind working, but it seemed her curiosity won out, and she laced her arm through mine.

I walked her around the end of the east wing, so we could see the small cove on the beach through the windows. Only the castle had access to it. It was surrounded by high sea cliffs, and I'd had one of my cohorts out to train despite the late hour. I looked at her face and saw the longing there, and I knew she would agree.

"You enjoyed training with the soldiers on the boat. Would you like to continue?"

She turned to me and raised her eyebrows, but then I saw that hope leave her eyes, "They wouldn't have me." She turned back to the window, that longing only growing stronger.

"They certainly would if I ordered it. I don't know how things are run in Niata, but here, soldiers obey my command." Her nose scrunched up, and I much preferred that look to the sadness I had seen creeping into her.

But then she turned to me again, those slate eyes holding mine as if I were staring into the heart of a hurricane, "And what do you want in return?" I could hear her heart beating faster. She had used her beauty and her charms on me more than once, working to get her advantage. But here, she knew she was the one bargaining, and I could tell she didn't know if she would be able to follow through with the price. Of course, I would never ask her for that, I never had. The chase was only fun when they succumbed willingly, but she didn't know that. And I wouldn't reveal it quite yet.

"I need you to get some information for me. From one of my guests tonight." I could feel her shock, but kept going, "Lord Plagis is in attendance, a fae older than myself, and quite the historian. He's also a dirty old man."

"Sounds like someone else I know."

I shot her a withering look, "Are you interested in my terms or not?" She pursed her lips together, and nodded, "I need any and all information you can get about the Diadem of Soraya out of him, discreetly of course."

"And what is that?"

"It's an enchanted object that belonged to Queen Soraya of the Eternal Kingdom. It is said to still hold a great deal of magical power but has been lost since her and King Soractes' fall." Yes, the infamous Queen Soraya and King Soractes, the last known fraternal twins. I saw that this was not lost on her.

"And you want this, why?" She narrowed her eyes at me.

"It's not for you to know why I add treasures to my collection. Will you take the deal or not?" She worried her lip as she thought, and it took all my self-control not to reach out and run my fingers over its plump surface.

"And how do you expect that I will extract this information from him? I'm surprised you don't just have Avlyn take him down to the dungeon, like in Metlin."

I stared at her then, but she held my gaze. Anyone who thought this princess was just a vapid, spoiled royal was in for a nasty surprise. She was clever, much too clever for her own good.

"Lord Plagis is an honored member of Hadeon's court. I don't think it would be wise for him to suddenly disappear while a guest in my home."

"I see, so subtler methods are required. Would you have me fuck him for this information? Play your little whore?"

She had surprised me twice today, but this time I wouldn't let it show on my face, even as anger wound itself through my ribs, "I'm surprised a woman as beautiful as you doesn't know how to get what she wants without such extreme measures."

Now it was my turn to surprise her, and seeing that small hit of color come to her cheeks was immensely satisfying, "Besides, it almost sounds as if you were trying to make me jealous, Princess."

She squeezed down on my arm with her hand, ever so slightly, "And, are you jealous?"

My skin buzzed where her hand made contact, but I focused, "I have no need for jealousy, Princess. Once I've had you, you will be so undone you won't remember any that came before me. But I do appreciate how hard you are working to upset me." Her cheeks turned a brighter red and she narrowed her eyes at me. But before she could retort, I said, "So, do we have a deal?"

She bit her lip in that excruciating way, but she turned her feet and began pulling me toward the throne room, "We have a gala to get to."

Chapter 17

Tori

I didn't trust this deal with the king, but I couldn't resist it either. He knew I wanted to train, so I was willing to play the spy. We reached the throne room, and I could hear music through the double doors.

Just before we entered, he paused and I turned to him, "Ready, Princess?" I saw him pull on that cold, aristocratic mask, the one he had worn when we had first met. I hadn't realized how much I had gotten used to him not wearing it during our journey. I pulled on my own, my courtly smile cranked into place, "Of course, Your Majesty."

He pushed open the doors, the muscles of his back and shoulders strained against his tight-fitting jacket as he moved the massive blocks of wood. It most certainly did not send a wave of heat through my stomach. A herald inside announced us.

"King Abraxas Corignus accompanied by Princess Tori Khato of the Pearl Kingdom." Almost all the eyes turned to him as we entered. I felt it then. I had seen him as a general, as my captor, but now I finally saw him as a king. The noble fae of his realm all gave him reverential bows as we walked past. But even after we had passed, I felt their eyes lingering.

"I guess they all really missed you."

He chuckled, "They aren't looking at me, Princess." I saw it then, the way their eyes lingered on my face, like I was some exotic animal at a traveling minstrel's show, and I felt the indignation and anger rising within me.

He must have felt me stiffen, for he leaned in and whispered to me, "Forgive their rude behavior. It's been quite a while since we've had any fresh meat at court. I'm sure, shortly they will get to know you as I have and learn to keep their distance for their own safety." I could feel the smirk on his lips, where they practically rested on my ear. I tried to wiggle away, but he held me fast, "Tonight, use that to your advantage."

And then he pulled away, and it was as if a dam had broken in the room. The nobles who had held themselves at a distance, all convened on me at once. Greetings and curtsies abounded, and I tried to remember names as numerous introductions were hurled at me. The mannerisms here were all different, curtsies instead of bows, and different formal greetings. It had me at a disadvantage, and I hated it. It seemed that Ciara had indeed chosen a conservative gown for me by the way the others dressed.

The men had fashion similar to the king's, mostly well-tailored jackets with short collars, embroidered with lavish embellishments. Some mimicked the sheerness of my dress with panels that showed off the wearer's skin underneath. I particularly liked one that revealed an elaborate tattoo on the chest of the man who wore it. The women were each like jewels, their dresses in every shade, and the undergarments ranged from scandalous to non-existent. But they wore them with confidence, and I found myself doing my best to mimic that.

A particularly boisterous woman soon dominated my attention. Was her name Lady Lovatia? She had a head of long, pale blond hair tied in elaborate braids laced with jeweled beads. She took my arm quite boldly and started leading me around the room, introducing me to all the other noble ladies. "Yes, this here is Lady Bogata, she oversees much of the agriculture in this region, and this is Lady Pascala, she's widowed, so she oversees her whole estate in the Mist District in the city." She handed me a long-fluted glass, and I was happy just to have something to occupy my hands and give me an excuse not to talk. The efferves-cent ambrosia sang on my lips. It was ridiculously expensive, and one of the few substances that could have full fae feeling inebri-ated. If humans drank it, well, they were lucky if all that happened was losing the memory of a few days.

Lady Lovatia kept showing me around the room, making more introductions, and I did my best not to feel like a prize-winning pig before the slaughter. But soon I regained my feet, and the niceties of court came back to me. I didn't know their traditions, but I could mimic them. The ambrosia helped. I had been doing this for almost two centuries after all.

"Ah, and here, Your Highness, is Lord Plagis, a famous histo-rian of Adimos. We are so pleased to have him visiting our kingdom now." Plagis might have been handsome once, but age and something more malevolent had stolen that from him. In fact, I don't think I had ever seen a fae as old as this male. He had heavy-set wrinkles around his mouth and deep furrows on his forehead. He likely once had fine dark hair, but it was almost entirely white now, with only a few stripes of the dark remaining near his temples. He had deep-set watery eyes, like a puddle on the sand at low tide, just moments from evaporating. He was not discreet as he eyed me up and down, and the smile that broke his lips was not flirtatious, but something much more sinister. I suppressed a shiver.

"A pleasure, Princess Tori." I hated the way he said that. He reached for my hand and pulled my knuckles to his lips. It took everything I had to not snatch it away. But I thought of the soldiers training on the beach, the feel of a sword in my hand, and held my smile.

“The pleasure is all mine, Lord Plagis. I have never met a scholar of such renown before.” I saw his lips twitch, his ego stroked. This would be easy, maybe even a little fun.

Lady Lovatia moved to pull me away, but I gracefully slipped my arm out of hers, my gaze fixated on Lord Plagis. "Lady Lovatia, would you excuse me? I was hoping that Lord Plagis would be kind enough to entertain a few questions I have." Lovatia's disappointment was evident on her face, but as a court-trained lady, she swiftly concealed it. With a slight curtsy, she excused herself and departed. Now alone with Plagis, I observed his eyes dilate.

"What can I assist you with, my dear? I must say, it has been a while since I've encountered a lady as captivating as yourself, displaying such a keen interest in our rich histories," he remarked, every one of his teeth showing in his smile. I offered a grateful smile in return, lowering my chin to look up at him through my lashes. I observed the way his eyes lingered.

“Even on Niata, I have heard so much about your writings, My Lord. I even read a few in my studies, but it’s nothing like talking to the man himself.” I gave his arm a gentle squeeze then, and he certainly didn’t miss it.

“You flatter me, Your Highness. Yes, my years as Hadeon’s closest advisor have come to a close, and I have enjoyed myself in more scholarly pursuits, among other things.” He flashed that grin again, and I leaned into him.

Placing my other hand gently on his chest now, I continued, “I do hope you don’t think I’m a bother, but I was rather hoping you could *satisfy* my curiosity on a few subjects.”

Plagis grinned, “Your Highness, there is nothing I would rather do tonight than indulge you.” I noticed him moisten his lips, and he placed his other hand on top of mine, his knuckles ever so slightly grazing my breast as he did. I repressed a gag.

I began with simple inquiries about the histories of the kingdoms and recent minor uprisings, prompting him to provide more elaborate responses to each question. I made sure that he always had a full glass of ambrosia in his hand and laughed at all the appropriate times. He seemed more than willing to drone on and on about each subject, a man certainly very pleased by hearing himself speak. I said very little, and he didn't seem to notice.

I turned from him for a moment to grab another glass of ambrosia. As I looked for a servant, I locked eyes with the king. Had he been watching me? Making sure I was upholding my end of the bargain, I was sure. But as he lifted his own glass of ambrosia to his lips, I could feel dark menace rolling off him, as he kept his eyes locked with mine. Right, I had work to do.

I turned back to Plagis as he rambled on about the Great Prophecy of the Third Age.

"Ah, the Great Prophecy. Witnessing its fulfillment has been an immense blessing bestowed upon me. Rarely does one have the fortune to witness such transformative events that shape the course of history and emerge unscathed. The Divine Emperor Hadeon has graced us with his rule, and to know I had a hand in that, well, I can say that with no small amount of pride. Did you know that I was present when he vanquished the World Breaker? It was an extraordinary display of power, unlike anything the world had ever seen—a defining moment for our great hero." He practically hummed with admiration while anger surged through me.

Maintaining a smile, though my teeth ground together, I gazed at him with soft eyes.

"But, my dear, surely you were aware of all this even in the Pearl Kingdom? What is it that you truly wished to inquire about?" I sensed my opportunity, but I could practically feel the king's glare searing into my back. Guiding Plagis towards the shadows at the side of the room, I positioned us in a secluded alcove, necessitating our bodies to draw closer together.

I drew nearer to him, my voice a soft and vulnerable whisper, "I find myself wondering, Lord Plagis, if you could offer me some insight into the mysterious Eternal Kingdom."

He recoiled. *Fuck.*

"Your Highness, such matters are not meant for polite conversation," he replied, attempting to extract his arm from my grasp. *Fuck!* How had I misjudged this so terribly? Abraxas' voice echoed in my mind, urging me to turn the situation to my advantage. Engaging in a struggle would only arouse suspicion, so I knew I didn't have many options left to me.

"I beg your pardon, My Lord," I let a tremor enter my voice my eyes glistening with unshed tears. He froze, "I never meant to offend. It's just that you possess a wealth of knowledge, and I'm filled with an *insatiable* curiosity," I practically pinned him to the wall with my body, making sure my breasts were heavily pressed against him. He didn't seem to notice that I was preventing his retreat as his pupils flared again.

"You see, I am a twin myself, and I yearn to uncover the secrets of our shared past. There is so much hidden, so much I long to understand." He hesitated, his curiosity outweighing his need for self-preservation.

He snaked a hand around my waist then, and I moved my lips even closer to his, "What is it that you seek, Your Highness?" he inquired, unable to resist the temptation.

I skated my hands over his chest, but I had already failed at this once. I had to give him something else, even if it wasn't true.

"You may not believe me, but I carry within me a secret. A secret that has burdened me for far too long. I have always been drawn to the Eternal Kingdom, its legends and artifacts. I have dreamt all my life of ancient powers and forgotten treasures. But it is more than a mere fascination. It is a connection, a piece of myself waiting to be uncovered." His gaze sharpened, and I could see his desire then, but it wasn't for my flesh. I had him all the same.

"Tell me, Your Highness, what is this secret you bear?"

I glanced around, ensuring we were concealed from prying eyes, before leaning in closer, my lips tracing the shell of his ear, and I felt him shudder, "I am not who they think I am," I confessed, my voice barely a whisper. "I am not just a princess from a distant land. There is something within me, dormant but yearning to be awakened. I believe the Eternal Kingdom holds the key, the answers to the mysteries that have haunted me since birth." I practically saw his defenses crumble under the weight of my revelation, my lies.

"Well, much of what the King and Queen had was destroyed, and anything that remains..." I leaned in closer, letting my lips just barely graze the skin under his ear, "Well, there isn't much more known, because it was all buried in the castle with them. The ruins still lie at the heart of Tenebrae Forest." His eyes grew hungry again. "What draws you to them?" I was about to make up another elaborate lie when he very hastily shoved me off of him.

"You-r Maj-esty." Plagis stammered the words, sweat beading on his brow. Abraxas loomed over us, nothing but pure menace. It reminded me so much of when I had first seen him, I almost thought he might reach out and remove Plagis' heart, or maybe mine. But instead, he reached for my arm and painfully pulled me to him.

"Ah, there you are, Princess. Lord Plagis, I'm afraid I'm going to have to reclaim her from you." I felt his eyes fall to my neck and a fraction of that menace receded. But he turned back to Plagis, who withered under the stare.

"Of course, Your Majesty. Princess Tori, I do hope we can

continue this conversation soon." And he strode off. Now Abraxas returned his gaze to me. I gave him a small nod, which he didn't react to, just held my stare. It suddenly became very difficult to push away the memories of his body pressed against mine, and his hand around my throat, that look he had given me when I stepped out of the bathtub. For a few more moments we stood there, my heart beating in my ears. But then he pulled me out of the alcove, and we returned to the party.

After another hour or so of socializing with various lords and ladies, I found an arm laced through mine again. I turned to find Avlyn, not in their armor for once. They wore a lavishly decorated vest, that I realized was actually boned and cinched like a corset, and tight-fitting pants. I showed off the narrowness of their waist and the curve of their backside.

"No need to stare, Princess, I know I look good."

"You do." I didn't say it in flirtation, just as fact. It was funny how seeing someone out of their element could really change your impression of them. In fact, I saw some color rise to Avlyn's cheeks, and it was very endearing.

"Well, it's past your bedtime. May I escort you back to your room?" My feet and soul ached from so much socializing, so I was more than happy to go with them. I turned for one last look at the hall and felt the king's eyes fall to me again. He was across the room, but our eyes locked. He gave me the smallest nod, and Avlyn led me off.

But as we made our way down the hall, we passed the door I knew was mine. A few doors down, Avlyn unlocked another and led me in. The room was very similar to mine. In fact, the bed and sheets were the same, and I saw all the books Avlyn had brought me had been placed on a small bookshelf.

I gave Avlyn a pointed stare and they shrugged, "This room was better." I was about to ask more when they cut me off, "Did you learn anything from Plagis?"

I recounted what he had told me. Avlyn swept their hand over their face and braided hair, "Fuck, Tenebrae— the Forest of Darkness, huh? It can never just be easy, can it?" I once again wondered why the king wanted this diadem so badly. Seemed quite troublesome for just another treasure.

"How did you get the information out of Plagis?" I explained my lie, about a secret power waiting to be awakened. Avlyn let out a hearty laugh and I grinned as well.

"Honestly. I'm surprised he bought it. Must have been because he doesn't know me. Anyone who did would have seen right through it."

I waited for Avlyn to laugh again, but instead, they just flattened their lips together. They rose and made for my door before I could inquire.

"You did well today. I'll see you in the morning for training. Be ready."

I pulled off my formal attire and was about to crawl into bed when something nagging sent me to my washroom. Inside, I found that this room didn't have a bathtub. Instead, I found a peculiar waterfall that emerged from the wall and would turn on and off with a valve. That domineering asshole.

Chapter 18

Tori

The next morning, I awoke with a twist in my stomach that for once wasn't helplessness, but anticipation. I pulled my leather leggings and loose tunic on, but before I could get out the door, Avlyn had arrived. They led me through the castle and, as always, I tried to memorize all the paths I could. But Avlyn led me deep into the castle, and without windows I eventually lost my bearings. We eventually emerged on the beach from a door on the lower level.

We were in the small cove bordered by the high sea cliffs on both sides that jutted out into the water, the castle formed the third wall further back from the ocean. The sand here was black, just as I had seen from the ship, and the ocean wind whipped my hair about. I saw a few different cohorts of soldiers already lined up on the beach, starting their morning exercises. Avlyn jogged over to them, and I scrambled to keep pace. They reached into a training rack and threw me a practice longsword. I thought about making a comment about no more wooden weapons, but I could feel the wary eyes of the soldiers on me, and I just kept my mouth shut for once.

Luckily, Avlyn was a strict commander, and soon I was sweating and working so hard I couldn't think about my discomfort. We trained harder on the beach than we had on the ship. Even with the cold sea breeze, I was drenched in sweat by the time we reached the first water break. It played out much like my first time training with them, but this time I anticipated Kaleos, and dodged his back-breaking slap.

He laughed, "Ready for our duel, little lady?" I heard a few murmurs from the soldiers around me. My stomach dropped, ashamed to admit I wouldn't be allowed to.

"Not a bad idea, Kaleos, a little friendly bludgeoning might beat some of the sass out of her." Avlyn smirked at me. Was this real? Was I really going to be allowed to duel? I was too giddy to think of anything to say. "Soldiers, clear the ring," Avlyn shouted.

It turns out *the ring* was just whatever patch of sand the warriors decided to all stand around. They were apprehensive, and unnervingly quiet as they surrounded Kaleos and me. But I had to focus on my opponent, not anyone else. Kaleos was half-fae, but he had clearly inherited his size from his fae ancestor. Even compared to me, he was tall and basically a wall of studded muscle. He would have almost every advantage over me because of his size, but I had to assume I was faster.

He pulled off his shirt, to a few hoots from the crowd. I raised an eyebrow to him, "Trying to distract me?"

He gave me that broad smile, "I'll take any advantage I can get." He raised his sword as I did the same. We gently tapped the edges together and stepped back, and then the duel began.

At first, we just circled each other, but Kaleos wasn't shy and took the first strike. I parried, but it was sloppy. It had been weeks now since I had actually dueled with another person, and it had probably been years since I had done so with a longsword. Kaleos didn't miss that and sent a flurry of strikes my way. I blocked a few and spun to dodge the rest. The sand here might have tripped others up, but I had trained on beaches my whole life.

I lunged at him, but he easily parried, our blades clashing in the air. But as my lungs worked and muscles strained, the energy of the fight hit me, and I used it. I struck again and again. Kaleos countered, but I kept my pace and saw him begin to falter. I worked to exploit this and managed to get inside his defense. I struck a small blow, but his long reach and my weakness with my heavier sword slowed me too much, and he landed a heavy strike on my leg. My knee buckled, and he swung down from overhead. I barely managed to block the crushing blow, but as he held our swords together firmly, I kicked my leg out and swept him off his feet, at least partially. Our blades both fell as we stumbled to get up.

"Full of surprises, Princess."

We circled each other again, but this time I could hear the gathered crowd engaging, as cheers came from around us. Some of my tension melted away, and I lunged again. We clashed in an exchange of blows, matching each other well, and I felt the crowd swell. As we moved, I saw it, after each third blow, he would swing a bit too far, leaving the smallest opening. He came at me and I parried his sword away, and slashed down through the tiny opening. I snagged his waist, and even with the practice swords dulled, I knew it was painful.

"A fatal hit, victory to the princess," Avlyn yelled.

The cheers from the crowd were quite rowdy now, but I dropped my sword and placed my hand on Kaleos' arm. He had moved both his hands to cover where I had struck him, and I saw a faint hint of blood.

"Turns out both my pride and my body are getting hurt today," he smiled at me, but I felt terrible.

"Kaleos, I'm sorry, it's been a while since I dueled, I should have pulled the strike."

"What, this? It's nothing. Besides, it looks like my plan worked." I looked where his eyes were focused, and I saw the soldiers around us jostling each other as they came close. Many of them proceeded to slap me on my back the way Kaleos had and congratulated me on my win. The tension from before slipped away. Avlyn worked to get everyone back into the ranks for more practice, and I grasped Kaleos' forearm, helping him to stand. Despite his injury, he moved fluidly, and it hit me.

"You did that on purpose. You left that opening for me."

He let out a small laugh, "Only a well-trained fighter would have seen it, and besides, I figured you hadn't dueled in a while, it would be good to get your confidence back up." His smile was so genuine it hurt my heart, "Don't worry, I won't make that mistake again." He got to his feet and moved to head over to the racks with medical supplies.

"Thank you."

He must not have expected that from me, but he smiled again, "Welcome back, Princess."

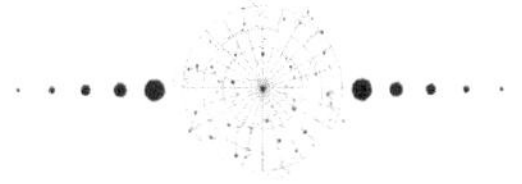

Kaleos might have thrown our first fight, but he certainly kept his word not to do it again. I spent my days training with the cohort, but now I dueled regularly. Kaleos certainly proved that he was a great fighter, beating me almost a dozen times before I was able to best him again. But slowly, more and more of the soldiers dueled against me. There, my performance was more even, winning and losing in equal measure.

As the days passed, I got more comfortable with the long sword, and I saw my skills improving and my losses became fewer. But I almost didn't care about that, because most days I now spent lunch dining with the soldiers in the barracks, and I found that even more enjoyable than the fighting. They had gotten comfortable with me again, and we would eat and drink cheap beer and tell rowdy stories late into the afternoon until they were often called away for various patrols.

The routine was similar to home, but my father's soldiers had always kept me at arm's length. They'd always been too wary of a princess amongst them to get comfortable. I'd fucked most of them, but that had never meant anything. They feared my father, and as my skills had improved over the centuries, they feared me as well. Nothing made men more uncomfortable than a woman who couldn't be controlled. Well, at least that is what I'd thought. Here, it was different. I almost felt like I was one of them. So much so, that I hadn't even tried to pursue a single one of them.

Avlyn, it turned out, was the most obnoxious of the bunch, always standing on tables, recounting stories of all their heroics and, much more amusingly, their failures.

"So, it's the middle of the night, see, and Noki here is supposed to be keeping watch. But this bastard had stayed up all night the night before, losing at cards at some shitty tavern."

They waved their hand at Noki accusingly, "Hey, in my defense, the bartender said I couldn't lose."

"You just thought he was pretty."

"No, I thought he was verrrrry pretty." His seatmates jostled him as they all laughed.

"Like I said, Noki was being an idiot, so he fell asleep on watch. I wake up to him snoring, so I go out to lay into him and find it's not him snoring at all, but an enormous hellcat who has gotten into our food stores and passed out. I go to sneak up on the thing, but I fucking trip over Watchman Snooze over here. Scare everyone awake. I don't know who screamed louder, the beast or Noki. But that thing's tail fluffed up like a goddamn housecat and booked it before I could lay into *him* for eating all my sausages." Everyone was laughing now, myself included. Avlyn's eyes twinkled as they looked down at me, "Too bad you weren't there, Princess, you probably could have had the thing eating out of your hand." I made a rude gesture at Avlyn, but we both laughed. Kaleos prodded me in the ribs, "Yeah, we all know how these beasts really fancy our princess here." We all laughed, and it was easy.

But as the afternoons crept on, no matter how many books I read, or guarded walks I took around the castle to explore, the darkness would always creep back in, like the tendrils of the Leviathan itself, coming to pull me down into the deep. This wasn't my home and guilt about how easy I found the mornings ate at me. I should have been doing more. Working harder to plan an escape, working to find more information about where Jun was, what had become of Niata. Memories of blood coated my dreams, and I could find no respite there.

I rarely slept well, and tonight was no exception. I had dreamed of thick red blood running down the marble-white sides of the Niatan palace, and I heard my mother and father screaming to save Jun, to take anyone but Jun, while I stood still, unable to move. I awoke, my hair plastered to my face with sweat, my jaw aching from grinding my teeth.

I had to get to Jun. My stay in the Dragon Kingdom could almost be considered pleasant— almost. But Jun had been taken by Hadeon himself, and I remembered the look in his eye when he had pulled Jun up to the dais. Like a snake, coiled to strike and swallow Jun whole.

I scrambled from my bed and tried to pry open all my windows again. I had tried the first few nights, hoping that by switching my room, they might have forgotten that detail. They hadn't. But my mother's screams still rang in my ears, and I pried at the frames, until one of my nails broke, bleeding freely. I muffed my aggravated yelp. I listened, but neither of the guards outside my door moved, so they must not have heard.

I stomped to my washroom to clean up my hand. The nail had already regrown. The moon was full, and light shone through the tiny window inside the shower stall.

My breath caught. The window was small and high up but was likely just large enough for me to wiggle through, and I hadn't tested it. My hands shook as I pulled in a small end table and used it to hoist myself up to the window. It opened without resistance. It was only designed to open a small amount, but I snapped off the bar holding it in place easily and was able to swing it wider.

I pushed my head out, and the frigid night ocean breeze blasted me, but it felt like freedom and was exhilarating. I looked and saw my room was on a corner, which wasn't surprising based on the hallway layout inside. There must have been a room nearby, maybe I could reach it and sneak out. The only problem was I was more than three stories above the rocky cliffs that held the castle and would be climbing in the near dark. But that had never stopped me before.

I pushed my shoulders through the window, and it was tight, but not difficult. I hooked my hands on the inside ledge of the windowsill and used the leverage there to slowly send my backside and legs out, unfurling along the castle wall until the muscles in my arms screamed. I managed to flip one hand, and then the other, turning my stomach to the wall, and found a tiny crack between the bricks that I could place my toes on. *It's no different than the sea cliffs back home.* I repeated it to myself a few times until I almost believed it. But I couldn't hang there forever, so I started to move. I slid my toes along the crack and found tiny but usable holds for my fingers. I reached the corner of the building and was able to peer around while the wind grabbed my hair.

I nearly yelped with joy. The next room over had a balcony, and I was only a few feet from it. I scrambled then, basically launching myself over the railing. The doors to the room weren't even locked. It looked unused, a fine layer of dust covering everything. I made my way to the main door and it was locked, but a quick search revealed the key in a vanity. Most people didn't expect a break-in from the inside of a room. I unlocked the door and opened it the smallest crack I could. No one was in the hall. I knew my room was around the corner, but the guards weren't going to change their shift for an hour.

My gut screamed *run,* but for once I didn't listen. I knew my best shot was to explore, learn more about the castle, and make an escape plan later. I pressed out of the room as silently as I could and made my way down the hall.

So, I spent my days training and my nights exploring the castle. Occasionally, this would be broken up by a gala. I learned what I could from the nobles, but I found the conversation to be very similar to those of the court at home. That is to say, shallow and almost completely worthless.

Each night I climbed from my window and returned the same way before dawn broke. I mapped the castle, both its main halls and its secret servants' passages, and every night the thrill of sneaking gave me the taste of freedom I needed to quell the guilt in my heart, at least a little bit. I even found a massive library, and on most nights I went there to read from some ancient tome. I memorized the route through the mountains from Xyr to Koron on massive maps, planning the route I would take and where I could stop. I tried to read about Hadeon and his magic, but everything was basically a love letter to our esteemed hero, and none of it was useful whatsoever.

But still, I continued planning, only daring to write the tiniest scraps of information in a small notebook I had *acquired* one night in the library, lest anyone discover it. But each stroke of my pen was a defiance, a small piece of myself that was still free. *Jun, I was coming for you.*

Chapter 19

Tori

My cohort was obviously one of the more advanced groups of soldiers, and as such they had more duties around the city. Their afternoons were often spent out on guard runs. Niata had a very small army, so most of the lords had taken up small private bands of mercenaries to patrol their lands. But in truth, these bands were used more to police their own people than protect them. I had visited a few estates where the intimidation had been so blatant that the people rarely left their houses outside their working hours.

I hated to admit that I had come to truly enjoy the company of my cohort, so I hated to think of them out in the city, stalking the citizens, for they were truly an intimidating force. I did my best not to think about it. That was until one day when it was my turn.

"I'm tired of having you mope around the castle all afternoon, Princess," Avlyn had declared. "Besides, what better way to have you out and about than with seven burly escorts." It seemed that guard runs were performed in groups of eight, and I counted as one of them, except I wasn't given a weapon.

But after our rowdy lunch, Kaleos, Noki, Raula, and I joined the others and made our way out of the castle. We marched around the outer wall that bordered the rolling green fields of the Dragon Kingdom. I could see the edge of the cliff that dropped off into the bay where we trained every day and the rolling ocean beyond. We marched two by two, and I was paired with Noki. It took all of five minutes for him to start complaining.

"Ugh, wall duty is so boring! Nothing is ever out here, why do we even bother?"

Raula, ever the orc, quipped back, "Those are the orders, and we follow them."

"Bah, don't act like you don't get bored out here too. Let's head into the city, much more entertaining there." My stomach sank.

Raula and Noki bickered for a bit longer, and I did my best to calm my mind, staring out at the mist and waves of the Shadowed Sea. I couldn't bear the thought of acting the enforcer with them, seeing that side of them.

Finally, they turned to Kaleos, who cracked a grin, "What the Commander doesn't know, can't hurt them." He turned our group westward, away from the castle and back toward the city. We had to crest a huge hill before we reached the city, and I let the fast pace Kaleos set drive the thoughts from my mind.

When we reached the top of the hill, the view of the city was spectacular, it sprawled before me like a great, colorful tapestry, woven through with streets and plazas. I could see the citizens mulling about their day even from this distance. The weather had been bitterly cold, clouds covering the sky like a storm was rolling in, but still, almost everyone was out and about. Snow littered the rooftops, and some clung in patches to the grassy land around us. To the south, I could see the Vitmos River curling across the grassy landscape like a lazy garden snake, unperturbed by the harsh wind that battered it.

All this stood in great contrast to the sight in the north. Where the Dragon Kingdom was covered in grass and small expanses of trees, the north of us was a great bare plain. The volcanic soil a deep black, as if the earth had been scorched long ago and never recovered. The great wound in the soil extended hundreds of feet in each direction and reached out over the cliff that disappeared beyond my sight.

My feet stopped as the wind changed and blew towards me from that wasteland. It felt wrong, like a disease that had festered into something putrid. The whole company stopped as I stared. I felt Kaleos lay a surprisingly gentle hand on my shoulder.

"That's where it happened, where Hadeon slew the Dragon Malech." The wind whipped around us again, as if summoned, the wrongness of it chaffing my skin. I saw through that horrid place, a land I wouldn't have dared touch, a small path that had been carved by hundreds of feet. At the edge of the cliff lay a small shrine with flowers and offerings scattered out.

"People walk across that to leave offerings for the saving of the world?"

Kaleos tightened his lips, but Raula answered, "It affects some more than others. As an orc, it doesn't bother me as much as those with fae blood. Humans barely feel it, I think they do most of the tending."

My skin was crawling, and suddenly going into the city seemed a pleasant alternative to standing here. The others seemed to agree, and we turned away from that place and the saturation of death. I was almost relieved enough to forget my anxiety from before.

We quickly entered the city, the first time I had since my arrival. We entered a neighborhood comprised of brick houses, mostly two stories, that lined clean cobblestone roads. I saw many children playing in the road and yards, and a few merchants were setting up booths in a small plaza. The group approached, and my palms were sweating as I waited for the scent of fear. But instead, our group was quickly greeted by warm smiles. Kaleos handed out his signature back slaps to many of the merchants and it seemed many were on a first-name basis as they chatted about everything and nothing.

"How are the kids, Amalthea?"

"The loves of my life and the bane of my existence," a young human woman smiled at Noki, handing him a fresh loaf of bread, which he refused.

"Anything we can help with today?"

"My wagon wheel has been squeaking, can you take a look?"

I saw then that Kaleos was already helping set up the awning of one of the merchants, and Raula was unloading crates for another. The others in our group had found similar tasks, all helping and chatting with the locals. I suddenly felt very out of place. Noki waved me over.

"You're full fae, lift this cart so I can get this wedged underneath." The cart was fully loaded with sacks of flour and other food items, but I was able to lift it just enough for him to slide an empty crate underneath before he shimmied under it himself. Occasionally, he would ask me to hand him a tool, but mostly I stood there, transfixed with the scene.

It was so comfortable, everyone helping one another, no hierarchy of enforcers and enforced, just a friendly community.

Amalthea came up to me and smiled, "We always love when a cohort wanders in on market day, makes everything so much easier. I'm Amalthea." She extended her hand. Her nails were caked with flour, and I could smell fresh bread and a wood fire on her.

"I'm Tori, a new recruit."

"A pleasure to meet you, Tori. Would you mind helping me set up my booth?" She gave me a beautiful smile.

"Of course not." Noki had the cart handled, and I followed

Amalthea a bit down the road and laced a thick canvas fabric around the posts of her booth with her.

"What made you decide to join the army?" She motioned at me to raise my corner a bit higher. I climbed up onto the table to get more leverage. Right, I was a new recruit. I couldn't see him, but I had a feeling that Kaleos was listening to my answer from the booth over.

"I've always been skilled with a sword. I wanted to use that skill." A true enough answer.

"And here you are helping me set up my booth instead!" Here I was indeed. She continued, "Well, we appreciate everything you do. Especially what you do to keep my little ones safe." She waved further down the road to a group of children playing some game on the ground. "Even if all they do is get into trouble. *Hey*! What did I say about playing bones in the street!" Not one single head turned around. She sighed in a way I had heard many mothers do, and couldn't help but laugh.

But then the wind whipped up to a harrowing gale. The sky darkened even more, and the street that had been lively before suddenly transformed into a tempest. The canvas roofs we had just tied down whipped free as heads of cabbages and bread loaves were picked up and rolled down the pathway.

I heard a sickening crunch, and saw the cart slam down to the ground and start rolling down the street. Noki had been clear of the cart, so no one could stop it as it started accelerating towards the group of youngsters in the street. I couldn't reach them in time to stop it, but I could do something. *Something stupid.*

I threw myself in its path and slammed my shoulder into its side as we collided. I felt one of my knees pop as I tried to stop the cart, but I managed to keep my feet under me. I felt the boards of the cart split, but we slowly came to a halt. I didn't dare move, even though my shoulder felt oddly warm, and my knee ached.

A few moments later, Raula was pulling me away gently, and I saw other soldiers grabbing the cart. Raula's hand was red with blood.

"You're hurt?" I asked her. She gave me a worried look. I saw then that a large piece of wood was sticking out of my left arm. *Oh*. People were fluttering around me, but I barely heard them. Without much thought, I reached up and pulled the wood out of my arm. I flashed back to reality as the pain hit. My knee was more than aching, and the pain in my shoulder was immense, but I could see my skin at the edge of the wound already closing.

"I'm alright, just need to clean up." Raula still held me tight, but my head was already clearing, and the pain had begun to pass. I shook out my leg and felt my knee pop back into place.

Pain laced my arm again as a small body wrapped itself around me. "Oh, thank you, thank you! I told them not to play in the road! I can't imagine what would have happened." Amalthea's face was streaked with tears, and her linen gown was now covered in my blood.

"It's fine. Anyone would have done the same. Good thing I'm fae. See? Almost all better." Only the deepest part of my wound remained, as I pulled myself free of the woman.

"I'm glad we were here to help, although maybe we caused the problem in the first place." Amalthea shook her head and tried to hug me again, but Raula intercepted the woman, and I felt a warm cloth being pressed to my wound by Kaleos.

"I think that's enough excitement for one day," Kaleos gently pulled me away from the gathered crowd, the rest of the cohort settling and calming them as we walked. "It can never just be an easy day with you, can it?" His tone was serious, but his eyes were laughing.

Chapter 20

Abraxas

"I made them take me." The princess stood before me her arm still pink where I could see the new flesh had healed. Avlyn had brought her to me after I had heard about the afternoon's events. I had demanded to see the entire group, but Avlyn had informed me that Tori had refused, and in their words, "I can't deal with her attitude and yours at the same time."

I stood from the table I was sitting at and approached her. A few weeks ago, she would have flinched at that, but today I saw nothing but defiance in her eyes.

I quirked a brow at her, "Oh, so you managed to convince *my* soldiers to disobey orders and take you into the city?"

She mirrored my raised brow, "I can be *very* convincing when I want to be, Your Majesty."

I shifted slightly as her words coursed over me, tantalizing on my skin, "Oh, of that I have no doubt, Princess." These past weeks with the cohort and court had been good for her. She was growing bolder, stronger, and it only made me want to grab that defiant chin and claim her even more.

"Nonetheless, if that is the case, they disobeyed me and shall receive proper punishment."

She stepped toward me then. One more step and our bodies would have been pressed together, and said, "I won't have them punished for what I did. I am to blame." She had become very defensive of her cohort; Avlyn had told me as much. And here she stood, as if she could stop me. But perhaps I would let her.

"You seem eager for punishment, so very different than on our journey here. I wonder, have you been dreaming of me, little bird?"

I felt her shift, and I knew it was true. With our rooms so close on the ship, I had felt every time she had brought her own hands between her legs, and it had taken every ounce of my control not to rip down the wall between us and get on my knees before her. And now with her here, and that same delicious scent of defiance and arousal spilling off of her, my control was even weaker.

She scrunched up her face, "Don't flatter yourself. I think we already know what I dream about doing to you."

I recalled the dagger across my chest but couldn't suppress a laugh. "Well then, I suppose if you crave punishment, then a month without training should be sufficient."

Immediately, she shrunk. Every ounce of rage was gone. "You wouldn't." I hadn't expected her to deflate so easily. This must have been more important to her than I realized. But I needed her to fight.

"Oh, I would, Princess. Worried your lovers will forget about you?" I saw that ember come back to her eyes.

'It's not like—Wait, are you jealous?" She shifted her body, and took that final step between us, pressing herself into me and tracing her hand up the collar of my jacket, "I thought you didn't get jealous, Your Majesty? If I were fucking them, what would you do?"

"I'd rip their hands from their wrists for daring to touch you." I wasn't sure that was a lie.

"So possessive. But no matter how long you keep me here, I'll never be yours." Deep inside me, something dark and feral stirred, and only the very thin veil of my will managed to hold it in, but I could feel it tearing through. This had just become much more dangerous.

"Oh, Princess," I couldn't stop myself as I laced my fingers over her jaw, drawing her even closer, "You don't know it, but you already are."

She pulled herself away from me then, and I could finally breathe, "I would rather jump from the sea cliffs."

I wanted to keep this going, but I knew that if I didn't stop now, it wouldn't end until I had her bent over my desk with my cock buried in her. And I had to wait. She had to take that first step.

"Well, then, to avoid any unnecessary bloodshed, a compromise." I had caught her off guard, but she didn't interrupt "No training with the cohort until you fix Amalthea's cart." She continued to stare at me with a puzzled look.

"I hear it was quite damaged when you used yourself as a blockade, and it is important to her livelihood. You can return to training once you have repaired it."

For a moment she just gave me a blank stare, but then she nodded her head, "Fair enough."

I should have let it lie there, but my mind was still caught on the irresistible scent of her, "What caused you to throw yourself between a fully loaded cart and a crowd of people you didn't know?"

She locked those deep, metallic eyes with mine, "It's what anyone would have done."

"You and I both know that isn't true."

She straightened her shoulders again, "Well, it's what I would do." Indeed, it was. My reckless and protective princess.

I waved my hand in dismissal, at which she rolled her eyes and turned from the room. As I watched her walk away, lecherously staring at that perfect ass in her training uniform, I wondered just how much more of this torture I could endure.

Chapter 21

Tori

It took me four days to fix Amalthea's wagon. After two, Avlyn showed me some pity and let Noki give me guidance. It was frustrating. I'd lived for over two centuries but couldn't fix a simple wagon! But with Noki's help, and a lot of work, we managed to create something that at least rolled on four wheels. Amalthea was ecstatic, and I was more proud than I wanted to let on.

A part of me wanted to show the king, rub it in his face that I had managed to complete his task. But after our last encounter, I avoided him at all costs. I had gotten too out of control. It had felt far too good to press myself against him and feel his heart pounding against his chest. *It's just a game,* I kept reminding myself. But with each day that passed, it was harder to believe.

I busied myself with the cohort once again and spent my nights wandering the castle and making my plan to rescue Jun. What had begun as a way to avoid the dark thoughts that crept in at night, I now used to avoid very different thoughts of Abraxas' hard body and promises of punishment.

That was until one night in my wanderings of the castle, I

passed one of the main meeting spaces and heard clipped voices. I had found a servants' passage that led into it, so I backtracked. I followed it and hid behind a tapestry in the room.

"We can't keep sending them there to die. We've lost three cohorts already." After being so adept at avoiding him, his deep rumbling voice surprised me.

"There is a reason these things are lost. No one has traveled to the Eternal City in memory, maybe we can find another—"

Abraxas stood and slammed his fist on the table, "There is nothing else; we need that diadem."

Avlyn dismissed the other officers until it was just them in the room. Abraxas sat back down, the rage ebbing from him. "We have been looking for decades, Avlyn, you know that. There is no other way." He rubbed his fingers over his eyes, "I'll just have to go myself."

"Out of the fucking question. There is no way I let you take one step into that cursed forest." Avlyn's voice softened, "You can't give this all up in your quest for revenge, Abraxas. This kingdom needs you. We need you."

"I'm tired, Avlyn, I'm tired of living this way. I don't even recognize myself anymore." I was shocked by the raw emotion in his voice. So very different to the arrogant man I had fought with just days ago. I heard Avlyn move over closer to him, and something knotted deep in my stomach, but they spoke again, "I can't begin to understand, Abraxas, but know that you have my loyalty, through all this."

"Never doubted that, Commander." They stood silent for a moment.

"I'll send in just a few scouts, tell them just to go in and out—one day—see what they can tell us. Maybe some clue to what keeps happening to the others."

Abraxas hummed his approval, and Avlyn seemed to take that as a dismissal.

I tried not to breathe, as the room grew more silent. The king rose, but as he made his way to the door, he closed it and turned around, sitting back down. I tried to move silently, making my way back down the tunnel when, "No need to hide anymore, Princess, I know you're there." I froze. I felt the tapestry pull back behind me, and he motioned for me to step out. He was backlit by the fire in the room, so I couldn't see his face.

I moved slowly, extracting myself from the tunnel, and stood face-to-face with him.

"How did you know I was there?"

"I always know where you are, Princess." *Asshole.* He seemed to read the unspoken words on my face, and he laughed, "You think I didn't know about all your late-night wanderings these last weeks?" My mouth dropped open, and he laughed again, which caused me to snap it shut.

"Why did you let me wander if you knew?"

"Despite what you think, you aren't a prisoner here, Princess. If you wanted to explore, all you had to do was ask," he smirked then. "Although I must admit, I did like watching you shimmy out of that window every night." My heart started to beat faster, and blood was pumping in my ears.

"Oh, so I suppose I could go down to the city and get on a boat whenever I wanted?"

His brow furrowed, "No."

I crossed my arms, "Seems my freedom has its limits."

"You are royalty, I thought you would already be used to that." He was right, of course, and I had a feeling he wasn't only talking about me. My life had always been dictated by the needs of my family, the needs of my kingdom, and all the limitations my society had required. I had fought them, but it hadn't changed anything. In fact, it had almost killed me. But I wasn't about to let him know he was right.

"Why are you keeping me here? What purpose do I serve? As

you can see, I'm no master spy." I motioned to the tapestry, then the drawings I saw littering the table, all maps of the Forest of Darkness, or at least pieces of it.

He didn't answer, but I kept looking at the drawings. The maps were created by scouts in the forest. Each was dated, but despite all originating from the same place, they were completely different.

I ran my fingers over the path drawn on the closest map but snatched my fingers away as if they had been burned. I looked up at the king, but his expression was muted.

"It doesn't make any sense, does it? How can our reports be so different just days apart." Was he asking my opinion? I looked back down, comparing the reports.

"Is it true, that the forest is shrouded in an unnatural darkness, day and night?' I asked.

"Yes."

"What happened to the cohorts?"

Deep worry creased his face, "We don't know. They enter but never come back. Our scouts find no trace of them."

"It seems like a place tainted by evil." I thought of the wasteland outside the city and shivered. "Somewhere that light cannot go. Is this diadem really worth the trouble?"

"Yes." He didn't elaborate. What was he holding back from me?

"Why are you keeping me here?" I asked again.

"I have heard you have become quite the warrior. Maybe I just have a very involved process for new recruits." He smiled then, and I saw it. That mischievous part he kept hidden away. I thought about the vulnerable side he had shown Avlyn, and apparently shown me as well. I thought of the hurt in his voice, and how at odds it was with that aristocratic mask he wore every day. Perhaps his vulnerability let my own slip.

"If you are keeping me as some sort of leverage against my

father, know that it's pointless. He's likely happy to see me gone." I had meant it to be an attack on the king, for his lack of foresight, but my breath hitched at the end, and I hated myself for it. Almost as much as I hated the sadness I saw creeping into the king's eyes.

"I'm sure that's not true, you are his daughter."

"No, I'm just the spare he's had to deal with for the last two centuries." I could feel the tears burning in my eyes, and I turned away from him. I wouldn't let him see that.

But I felt his hand gently trace under my chin, as he turned me back to him, "Tori..." I couldn't stand it, the way he said my name, that look of pity in his eyes, "Any man would be a fool to not see the value you have." The warmth that flooded me at his words had to be stopped.

I didn't have a weapon, so I attacked how I could. "And what value is that, Your Majesty? Pissing everyone off?" He didn't answer, just held my stare until I couldn't bear it any longer.

"Our relationships with our fathers can be complicated, can't they?" He pulled away like I had slapped him. I didn't stop. "What do you want revenge for?" In an instant, there it was again. That ice-cold expression. Any tenderness gone.

He moved towards me, and once again, I found myself pinned between him and a wall, his arms blocking me on either side.

"So many questions tonight, Princess. I can think of so many better things to do with our time together." He was playing the same game I was, trying to distract me. But I wouldn't let him. I slammed my palm into his chest, directly over his heart. I wasn't as strong as him, but the hit sent us both flying. But it wasn't from my strength. A bright light filled the space between us. I was so close to the wall I knocked my head on the stone as he toppled over the table. My world spun, and visions danced before my eyes.

A man with long dark hair and pale skin stood before me, wearing fine clothes. I could see strands of silver blonde hair whipping around my face in the wind. We stood at the cliffs at the edge of Xyr, looking out over the ocean and the sea mist. King Amaros pointed out to the sea, and I felt a huge grin spread over my face. The king didn't say anything, but I could feel the unadulterated joy leaking from my heart as I dashed towards the sea.

My vision shifted, and I was training out on the beach. I dueled with Dragon Kingdom soldiers, my sword whirling through the air like a bird riding the sea breeze. My movements were blurred with speed, and my grace was unmatched as I deflected blow after blow from my opponents. The match quickly ended with all of them disarmed, and my muscles sang with exertion and familiar rhythm. My companions laughed and jested after the fight, and a young, dark-skinned fae with long braids ran to me and practically climbed up my tall, male body to sit on my shoulders. I laughed and held young Avlyn's legs as I pointed out fighting techniques of the other soldiers who had started sparing.

The fighting of the soldiers blurred, but I could still hear the ring of swords clashing and shields smashing. But suddenly the beach was covered in blood, the bodies of soldiers lying everywhere. Then I was running through the streets of Xyr, a gangly teen Avlyn close behind. A deep red fire rained down from the sky. *Dragonfire.* A great roar shook the very earth, and the sky darkened as maroon wings covered the sun. I grabbed the young Avlyn and shoved them into a doorway as a great crash of bricks and dust rained down. Enemy soldiers flooded the streets, and the screams of citizens could be heard from all directions. I broke down a nearby door, and a group of enemy soldiers looked back at me. They didn't have time to react before my sword was in the first's neck. I wretched it free, blood shooting out and covering my face, but I kept moving. Stroke after stroke, soldiers fell, until they were all dead before me. Blood dripped from my long pale hair as I bolted up the building's stairs, to the roof with Avlyn close behind.

My head spun, but my vision cleared, and I was back in the room again. I tried to stand, but my head throbbed from where it had hit the wall. I heard the chair scraping against the floor as Abraxas rose. He looked about as confused as I felt. His eyes locked onto me, and he pushed aside the prone furniture to scramble to me. He grabbed my arm and lifted me to stand roughly.

"What did you just see?" My head was in a daze, I still couldn't comprehend what he was saying. He shook me, his voice raising, "*What did you see*?" I looked at him, and he was afraid. I could smell the fear on him, lurking under his anger.

"I saw...I saw the World Breaker, attacking Xyr. I was there, with Avlyn, and I was trying to get through the city..." I clutched my head, trying to remember which made it feel like it was splitting open.

"What else? Tori, what else?" I rubbed my eyes.

"I can't remember. What the fuck was that?" I looked at him, the lines of his face seeming deeper than I had ever seen them. "Was that a dream?" I thought about the perspective, and it became obvious whose eyes I was seeing through.

"Was that...you?"

"What else did you see, Tori?" He was drawn so tight, like a bow ready to be released.

"I saw your father." He stiffened even more. "But I think you were very young, and you felt...happy." It was all becoming so blurred, slipping away just like a dream would. "I can't remember anything else." I felt him exhale and he seemed to relax. "What just happened?" But then Avlyn stormed into the room, sword drawn.

"What's going on? I heard—" their eyes locked onto me, "Ah, I see you finally got caught, Princess." Gods, did everyone know about this? I suppose spymaster would certainly be taken off my list of skills.

"Time for the princess to return to bed." The king's tone was final, but fuck that.

"What the hell is going on? Was that magic?" Avlyn's gaze darted between me and the king. He slowly nodded to them, and they stepped out of the room and closed the door behind them. My mind was racing. Trying to hold on to those memories, those pieces of him I had seen. It felt invasive, but I couldn't stop myself from trying to cling to them. "Did you see my memories as well?"

"Always so many questions, Princess."

"Always so few answers, Abraxas." I think it was the first time I had used his name. I felt him linger on it, then he let out a huge sigh.

"Walk back to your room with me, and I'll answer what I can." He held out his arm, and I slipped mine in without a second thought.

"I don't know what that was. It certainly felt like magic, but different somehow. You are too young; magic had already almost completely left our world when you were born. But I remember when it was ripe, the earth was saturated with it. That moment was like a flash, a single bolt of lightning in a thunderstorm. A hint of magic perhaps."

He paused then, "I did see your memories. It was only pieces. I saw you very young, with your brother, I think. You were upset that he beat you at some board game I have never seen." He gave me a sideways glance with so much mirth, I screwed up my face. I could see the small black and white pieces in my mind. I never had the patience or long-term strategy for the game, Jun always beat me. But then the smile faded from his face, "I saw you at court, how easily you manipulated the nobles, solved arguments. Perhaps I should have you working as a courtier instead of a warrior or spy."

We had reached my door. The look he gave me made me feel like I needed to defend my actions, "It was easy there. Nobles are simple, greedy things, and I could always read them. A squabble between two lords over where a wall should go, who had rights over the rain that fell to a shared stream, those sorts of things."

He raised an eyebrow, "Those are simple?"

"People just want to feel seen, feel they aren't being taken advantage of. You can often find a solution where both parties feel like winners, or in a worst case, that their neighbor at least got equally fucked." He laughed then, and it encouraged me, "Nothing here is as simple though. I can't read people here, discern their motives."

"You will learn, just as you did there. All my soldiers are already disobeying orders for you. Hmm, perhaps I should be more concerned about that." He opened the door to my room. This was the most I had ever spoken with him, and I wasn't ready for it to end. Besides, I knew there was more to tonight than what he had told me.

"I haven't been able to read you at all." Oh gods, I'd done it now. His eyes darkened into something dangerous.

"I thought it was very obvious what I wanted from you, Princess." He leaned in then, surrounding me.

I blurted out, "What else did you see?"

He pulled back, "Nothing." But it was a lie.

"What did you see?"

"Good night, Princess." He'd seen something private, something he wouldn't tell me from my own memories. Anger replaced whatever I had been feeling, and I lunged at him again, but he caught me easily this time. "You need to change your tactics, or an enemy will be able to predict your attacks," he said.

"So, you are back to being my enemy then?"

"I didn't realize that had changed."

Yes, he was right, once again I had gotten complacent. I had gotten vulnerable with this male, who was nothing more than my captor. Keeping me from Jun. Weak, I had been so weak.

"Good night, Your Majesty." I closed my door and dashed to the small notebook I had kept from the library. I added what I could recall of the king's memories before any more slipped away.

Chapter 22

Abraxas

I had lied to her. I had seen more of her memories, and she knew it. She said she couldn't read me, but I hadn't been able to slip a lie past her in quite some time.

But I couldn't tell her what I had seen— what I had felt. I played the memory again in my mind, anger rising within me. I, or rather Tori, stood before her father's throne. Her mother sat to the other side, and a fae male stood beside her father. I didn't know the man, but Tori did, and I could feel her thoughts as if they were my own. A younger lord, but one who had been fighting for power in all the ways Tori despised. Lies— deceiving his neighbors into bad deals to gain their land. He'd sent his soldiers to small towns to scare the villages into working longer hours in the fields. Nothing too grand, nothing he could be punished for, but it showed who he truly was. But it seemed his greatest sin was attempting to become Tori's betrothed.

Her father spoke, "Am I to understand, Lord Quen, that you believe my daughter has slept with your brother, and this nullifies your betrothal?"

"Not just my brother, but my captain of the guard as well!"

"And what proof do you have of this?"

"Proof? I don't need proof; she freely admits it!" King Rahul's head turned to Tori now, his look withering. But she did not hesitate.

"Lord Quen's brother is much better looking," she shrugged her shoulders, "and from what I have experienced, a much better lover as well."

"You see? Do you see how she mocks me? I will not stand for this insult from a whore such as—"

"That is enough, Lord Quen." King Rahul's voice did not carry any anger, and that upset Tori far more than the insult thrown at her. "Leave us, I will deal with my daughter." He turned and strode out, but not before Tori blew him one last kiss, and his face turned completely red. I felt her petty happiness swell before it all came crashing down. Rahul stepped up to her now, and as soon as the lord had left the room, slapped her across her face. I felt the sting on her skin, but it was the gaping pit that opened in her stomach that hurt far more. I felt the queen shift on her throne, but she said nothing.

"You sully the name of this house with your actions. How many betrothals have you ruined now?"

"Perhaps if you stopped trying to sell me off to the highest bidder. I have told you; I don't wish to be married to some liege lord. At least give me the honor of marrying me to someone decent, not some land grabbing merchant."

"At this rate, you would be lucky if any man would marry you with your reputation."

"I do nothing more than every other fae in this court!"

"You are not any other fae, you are Princess Tori Khato, and you shall control yourself." He never raised his voice, but it didn't matter. The last words hit Tori harder than his slap. She looked to her mother, who simply turned her head away. The pit in Tori's stomach opened even further. She looked down, unable to meet her father's eyes.

"I could be so much more than someone's bride, Father."

"What, with all the fighting you do? Or maybe with all your failed lessons and foolish exploits? Perhaps one of these days you will finally fall from those cliffs and give me some damn peace."

I felt the hot sting of tears in Tori's eyes, "Yes, Father, that would be easier for all of us, wouldn't it?"

She'd left the room calmly, and I'd felt nothing but a deep, unending darkness that seemed to grow with every step. This was not the first time this had happened, but today it would be the last. She reached her room and pulled open the drawer of her vanity. Inside sat several small vials of a milky white potion. She quickly unstoppered one, then two, downing the contents in a single gulp. She didn't stop until seven vials lay empty, and her body began to give out beneath her. Then everything went black.

I slammed my fist into the stone wall in front of me, leaving a crater as small pieces fell away. Rahul was lucky I hadn't known these details when we had met, or I'm sure he would not have survived the encounter. He was more of a fool than I had imagined. My blood boiled as I thought about how close I had come to losing her before I had ever even known her.

I paced my room, sleep eluding me. This connection between us had become dangerous. I was lucky she had seen the memories she had. Perhaps it was because of my conversation with Avlyn, my mind had been caught on that fateful day. I shook my head. No point in dwelling on it now. A knock came at my door.

Lord Nalux stood with two beautiful half-fae women outside my door. "I heard you could use some company tonight?" This man always seemed to know when I was in a foul mood and needed a distraction. I allowed him and the women in when I saw Avlyn lurking in the hall. I excused myself and stepped out.

"A message, Abraxas."

"Out with it, Commander, I'm a bit occupied."

Avlyn rolled their eyes, "Well you aren't gonna like it. Emperor Hadeon is on his way and expects a celebration for his visit."

"Fuck him. Always with the dramatics. What, he expects a delayed solstice celebration because we were off fighting instead of drinking and fucking?" Avlyn nodded their head, "I suppose I can't keep the princess away from it either?"

"He specifically requested for her to accompany him."

At that, my chest burned with rage. "She's not ready. She won't be able to handle him."

"You give her too little credit, Abraxas. She holds her own with the cohorts, and she got us more information from that tight-lipped Plagis than anyone else had managed before. She's capable." I imagined Hadeon's arm around her waist, running his fingers through her hair and getting to inhale her delicious scent. If he saw how strong she really was, how cunning, but still so vulnerable, he would sink his claws into her and never let go. I didn't blame Avlyn, but they didn't understand. It was Tori's capabilities that made her a target.

I dismissed them and returned to my room. Nalux was already naked with both women on top of him, one astride his face and the other with his cock in her mouth. He pushed the first aside when he heard me enter.

"Oh no, I know that look. Good thing I already versed these ladies on the rules."

I pulled off my night robe and gripped his face in my hand, "Good, because until you say red, I'm not stopping tonight."

Chapter 23

Tori

I readied myself for training like I did every day, when a knock came at my door. I opened it to see Ciara and Avlyn waiting expectantly for me. Avlyn shoved their way in without hesitation, but Ciara gave me an apologetic curtsy and waited for me to invite her in. They sat themselves down on my small couch, and Avlyn launched right in.

"Right, so the bad news, or the worse news first?"

"Avlyn, must you always be so dramatic?"

"Yes, and well, ok, bad news first. Emperor Hadeon will be here in a week for a grand ball." The ocean of my mind that I had managed to keep calm despite my encounter with the king suddenly bottomed out, like a tidal wave approaching the shore.

"And the worse news?"

"He expects you to be his escort during his visit." The wave hit me, and I couldn't breathe. It was just like the carriage ride, as if a great weight sat upon my chest, and I couldn't fill my lungs. I felt my knees meet the carpet, and my head buzzed. I could just make out Avlyn and Ciara holding me up, Avlyn telling me to breathe. I felt Ciara's soft hands rubbing along my back, cooing soft noises at me. An eternity seemed to pass, but the weight lifted, and I could hear again. I was still on the floor, Avlyn and Ciara still around me.

"Avlyn, I can't— I can't be with him— he's the one—"

"I know what he's done." Avlyn's face was the darkest I had ever seen it. "But I also know what you can do. You can handle this, Tori. It's only for a night." Avlyn's faith eased a very fundamental part of me that hadn't seen kindness in quite some time. I felt Ciara's hand on my back and couldn't remember the last time I had felt a gentle touch like that. I shook both off before they overwhelmed me, standing quickly.

"Being able to fight has nothing to do with being able to play nice at court."

"Yeah, but I've seen you do both, and don't forget, I may be the most beautifully rugged warrior you have ever seen, but I've done my time at court as well. I know how similar the two skill sets can be. Both just a dance, reading and anticipating your opponent." I thought about the memories I had seen. Avlyn was there when the World Breaker attacked. I had never really thought about how old they were, but they had to be at least five centuries. I'd spent so much time with Avlyn these last few weeks, but how much did I really know about them?

They interrupted my chain of thought, "Actually, that gives me an idea. I know exactly what you need to boost your confidence. Yes, this will be good for the both of you." They wore a grin so mischievous it put Abraxas' to shame, and I couldn't help but worry.

"Avlyn...what are you planning?" The grin showed every single one of their teeth now, "Oh, you'll see, Princess. But until then, I brought Ciara to measure you for a new gown." I glanced over to my closet full of garments I hadn't worn, as none of them really suited sword-play on the beach.

"I have plenty, why do I need a new one?"

"King's orders I'm afraid. I'll leave you lovely ladies to it." They excused themselves and were out the door.

I turned to Ciara, "I really don't need a new gown."

"Nonsense, if the king wants to spoil you, I say let him." Her grin was so genuine, that I stayed silent. She had me stand then, taking out a cord tied with knots at even intervals to take measurements of my body.

She whipped around me, placing the chord over me in every direction, "You know, Your Highness, I have heard a rumor. There is a betting pool among the servants over when you and the king will announce your engagement." I choked on nothing. "Oh, no need to be coy, Your Highness. I am not one of the women who wept for days knowing they had missed their chance at the long-term bachelor." She came around my front, and her eyes were twinkling.

"Ciara, are you teasing me?"

"Not at all, Your Highness, I am simply hoping that you will help me place my money on the correct date. I've had my eye on a set of earrings outside my price range for some time now." Was she serious? How could anyone think that I, a princess—one of two currently in existence due to the low birthrate of fae royals—would be getting engaged to a king who had long resisted producing an heir to his bloodline, as I stayed as a ward in his kingdom? Alright, perhaps I could see how this rumor had started.

"Ciara, I hate to disappoint the gossips, but the king and I are not to be engaged. I am here merely to improve relations with Niata."

"Oh, of course, Your Highness." But that cheeky grin never left her face. I scowled, and she laughed. I had to change the trajectory of this conversation.

"Thank you, for your kindness before." Her face fell immediately.

"Of course, Your Highness."

"Tori." She smiled but did not give in.

"I know better than most the cruelties that the emperor possesses. I was lucky that I was able to flee here, to the Dragon Kingdom. I grew up in Koron, my mother was a human slave in the palace there. Who knows who my father was, but as half-fae, I was lucky enough to not be born into slavery as well." Her face told me she didn't feel lucky at all. "I actually met Avlyn when they were there with the king, and they helped me move here, and set me up with a job in the palace." She gave me a melancholy smile that I knew all too well, "I owe them quite a lot."

"I had always heard of him as the Great Hero, the savior of the world. How could it be that he has been allowed to rule like this? He seems to possess nothing but cruelty."

"Most on the continent don't see this, only the acts of a generous emperor, who provides protection and peace. Besides, who would stand against him? I'm sure you saw it, Your Highness. His power can decimate entire armies, and with King Abraxas at his side..." she trailed off. Yes, Abraxas had been the enforcer, the dark Dragon King who haunted nightmares. The man who had murdered his father for power. How easy it must have been for Hadeon to seem the benevolent overlord, while Abraxas took the blame.

I worried my lip, then shook my head. No, Abraxas *was* to blame. Every uprising, every threat to Hadeon's peace these past centuries, Abraxas and his soldiers had been there to enforce, to terrify. Those had been his actions, there was no excuse.

Ciara surveyed me with worried eyes, "People do the best they can to adjust their lives to their circumstances. We would rather slowly boil than rise up out of the flames."

But it seemed this conversation had become too heavy, for she flitted back around me and pulled her smile back on.

"But enough about that, you need to be ready for a gala fit for an emperor. With your eyes, I'm thinking something dark blue." She moved to a box full of fabric samples, but I barely paid attention, my eyes instead taking in this brave woman, who still had the courage to smile through it all.

Chapter 24

Tori

Something was different about today's training. I could hear the troops hollering from across the beach, various jeers and shouts breaking loose, and instead of standing in formation, they were all gathered around in a circle as Avlyn and I approached.

"Move out of the way, soldier. Move! What are you assholes doing?" Avlyn shoved our way through the crowd. I could tell by the sounds of clashing swords that some of them must have been dueling in the center. Not so uncommon when Avlyn wasn't around to wrangle them, but normally they didn't get this worked up about it. The idea of getting a good fight in sent my stomach churning.

I inserted myself between Noki and Raula to get a better look. I saw two fae soldiers rush at a third, but he parried them both off easily. As the two attackers side-stepped to try a new maneuver, my heart stopped.

The defending fae was Abraxas himself, and it was almost comical how fucking stunning he looked. Almost.

He wore traditional black training leathers that clung to his strong legs and had forgone a shirt, like many of the soldiers did. Instead, he wore a black leather pauldron on the shoulder of his guard arm, a single strap of leather bound it to him by wrapping it under his chest. He wasn't as ridiculously defined as some of the other young soldiers, but there was no doubt that he was nothing but solid muscles, the veins in his arms standing out from the effort of the swordplay. A large scar cut around his ribs, and I could hardly imagine what kind of injury it would have taken to leave a scar like that. He had that mesmerizing V of definition that led me exactly to where I needed to avoid.

He had tied his hair half back, out of his face, platinum locks still trailing him as he easily dodged another attack from his opponents. But it was his face that stunned me most, a hungry and youthful expression, one I had seen so often on the other soldiers when they riled each other up. Pure male bliss. It curled heat deep in my stomach and I did my best to swat it away.

He moved to the offensive now, but his attackers didn't know it yet. They flew at him again, but this time as he parried, he sent one of the other soldiers flying into the other. They stumbled over each other, and Abraxas used the opportunity to engage one of the soldier's swords, twirling his blade and disarming him. He tripped trying to reclaim his sword, and Abraxas slapped the training sword over his back, a clear defeat.

The second soldier corrected, however, and reengaged. Sparks flew as their swords met, drawing jeers from the crowd.

As the clash of steel echoed through the training ground, I couldn't tear my gaze away from the captivating display of skill and power unfolding before me. Abraxas moved with grace and precision, each strike executed with calculated finesse. The intensity in his eyes was undeniable, a hunger for victory burning within him.

The second soldier fought with renewed determination, refusing to yield to his king. Their swords met in a symphony of metal, sparks dancing in the air, eliciting cheers and applause from the enthralled crowd as they were swept up in the exhilarating dance of the blades.

Abraxas, undeterred by his opponent's resilience, countered every attack with fluidity and expertise. With each swift maneuver, he inched closer to gaining the upper hand.

In a calculated moment, Abraxas seized an opportunity. As the second soldier lunged forward, he expertly sidestepped, causing his opponent to overextend. With lightning-fast reflexes, Abraxas executed flawlessly, slamming his elbow into the soldier's nose, and sending his weapon clattering to the ground.

He hadn't even broken a sweat. A few of the soldiers from the crowd tried to help the loser with his broken nose, but he was obviously more embarrassed than anything else. Some of the others clapped Abraxas on the back and jested with him.

"Not too bad for an old man who sits on a throne all day?" He chuckled, and the other soldiers bantered around him.

"Not too bad?! If two fae soldiers can't stop you, then my half-fae ass surely won't try," one of them said.

"He may be on the throne all day, but all night is a different story," quipped another.

"Hell, I fuck all the time and I don't fight like that."

"That's cause you're a fuckin' liar."

A part of me wanted to melt away, to vanish from the crowd before he saw me. Seeing him joke and boast like this was a side I hadn't seen much of, and it felt like early mist that would soon be burned away by the morning sun. But another, bigger part of me wanted to stay— craved to stay.

The crowd started to disperse, Avlyn doing their best to get the morning formations started, and slowly everyone started falling in. As people moved away, Abraxas' eyes locked on me.

"Ah, Princess, I was just getting warmed up for you." He

crossed the sand to me in three strides. "Are you ready for our match?"

My head whipped to Avlyn, who gave me a wink that made me want to punch them right across their smug face. Was this what they thought would prepare me for Hadeon's arrival? They were in for it later.

"I don't think it will be much of a match, Your Highness." It wasn't a lie, not really. I had seen him fight just now, and he hadn't even been trying. Besides, it would be dangerous to show him how well I could fight in an even match. That was my card to hold.

"Never seen you this modest, Princess. I have always admired a woman who knows how to handle a blade." He tossed a long sword at me. I could practically feel the necks of the soldiers snapping as they looked back at us, but Avlyn shouted louder, getting them back in line.

I took my position across from him and dug my toes into the sand. I raised my sword up to my first stance lazily, and he batted the tip with his own sword, sending me off balance.

"I do hope you are taking this seriously, Princess, because I certainly am." With that unnatural speed he came at me, and without even engaging our swords, he swept my legs out from under me, and I landed flat on my back with a thud.

"Again." I parried his first strike, but again he quickly got inside my guard, knocking me down again. We repeated this several more times, each time with him quickly disarming me, and on the last pass, he managed to graze my arm. The sword wasn't sharp enough to cut, but it stung.

"You aren't even trying." I shrugged my shoulders. I could see the anger rising in him, but then a shadow passed over his face. "Well, I guess I shouldn't be surprised at your training, considering who taught you. No wonder Niata fell so quickly." I swung my sword overhead uncontrolled, and he parried, but not before I shifted my body inside his guard and struck him with the pommel of my sword. I was very satisfied with the grunt he emitted, as he stepped back. He had that stupid grin on his face, "Better."

He came at me again, but this time I engaged. But I couldn't get inside his guard again, he'd already anticipated me and adjusted his technique. I tried to outpace him, as was often my strength, but he was too fast for that. I tried a series of fast strikes to throw him off, but he parried me easily, and my speed overran my footwork, and I stumbled. He used the opening to his advantage, striking my thigh with his sword.

"Not bad technique, but you aren't able to execute well enough. Maybe if you had more control..." He swung again, forcing me to take a step back, and he managed to land another blow across my ribs this time. Now he was really pissing me off. I knew what he was trying to do, and it was fucking working.

Almost all the soldiers were completely ignoring Avlyn now, fully focused on us. I paced around him, trying to find an opening. But it was useless, he had speed he shouldn't have had for his size, and his reach was longer than mine. I would have to use close quarter fighting to win, but I couldn't do that with the long sword.

"I didn't realize there was this much talking in a duel. Guess I never learned that either." I slid my feet across the sand and thrust at him again. He parried lazily. "You're still holding back."

"I'm not."

He came at me again with a rush of strikes. I countered them all, but each one fell later and later until he was able to snag the pommel of my sword with his tip, and it flew out of my hand. I lurched for it, but he grabbed my arm and twisted me until he had me pinned against his chest, the base of his sword at my throat. I felt him push his lips to my ear, "You sure about that?" I felt the words flutter across my sensitive skin before he pushed me away. I turned to him, now disarmed, my heart pounding.

He frowned, motioning to a soldier from the circle that had gathered around us. "Bring the princess a bladed sword." Surprise passed over the soldier's face, but he ran to the weapons rack without question.

"How about this, Princess? If you say stop, I'll stop, but until then," he flung the blade with a lethal edge at my feet, "you fight me how you really want to."

I stared down at the gleaming blade, obviously not a practice weapon. *Don't do it. Don't let him see.* But it was too late. The fight had gone to my blood, and I was past the point of no return. My mind was fixed on the images I fought to keep away at night. Niata burning, the Dragon Army loading up dead bodies to burn, and him, standing on that stage, that cruel smile mocking me. No matter what had happened in the last weeks, I couldn't waste this opportunity, even if it was madness.

"Any way I want?" The king nodded.

I quickly spun, surprising the soldiers behind me, but they parted so I could reach the weapons rack. There I found exactly what I was looking for, what I had known was there from my first day training on the beach. I grabbed two sharp scimitars. They weren't exactly the swords I was used to, but they were about the same weight, and more importantly, the same length. I walked back to the circle, the king examining my new weapons, and his pompous grin only grew. I tossed the bladed longsword at his feet.

"It only seems fair."

He tossed away the practice blade and picked up the new weapon. He ran his thumb along the edge, and I saw the faintest hint of blood bloom from the soft pad at the tip.

He looked at me, "I won't hold back."

I gripped one sword in each hand, feeling the leather on the pommel cut into my skin. Adjusting to their weight felt like coming home.

I took a final steadying breath, "Good." And I was on him.

Dual wielding of weapons had its disadvantages. It was much harder to block with a sword than say, a shield in the offhand. They were also shorter, which was a disadvantage to a larger two-handed sword. But I was fast, and up close with my training in hand-to-hand, I was much more deadly. I used both swords to knock his long sword out of the way, and immediately got much closer to him. He wasn't prepared for this, and lost time trying to adjust his feet to the closer combat.

I came in with a flurry of strikes, and he was able to block, but now it was him on the defensive, trying to keep pace.

But he was an expert swordsman, and I saw him slowly closing the gap between us, his blade matching my strikes again. I changed tactics again, moving in even closer. It could have been deadly for me, but I twisted my body all around his, dodging his blows and tripping up his feet with my own. Steel rang out as our swords collided again and again, and I searched for my opening. I saw it and struck, my offhand sword slicing over his thigh, leaving a trail of blood. He staggered and I landed another across his ribs. Both were grazes, he would heal in a matter of moments, but seeing his blood hit the sand surged the bloodlust through me. I moved faster then, pushing my muscles past their limit. I threw elbows and knees at him along with my blade. He had shifted as well, the fight taking over him, and he struck.

He swung so hard I couldn't block him, and he sent the edge of my own sword back into me, pain lacing across my shoulder. I barely felt it as I spun, but he anticipated me now, his sword coming up to greet mine.

One of my weapons flew across the sand, leaving me exposed. The king hesitated on the final blow, but I did not. I used the movement of my already tumbling body, and grabbed with my now empty hand onto the pauldron he wore. I threw my head down around the lever of my arm and flung my feet up until my legs wrapped around his neck. My weight and the inertia of the motion tumbled him forward and flipped him so he landed flat on his back, and I twisted myself so my ass pinned his chest down, my thighs framing his face. I slid my remaining sword over his neck.

The entire beach was silent, even the waves didn't seem to crash. All I could hear was our labored breathing and the blood rushing in my ears. I pressed the edge of my blade into his throat until a faint red line dripped from beneath it. I looked deep into his eyes as I prepared to end him, but instead of seeing that twisted smile, my mind brought me the image of his eyes laced with concern as he gently held my face. *Any man would be a fool not to see your worth.*

"There you are." He was calm, far calmer than he had any right to be, and I couldn't read his expression. I could end it all, right here. I tensed my muscles to gut him, and he didn't even flinch, just continued to stare at me with those eyes that seemed to glow. It was my turn to hesitate.

"Put the sword down, Princess." Avlyn's blade slid against my throat.

"There is no need for that, Commander." The king gently placed his hands on my hips, and lifted me enough that he could sit up, as if I weighed nothing. He pressed further into my sword as he did, but I didn't have any pressure behind it anymore. I hadn't pinned his arms, for if this had been a real fight, his head wouldn't have been attached to his shoulders by the time he had recovered from my takedown. *This was supposed to be a real fight.* My heart raced, and it was as if a piercing noise had shattered my eardrums, and I was blocked from the sounds around me. I didn't hear what was said, as I was brought to standing. People were moving around me, maybe speaking to me, but all I heard was buzzing.

"Princess, Princess Tori..." My name snapped me to the

present. The king had captured my chin between his fingers. "I said, I think it's time you returned to the castle." His face hovered before mine, and all I could do was stare into his eyes. I had never really looked before, and I could see now how deep green they truly were, like the moss lost in an ancient forest, deep below the canopy. But near his pupils, I saw flakes of gold, like the beams of light from the summer sun just peeking through the leaves above. I hated nothing more than the soft look they gave me now.

I couldn't speak, so I simply turned and sulked across the beach to the castle. I don't know what Avlyn had intended for me to feel after this duel, but I doubted it was this.

Chapter 25

Tori

Servants had been buzzing around the castle for the last few days, preparing for our belated winter solstice celebration. Greens filled with red berries were draped over almost every doorway, symbolizing the blood of the World Breaker that had been spilt.

The weather seemed to be in agreement with the delay. Harsh winds whipped in from the ocean, coating the city and castle in a fine layer of ice, and I saw snow gathering on the mountains further from the coast. Even inside my comfortable room, heated by a roaring fire, I wrapped myself in a warm blanket. Niata had been a balmy place, the air always rich with humidity and heat. You were more likely to find yourself cursing the sun than shivering. All of this only seemed to rub my nerves more raw than they already were. The ocean of my mind churned along with the sea outside. Even going through my routine of breathing and movement seemed to do nothing to quell the squall.

Ciara had arrived early this morning, buzzing about with my own preparations. I had hoped to get some training in to burn off the energy that seemed to be crawling over my skin, but looking at the weather outside, maybe I could be grateful I had missed it.

"Like I said, Your Highness, the dark blue is stunning on you." Her eyes twinkled with delight. She was right. The dark navy fabric was draped beautifully, and decorated with silver stars that mimicked the late winter sky. My underlayer was made of small metallic scales that were held together by chains.

"Like armor, Your Highness," Ciara had said. It made me grin. This would have been the worst armor anyone had ever seen, but somehow it did make me feel more secure. Perhaps I was getting used to this court's ridiculous fashion. I could appreciate how it certainly emphasized the best parts of my body. I had gotten strong training with the cohort, and my legs were toned in a way I hadn't seen in years, my arms showing off lines of muscle with each twist.

Despite previous failures, Ciara was trying again to tame my hair into some kind of updo. I always let her, knowing she would eventually settle for just a single pin when all my other hair escaped.

"Ciara, I have something for you." She paused, more of my hair falling out of the pin she held in place while she wrestled with another. I reached into the drawer of my vanity and pulled out a small box to hand to her. She cautiously lowered her hands from my hair and opened it. Inside sat a pair of earrings. They certainly weren't elaborate, but they were beautiful, with a small ruby connected to a larger yellow topaz hanging below. The jewel and gold metal offset her eyes perfectly.

"A little bird told me that these were the ones you had been looking at. I couldn't help you win the bet, so I figured I could make up for that." She stared at me, and as was becoming uncomfortably common, I couldn't read the emotions on her face.

"I cannot accept this, Your Highness."

"You can and you will." I didn't let her protest before I

grabbed one of the earrings and started placing it on her ear, just as she had done to mine. She kept silent as I added the other. "Just a belated solstice present." They did look lovely on her and didn't seem out of place with the finer clothes she wore for the celebration.

"Thank you." She busied herself with the fabric at the hem of my dress, and I let her be.

Shortly thereafter, my door opened without a knock. That could only mean one person. "Your Majesty." I didn't turn to greet him.

"Ciara, you have outdone yourself," he spoke to the half-fae woman at my side. I looked at her and saw her swell with pride, that lingering awkwardness vanishing.

"Isn't she gorgeous, Your Majesty?" I saw that mischievous gleam in her eye then.

"Indeed." I would not let that affect me, I would not.

"Time to go." I held out my hand to him, and we were off.

As we made our way down the halls, he was unusually quiet, and not in the typical icy way I knew. I looked at him, but he refused to look back. I listened in the stillness of the hallway, and I could hear his pulse racing.

"What's wrong?" He didn't answer me, so I stopped, holding him back. "I can handle Hadeon." I wasn't entirely sure if I believed myself, but I would say it until I did. I continued with a sing-song voice of mockery, "Are you worried about me, Abraxas? Best be careful or I might start to think you care."

He finally looked at me, "Hadeon has brought your brother with him."

My heart stopped, "Jun...is here?" That restless anxiety I had felt all day exploded like fire all over me. It was so different from the crashing waves I felt in my mind, and it worried me. It compelled me to act, and I knew that was dangerous. But I couldn't fight it.

I pulled at the king's arm, "I must go see him, take me to him now!" But Abraxas wouldn't move. I tried to release his arm to run, but he held me fast.

"This is a trap, Tori." He stared at me with those emerald eyes, the intensity locking me down more than his grip, "I don't know what he is planning, but you must be cautious."

"I know that; let's go! I can't—" He caught my cheek in his hand, his gaze only intensifying. I thought I imagined it, but he ran his thumb over my jaw gently, and it seemed to calm the fire eating at me. I saw now the faintest pink line on his neck where my sword had marked him. My heart beat faster now, but for an unforgivable reason.

"If I didn't know better, I would think you were jealous of me accompanying Hadeon. I would have thought you would be happy to show off your little pet to your emperor."

His voice was deeper than usual, "I don't like other people touching what's mine." I finally managed to wiggle my hand free from his arm.

"Abraxas, I will never be yours."

That soft look was immediately gone, "Well then, I suppose it's time for me to deliver you to your new master."

He gripped my hand in his, but it wasn't kind this time. I felt my bones press together as he dragged me down the hall. We rounded a corner into the entryway and were greeted by a throng of people. At its center, the emperor stood, surrounded by adoring sycophants. I scanned the crowd quickly, looking for Jun as the king dragged me forward.

I finally saw him behind Hadeon. He wore a finely tailored jacket with a high collar and slim pants, the fashion of the Court of Flames. I had never seen him in anything but the robes of our home, so it took me a moment to spot him. His posture was slouched, and his long dark hair was falling out of his high bun.

His eyes were unfocused, his mouth slightly slack, almost like he drank too much ambrosia, but I knew better.

I tried to catch his attention, but Hadeon stepped between us.

Abraxas released my hand, "Princess Tori Khato, as you requested, Your Eminence." Hadeon raked his eyes from my head to my toes, but I barely noticed as I tried to lock eyes with Jun.

But then Hadeon laced his arm through mine and pulled me in the opposite direction, "My lovely Pallas couldn't accompany me this time, but I think I shall enjoy the evening nonetheless." I couldn't turn my head to see my brother without basically bending over backward now. I finally turned to face Hadeon, and was greeted by the look of a wolf who had cornered its prey.

But we were quickly surrounded by the nobles of both his court and the Dragon Kingdom. I took a deep breath and focused on the stillness of the sea. I plastered on my best smile. I could do this; I could pretend for one evening. For Jun, I would manage.

I didn't say much of anything, as Hadeon paraded me around like the dancing monkey I was. He was courteous with the nobles, the picture of our Divine Emperor. The only hint I had of his true nature was the iron clad grip he held on my arm.

Lady Lovatia practically clung to his other side, "Oh, Emperor Hadeon, since we are celebrating the Solstice, please, please tell us about your battle with the World Breaker. About how you saved Xyr!" At that, I saw Hadeon's gaze twist over the heads of the crowd for just a moment. I looked where his eyes fell and saw Abraxas, engaged with a few nobles of his own.

His face changed to one of annoyance for just a moment, but he quickly regained himself. "My Lady, I have quite the surprise for you later, I wouldn't want to spoil it with a story you have all heard before."

Lady Lovatia practically buzzed in excitement, "Oh, you must tell us what it is!"

Hadeon's grip on my arm tightened, and I felt it tingle as he laced his power through it. He locked his eyes on mine, "Oh, I don't think so. You know your emperor loves a great reveal." Lovatia was still muttering something, but Hadeon had me locked in his gaze, and I saw absolutely nothing but cruelty.

"I have never heard the story; I would love to know why you decided to kill the Dragon Malech." The chatter around us died as if I had just uttered a great insult. Hadeon's face twisted.

"Why? To save Adimos, of course. Who would stand against the Breaking of our world if not me, the last fae with magic?"

"Who indeed? And how did you do it?"

He scoffed, "Niata truly was a wasteland if you haven't heard the tale."

I let his insult roll off, "I would prefer to hear it from you, Your Eminence."

We stood at an impasse, but then the band struck up a lively tune, and he used that as an excuse. As he dragged me to the dance floor, I heard him whisper in my ear, "If all the old gods are dead, who are the new gods?"

I had avoided dancing at any gathering thus far, but it seemed my reprieve was over. Hadeon swept me into a dance that I very much didn't know. I did my best to mimic what I saw around me, but Hadeon didn't lead me so much as shove me around, and I was tripped constantly. I was already losing this battle. When I wasn't watching my feet, I only saw his nefarious smile grow. The song ended, and I tried to push away from him, but he slung his arm around my waist, pulling me up against him as an even faster song began.

Don't overthink it, Tori. You can do this. I stopped trying to dance, and instead just shuffled my feet along to the beat and found that at least I wasn't tripping now. Hadeon's smile only grew. "I had heard such good things about you, Princess, that you are a delight to have in court these last few weeks. My guess is no one has seen you dancing."

"I'm still learning the steps, Your Eminence. Forgive my clumsiness."

His wicked smile turned into a frown. "No need to play nice anymore, Princess. I was hoping for some entertainment tonight."

"I'm afraid I don't know what you mean, Your Eminence. Is this not how a princess should treat the emperor?"

He snagged my chin between his fingers, his nails cutting into my skin, "How very disappointing it would be to find that you have turned into this simpering, weak thing so quickly. How very similar to your dearly departed mother."

Without thinking, I snapped at him, trying to snag his fingers between my teeth. He jerked away, but that smile laced with cruelty returned to his face.

"Oh, there you are, my little hellcat. Finally, we can have some fun." He ran his hand over my back, pulling me even tighter to him. "I always did enjoy the fashion here." His fingers landed on the metal chain of my underwear, and I felt a jolt as he sent lightning dancing over it. It landed directly on my clit, and I stumbled at the extremely intense sensation. Hadeon loosed that cruel laugh, just like he had in my father's throne room. It took every ounce of my control not to slap him across the face. But I was done hiding.

"What have you done to Jun?" I was sure my hatred was plastered all over my face. He laughed again, even more wicked.

"Such a ferocious little thing. No foreplay it seems." He raked his fingers through my hair, pulling my face right up against his. "Your brother has been well cared for in my court, as I promised. I don't think you will have much chance to talk tonight, since you will be with me, but if you did, I'm sure he would tell you that it has been quite pleasurable." I had to choke back the bile in my throat.

"You will not touch him." I threw it at him like acid.

"Oh, darling, I think you will find I can do whatever I want. And someone as small as you certainly wouldn't be able to stop it." He laced his words with his magic, and it flayed over my skin. I swore I could smell my flesh burning as the pain rippled over me. But he left no marks. My body seized, and I fell out of whatever dance step I had managed to maintain up until that point and crashed into him, my face much too close to his, "But you could be so much more." I shoved off him.

"You hate me so, Princess. But I wonder," he pulled me up tight against his body again as the dance continued, "do you feel the same about your warden?" He looked over my shoulder and then turned me so I could see Abraxas, dancing with another lady of his court. "He and I, we are the same, you know. I did so enjoy watching him conquer Niata. Quite ruthless, isn't he? Did you know it was his idea to bring the trebuchets? He said a fast and devastating attack would destroy morale. Make it easier to decimate the army." I shook my head as the words bubbled up, *He is nothing like you.* What was I thinking, of course he was. They were both monsters bound by nothing but their own desire for power.

People think they want sex and power, but it's always more than that. I couldn't reconcile Abraxas with the man who had held me in the hallway, that dangerous emotion in his eyes.

I had first seen them together, side-by-side. Hadeon the glowing sun, and Abraxas the darkness that made Hadeon shine even brighter. Then I had seen Hadeon's cruelty and thought them just two sides of the same coin. But seeing them here, together again, I saw the truth.

They weren't the same. Hadeon was an erratic animal, barely caged inside his illusions of charm. Abraxas was calm and calculated. He was mischievous, but I remembered the feel of his hand on my face as he looked at me with those eyes so full of worry and compassion.

As my thoughts raced, Hadeon continued, "It's really a shame. I had hoped for more of a fight, it has been so long since we've had a reason to raise the army." My teeth felt like they might crack, I ground them so hard. I was sure he saw it as well, delight dancing in his eyes, "In fact, the only fight I saw was with you, my little hellcat. Oh, it's been so long, I had forgotten how much fun that is." He wrapped his hand tighter around my waist, "We could have such a good time together."

I felt his power again, the electric shocks traveling across my skin, sitting on the razor's edge between pain and pleasure as it raked over me. My nipples hardened in response, but all the courtly training in the world couldn't have kept me there, any pleasure I felt was absolutely decimated by disgust. I shoved out of his grasp.

"You killed my mother." I let the words hang there, but he stepped right over them.

"That pathetic little creature? Oh, Princess, don't you see, I freed you from her, and from your father. You can be so much more without them holding you back. You can let free that power that sleeps inside you." What the hell was he talking about? That enormous weight threatened my breathing again, and I tried, damn me, I tried to get it under control. I wouldn't let him see me like that. I took another step back and ran into a hard body. I felt Abraxas' hand come to rest at my waist ever so softly.

"Everything alright here, Your Eminence?" Hadeon's eyes snapped to Abraxas' hand, but only for a moment.

"The Princess and I were just discussing her future, Abraxas. In fact, Lord Plagis has blessed me with some very interesting information. I wonder what it might take to prove my theories." I felt Abraxas' hand squeeze down on me, ever so slightly. I cursed my lies to Plagis. I should have known that was too dangerous a tactic, but I didn't know it would have been intriguing enough to pass to the emperor himself.

"Perhaps in his old age, Plagis' mind is slipping. I don't remember discussing anything with him that was all that interesting. Perhaps he misspoke in the hopes of garnering your favor." Not a very good lie, but my mind was racing too much for anything better. The emperor's eyes sparkled with greed.

"But, Princess, I have already seen the proof I need." He waved his hand, and Jun emerge from the crowd. He slowly shuffled over to us, and again it appeared as if he were drunk.

"Jun!" I wrenched myself from Abraxas' grasp and flung myself at my brother. I wrapped my arms around his neck. Normally we could say so much to each other without even speaking, but it was like he was mute.

He didn't even raise his arms to me, and simply said, "What do you need, Your Eminence?"

"Perhaps a small performance for us?" Jun pulled from my grasp like I wasn't even there. I tried to keep a hold of him, and it pulled open the high neck of his jacket, revealing a small glimmer of gold underneath.

I moved to follow him, but Abraxas grabbed my wrist, "Let go of me!" But with more force than he had ever used on me, he pulled me to him and pressed his lips to my ear.

"The collar." It was so soft I almost didn't hear it, but he turned his gaze to Jun.

He walked to the dais where the throne stood. A moment later, the music from the band died down, and the dancers halted. I saw it then, his jacket was still pulled open, and he hadn't bothered to correct it. The gold underneath was a flat collar that lay against Jun's throat. In the center was a purple gem that I could see laced with the faintest hint of lightning.

Then Jun started to sing, and the room was transformed. I

had heard numerous performances from Jun all my life, and they were always beautiful, but this was something else. It made me think of when the forest stopped moving to listen. Just as it had then, the room seemed frozen, each person mesmerized by the sound of his voice. The song had obviously been chosen for its impact, full of powerful choruses followed by soft verses that displayed the beautiful tones Jun brought to the music. The lyrics were about the final battle against the World Breaker outside Xyr, Hadeon's surprise.

I tried to pull away from Abraxas again, but he held me fast, his hand immobile. I looked into his eyes and was shocked to find tears dancing there. He was trapped in the same spell as everyone else. I looked at Hadeon, and it seemed we were the only two awake.

His lips curled, and his body shook as lightning circled around him. He looked at me with those shocking violet eyes, and I felt his power thrum. Somehow, I knew that power came from Jun, I could feel it being sucked across the room.

The song reached a dazzling crescendo, and my eyes locked with my brother. His eyes, suddenly clear, focused directly on me. In that moment, we connected again, and with just the smallest twitch of his brow, I knew. I knew he was fighting whatever it was that held him. He was pleading with me to help him.

I tried to move to him, but even though I was awake, it seemed my legs were not. I fought, freeing my hand from Abraxas' grasp, and willed my foot the tiniest step forward, and then another. But lightning laced fingers gripped me around my neck as Hadeon leaned over my shoulder.

"You can't hide from me, Princess. Your brother's magic is delicious. I wonder, what will yours taste like?"

"Get the fuck off of me. I don't have any magic!" I tried to shove him away and failed, every muscle of my body seized up.

"Hmmm, we will see about that, Princess. Maybe I'll let

Abraxas play with you a little bit longer, but you will be mine." I was fucking tired of these men thinking they owned me. To hell with control. I locked eyes with Jun and passed him one last message. *I will come for you.*

With every ounce of my muscles gained from weeks of training, I fought the hold on my body. I threw one arm up to free me from Hadeon's grasp, then swung my other back, shoving my elbow into his stomach. He let out a groan, and I smashed my fist into his face. It was like we moved through thick syrup, but I felt myself surging through, even as my skin felt like it was burning off. But then Jun's song ended as his knees hit the floor and he slumped down.

The spell that had held the room broke, and I lunged for the emperor. But a strong arm barred across my chest, holding me back. I snarled as Hadeon moved his hand up to wipe the speck of blood at the corner of his mouth. His eyes filled with unadulterated rage. I tried to pry myself free, but Abraxas held me fast.

I barely heard him whisper, "Tori, Jun's not safe yet." It hit me like a bucket of ice water, and I saw my brother escorted by Hadeon's guards off the stage. His eyes had dulled again, and his steps lilted.

But Hadeon rounded on me, and I felt the immense pressure of his magic engulf me, pain shooting through my chest.

"I want her submissive at the party tonight, Abraxas." I felt him flinch around me.

"No." His arm tightened over my chest. The rage that had been directed at me suddenly turned on the Dragon King, and I felt the pressure in my body release the smallest amount.

"No? I know you don't like to share your toys, Abraxas, but this one—"

"I haven't broken her yet." Hadeon paused at that, and I seethed. But before I could snap anything, Abraxas brought his hand over my mouth.

Hadeon raised an eyebrow, "Taking your sweet time with this one, I see. But I see the appeal. I won't deny you that pleasure, old friend." He sighed dramatically, "I suppose it's for the best. Her brother will join me, and even I have limits on my depravity." The pressure in my body fully released then, and I struggled against the hands that bound me with new ferocity, but it was to no avail. Hadeon turned, and in that bored tone said, "Get her out of my sight."

Abraxas wasted no time dragging me from the hall, many of the nobility staring as my feet flailed uselessly. He took me all the way back to my room before kicking open the door and tossing me inside.

"That was the stupidest fucking thing I ha—" he yelled, but I lunged at him. I slammed my arms around his waist, and he must have been off balance because he fell backward to the floor. The breath left him, and I was able to smash my fist into the side of his face once before he caught my hands. He rolled himself on top of me and pinned my hands over my head.

But still, I struggled. "I need to get to Jun! Let me go, he needs me!" But I was completely trapped, and I couldn't fight him. I tried to resist but the sobs flew out of me, tears streaming down my cheeks, my breath catching. "He needs me, he needs me..."

"Tori..."

"Don't fucking call me that." I tried to search for my rage, but all I felt was the bottomless pit of despair I had worked so hard to hide from myself these last weeks. More sobs escaped me, "Abraxas, please, I need to go to him."

"This isn't how I wanted to see you beg, Princess." But I couldn't take his bait, I was too far gone. More sobs. "He will kill you, and he won't hesitate."

"Why do you care? Just let me go, let me fight."

"I can't do that."

"Why not?"

"Because you are mine to protect." I was suddenly aware of how our bodies had settled together. How my legs had opened in my struggle, and he now lay between them. How very close his face was to my own. How very natural it felt. The need to escape cleared my mind.

"I thought I was yours to break?" Guilt flashed in his eyes. I shoved at him again, and this time he let me. We separated, both still sitting on the floor.

He sighed, "You can't fight him, Tori, not like this. Especially not while he has that collar on Jun."

"What is it?"

"I imagine it's some sort of enslavement enchantment. Very old magic, powerful. Very difficult to break."

"But you know how?"

"No, just that it can be done." *Fuck.*

"The party tonight, take me to that. I need to see him again, maybe I can learn more about it.

"No." His face was blank.

"What do you mean no?"

He rubbed the bridge of his nose. "You will stay in your room tonight. No exceptions."

"What happened to 'I'm not a prisoner here?'"

"Tonight, you are." I was stunned into silence, and his face was pure ice. "Fuck you!" I made a dash for my door, but as always, he was too fast and had me pinned to the ground belly down again. I screamed, but he just lifted me over his shoulder like a sack of flour, and then tossed me on my bed. I scrambled to get up, but he was already out the door, closing it behind him with a firm slam. I ran to the door just as I heard the lock slide into place.

I slammed my fists into the wood over and over, but it was useless. I screamed, "Fuck you! Fuck you. Fuck... you..." but the words quickly turned to sobs. My fists slowed, my knuckles bleeding, and I slowly slid down the door. My shoulders shook, and my legs collapsed under me. I laid my forehead against the hard grain of the wood, "I hate you." I ran my hands over my neck, and for a moment I could almost feel the weight of Jun's collar, as if I were him instead. But my neck was decidedly bare, only the smallest of scars remained from where Abraxas had bitten me. Darkness swallowed me, but not before I knew what I had to do.

Chapter 26

Abraxas

After the party, a small group returned to my room, as was often the case. Most had already left, but Nalux lingered as he often did. I normally didn't mind his company, but I was in no mood tonight. I pulled on my robe and slunk away from the bed, trying to signal as much to him, but he followed after me.

"Are you going to tell me what is wrong, Abraxas?" I turned to him, to find him staring me down, arms crossed.

I sighed and walked to pour myself a drink of malt ambrosia from the crystal decanter I kept near my fireplace then poured a second for Nalux. The golden liquid caught the firelight as I walked over to the half-naked man.

"What makes you think something is wrong?" I handed him his drink.

"Tonight, you were acting much more...intense." I raised a finger to his swollen lips, tracing their pillow soft surface. Pleasure and pain had always been something I had enjoyed mixing, but I prided myself on my control.

"Nalux, if I went too far tonight, you should have said something." He batted my hand away.

"No, no. But I know you better than you might think, Abraxas, and I can tell there is something on your mind." I took a sip from my drink.

"I don't know what you are talking about." Now it was his turn to sigh.

"Abraxas, we have been lovers for years now, you could at least respect me enough to not lie to me." I'd hurt him, but before I could apologize, he boldly asked, "It's the princess, isn't it?" I was stunned into silence for a moment too long. A mischievous twinkle lit his eye.

"I'm surprised you haven't invited her to any of our little parties. She seems like she would go quite feral, especially based on what I saw tonight." I hummed a response, but my face must have revealed something. Nalux's eyebrows shot up. "By the gods, you haven't...Interesting."

I shot him a look over the rim of my crystal glass as I took another sip, avoiding answering him, but a knowing smirk crossed his lips.

"Very interesting." I turned from him, partially to set my now empty glass down, but mostly to avoid his eyes. But as the container clacked onto the serving tray, I felt his hand slide in a familiar way across my back, as he came to set his glass down as well.

"I think it's about time you met your match, Your Majesty. I'm happy for you." A true smile lit his beautiful face, and he gently placed a kiss on my lips that felt an awful lot like goodbye.

Sleep never found me. I normally made this journey on the solstice itself, but this would have to do.

The moon was full, its light dazzling off the sea beyond the cliffs, and the storm that had threatened the skies early had disappeared. But I didn't need the light to trace the path I had taken for over five hundred years.

As I approached that scorched land, every fiber of my being begged me to turn away. The pain lodged in my chest, and it felt as if needles were being driven into every inch of my skin. The wind whipped up again, but I calmed it, the focus helping to drive away some of the torment.

I finally reached the edge of that great wound, that place that had changed everything on that fateful day. I kept to the path that had been worn down by the humans, as it was always the easiest for me to traverse. Each step seemed to draw more and more of me away until I was nothing but an empty husk. But this was my penance, and I gladly paid it.

I reached the edge of the cliff and saw the small stack of rocks that had been built by hands that had likely been dead for centuries. A few recent tokens remained. A small bundle of flowers, a set of golden pastries, and numerous dragon figurines both carved and folded.

I fell to my knees, and as every year, I wondered if this would be the year I wouldn't survive this short journey. But deep within me, a small golden light clung to my heart, as it had never done before in this wasted place.

"Everything is different now," I spoke the words out loud, and they were whipped away by the wind. "For so long I have had one goal, one focus. Now, in just a few weeks, she has changed everything."

I wasn't the man I had been a few centuries ago. I had let my anger swallow up all my pain and fear, along with everything else until I felt nothing at all. I had become the monster they all said I was. I could almost laugh about it, another self-fulfilling prophecy.

A younger me would have hated who I had become, but he hadn't lost everything. He hadn't survived these past centuries on rage alone. But seeing her in Hadeon's grasp tonight, fear had cut straight into my heart.

I looked up at the stars, and as so often was the case, I wished I could hear what they were saying. "I wish I had never gone to that gods-damned island."

That golden light inside me seemed to spark with a familiar annoyance. I knew it wasn't true.

I looked at that stack of rocks. So small a thing seemed so inadequate for what had been lost here. But I would not lose her. Hadeon had taken everything from me once. I would not let him do that again. I would not let him have her.

I had been harsh with her tonight, but I had no other choice. I would keep her— keep her safe, no matter the cost.

I reached into my pocket and drew out a small candle. As I had done for centuries, I tried to light it. It had become more and more difficult with each passing decade. But tonight green flame danced easily between my fingers. I shouldn't have been shocked. Everything else in my life had changed, why not this as well? I set the small light atop the rock and began my long walk back to the castle.

Chapter 27

Tori

After weeks of absence, my sleep had been filled with nightmares of blood running down the white marble steps of my home. But this time, I tried to run in— to fight, but strong hands held me back. I had barely slept a wink.

Avlyn had come to accompany me to the beach. I looked terrible, but they had the good sense not to mention it. We didn't speak at all as we made our way out along the sand. They lined us all up for our morning warmups, and I made sure I ended up at the far end of the line. When we broke formation for the first water break, I lingered as all the other soldiers made for the barrels. I took off my shoes and waited. After a few moment, I ran.

I ran as fast as my legs could carry me. The sand slowed me, the sharp rocks of this barren shore cutting into my soles, but I didn't care. I could smell my freedom, and it lay just beyond that rock wall. I reached the base of the cliffs and allowed myself three heaving breaths to look at the wall and choose a route before I was off. My hands found purchase in the cleft between two of the massive basalt columns, my feet following behind. I continued to climb, hands and feet moving together at a rapid pace, finding my balance and keeping myself close to the wall.

As I moved up, it became harder, the rock no longer worn by the sea, but my body remembered how to move, using my legs to counterbalance, and swing from one hold to the next.

I could hear shouting behind me, but it was mostly drowned out by the crashing waves. I allowed myself to look back as an arrow hit the rock wall next to me. Would they really shoot me? I couldn't believe it. I looked back to see Avlyn punching the archer straight across the mouth, laying him out cold on the sand. I could see their mouth moving and shouting at the other two guards who had raised their bows, and they lowered them slowly. The whole cohort stood watching me. Kaleos made to climb the cliff after me, but Avlyn swatted him down as well. They knew the truth as well as I, he would never catch me, and if he did, the only result of our meeting on the wall would be one or both of us falling to our deaths.

I kept climbing. In order to find my footing, I had to travel sideways, out over the sea itself, but then I was able to keep climbing. The waves crashed beneath me, and I saw the jagged rocks that cut out of the surface. Yes, a fall now would destroy me, my body raked over those sharp rocks by the sea, but I didn't intend to fall.

I could just hear Avlyn shouting my name, but I didn't turn back again. I kept moving, up and sideways, further out over the ocean. I crested the edge of the rock and the harsh wind whipping around from beyond the bay. I saw another similar cliff about twenty feet from my back, as if the cliff I was on had been split by an invisible hand a millennia ago. On this side, the climb was much easier, and I moved up quickly. I could no longer see Avlyn and their guards, the wall protecting me from them. But as I reached the top of the cliff, my heart dropped as I heard the clink of armor.

I looked up and saw Noki reaching down for me. "Princess, take my hand!" He spoke as if I had fallen from the cliff and hung on for dear life, not climbed there myself. Two more soldiers joined him on the edge, waiting for me.

How had they gotten there so fast, how had they known? The answers were really irrelevant, the only thing that mattered was that they stood between me and my freedom. I looked around. The other side of the cliff that had cracked away from my own taunted me. It was a long jump, and I would fall a great distance before hitting the wall, only adding to my momentum. But if it was like the twin wall I climbed now, it was well textured, and I should be able to catch myself. The fissure ran a great distance down the top of the cliff, and the soldiers would need to go around it before they could catch up to me.

It was my only option. I climbed up higher, seeming as if I meant to take Noki's hand, but really, I just wanted more leverage for my jump. I reached out to him, and just as he was about to reach me, I coiled every muscle in my body and then released, pushing from my wall toward the other side.

I could hear them shouting as I fell through the air, the opposite cliff approaching me at a sickening speed. I hit the wall hard, the rock etching itself into my skin as I scrambled to hold on. But this wall was much slicker than the one I had been on. Something about its positioning allowed the sea mist to cling to it. I continued to slide down; my tearing flesh the only friction slowing me down. Despite the pain, I pressed my whole body into the wall, even my face, begging to slow down. The cliff disappeared from beneath my feet as I finally managed to grab a single handhold, just above the edge.

The cliff had cut back into a cave carved by the ocean, and I hung on now by a few fingers just above that cave. Below me the sea swirled into a vortex that seemed to gurgle and roar like a hungry animal, waiting for me to fall into its maw. My fingers began to slip, so I swung my other arm wildly, trying to catch hold anywhere as my legs dangled freely. The sharp rocks cut into my already battered fingertips, but I managed to grab on with my other hand just next to the first.

Then my stomach dropped as an unmistakable crumbling sound ripped from the wall and my holds came loose. The last thing I remembered was the ocean capturing me in its icy embrace.

Part II

Chapter 28

Tori

I dreamed of light. Small dancing lights, that floated in the air above me like fireflies. I tried to reach for them, but it was as if my body were made of stone, as if the very earth had come up around me to hold me prisoner. But the earth was warm, and soon I found the embrace comforting. I dreamed of the arms of my mother, her sweet song rocking me back into deep sleep.

I dreamed of a great beast. His scales shone an iridescent red, like old blood had been crystallized. His eyes glowed orange, like the depths of Ashenforge Peak, molten and laced with the ancient magics of the earth. His black horns rose in great waves behind the collar of spikes at the back of his head, leading into his long neck and body. But his wings rose up to unfathomable height, each tipped with black claws. His silver teeth glimmered with the same iridescence as his scales, and his hot breath was laced with ash and death. But as I stood before the dragon who had almost broken the world, I didn't feel rage or destruction from him, only sadness burned in those deep eyes.

I dreamed of warm arms again. They weren't rigid as of stone, but soft and strong. Instead of reaching for the light, I was filled with it, a deep golden light that began at my heart, and spread outward. It burned away the blackness that filled every crack in my chest, every bruise on my body. It flooded from my heart and out through the tips of my fingers and toes. And as it filled me, I heard its deep voice whispering my name.

I dreamed of blood. The hills outside Xyr were drenched with it. Emperor Hadeon's army surrounded the great dragon. Hadeon engulfed himself and the World Breaker with a shell of lightning, blocking out the rest of the world. The dragon was injured, but he continued to fight, matching each of Hadeon's lightning strikes with blows of his own. Hadeon fell to one knee, and the dragon descended. But as he moved to make the final attack, Hadeon lifted something in his hand I could not see. Malech froze, and Hadeon's malicious smile that haunted all my dreams spread. The dragon lowered his head, and Hadeon struck.

I dreamed of a lake, which glowed with soft blue light. I looked over the edge to my reflection, but a different face looked back. A face lined with age, so worn and ragged that it seemed she was carved of the earth itself. Age spots and wrinkles shifted as a smile pulled at her lips, revealing toothless gums.

I dreamed and dreamed again. Some stayed with me and some floated away like the clouds that hugged the mountains in their deep wintery embrace. I lay in a river of stars, the current slowly taking me somewhere from which I could never return. But it was peaceful, and I longed to rest, I longed for the freedom that it brought me. But still the light danced in front of me, calling me back. Its low voice a lure I could not ignore.

Chapter 29

Abraxas

This princess was brave, but also stupid. I had expected her to try and escape again. Hell, I'd even had patrols on the upper cliff just in case she tried to climb out, but I never truly expected her to take that route. She probably didn't know that the young recruits who trained on the beach had actually been forbidden from taunting each other into climbing the wall. So many had fallen to their deaths over the years, swallowed up by the unforgiving sea.

Now she lay here, battered and broken, and I knew that I had almost lost her. She had crashed into the underwater rocks, her arm nearly severed and severely crushed from the fall, along with severe internal bleeding and bruising. Only the cliff's proximity to the castle had saved her.

Now, I sat with her as she recovered. I had carried her down, deep into the earth as her blood ran down her in rivers, leaving a grisly trail in our wake. She was sopping wet and covered in seawater, the salt slowing any healing that Tori's body could do. Her breathing and pulse were almost non-existent. But I had laid her into the grotto beneath the castle, begged the ancient magic that still lived in that hidden place to save her. It hadn't been enough, not nearly enough to heal her, but she still breathed.

We couldn't remain there long, and Tori's body still lay broken before me, her recovery slowed by a fever and the severity of her wounds. The healers came and went constantly, but they always seemed to have the same answer. She would have to wake on her own. They spoke the words softly, likely knowing how close I was to ripping their heads off every time they said them. But it was not their fault she lay like this— it was mine. I had held her too tight, and the bars of her cage had bit into her until she could think of nothing but escape.

So, six days after her fall, I sat with her, my fingers threaded with hers on her uninjured arm. I traced the lovely curve of her cheekbone and pushed her raven hair behind her pointed ear.

I sighed and let my fingers drift over her forehead. A light coating of sweat covered her from the fever, but she felt cooler to me than she had in days, and that gave me hope. I leaned in, hovering over her ear, as I had the last six days, "Wake up, Princess." She didn't move at all. I leaned in closer, my lips just brushing her skin, and in a whisper even I could barely hear I begged, "Come back to me, Tori." Still nothing.

The beast in my heart roared, pushing against my ribs, sick with rage that threatened to burn all that lay before me, to hurt any who had harmed her. But I knew the truth, and all the creature had managed to do was break cracks in the ice that had surrounded my heart for so long.

I couldn't help myself, as I laid a soft kiss upon her forehead. I imagine the aghast look that would cross her face if she knew what I'd done. I couldn't help the small laugh that escaped me, even though my heart cracked a little more. *What I wouldn't give to have her scowling at me right now.*

But then, for the first time in days, her lips parted, and she emitted a small groan. I froze in place, afraid I had imagined it, but a moment later, her eyelids fluttered slightly. "Tori, Tori, open your eyes." Just as I spoke the words, my healer, Oryx, walked in and rushed to her side. Her eyes kept fluttering, as if she were in a dream. "What's happening?" I meant to speak the words calmly, but they escaped as a ragged shout.

Oryx touched her neck and pulse, his other hand on her chest, feeling her breathe. "Your Majesty, she—" but then her eyes flew open, and she sucked in a deep breath. She seemed to try to move, to swing her arms, but the bandages and I'm sure the pain held her back, and she sunk back into the bed, another moan escaping her. Oryx dashed off to the alchemy table they had set up in the room, the smell of herbs being crushed meeting my nose as Tori's eyes darted around.

"You're alright, you're in the castle." Her eyes were unfocused despite their movement, but then they locked onto me, and I saw her coming back.

"I'm...alive?" Her voice was hoarse from lack of use, barely a whisper.

"Yes, you are safe." She seemed to relax at that, her eyes leaving me and drifting towards the ceiling,

"I must have dreamed...I was flying, soaring through the air, over the seas and mist and mountains. The wind lifted my wings..." She trailed off, then snapped her eyes back to me, her face hardening, as if she hadn't meant to share that.

"What happened?" she asked.

"You fell from the cliff during your escape. Avlyn rescued you and brought you back here."

Her eyes seemed to gain back an ember of her fire from before, "I won't apologize for that." There she was. I couldn't help the true, rolling laugh that escaped me. Both Tori and Oryx locked their eyes on me as if I had gone mad.

"Here you are, laid up in bed on the edge of death while I heal you back to health, and still, you must defy me."

Her eyes shifted, that beautiful slate turning from the hard grey of the sea to something softer, like the tones of the sky as the sun just breaks the horizon in the morning.

"You...healed me?" Her face was soft, perhaps the softest I had ever seen. I ignored her question.

"When you fell, you almost completely severed your left arm. It is still healing, but so far, we have not seen an acute infection. The healers were able to recover enough of the bone to set the arm back in place, and you should regain a great deal of your function. The rest of your body was battered as well, but nothing so severe as your arm." Her eyes drifted down to her injury, and I could see her trying to move her finger.

"No, Your Highness," Oryx piped in, setting his hand gently on her arm. "You must not move yet. The ligaments and muscles are still regrowing."

"Yeah, I can feel that," she huffed as her face turned red from the pain.

"Now that you are awake, we can give you more potions that will significantly speed the recovery of your arm, as well as your ribs and other injuries. I have one here for you, and one for the pain." He held up two small cups that smelled of the herbs he had been crushing.

Tori looked to Oryx, and spoke with a tone more vulnerable than I could bear, "It won't put me back to sleep, will it?"

"No, Your Highness, although you should rest, we will let your body decide when to sleep. This should just reduce the pain of your bones regrowing." She grunted at that, the pain obviously front and center of her mind.

She moved to lift her head to take the medicine, but she couldn't. Before she could object, I unlaced my fingers from hers, and slid my hand under her head to help lift her. She groaned again, but then drank the potions down, gagging.

"Yes, they taste terrible, but I find it's better not to mention that first." Oryx winked at her. The beast in my chest stirred, but I tamped him down.

"Thanks for that," she mumbled as she drank some water offered by the healer.

I lowered her back to the bed softly, and she locked her eyes with mine, something in her gaze I couldn't read.

"Oryx tells me you will need to be in bed at least a week more for your injuries to heal well." I stood, knowing Oryx would have much work to do, and I would likely now only get in the way as a few of his assistants entered the room. As I moved away, I saw her flexing the fingers on the hand I'd held, as if adjusting to their emptiness.

"You're leaving?" The vulnerability there cut straight into me. I longed to hold her in my arms and tell her she would be safe with me, and I would stay until the breaking of the world. But I needed her to fight.

"You are my ward. And my responsibility. I will be here to provide whatever assistance is needed in your healing." The tiniest of smirks crossed her lips, "Good, I can't wait to see you in one of those little outfits." I truly laughed again as I stepped out of the room, comforted by the embers I could see kindling in her again.

Chapter 30

Tori

The warmth that filled my heart at hearing the king's laugh almost made up for the completely agonizing pain coming from my arm and the rest of me. While my body felt like it had been pressed under a giant vice, my arm flared with hot white pain any time I even thought about moving it. It was the muscles regrowing, and a good sign, according to Oryx. I think we had very different perspectives on this.

But I was happy to be awake. I was told I had been unconscious for six days, and the thought made me sick. How close I must have been to death, and how lucky I truly was to be alive. I had longed for freedom, but the freedom of death was something else. I told myself over and over that I didn't want that. I almost believed it.

In truth, I had thought I was dead, my coma had been filled with dreams of flight, which I had admitted to the king. But I hadn't told him of the other dreams. Everything had been blurred and dark, but I had felt warm as if wrapped in a tight embrace, supported and floating weightlessly. A deep voice had called to me, calling me *home*. Not Niata, but my true home, where my soul was full. I thought if this was death, then perhaps it wasn't so bad.

But with every hour I was awake, the warm feeling drifted further and further away, the way that dreams fled the morning light. For that was all they had been, dreams. Now all I felt was the slow and steady pain of my body regrowing itself. Oryx was kind, a half-fae male knowledgeable in medicinal herbs and healing. His short-cut red hair bobbed around the room all day as he worked, gently moving me to change my bandages and check my wounds. He also had me run a series of strange tests, holding a candle in front of my eyes, and asking me questions about various events in my life. It seemed I passed, as he smiled and jotted some things down in his little notebook.

Whatever he was happy about, I wasn't in on it. He hesitated but let me look at my injured arm when he changed my bandages. Just above the elbow was the gaping wound where I had fallen on a sharp rock. Angry red and purple striations still ran up and down from the injury, and huge stitches still held my arm together. I could see scar tissue already forming, and every time he rewrapped it, the redness seemed to decrease. The worst part was when he massaged the wound to prevent too much scar tissue from building up. That sent lightning from my head to my toes, and I ground my teeth to keep from screaming. It didn't always work.

My body seemed to only grow more painful. The potions helped a bit, but not enough for me to fall back asleep. Part of me was grateful for the pain for grounding me back to the earth, but after being awake almost a full day, I could hear Oryx and his assistants whispering worriedly.

The king had stopped by a few times already to check on me, but not much had changed in my recovery, so he stepped out quickly. The little voice inside me bubbled up gleefully whenever he would appear, but I let the pain drown it out. It was easy to do. But I couldn't stop thinking of the feeling of his hand intertwined in mine when I had first woken, holding on to me as if he could anchor me to this plane.

Oryx had called him in again since I could not sleep, whispering to him and making frantic hand gestures that did nothing to calm me. I saw him turn towards me, that regal nose cutting a handsome profile against the light of the apothecary table. He walked towards me then, and I cursed my stomach for clenching. But it didn't feel like it was clenching with fear.

He knelt down beside my bed, his face very close to my own.

"Can't sleep? Oryx tells me you have nothing to fear from sleeping now. The tests he ran today indicate your brain is almost completely healed from the bruising."

"It's not that, I just can't...there is too much pain." I hated to sound weak, especially to him. But my body craved sleep, and it was overriding everything else. The king turned to Oryx, but he shook his head.

"She has already had the maximum of the pain relief I can safely give her, and while her brain is healed, a sleeping potion is too risky." The king turned his gaze back to me, and my stomach fluttered again at the look of concern in his eyes. I longed to reach for his face then and trace the hard line of his jaw, but instead, I fisted my hand. The absence of his hold was even more present.

He saw the motion and the worry grew, so I said, "It's just, I've been in this position so long, and my arm, and—" I was rambling, "I just wish I could move a bit."

He nodded and called out, "Oryx, come help me move her."

"Your Majesty, I don't think that's such—"

"Now, Oryx." That commanding voice sent a shiver down my spine, and the little voice inside me purred.

It practically sang as the king slid his arms under my back and knees, and gently lifted me while Oryx delicately held my arm. The pain flared and I ground my teeth, but then he set me back down, on my side now, and then helped Oryx place pillows to support my arm. Once I was settled, the pain ebbed, and gods it did feel good to not be laying on my back anymore, even if my arm throbbed.

"Better?" He asked.

"Yes, much better."

He smiled at me, "Good girl."

The muscles in my lower stomach curled up and pulsed, going molten, I certainly couldn't pretend it was from fear anymore. My brain must have been more injured than they were letting on. Perhaps he had read it on my face, as his smile slowly slid into a smirk, "I have one more thing for you, I'll be right back." He left the room, but promptly returned with a small object in his hand. He returned to the chair next to my bed, then leaned back and crossed his left ankle over his right knee, getting comfortable. I saw then that the object was a small white book. He cracked it open and began reading.

"Alright then. Once, long ago—"

My cheeks flushed in embarrassment, "I am not some youngling who needs a bedtime story," I huffed.

"Hush now, this story is quite a bore, and always sent me straight off to sleep." I rolled my eyes, but he smirked again and continued. "Once, long ago, the Lord of Alfhiemshire sat by a pond, pondering the ripples and flowers that bloomed..."

Perhaps the story really was boring, or maybe it was the soothing deep sounds of his voice and my back finally being relieved, but the pain didn't seem such a bother anymore, and I drifted off to sleep. I dreamt of strong warm fingers stroking my hair, and a light kiss upon my brow.

Chapter 31

Tori

After that first day, my recovery went swiftly. Even Oryx was impressed with the progress. I heard him muttering to himself about my internal healing being mostly diverted to my brain initially, but now focusing on my body, allowing more rapid healing. I didn't much care why because every hour my body seems to hurt less, and I was able to move more. The next day Oryx had me getting up and walking with my arm in a sling, if only for a few minutes at a time. But those few minutes felt exquisite, my body craving the motion again.

He then had me start moving my arm more and more. That was less exquisite. Movement still shot pain from my fingertips to shoulder and my range of motion was frustratingly small, but Oryx assured me that it would increase, but only if I kept up the exercises.

He kept me distracted during my sessions by regaling me with stories of his life. He and I appeared around the same age, but it seemed he was about eighty years old. His father had been a fae who had fallen in love with a human woman who was a healer and midwife. They had met during a skirmish with bandits at the edge of the Dragon Kingdom territory. Shortly after they had met, Oryx had been born, but his father's family had not approved of the union— or their child. While his father had sent support to his mother, he had been forbidden from seeing the boy. Oryx didn't linger on this part of the story, instead focusing all he had learned of herbs and healing from his mother, their years spent in the forests outside the Cold Mountains foraging and experimenting with healing.

Oryx forced me to try lifting my elbow up above my shoulder, and I was not enjoying it one bit, so I nearly bit my tongue asking, "Do you ever wish you knew your father better?" He didn't relent in forcing me to complete my exercises, but I could see his blue eyes shift in contemplation, the smallest wrinkle settling into his nose. He had a smattering of red freckles all over the bridge of his nose and cheeks, and I found them quite charming.

He made me lift my arm again, and a hiss escaped me, prompting him to answer, "Now that I have lived at court so long, I see that my story is not an original one. Many of my fellow half-fae don't know their fae parents, or if they do, the relationship is not a simple one. It has helped me understand my father better. And unlike many, he supported my mother. He worked with the king to make sure my mother was a protected citizen of the Dragon Kingdom, which allowed her to not be burdened by working for a lord and gave us more time together during her life." His eyes shone then, like the top of an alpine lake under the moonlight. His mother was human, so I was sure with his age she had already left our world. I extended my arm through the pain and squeezed his hand gently. I let the pain drive away the thoughts of my own mother.

He gave me a sad smile, "My mother was an amazing woman who lived to a ripe old age and loved me with abandon." His smile lit up then, "I had everything I needed with her."

His smile and pure adoration threatened to crack open my heart. "Tell me about her." His smile widened, and he spent the rest of our session waxing poetic. I tried my best not to let the toxic threads of jealousy enter my mind, but luckily, he had me start doing more difficult exercises and all thoughts fled my brain.

As our session came to a close, Oryx gave me a pain relief potion and started massaging my arm. Before I could even hiss, the king walked through the door. His eyes immediately locked on where Oryx's hand lay on my exposed arm, something sharp in his expression as he examined my exposed wound. He had been so kind to me these last few days, I had almost forgotten. But all danger of my recovery had passed by now, and so perhaps it would be time for me to reap the consequences of my actions. I had disobeyed, tried to escape, and nearly died. I had no doubt the punishment would be harsh.

I could feel my insides shriveling as he continued to stare down at me. Somehow these last few days, I had forgotten all about my ebony cage. How much smaller would it become now?

"I'll take over that Oryx." Oryx immediately hopped away, busying himself at his apothecary table. The king took his place next to me and placed his hands on my arm. I couldn't appreciate the warmth of his fingers before he squeezed down on the scar tissue firmly as a very feral sound fled my lips. "Not exactly how I wanted to have you moaning under my touch." I shot him daggers with my eyes, and caught the laugh hidden behind his smile. But he continued his ministrations, and I couldn't do anything but bite down on my cheek to stop more sounds emerging from me. Even with my best efforts, a small low note escaped as his fingers worked apart the scar tissues and adhesions. It felt like my arm was coming apart all over again.

His face grew more serious, focusing on his work. His fingers moved firmly and swiftly, long expert motions that as he worked, hurt less, and I could feel the arm relaxing.

"You have done this type of work before?" He moved his hands away from the scar now, and massaged down my forearm, activating the muscles there.

"I have lived through many wars and had a kingdom to put back together after. Healing is an important part of that." He didn't elaborate, instead focusing on stretching my fingers individually.

"But surely, as the king, you had other things to focus on?" He took my gaze then, that serious look absent of any teasing. "A king is beholden to his people in all ways, whether that be to rule from the throne, or travel through a burned down village and the injured."

"There are many who don't hold that view."

He held my stare, a challenge, "And what view do you hold, Princess?" The seconds that passed between us seemed to last for an eternity. But it allowed me to speak the truth.

"Many treat their subjects as slaves, or worse. Worth nothing but what value can be extracted from them. But the truth is, what would we be without them? Yes, it is us who are beholden to them."

He continued to stare at me, not answering. But I realized his hands had stopped moving, his fingers resting in mine again, his thumb lightly tracing the web of skin between my thumb and forefinger. It sent a completely different type of lightning up my arm. He seemed to realize and gently moved his hand away and turned as if to leave.

"Where am I to be confined to?" He paused and turned back to me with a confused expression. "What is to be my punishment for my escape?" I couldn't bear to wait, couldn't bear his kindness knowing it was all going to come crashing down soon. Better now than later. His face became unreadable. Oryx quickly excuse himself from the room.

"Escape *attempt*. You didn't manage to get anywhere." His

reply stung deeper than I think he intended, and I could feel tears rising in my eyes. But he didn't say anymore and turned to leave again. I stood so fast my head swam, and my knees buckled. Instantly his hands were there, catching me, one gripping my good arm, the other resting on the small of my back. I looked up into his gemstone eyes, veins of malachite and emerald bleeding into that golden center. Heat seemed to radiate from his hand on my back, and my knees still shook. Gods, I was so weak, and this man only seemed to bring it out in me. Tears came to my eyes truly then, and I could feel the ocean of my mind churning as it threatened to drown me.

All the thoughts the pain had allowed me to suppress these last days boiled to the surface. Each one seemed to chain itself to me, dragging me under the waves. My resolve disappeared, the tears streaming freely as the words escaped me, "Please, I can't—I can't..."

He snapped away from me then, standing tall as that icy sneer returned to his face. But it didn't seem to reach his eyes. "Don't beg. It's unbecoming of a princess." He stepped into me then, all menace, the warmth of his hands on me before vanished. He towered over me, "Unless of course, you would like me to punish you? I can think of a number of things I would enjoy... Watching you come undone before me." Those words would have normally sent waves of heat through me, but I was too far gone, drenched in the icy coldness of my own mind.

He bore down on me again, making me take a step back, and then another, as his hand snaked up to my throat. He held me tight, but didn't block my air, not yet. But I didn't resist, didn't fight him. This seemed to anger him more as he pushed me back into the wall, pinning me with his hand. My arm throbbed as it was jostled, my throat constricted as I let out a small yelp. His face was inches from mine, his sneer frozen in place, but something was different about his eyes. They didn't hold that malice, in fact, I could almost imagine I could see his thoughts through them, and they said, *Fight me, fight back.*

But I couldn't find it, couldn't find that spark. I didn't move. And then he tightened his grip on my throat, constricting my air, and it was as if I truly was drowning.

My mind flashed back and I was falling, then swallowed up by the cold sea. Pain ripped through my arm, and the metallic taste of blood and the brine of the ocean filled my mouth and lungs. I kicked then, kicked for the surface, reaching for the light that streamed down in rays through the cold blue water. My arm felt like an anchor, useless and dead dragging me to the bottom, but still, I kicked. I would not die like this; I wouldn't let this ocean have me. The surface moved away from me, and my lungs burned along with my arm. The light moved further and further away, but I still fought. Then, as if the ocean acquiesced, a strong current lifted me to the surface.

Back in the room, my good arm sprung out, shoving him away. He took an easy step back, but the smirk on his face now reached his eyes. "Wouldn't you look pretty, on your knees, your pink lips wrapped around my—" The slap resounded through the room, and my hand hung in the air. The faintest pink blossomed on his pale cheek.

He slowly reached out and grabbed my hand as it hung in the air. My palm stung from where it had collided with him, and he lifted it to his lips, placing the lightest kiss against my skin. He then slid my hand over to the cheek I had struck, and I could feel the heat blossoming beneath his skin.

"In a week, we will celebrate Lupercalia. I expect you to accompany me into the city for the celebration." My heart stopped. He held my hand against his skin still, and it did nothing to quell my rising suspicion. I had never been allowed to leave the castle grounds. Why was he allowing this now? *Why?* When he answered, I realized that I had asked the question out loud.

"Consider it your punishment," he spoke with his lips grazing over the palm of my hand, sending shivers over my skin. "A lesson in obedience. I expect you to be on your best behavior." He finally dropped my hand.

As I watched him leave, I hadn't even noticed that my mind had gone completely still.

Chapter 32

Tori

The next week passed in a blur. Oryx released me from his care, and I was able to return to my room. He still visited me daily to run exercises, but they were getting easier. My arm was no longer bandaged, all the red and purple of a fresh wound finally gone, but a truly grisly scar wrapped around the entire bicep, like a thick white vein through the tanner marble of my arm. Even though my range of motion was coming back, I could tell I would never have the abilities I had before. It felt as if the arm were shorter now, and my balance was off. I did everything I could to not think about how this would affect my swordsmanship.

I had resumed my breathing practices and motions, using it to keep the anxiety down about the upcoming celebration. But I was basically a fledgling all over again, needing to truly focus on the motions as I went through them, and finding it difficult to reach that place of body and mind working in tandem.

Despite my best efforts, some thoughts still slunk in. We had celebrated Lupercalia in Niata, but it had become a minor holiday. However, it was much more widely celebrated across the continent, a time to remember the great cycle of life and death. The legends said our world had been born after the last was eaten by the Great Dragon Remus, and Lupercalia celebrated that. Many of the different kingdoms had adjusted it to their own desires, with the Dragon Kingdom carrying out the largest celebration of them all. It was always whispered that their celebrations included gambling and general debauchery, but more whispered were the rumors of blood sacrifices to the old gods paired with public spectacles of sex and pleasure. As younglings, it was common to speculate on the types of activities that would happen, but I had never met anyone who had attended. I would know someone now.

Ciara came to my room the morning of the festival, carrying a new dress. It was by far the most scandalous of any the king had given me before. Instead of containing a sheer dress with a decorative undergarment, this dress combined the two in a red, the color of fresh blood. The corset style top was fully exposed, with drapes of translucent fabric extending over one shoulder, and gathered at the hip to flare out, A long slit ran from the bottom of the corset all the way to the ground over my right leg, so no undergarments could be worn, and only the heavy draping of the fabric at the hip prevented me from being completely exposed. The garment only had one sleeve that conveniently covered my scarred arm.

Ciara dressed me, then fussed with my makeup. As always, my hair didn't need much fussing. She also dotted my collarbone with oil that smelled of musk and roses, traditional for Lupercalia. She slipped on some of the ridiculously uncomfortable heeled shoes of the court, these lacing halfway up my leg. I prayed that we weren't going to be walking much on this outing, or I would certainly need to remove them. I was sure carrying one's fancy shoes around wasn't 'being on best behavior.'

I hadn't seen the king since the night I had slapped him.

After returning to my room, the guard who used to accompany me everywhere was gone, but it felt like a trap. Was the king waiting for me to try and escape again, just to catch me? I really didn't know his motives, but I hadn't wanted to push. Despite my nervousness about the festival, I was also excited. I longed to see the city, if only to be free of the castle. The little voice inside my head reminded me that the king had asked me to accompany him specifically, and it preened at that. I did my best not to read into it, not think about the tradition of finding a 'partner' for Lupercalia to enjoy the festivities with, and what that might imply. But when I took one final look at myself in the mirror, with more of my skin on display than I had ever been comfortable with before coming here, I knew exactly what it implied.

Ciara walked me out of my room and down to the entrance of the castle. In the great entrance hall, with its staggering chandelier, the throne room stood to the left through the massive ebony double doors. Mirroring those were the doors I hadn't passed through since I had entered the castle weeks ago. They stood open now, and I could see the king waiting by a carriage outside.

The entrance framed his striking figure. He wore a formal outfit made of a mix of black materials. The long velvet pants and shift covered most of his body but were tailored to fit him perfectly. Over top, he wore a long, sleeveless leather duster beautifully embossed with black-on-black designs of dragons cutting through the night sky. The craftsmanship was impeccable, but it was all dwarfed by the crown atop his head. I had never seen him wear it before, and it truly completed him as the Dragon King. The crown was topped with seven dragon fangs, each more valuable than any jewel. They shone a deep metallic grey in the midday sun but would shift with a golden flash as he turned his head to greet me. His eyes roamed lazily from my head to my toes, not at all concerned with how I glared back, even as I shivered under the attention.

I stepped through the front gates, and immediately the cold wind reminded me it was still winter, and goosebumps rose all over my exposed flesh. I had to snap my hands down to keep my skirt from flying up and revealing what was obviously not covered underneath. The king waved his hand, and a servant brought me over a large fur-lined cape that I quickly wrapped around myself. After I placed it around my shoulders, the king held out his hand to me, to assist me into the carriage. I took it, and he quirked an eyebrow at me as if he had expected me to resist, but the wind whipped at my cape again, and I all but threw myself into the carriage. It was much warmer inside. The king very nimbly entered and sat himself opposite me as the carriage lurched into motion.

He stared down at me, all his aristocratic postures in place. I couldn't bring myself to hold his stare, so I flipped open one of the curtains and looked out the window. We rolled out of the main courtyard and passed the outer wall. I saw a legion of guards standing along the parapet as we passed through the gate. The road sloped down and into the city. The first buildings we passed were large, obviously the homes of the aristocratic elite, with well-maintained stone and wood walls, but I was surprised to see no guards at any of the homes. I remembered the route from our arrival and knew we would take the main road down to the large plaza at the center of the city for the festivities. I was shocked as the carriage suddenly took a turn down a much smaller road, leading off towards the hills surrounding the city. I turned to the king with my eyebrows raised.

"I thought we might take a more scenic route today, let you see more of the city," he grinned, "I wouldn't want to disappoint a subject of King Tour Guide." His eyes sparkled with mischief. What was he up to?

"One of the few titles you hold with any respect," I said, but I couldn't help mirroring his grin.

He huffed, "Can't play nice for even a minute, can you?" But his grin only broadened, and I didn't like the way it made my stomach pull in knots. He shifted then and brought himself to sit on the bench with me, his leg and side pushed against mine as he reached past to pull the curtains of my window completely open. He left his hand at the window to point at various sights as we passed them, so I was essentially surrounded by him. He spoke softly, but the words seemed to float by me as all I could focus on was the feel of his body just slightly pressing into mine in the confines of the seat, and the way I could feel his hair just barely brushing my shoulders as he leaned over.

That was until we rounded a corner, and the buildings pulled away to reveal the rolling grass hills that surrounded the city. We had come to the edge of the city proper. In the distance I could see where the black volcanic sand still peaked out from the higher and sharper hills dusted with snow, but everything nearby was covered in waves upon waves of flowing green grass, resistant to the cold's embrace.

"Do you see that small village there?" He wore an unmistakably mischievous grin now, as he pointed out the window. I peered through, but all I saw was more grass. I frowned, and the carriage pulled to a stop.

"Is this where the festival is?"

"No, but it's just a short stop. Come with me." He held out his hand, and I took it without hesitation. He led me out of the carriage, but the shoes I wore were not compatible with the muddy road we had ended up on. He took one look at my shoes, then at the ground, and then swept me up.

"Put me down!"

"And ruin those expensive shoes I got you, not a chance."

"You can afford new ones."

"Of course, but I liked these. Stop squirming, if I drop you here, you will be absolutely filthy." He was right, and it wasn't like I could run anywhere in these ridiculous shoes. I finally let myself settle in, feeling the warmth of his arms behind my back and knees, and the feel of his broad chest.

The wind blew the scent of sweet grass and rich earth to me, with just some slight undertones of animals and their leavings. It was fantastic. He crested a small rise, and I could see a few pens of goats and sheep. They seemed out of place all alone in the grass field, but on closer inspection...

"The houses! They're buried in the ground!"

He chuckled, "In a way, yes."

We approached the small village, for now I could see a number of these dwellings, some painted white, some just raw wood, that looked like the homes of the city, but they had allowed the grass and earth to cover them like a blanket. We approached the nearest house with the animal pen attached, and the king set me down on a small path made of flagstones, so I could find my balance without sinking into the ground. He approached the adorable yellow door of the small cottage and gave it a polite knock. As we waited, I couldn't help but approach and run my hand over the edge of the grass where the roof met the ground. It tickled my palms and was still wet with the morning dew. Up close, I could see it was laced with tiny white flowers, and even saw a few bugs making their own homes. Somehow it felt like life, like I could feel the network of roots that grew here and as far as the eye could see.

The door opened a crack and the tiniest squeak emerged, "Your Majesty!" A very young human girl had stuck her head out the door.

"Hello, Emilia, would you fetch your father for me?" She bolted back inside, and a few moments later, a middle-aged human man with a handsome brown beard emerged. He wore his work clothes and wiped his hands on an already dirty rag.

"Your Majesty, we weren't expecting you with the festival. I'm sorry to be caught in this state."

Abraxas waved his hand, "I came unannounced, Bronn, it is no issue. But I was hoping that you might have something for me?"

"Of course, Your Majesty." Bronn turned back into his home, leaving the door ajar. Once he was out of sight, several sets of small feet snuck into the doorway. I counted six children in all, Emilia likely being the oldest.

"Ask him to do the magic!"

"No, Pa will be mad." They bickered amongst themselves, as I turned, raising an eyebrow to Abraxas. He gave me a grin before squatting down in front of the children gathered at the door. My heart stopped for a moment as he whipped a dagger out of his belt, but then he carefully rolled back one of his sleeves and drew a thin line across his forearm. Crimson blood welled up from the cut, and he held his arm out for the children as they gathered around, their greedy eyes wide in anticipation.

Almost as quickly as it had appeared, I saw his wound knit together. He wiped away the small line of blood that remained, revealing perfectly smooth skin underneath. The children's eyes widened further, smiles crossing their faces.

Footsteps sounded, and they all pulled back quickly, as Abraxas stood, rolling his sleeve back down.

Bronn returned, a frown passing his lips as he eyed his children, "What happened?"

"Nothing!" They all chimed back at once, betraying their guilt, but Bronn only sighed, holding a package wrapped neatly in white linen out to Abraxas.

"I took the liberty of adding a few extra things for you and—" he turned to me.

"Tori, just Tori. A pleasure to meet you, Bronn."

He nodded, but one of the small girls pushed past his legs and whispered, "Are you a princess?" It was my turn to squat down, looking into her round blue eyes.

I motioned to my head, "Do you see a crown? Wouldn't I need one of those to be a princess?"

She looked up at the vacancy, but then added, "But you are so beautiful!"

"That she is, indeed." My cheeks flushed at Abraxas' words, and I refused to look back as I stood, Bronn pushing the girl back behind him in a hurry. Abraxas then handed the man a purse of coins that he tried to wave off, before the king simply set it in the outstretched hand of one of the nearby children, who ran off with it. Bronn thanked him, shook his hand, and then we were off.

I made it to the end of the walkway before Abraxas promptly picked me up and carried me in silence back to the carriage. Once he had set me back inside, he retook his spot across from me.

"I find on feast days, ironically, my duties keep me from enjoying much of the food, so I thought we might have something now." He undid the knot of linen and revealed a beautiful spread. There was a log of fresh farm cheese, a loaf of bread, a small bottle of honey, and a sliced cured sausage. He very unceremoniously ripped off a piece of the bread and loaded it with the other toppings before holding it out to me.

"Bronn and his goats make the best cheese in the kingdom." I cautiously took the bread from his hand, and ignored how he watched me bring it to my lips. It was absolutely divine. The tangy cheese met perfectly with the crisp bread, and the sweetness of the honey offset the fat of the sausage. I greedily ate the rest of mine, while Abraxas made himself another. We sat in comfortable silence, taking turns tearing the bread and eating, until it was all gone. I leaned back and ran my hands over my stomach, now straining against the corset I wore. I let out a contented sigh and closed my eyes.

When I opened my eyes, the king was staring. "What?"

"It was a mistake." My stomach clenched uncomfortably.

"What mistake?"

"Not giving you a crown." I was startled at his answer. "It would have made you positively ravishing." I felt my whole body flush, and I was glad I was still wearing the cloak so that he could only see it on my face. He smirked then.

"Why did you take me there?" His smile vanished, and he looked lost in thought. "You once said that people's lives were a blessing to you. I wanted you to see some of mine." I was even more lost for words.

"I thought you just wanted an excuse to carry me."

His smile returned, "I'm thinking of banning paved streets anywhere in the kingdom."

But then the carriage ground to a halt. Our travel had passed so quickly, I hadn't noticed we'd reached the main plaza. His face returned to that of the Dragon King, and he extended his hand to me silently. I shrugged off my cloak and stepped out into the evening air.

Chapter 33

Tori

The air had gotten even colder, but the plaza was lit with braziers and bonfires that seemed to keep the chill at bay. Long tables—longer than anything I had ever seen—seemed to fill every inch of the plaza, save for a single, mostly empty corridor heading up the middle. Hundreds of people were already gathered, feasting and drinking. Many were dancing in the open spaces as music rained down. I looked to see many bands had gathered on the balconies of the buildings surrounding the plaza, as well as many more partygoers.

Revelry could be seen in all directions, and it bombarded my senses. On a few of the balconies, I saw humans and fae alike waving ribbons decorated with sparkling beads at the crowd. As they did, I watched a woman from the crowd below lower her dress to expose her breasts, to much jeering and clapping. A fae from the balcony tossed a ribbon down to her, and she placed it proudly around her neck.

I turned to Abraxas, and he shrugged his shoulders, "A time honored Lupercalia tradition." I rolled my eyes, but couldn't help the grin that crossed my face, the atmosphere of the party was infectious.

We walked up the center aisle, the king's arm laced through mine. While the guards trailed us, they kept a large distance. Revelers parted to let us through smoothly, and as we passed, many shouted, "Long live King Abraxas!" or similar sentiments. Abraxas' face stayed neutral and calm, but he would nod and acknowledge his people as we moved past. Men from every race cheered him and raised their glasses, and I saw the women preening, many shifting their bodies to be on greater display as he passed lashes lowered, and lips pouted. I knew the move well and hated how it curled anger deep within me. But Abraxas merely kept his pace, nodding greeting to all.

We reached a great stage that had been set at the far end of the plaza. Tables filled with some nobles I recognized lined the stage, and a small band of fawns played the fiddle and drums, a riotous tune made for dancing. The center of the table was set with a large chair clearly meant for the king, and an empty seat for me lay to his right side. He escorted me to my seat, before making his way around the table to greet everyone. My stomach was still strained from the bread and cheese in my belly, so I didn't grab any of the feast before me. I noticed that while the feast was grand, it wasn't any more grand than the food I had seen on all the tables we had passed, full for the common folk. I reached for a glass, and a server quickly came and filled it with warm spiced wine.

I sipped it slowly, watching the spectacle before me. Acrobats had set up in the open area, stacking themselves and balancing in impossible shapes. The sun was lower in the sky now, and the bonfires were stoked to even greater heights. The crowd cheered and danced, and the whole plaza seemed to hum. It was as if the energy of everyone present had coalesced into a great primordial force, and a mischievous one at that. I saw more and more people pulling off articles of clothes despite the nip in the air as more mouths and bodies came together in the crowd.

"Enjoying the show, Princess?" A familiar voice rang over my shoulder. I turned and recognized Lord Nalux Ozmodus, a broad smile stretched across his face, "Have you ever attended a Lupercalia celebration before?"

"No, we don't celebrate like this in the Pearl Kingdom."

"No, I would think not." Something mischievous flashed through his eyes. "This is surely a spectacle, but it's just the beginning. I think you will like the part that comes later tonight much more." He winked at me.

"What comes later tonight?" His grin widened into something more akin to a cat stalking a bird than anything friendly, but before he could answer, Abraxas reappeared to take his seat.

"Good evening, Nalux, I hope you are enjoying the festivities."

"Of course, Abraxas. You know that Lupercalia is my favorite holiday." He smirked at the king, and I didn't miss that they were apparently on a first-name basis. "But it's so rare to have a virgin in our mists—to Lupercalia I mean. I wanted to get the princess's perspective." He turned his eyes to me, the question open. Abraxas kept staring at the man.

"It's fantastic to see so many of the people, and to see them enjoying the feast, just as we do." Nalux's smile softened at that, some of the wickedness banished. "Yes, our king makes sure that all get to enjoy our greatest holiday. How *benevolent* of him." His tone was teasing, and he reached out and touched Abraxas' arm in a very familiar way. I had a rapid intrusive thought of ripping his hand from his wrist but pushed it away.

"Ah, it seems that the party really is getting started now," he looked over the king's shoulder, "so I will take my leave. Enjoy your evening, Princess." He gave Abraxas' arm one final squeeze before sauntering off, and I imagined what it would feel like to break his fingers one by one. *So jealous for someone who isn't yours,* my inner voice teased me. *Shut up*. But they were right, as always. I flexed my fingers, the space between them feeling empty.

But I saw now what crossed the stage. A group of priests led a great stag, with antlers almost as wide as the stage itself. They had it harnessed with several leads being held by different men. As they brought it onto the stage, the crowd hushed, and the music stopped playing. One of the priests stepped in front of the stage, his voice booming through the plaza.

"Tonight, we celebrate Lupercalia," a great roar rose from the crowd, but quickly died down again as he raised his hands, "We celebrate the birth of the continent, and celebrate the great cycle of life. For with every death, there is rebirth, and with every birth, a death will someday follow. The Great Dragon swallowed the old world, so that this one could be born." He stepped aside, and the stag was pulled forward. But it heaved at the reins holding it, even managing to pull one priest off his feet before they got him under control. His eyes were wide with fear, and his mouth foamed.

I felt Abraxas leave my side then and make for the center of the stage. He approached the stag, and the animal went wild, death at his side. But Abraxas raised his hands to the creature's snout and neck and held him despite the stag's size advantage. The creature fought, but I saw Abraxas whisper in his ear, and stroke his neck, a hand still on his muzzle, letting him adjust to his scent. Slowly the creature calmed, and Abraxas continued to stroke him. Once his breath had evened, and his motions stopped, Abraxas slid his hand down the chest of the beast.

Then I heard him whisper, in a voice so quiet maybe no one else had heard, "Thank you, brother," as he pushed his hand into the stag's chest. The stag didn't even have time to react before Abraxas pulled out his heart, a gush of blood following from it as the creature collapsed dead to the floor. Abraxas held the heart aloft, blood pumping out of it and running down his arms and over his crown.

"With your sacrifice, we are born anew. Let your blood fertilize our fields and bring new life to the Dragon Kingdom."

The crowd exploded. As blood ran down the stage and across the plaza, I felt that great surge of energy return. But it was something greater this time. As if the life of the crowd met the death of the stag in a great wave, and the resulting collision spread up and over everything. The wind whipped around us, picking up embers from the bonfires, and seemed to circle around the king and the heart he held.

"*Morka Tempeli!*" he shouted, and the music resumed at deafening volumes. People across the plaza danced and screamed with abandon, and the bonfires rose even higher. But Abraxas' job was done, and he lowered the heart, passing it to the priest, who placed it with the rest of the stag, where they were dressing the body as he wiped his hands clean.

He walked back towards the table, blood still clinging to him, but my mind remained on the great pressure that seemed to leech from the air itself, from the way the fires had come alive, and the whole plaza buzzed like a great beast rising from its slumber.

As he sat in the chair next to me, I looked at his face, and time slid back, to when he had held another heart. The blood covering him was almost the same, but now he seemed calm, whereas before, he had been nothing but rage.

"Are you alright, Princess?" He had been staring at me, and I hadn't even noticed.

"Yes, what did you say, up there?"

He pressed his lips together, "It is the language of the old gods. It means, death is the beginning." I had so many more questions I wanted to ask, but all I could do was stare at him and try and reconcile these different parts of him in my mind. The killer, the benevolent king, the war general, my warden... my savior. He reached his hand forward and slid it into mine, and I felt the warmth of a drop of the stag's blood slide between us.

"Your Majesty! Would you honor me with the first dance?" Lady Lovatia had approached us without my notice. The king immediately dropped my hand, and turned to her, his kingly manners in place.

"It would be my pleasure, Lady Lovatia." He stood and made his way around the table, and she placed her arm in his, and led him off the stage to the plaza, where rings of partygoers now danced in coordinated movements. I slid my thumb over my palm, feeling the blood there, and once again the emptiness my hand felt.

Another body approached me, and I looked up to see Lord Nalux had returned. "Honor me with a dance, Your Highness?" His eyes still twinkled mischievously, but it seemed whatever malignancy that had been there before was gone.

"I don't know the steps, My Lord."

"Never stopped me." He smiled again, and I let the energy of the festivities override my impertinence. I took another deep sip of wine, then stood, and joined him as he led me off the stage, my own courtly smile plastered on.

As we descended from the dais, I saw that the priests had cut the stag's skin into long, bloody strips. They had also stripped themselves bare, and were running through the crowd, using the strips as makeshift whips, lashing them at passersby. I raised my eyebrows, and Nalux laughed. "It brings fertility in the new year. A blessing!" He laughed again, but I could see now that many young ladies were conveniently standing in the path of the priests, backsides outstretched. But before I could observe further, Nalux had whipped me into the circle of dancing at full speed.

I ground my teeth as he tugged on my injured arm, pain radiating from my fingers over my shoulder. I once again imagined breaking all his fingers, but I couldn't concentrate on that as my feet barely managed to stay underneath me.

"You're overthinking it, Princess, just listen to the music." I stumbled along, but despite my desire to resist, I did find that letting the beat of the drums lead my body instead of my mind eased the movements, and after a few more beats, I found myself moving with him rather than against him. He swung me round and round, joining the other dancers in a great circle around the closest bonfire.

With my feet now under control, I was able to observe my surroundings, and quickly my eyes fell on Abraxas, who danced nearby with a new partner.

"Can't keep your eyes off of him, can you? Not that I blame you," Nalux laughed, and I felt my face burning. Before I could open my mouth, he spun me away to a new partner. He was a human man, about half a head shorter than me. His eyes widened for a moment, but then he led me off in the dance. He obviously knew what he was doing, and led me well, so I allowed myself to fall into rhythm with him. Before I knew it, a smile had blossomed over my lips, and he returned it, as we let the rising crescendo of the music guide us.

The songs of the plaza had no beginning and no end, each blending into the next, only the beat of the drum changing tempo to change up the dances. I was passed from partner to partner, human and fae alike. I even danced with a great Askadryad, although I was careful not to snap any of her delicate woody fingers in my grip, and she certainly kept us away from the fire. I danced until my feet ached in my high shoes, and I couldn't imagine how the humans seemed to keep up the pace as my heart raced. I spun, and spun again, and then collided with the solid body of my next partner. I looked up into the king's face. He was flushed from the dancing and fires, and I could see the smallest bead of sweat forming on his brow. For a moment we paused, facing each other, and then he gripped my hands to lead me.

I winced as he moved my bad arm and I saw his face tighten. He removed his hand from my grip and placed it to rest on my waist. He pulled us in closer together, and my hand came to rest on his upper arm, my injury relaxed. I looked up into his eyes. He smiled, and it transformed him into the most beautiful sight I had ever seen, "Hold on, Princess."

We danced and spun until I felt our hearts beat in sync. As we spun, he wrapped his fingers tighter around my waist, holding me to him, only to release me and let me spin away, our arms outstretched. But he would always pull me back in. When I occasionally lost my steps, I would crash back into him, but he would just smile and guide me back into the dance. It felt natural, and whether it was the wine or the music or the great ecstatic energy that filled the air, I didn't care. I didn't want our dance to end.

The sun had nearly set, and the sky was alight with reds and oranges, as if our whole world was captured in a great ember, floating through the darkness of the night sky. The music reached a great crescendo, and he lifted my hand, and spun me around and around until I didn't know up from down. The music finally ended, and I once again crashed into him, but his arms embraced me, holding me tight to his chest. I looked up again, and our faces were so close, I could feel his breath ghosting across my face. The moment held, both of us on the precipice from which we could not turn back. My heart hammered, and I urged my toes to lift me just a little higher, to close that last space between us.

But a great horn blared, and the moment shattered. He released me from his grip, and I fell away, the cold night air lashing against my skin.

"It's time for us to return to the castle, Princess." The party didn't seem anywhere close to over, and I felt the bars of my cage closing in around me again. My shiver had nothing to do with the night air. The king laced his arm through mine once more, and I did everything I could to settle my breathing as he led me back to his carriage. Again, the people around us nodded and cheered for him, but they seemed much drunker now, and I could hardly hear any of it over the sound of the music. I stepped into the carriage and as the king closed the door, the sounds of the festival were suddenly shut off, like a candle being extinguished. I shivered again as we rode back to the castle.

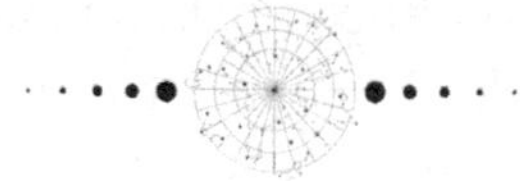

When we arrived at the gates, I could see many other carriages already gathered. "Is there going to be a ball tonight?" My dress was filthy, plastered with dirt and spilled wine, and blood clung to the hem.

I thought about what I would wear, when he abruptly said "No." I looked at him puzzled, as our carriage pulled to a stop.

"You will be returning to your room and will remain there for the rest of the night." More carriages pulled in around us and nobles spilled out, laughing and falling over each other, clearly not done for the night. I saw Lady Lovatia step out of her carriage, but she was no longer wearing her attire from earlier, but just an elegant night robe. I looked back at the king with a frown.

"For once, will you just obey?"

"For once? I haven't been allowed to do anything else." The laughing face of the man I had danced with disappeared, and that ice cold demeanor he threw on so well returned.

"Interesting. I consider throwing yourself off a cliff very much doing exactly what you want, damning the consequences."

"So, one taste of freedom and then back in the cage. A fitting punishment indeed." He looked more taken aback than when I had slapped him.

"You have never been a prisoner here, Tori." His use of my name struck me like a wave in a storm, but it couldn't stop the flames of rage building inside me.

"Oh, I suppose the constant guard and locked doors were for my safety, were they?"

"Of course! You have no idea how dangerous this world is for you, how it would destroy something as precious as you." Some of that softness returned to his gaze, but I couldn't stand it, so I attacked.

"The only thing that's ever been a danger to me has been you! You stole me from my home, you dragged me here, you...you let him kill my mother!"

It had been too far. I had always gone too far. His face was blank.

"Abraxas, I—"

He threw open the carriage door, and two guards stepped up. He pushed past them and left me behind. They escorted me out. He turned back to me for one brief look.

"Stay in your room tonight," was all he said and then he stormed into the castle.

The guards escorted me to my room, and I formulated a plan.

Chapter 34

Tori

It turns out the elaborate plan I had cooked up to get out of my room was unnecessary. No guard had been stationed outside my door, just a few who walked by on rotation. After a short time of observing them, waiting for their armor to clink by, I figured out their pattern and simply snuck out while they patrolled the other end of the wing.

I hurried down the hallway towards the throne room, but soon found no sound from that direction. Instead, I heard faded voices and music coming from the direction of the dining hall. I diverted my course and headed that way. I ducked into a servants' passage that led into the hall.

I pulled aside the tapestry and ducked into the hidden corridor. I could hear the revelry from the far end. Loud music heavy on the drumbeats played, filtered with the sound of laughter and shouts. If I was not a prisoner, certainly I could walk through the main doors to join, but somehow that didn't seem like it would end well. Maybe just a swift refusal from the guards and sent back to my room. But I needed to feel the freedom afforded to me by sneaking around, even if it were only an illusion.

My slippers moved soundlessly down the corridor; the hem of the night robes so popular in this kingdom kissing my ankles as I stepped. Light leaked through the crack between the wall and another tapestry as I reached the end of my hidden passage. I pressed up against the great weaving with my shoulder, slinking into the room. As I had assumed, this put me in a very inconspicuous location. The torches that flanked this alcove left my hiding spot in the shadows, and a large set of crates had been moved in front of it, likely holding more supplies for the party.

I knelt down and snuck up behind the crates, carefully popping my head over to observe the party. It took all my self-control to not allow my jaw to drop to the floor.

After the festival today, I thought I had understood the rumors surrounding Lupercalia. The celebrations had been raucous and rakish, but I assumed all the rest of the rumors were just exaggerations. Well, it turns out they were not. Before me sprawled a literal cornucopia of debauchery. In the center of the hall, a huge tower of crystal glasses had been built, with two large crystal cages inside. Inside those cages, one naked human and one naked half-fae danced to the beating of the drums. A shimmering liquid I could only assume was ambrosia poured down from the top of the tower, over the dancers' naked bodies, and into more glasses below them, that revealers could take and partake from.

Around this glowing fountain, various tables had been set overflowing with a feast that was beyond what we would partake in on the highest holidays in Niata. Numerous roasted boars sat half carved, with pies and pasties of all sorts stacked into tiers all around. Roasted vegetables staged with cured meats and numerous types of aged cheese filled all the gaps on the table. Jugs of honey and sweet jams sat half spilled and dredged over bread in every form. Various partygoers stood or sat around the tables, filling plate after plate, many of which I saw littered about half-eaten and forgotten.

But I couldn't feel distressed over this awful waste as my attention was drawn to what was very clearly the heart of this party. Set away from the food, past the dance floor where party-goers of every race ground against each other, on a small dais raised inside a series of circular couches, was a pornographic spectacle. A large orc warrior, nothing but pure muscle and violence, knelt behind a petit human woman with a full round ass, his hands gripping the fronts of her thighs as he pounded into her. The woman's breasts swung obscenely in time with the sound of the orc's thighs slapping into her ass as he penetrated her. The woman's face was a mess of pleasure and pain, reddened and without shame as she moaned and mewled, the sound reaching me over the music of the hall.

The orc raised a hand and spanked the woman, sending shock waves through her flesh and a fresh yelp from her lips. A large welted red handprint remained when he removed his hand. She fell to her elbows, face now buried in the blankets that covered the dais. "Thurr, I need more, more!" she cried, pulling herself up and looking back at him.

"Give the lady what she wants!" My eyes were drawn away from the woman to see that numerous voyeurs around the couple were now engaging.

"Come on, Thurr, show the human what it means to be with an orc!" I couldn't see the faces of those around the dais, the lighting obviously highlighting the stage itself, but I could see many watching the show with rap attention. Several were couples, clearly getting their own shows started. In the second row, two fae males were obviously fucking, the fae on top clearly enjoying drawing attention away from the main stage. One of the hecklers had a large breasted human woman on his lap, completely topless, with his mouth around her nipple when he wasn't yelling at the orc on stage.

A devious smirk crossed the orc's lips as the woman looked back at him pleading. He slowly, so slowly, removed his cock from the woman, her lips uttering another whining plea at his removal. Now that I could see him on full display, it seems what they said about orcs really was true, and his cock was unreasonably large, tinged a darker green than his skin, and laced with veins. I was truly contemplating how such a thing could even feel pleasant when he rubbed himself with a liquid he had grabbed from somewhere on the stage. His hand traveled up and down his length, milking a small bead of white from his head. He placed a hand on the woman's hip, and a tender look crossed his eyes as she looked back at him, giving him a small nod.

Then, to my shock—although that anything could shock me at this point was unbelievable—he placed the head of his cock at the entrance to a place even less likely to enjoy the size of him, and pushed inside her. The sound that escaped the woman was obviously laced with more pain than pleasure, but he moved slowly. She gripped the sheets in her hands, twisting them violently, but as he moved more and more, she relaxed, her breaths coming back in those heady pants. The audience was going wild, hooting and hollering and making their own obscene sounds along with the show.

I stepped back from my hiding spot. Heat coiled deep in my core in a way I had not experienced before. I had to tear my eyes away from the stage, but when I did, I saw that in the distant parts of the hall there were more of these stages, all with similar performances and audiences. My mind reeled, as I stepped back again, this time my body smacking into a solid, warm obstacle.

My mind had been so lost in the scene that I hadn't noticed a man step up behind me. As I jerked away, a firm hand came to cover my mouth, and another gripped me around the waist.

"You must be careful wandering these halls at night, little bird, otherwise a dragon might sneak up and eat you." The king's warm breath tickled the shell of my ear as he whispered to me, sending shivers down my spine, curling down to join the heat already pooled at my core. He used the hand covering my mouth to tilt my head to the side, revealing my neck to him.

"Do you like the show?" I couldn't think of an answer as I felt his lips gently kiss the skin of my neck just under my jaw. If it were possible for me to melt even more, I would have, but the show and his warm body and the feel of his tongue sliding over the sensitive skin of my neck had me in place beyond recovery. He smelled delicious, of crisp evergreen mountains and a bonfire on a midwinter night, all mixed heavily with ambrosia, of which he had obviously been partaking. A moan escaped my lips under his fingers, and I could feel his lips curl into a smirk against the skin of my neck.

His lips parted and his teeth came together, gently but firmly squeezing the flesh of my shoulder, eliciting another moan from me. "You taste delicious, little bird, like the wind that passes through the meadows of spring. I wonder what the rest of you tastes like?"

I was frozen, my body unable to fight or give in, feeling the heat of his body behind me, feeling the graze of his fingers on my ribs as he moved the arm around my waist, slipping his hand below my robe. Those fingers traced down my side and caught the loose band of the silk sleeping shorts I wore, slipping underneath. The heat in my core pulsed with so much strength I was sure he could feel it through my skin as he moved his fingers lower, grazing the top of my panties. He didn't push his fingers underneath them, instead continuing to travel over them until the tips of his fingers reached the apex of my thighs, pushing down firmly on the flesh there and sending a shockwave through my legs.

As my legs wavered, my body fell forward, and I managed to push away and spun to face him. The torches played games with the shadows on his face, and made it seem I could see flames burning in his eyes. The heat in his gaze was unlike anything I had seen before, showing me that everything up until now had only been a hint of what he was capable of. The look on his face wasn't flirtatious now, it was downright predatory. And his sights were set on me.

"You are so beautiful when you are flustered, did you know that?" Cocky bastard. He gave me that smug smile that curled anger deep in my stomach. I would do anything to wipe it off his face. Anything.

"Domineering asshole." I grabbed the collar of his robe and slammed my lips into his.

It was more a battle than our duel had been. His hands clamped at my neck, my lower back, pulling me into him. I gripped his robes harder and pulled his mouth deeper onto mine. I reached up and raked my fingers through his hair, letting my nails slide over his scalp. He claimed my mouth, the taste of him washing over me like a heady drug that only left me desiring more. I felt my finger sink into the firm muscle of his chest, and his hand sank lower, pulling my hips into him. He traced his hand over my ass and hooked it under my thigh, so my leg was pulled up over his hip. This placed my molten sex directly against his hardness. I groaned, and his hands gripped me harder.

But a drunken couple crashed around the crates in front of us, engaged in much the same way we were. I don't think they even realized who we were, as the male giggled, "Looks like this spot is taken." They stumbled away, still giggling, but my skin had gone icy, and I shoved out of the king's arms.

The fire vanished from his eyes, replaced with that cold look I was so used to. He stood tall, shifting his body away from mine.

"Run off to bed, little bird, before someone more dangerous

than I finds you." It wasn't a request. His cold gaze bore into me as I slunk around him and back behind the tapestry. Finally, out of his gaze, it seemed I could breathe for the first time in minutes, my lungs filling with the musty air of the corridor. I leaned against the wall, my chest rising and falling slowly. But something had shifted, and I knew there was no going back.

Chapter 35

Tori

The hour was late, or very early depending on how you looked at it, but sleep eluded me. My mind raced with all that had happened in the past few hours, my fingers tracing over the path the king's lips had taken down my neck. I had slipped my hand between my legs and found release over and over playing those images in my mind, but relief seemed even further away from me.

I cursed my body, even as the thought of the king's hands and lips on me set me ablaze again. I let out an exasperated sigh and rolled to my side, twisting the silk sheets into even more of a mess than they already were. I slipped my hands under my pillow and closed my eyes, as if this would be the time sleep finally came. But again, the same thoughts ran through my head.

He was my enemy, my warden, despite how he claimed otherwise. Images of Niata covered in blood filled my mind, but I shoved them back to the far corners of my mind, as I always did, tossing them beneath the waves. He had been there, had a hand to play in that. But these past weeks had been.... We had always played our games, but tonight had changed something.

My hand fell between my legs, I brought back up the images of the orc fucking that soft human woman, of the king tracing his fingers between my thighs, anything to distract me from the darkness that seemed to creep forward in these late hours. I began moving my fingers inside me, but the thoughts just kept coming. What if tonight had ruined this? The king had thought I had rejected him, even though the truth was far from that. Even more, he had let me reject him. I would think more about the implications of that later. For now, I'd made up my mind. I wasn't done with tonight, not yet.

I ran to my wardrobe, sorting through my underthings. I had options but settled on a pair of black panties with a thin lace waist where the openings traveled up over my hip bones, with a matching top. It wasn't too ostentatious, something I could handle for what I had planned. I pulled them on, then added the night robe, and was out my door before I could allow my nerves to stop me.

I walked down the hallway with my chin and shoulders high as if someone would see me, and my posture alone would show I had nothing to be ashamed of. Luckily, I didn't encounter anyone on the short walk to the king's quarters. The huge ebony double doors seemed so much more imposing in the dark, or maybe it was just my nerves creeping up on me. I raised my hand to knock, but my hands shook.

I shook my head and balled my fists. *Tori, you have slept with how many people in your life? He is just one more.* It sounded like a lie even to me.

I shook my head again before I could let the thoughts derail me and knocked. I heard nothing. After what seemed like an eternity, but was likely about ten seconds, I knocked again. I pressed my ear to the door. Could I hear voices inside? Oh gods, I was a fool. Of course, he wouldn't come back from that party alone, he was the king for fuck's sake.

I turned to quickly make my escape when I heard the door behind me crack open.

"What do you want at this hour, little bird?" I turned back to see the king's emerald eyes studying me. He leaned with his arm braced above his head on the frame of the door. He wore a night robe as well, but it was tied loosely, and I could see his bare chest underneath. It allowed me to see the large scar that marked his birch-colored skin, and I once again wondered what it could have been from.

"Yes, Princess?" His voice was filled with the smirk I saw on his face when I finally raised my eyes up, after I had been obviously staring at his chest. This was it. I was knocking on his door in the middle of the night, it was obvious what I wanted. No point playing coy now.

"I was in my room finding my own pleasure after tonight's performance, when I realized that was foolish when I could come to you for assistance." The words tumbled out of me, not nearly as sultry as I would have desired, but they seemed to hit their mark. For a moment, I saw the smallest expression of surprise cross his face, before he controlled his features once more. Then that snobbish grin crossed his face, the one that I hated, that I could never seem to get out of my mind.

"And what sort of regent would I be to deny a princess the *assistance* she requires?" The way he drawled assistance captured all the seduction I wish I had portrayed and made my toes curl into the carpet beneath my feet. He moved aside and motioned for me to enter his room. But as I took a step to enter, he snapped his arm across my path, blocking me. The veins of his arms strained as he pressed his hand into the opposite door frame.

"But know this, Princess. Once you cross, you cannot turn back, because I won't be letting you go." Deep in my abdomen, pressure curled and released, as I drank in the heat in his eyes. I took a deep breath, ducked under his arm, and crossed the threshold.

His room was smaller than I imagined. With a castle the size of his, I had imagined a cavernous room to match his ego. What I saw before me was much more cozy. Near the door was a small sitting area with a table, likely for taking meals in his room, placed near a fireplace. The mantle was two carved dragons flanking the flames in an onyx stone, their eyes jewels that reflected the firelight. But instead of the ferocious creatures featured throughout the castle, these dragons seemed content and relaxed, soaking up the warmth of the fire beneath them. All around the fireplace were shelves upon shelves of books, the king's private collection. I almost moved towards them, desperate to see what he thought was worthy of the shelves in his room, when I felt his hand on my lower back, gently leading me further in.

Past the sitting area was a large and beautifully built canopy bed, made of deep ebony like his door, facing floor to ceiling peaked windows that overlooked the bay. His view was magnificent, and the bay was stunning in the moonlight. The silver light reflected off the harsh waves of the cold sea, softening them and the beginnings of the early morning mist twisted up and over the great rocks that lurked beyond the shore. The stars winked at me, like they knew my dirty intentions. It seemed that the king had not forgotten them either.

"So, my little bird, perhaps you could elaborate on what assistance you might need from me tonight?" I turned to him to see his eyes twinkling in the moonlight, the soft light highlighting the beautiful shadows of his face, the high cheekbones paired with his strong nose, his teeth gleaming behind his now predatory smile. I felt a blush rising in my cheeks, and the predator's gaze raked over me, the flames I had seen earlier tonight returning.

Then with all the speed he used in battle, he closed the space between us. One arm was around my waist, the other at the back of my head, tilting my face up to look at him. My breath hitched. He had captured me with those malachite eyes.

He wrapped his arm a bit tighter behind me and pulled me into him. My breasts rubbed against his chest and the lace fabric of my top stimulated my nipples as I felt them pulling taught. The flames in his eyes as he stared at me set that same heat pooling down my spine and between my legs. He slid the hand on my back down, pulling my hips into him. "Perhaps you have forgotten why you came? The hour is late, these things do happen." His eyes were alight now, the true image of a fae trickster just about to steal my soul in a one-sided bargain. "Perhaps I can remind you?" And this time, he closed the final distance between us, his lips gently landing on mine.

For a moment he held me there, his lips soft, his body taught, holding back as he waited for me. His last hesitation. I pressed myself more firmly into him, relaxing in his grip, as I tilted my head to the side and opened my lips for him.

And then any control he had before was shattered. His tongue darted into my mouth, claiming every piece of me. His hand in my hair held tighter, tilting my head more so that he could claim even more of me with his kiss. The hand on my back slid down and over my ass, cupping it firmly. I moaned then, as I felt his growing hardness pressed directly up against me, pulsing as I ground my hips up against him. He swallowed my moans, before releasing my lips and moving his mouth down my throat, showering me with kisses and small nibbles. I ran one hand through his long, pale hair as he spoke to me.

"Tell me, my little bird, what were you thinking about when you pleasured yourself tonight?" Oh gods, the blush rose on my cheeks again, mingling with the heated pleasure that already had every inch of my skin aching for him.

"I— uh..." moans left me, but no coherent thoughts. He kept

kissing my neck, his tongue darting over that sensitive spot beneath my jaw and his hand swept below my robe, cupping my breast.

He tweaked my nipple through the lace and had me gasping. "Tell me, tell me all those secret desires inside your head." He tweaked my nipple again.

"Oh gods...I—I was thinking of the party tonight."

"Yes, go on..."

"And I was thinking of you." That elicited a low growl from him.

He slid the hand on my ass down my thigh, lifting my leg up again, and he moved his mouth down my chest, opening up my robe. His hand on my neck laid me back, as he kissed my nipple through the fabric, biting down ever so slightly.

"And what was I doing to you?" All I could do was moan as he bit down on me again, and he ground me into his hips, so he helped me. "Were you sitting on my lap, little bird, grinding into me as we watched that orc fuck?"

"No—no, it was us, on display..." Oh gods, why was I telling him this? But I knew I had lost all control at this point. My core was on fire and if I didn't have him soon, I was sure that I would combust. If he was a fae trickster here to steal my soul, he could have it, all of it.

He had stopped torturing my nipple and I whimpered, begging for that contact back, but he had locked his eyes on mine, "Go on." A command.

"It was you and-d me, up there, but we were on your throne —" My world spun as he lifted me off the ground. I felt my robe pull away and my back landed on his silky sheets, his body perched above mine. His robe had come open, and I could see his black silk shorts, barely concealing the hard outline of him, more scars visible on his stomach, where a delicious V of muscles led below the treacherous material.

I tore my eyes away to see that his gaze had darkened to black, his expression unreadable. "Touch yourself, Princess. Touch yourself and tell me how I fucked you on my throne." Another command. Any playfulness I had seen in him before was gone, only the general of the world's largest fae army was left.

"But—I...your assistance..." What was I blubbering about? He leaned down on his hands, lowering himself to place a kiss just above the hem of my panties. Then he kissed up my stomach, between my breasts as his long hair tickled over my nipples, up my neck until his body was pressed against mine, his lips caressing the curve of my ear.

"Tori," the sound of my name on his lips had me shivering, "by the end of this I will have you coming so hard that you will be singing my name like a holy mantra, but right now I need you to touch yourself and tell me how I fucked you on my throne." He rolled to the side of me, propped up on one elbow. I looked at him there, his pale hair draping down his chest, his skin a glow with sweat and arousal, his deep eyes blazing, the very picture of male arrogance. I moved my hands slowly down my stomach.

He watched intently as I slid my finger beneath my panties, and when I moaned as my finger entered me, he dropped his lips to my neck again. "Tell me, Tori."

"The party was in your throne room; your whole court was there..." His kisses turned to bites, and I brought my thumbs up to stimulate my clit as I continued, "You were seated on your throne, collecting the tithe, but at my turn, I had nothing to give." My legs shook as my orgasm came closer, but he growled into my neck, spurring me on. "You said there is only one way I could prove my loyalty and unlaced your pants." He pushed himself against me, his hardness grinding into my hip. His hand brushed over my arm, tracing down the sensitive flesh. I moved to pull my hand away, but he gripped my wrist, holding me in place. Then he moved his hand down over mine, sliding his finger next to the two inside of me.

He groaned, "Finish your story, Princess," and he pushed his finger inside of me, along with my own. The sensation as I stretched to fit him, along with the heel of his hand grinding down on my clit almost sent me over the edge, but I kept going.

"I lifted up my skirts, and climbed onto your lap," His finger and mine pulsed in and out of me, "and I took your cock into me, and rode you for your whole court to see."

"Yes, they can all see who you belong to." He had finally freed my hand, and I fisted it into the sheets beside me as he slid another finger into me to replace it. He moved his thumb over my clit, pulsing with his fingers and I was seeing stars. "Who is your king?"

"You are, Your Majesty." My legs shook as every muscle in my body tightened. He bit down on my neck again and I yelped. "My name, Tori..."

"Abraxas, Abraxas—please—"

My body tightened, but just as I was about to cross over, his hand and body pulled away. An extremely pathetic whimper escaped me. That devious chuckle left his lips again. "I've waited this long for you, Tori, you can wait just a bit longer." He shifted himself off the bed, and grabbed the tops of my thighs, pulling me to the edge. The tension in my body throbbed as his head lowered between my legs, his lips grazing my inner thigh. My legs shook in earnest now, but he used his hands to steady me, all while opening me up further to him. It seemed a pattern now, but I couldn't move, I was under his spell. He placed his mouth over the flesh covering my clit, pressing down with his lips, his tongue, eliciting a feral sound from me.

"Abraxas, please." His chuckle vibrated through my core as his teeth came down and ripped the thin cloth off of me.

The lace snapped at my hips, and he was unleashed, his

tongue sliding through my lips, always coming to land at my most sensitive point, circling before he would move down to kiss all around my core. "More delicious than I dreamed," he groaned, and it sent vibrations through every part of me. My delayed orgasm came back for vengeance, and my legs thrashed, my fingers ready to rip through the fabric of his sheets.

"Oh gods..." He chuckled against me, the vibrations torture as he continued to tease me, taking me to the edge before backing away.

"I'm the only God here tonight, little bird. If you must pray, pray to me." He sent his tongue through every inch of me, before thrusting inside.

I was desperate now, and I ground my hips into his face. I slid my hands through his hair, holding him to me tighter as he continued to fuck me with his tongue.

"Abraxas, please..." He shifted his hands, one pulling me to him even closer, and the other replaced his tongue, filling me as he slipped his fingers back inside. He wrapped his lips around my clit one last time and sucked while flaying me with his tongue, and my body released.

It was unlike anything I'd had before. Every muscle of my body worked as a symphony, playing in harmony as they contracted and released. The climax I'd missed and the one I had now played together to give me something greater than the sum of its parts, as stars danced before my eyes and my skin flushed red.

How long I lay just panting and riding my waves of ecstasy, I don't know. When my mind came back to my body, he had crawled back onto the bed with me, lying by my side again. I tried to move my arms to reach him, but it was like the signal from my brain was cut off, and I couldn't move. He seemed to read my thoughts, and a smile lit up his face. A true smile, not his usual smirk, and gods was he beautiful like that.

I finally willed my hand to move, and I caught his face beneath my fingers, tracing the lovely curve of his cheekbone and jaw. His eyes turned soft, and he leaned in and kissed me gently. I could taste myself on him, but the gentleness of the kiss made this moment, wrapped in his arms, feel much more intimate than when his head had been between my legs just moments before. I allowed myself to soak in the gentleness of the moment before I started tracing my hand down his chest to find his pleasure. But as I did, he caught my hand in his, lacing our fingers together. I released our kiss, giving him a frown.

He gave another soft chuckle, "Little bird, I will have you in every way imaginable. But we have time. For now, you need sleep." He let his eyes slowly rove my body, and it made goosebumps rise all over me. "Besides, I get the feeling your legs aren't working properly right now, and I want you at your best for what I have planned." His eyes glimmered with mischief, truly a fae king. He was right. While I had gained control of my arms, my legs were still unresponsive, I was barely able to get a twitch out of them as they continued to throb.

"Sleep now, Tori." He rolled me over, so my back was pressed against him, and he stroked my hair and ear softly. He held me so close, like I was a precious treasure he had finally added to his horde, and a part of me wondered if he truly would never let me go. I pushed down the little voice who said, *I hope not*.

After a few moments, I felt him press a soft kiss to the point of my ear, and felt his breath deepen. I looked out his grand windows, and the sky was alight with green and blue light, ribbons that stretched across the sky dancing and intertwining with each other. I watched for a few moments, then let my eyes drift closed and fell asleep next to a man for the first time in my long life.

Chapter 36

Tori

When I woke, the curtains had been drawn to give me darkness. I could see the bright sun peeking around the edges, and I knew it was past noon. I shifted and found a fluffy linen duvet pulled over me and tucked in to keep me warm. I flipped over in the bed, hoping to find him there, but I knew he had already left. The fire had been left on in the hearth, and I saw my robe lying over the winged chair next to it. My destroyed underwear was nowhere to be seen.

I slipped out of bed, my legs wobbling horribly as I stood. I donned my robe, and when I grabbed it, a little white note fluttered to the ground.

Little Bird,
Apologies for not being there when you awoke, but I was called away. Should you have need of anything, please call on Ciara and she will provide anything you need. Try not to snoop too much.

~Abraxas

My fingers traced where he signed his name. Seeing it there so plainly twisted my stomach. Were we on a first name basis now? My mind raced back to the previous night, my legs wobbling again at the memory. It seemed so.

My nose twitched at his mention of snooping. Of course, I was going to snoop, I just hated how he always seemed to know my moves before I did. I folded the note up and tucked it in my pocket, running my finger over where I knew his name was one last time. Our game had become much more dangerous now.

I pushed that thought back in my mind where I kept all the other undesirables, and instead walked over to his bookshelves to snoop. Most of the books I found were recounts of ancient battles or books on war strategy. Not so surprising for a general, I supposed. A few books on the history of the continent, and one that looked relatively new on the history of Niata. *Interesting.* Well not really, I had read that particular book in my studies as a youngling, and it was quite boring in my opinion, but interesting it was there.

After several more shelves of war strategy, I saw a small section of fiction. Most seemed to be of the genre man versus nature. Not really my preferred reading so I hadn't read any of them before, but I took note of the title and author to see if I could grab copies later. At the end of the row, a little red book with no title caught my eye. I carefully pulled it out. The cover simply read *Poems* by Balthazar Ruin, an author I had never heard of. I cracked open the book for it to naturally fall open at a dog-eared poem, the spine worn as if it had been opened to this page many, many times. The poem was titled *Upon the Wind.*

On wings of freedom soaring high,
Amidst the boundless, open sky,
Where endless seas meet endless blue,
The call of freedom rings anew.

But in the distance, shadows grow,
A darkness stirring deep below,
And in the heart of sea and sky,
A great unrest begins to fly.

Yet still the sky is vast and wide,
The sea, a never-ending tide,
And from the depths of darkened days,
A new light comes to show the way.

So let the winds of freedom blow,
And let the seas of freedom flow,
For in the heart of sky and sea,
A world reborn, once more is free.

A knock rapped at the door, and I snapped the book closed, fumbling to get it back on the shelf like a youngling caught stealing jelly rolls. The knock came again, and I realized they were waiting for a reply. I tiptoed over to the door and pressed my ear against it.

"Your Highness, it's Ciara." I cracked the door open to see Ciara's kind, soft face peering at me.

"Ciara, I have told you not to call me that. Tori is fine."

The half-fae woman cracked a smile that was completely wicked fae as she said, "I was coming to check to see how you were doing this morning." She winked at me. I felt color rise on my cheeks. Her smile grew even more wicked, if that were possible. "Although, by my observation it seems to me you are doing quite well." I scowled at her, unable to come up with anything witty to say. I was standing in the king's room with no underwear on for fuck's sake.

She let out a friendly laugh that managed to coax a smile out of me, before her face became more serious and she said, "Your Highness, truly, do you have need of anything?"

"How about an escort back to my own room?"

The warm smile I knew well returned to her face and she nodded, "Of course, Your Highness."

"Tori."

"Of course, Your Highness."

She walked me down the halls back to my wing of the castle. I didn't speak, but it was nice to be walking with someone, as opposed to slinking back to my room. Ciara spoke casually of the plans for dinner that evening, it was past lunch after all, she added with a snarky wink, and of the new plants coming into the garden this week. We reached my door, and she opened it for me, I passed her in silence when she touched my arm lightly.

"Tori—" I paused at her use of my name, "You are not the first woman to succumb to the king's...charms. If you need of anything, please do let me know."

The knowledge that this was a common occurrence made something twist in my stomach, stinking suspiciously of jealousy. A look must have passed my face that she interpreted as regret, for she squeezed my arm.

She couldn't have known, but she squeezed my arm in just the way my mother had when I had been discouraged with my lessons as a youngling. One of the few signs of physical affection she ever showed me. A tear rose to my eye before I could suppress it. Horror crossed Ciara's face, and before I knew it, she had wrapped her arms around me in a deep hug. I froze. After everything that had happened the night before, this was too much. Not to mention this was a highly inappropriate breach of her station. My head spun, and that weight was pressed to my chest again.

I pushed out of her arms, "Ciara, I'm alright—I'm fine. I'll call if I need anything." I pushed her away, more forcefully than I meant, and she staggered back and fell to the floor. "I'm sor—"

"It's alright, Your Highness." She straightened her apron and stood tall, away from me, all formality returned. "Please, do call if you need anything." She closed my door and walked away, as a great whirlpool opened up inside of me, sucking me in.

Chapter 37

Tori

My mind raced all afternoon. Despite the activities of the previous night, my mind was caught on Ciara. She had been one of the people to show me kindness in my time here, and I had treated her like a spoiled brat. I berated myself for also thinking of her station when she hugged me. I had always praised myself for never judging others by their station in life, but here I had done just that with the closest thing I had to a friend. I paced the room, thinking of how I could apologize, wondering if she even wanted me to.

Being in this palace was driving me mad. And not just because I was a prisoner. I was so tired of trying to see the hidden motives behind everyone around me. Did they see me as the enemy? Or just as a captured spoiled princess they needed to deal with? Were Ciara, Kaleos, even Avlyn truly showing me kindness, or were they just doing their duty to the king? And the king...

No, I didn't let myself think about that. The ocean of my mind had been churning, memories rising up without my consent. All thoughts of the king I shoved forcefully back, thoughts of how my stomach had turned at the thought of him being with other people, the way his arm had wrapped around me, holding me to him last night, all filed away and tossed into the recesses of my mind.

I only allowed myself to think of the mind-blowing orgasm he had given me. That I understood, that was physical. I could have that, I could keep my feelings for him purely carnal, couldn't I? Surely, he was doing the same? I was just one of many to pass through his door. *Even if he had told me he would never let me go, and kissed me softly and tenderly wrapped in his arms...*

My memories threatened to rise up, but I slammed them down. The nervous energy in my body caused my injured arm to ache, small stabs of pain running up over my shoulder.

A soft knock came at my door. Thank the gods. I ran over, hoping to see Ciara, but a young human boy held a tray with my dinner. "For you, Your Highness."

"Oh, thank you."

"And this as well." From his pocket he drew a small paper-wrapped box, with a note tied to the top. "From the king himself, Your Highness." Well fuck, so much for putting him out of my mind. "Is there anything else?"

"Yes actually, would you be able to bring me a sleeping potion?" The darkness called out to me like an old friend. It had been since I'd left home. I no longer had the strength to deny it. I needed to sleep with no dreams, no thoughts, just for a little bit.

The boy was well trained, because his face showed no emotion as he reacted, "I would be happy to, but please know all the servants have been instructed to never bring you more than a half dose at a time, and I must watch you take the potion." I breathed deeply. This was a logical policy for a captive. It didn't mean anything. It didn't.

I nodded and the boy walked away. I took the tray of food and package into my room. I nibbled at the edge of the rustic bread and ignored the rest, staring at the package like it might combust any second. I took a few more steadying breaths and slipped the note out from beneath the deep green ribbon.

I have provided you with more appropriate attire for wandering the castle late at night. Should you need assistance again, wear this.

~Your King

Appropriate attire was certainly a stretch of the imagination. In fact, it took me a few moments to even identify the small lace garments located in all the silk padding of the box. The brassiere was exquisite, the black and emerald lace twined in delicate patterns that almost mimicked scales, completely translucent and hand-woven. The underwear—if I could call them that—had a small triangle of the same fabric in the front, but it disappeared into a thin ribbon that traveled up that back, meeting with the tiniest triangle of the fabric again that would rest just above the curve of my ass. A set of garters made with black silk straps completed the look.

Why was it that everything this man did had me feeling like a fumbling youngling again?

I set the gift down and curled up on my couch, knees tucked into my chest. How long had I yearned to be more than the disappointing spare? I'd longed to live outside the life my father, my entire kingdom had prescribed for me. And here I was, a princess in a foreign court, free of what I thought had been holding me back, and still I had done nothing. How comfortable the gilded cage I grew up in had become before I ever entered this ebony one.

Tears flowed now, and I didn't attempt to stop them. They were silent, and I didn't sob, but still, they came as I stared into the fire, willing it to burn me away. I cried, and all my thoughts came rushing back. I cried for my brother, trapped with a monster; I cried for my mother, dead on the floor. I even cried for Lyle who had never had any real affection for me, but had given me the comfort I needed at the time. Now he was dead too, buried with so many others under the rubble of my home. And mostly, I cried at the pathetic creature I had become, immobilized and weak.

A knock came at my door again. The young human boy truly was a marvel in his stoicism, as he handed me the requested potion, a small vial half-filled with a milky liquid. He nodded, ignoring my tears, as I swallowed the half dose. He collected the bottle from me and wished me a pleasant sleep. Not pleasant dreams, for no one ever dreamed under a sleeping potion, thank the gods.

I turned and immediately threw myself on my bed, letting the sweet shadows of the potion curl around me, and drag me under into a sleep like death.

Chapter 38

Tori

I awoke to the light of the full moon shining through my window. I groggily raised my head, and the clock above my hearth marked the time as half past midnight. It seemed a half dose of potion wouldn't keep me asleep all night. But now that I had opened my eyes, I heard the voice calling. *Wake up, Tori!* The waves of my mind no longer roiled, and the sweet darkness of the potion still clung to it, calling to me. I craved the safety of it, even though my mind knew it was an illusion. It was like a still lake on a summer day, placid and beautiful, but beneath the depths held dangers of unknowable monsters. *Wake Up!* I forced myself out of bed and to my fire, letting it burn the darkness out of me. I went to grab a book to pass the hours when my resolution solidified.

I would not be passive any longer. While I had not entered into the situation with this intention, an opportunity had presented itself to me. An opportunity to shift the balance of power. And if I had a little fun in the process, no harm in that right?

I snatched up the negligible undergarments from my couch. I

ran to my bathroom and washed myself under the waterfall that came from the ceiling. I moved to the collection of scented soaps and decided on one that smelled of pine and musk. Nothing too flowery tonight. I was not going to be delicate.

I toweled off, and pulled the tiny lace pieces on, then strapped some stockings into the garter. I admired myself in the mirror. My dark slate eyes were fierce. I practiced softening them, but not too much. Then I threw on a smirk and struck a pose, chest lifted and hips back to really accentuate the curves I had. It looked slightly ridiculous to me, but I had no doubts it would have the desired effect. I threw on my robe and was out the door.

As I walked to the king's room, I let the memories of the previous night come back to me. His finger along with mine pulsing inside me, his tongue dragging over my core, his head between my thighs. The heat curled in my belly, and I felt wetness already soaking through the tiny pieces of my undergarments. Perhaps it wasn't right to allow myself to feel this level of arousal for the man I was trying to manipulate, but it certainly made things easy that my body was clearly drawn to him. *Not just your body,* the voice in my head said, but I shoved it down.

I reached his door and knocked. Much quicker than last time, the Dragon King opened his door. "My, what would bring you to my door at this hour, little bird?" I felt him trying to see what I wore under my robe, but I held it closed tight. He inhaled deeply and flames came to his eyes as I was sure he had smelled my arousal. Perfect. "Do you need my assistance again tonight?"

I took one steadying breath and pulled on the persona of someone much more confident than I felt. "Not tonight, My King," I echoed his signature on my note, and gently grabbed the front of his robe, leaning my body into his, "I had something a little different in mind." His eyes darkened, and I leaned more heavily into him, using my weight to shift him back into his room. He stepped back, letting the door close behind us. For a moment

I let my eyes dart around, making a plan, until they locked on the wingback chair near his hearth. It wasn't a throne, but close enough. A wicked smile crossed my lips, as I twisted around, still holding on to his robe, now using it to pull him towards the chair.

"It seems you were so generous with me; I was hoping that I could give you a gift in thanks." I pushed him gently so that the backs of his knees hit the chair, and he gently sat. I stepped back, placing myself between him and the fireplace, and with no small flourish, let my robe drop to the floor.

His eyes swept over my body, locking on the gift he had provided. His lips curled, "It seems you can comply with my requests on occasion."

I held the snarky reply I wanted to say back, and instead I allowed my hips to push out, and turned slowly until I was on full display for him, and I heard him growl behind me. I turned to see the face of a man who was starving, and an elaborate feast had just been placed before him. "You don't know what you do to me, little bird." He moved to rise from his chair, but I dropped to my knees, and he froze.

"Oh, I think I have some idea."

I crawled to him then, just two paces, but his eyes had become pitch black. "Careful, Tori."

"Or what, Abraxas?" I hit with my most innocent look, while running my hands up his thighs, towards the hardness I could already see bulging under his robes. His hands snapped to mine, stopping me.

"Or," he leaned down, his long hair wrapping around my face, "I won't stop until that delicious cunt of yours is wrapped around my cock." My core throbbed with need at his filthy words, and I could feel the heat rising to my cheeks, but I had a plan.

"But that's not your present tonight," I stuck my lip out to emphasize the pout in my voice.

I slid my hands from his grip, and moved them up, opening

his robe. Beneath he wore similar silk shorts to the night before. I traced my fingers under the edge of those shorts and felt him lift his hips ever so slightly. His cue, his consent as I slid them down and off, revealing him. It was ridiculous to think, but gods he was beautiful. Fully hard, his cock curved up ever so slightly at the head, and I couldn't help but reach out and feel the velvet-soft skin there.

"Tori..." I wasn't sure if it was a warning or a plea, but I took the hand gripping him and slid down towards his hips, giving a twist as I did. "Fuck..." his head fell back on the chair, and his eyes rolled closed, and gods, I did feel powerful. I pulled up and pushed back down, tightening my grip ever so slightly, and drank in the moans he made. Seeing him come undone like this, being in my control? Yes, I could get used to this. But I had more planned.

But I also had a problem. My hand wasn't able to fit around his girth, and I had never used my mouth on a man of this size before, but I was thrilled to try. I nudged myself between his knees, and he shifted his hips forward, opening himself more to me. His head was still leaning back, enjoying my strokes, but as I leaned down and placed my lips around him, his head shot up.

"Tori—I—" But his words turned into a delicious moan as I slid him down my throat. I pulled back, using my tongue to tease the head of him, sliding around and through the small groove at his tip where a small salty bead had already appeared. Then allowing my lips to stretch as far as they could, I took him in until he hit the back of my throat. His hips bucked, and it spurred me on, taking him even deeper.

"Tori, gods, I always knew you had a wicked mouth, but this..." I felt his hand come to the back of my head, resting there gently. I couldn't help but test him as I pulled back to release him, I felt him push me back down. I chuckled internally. In some ways, men really were all the same. But now I was warmed up, and when I slid back down, I let my throat open, and felt him push even deeper. After a few more strokes, I had taken much more of his length, and I could tell he was really losing control of himself. His hips bucked harder now, and tears streamed from my eyes as I stopped myself from choking. I could feel him pulse inside me and I knew I had him. I slid up, but as I did, his hand shifted, weaving into my hair, and lifted me away from him, wiping my tears. I looked up, those gemstone eyes showing me an expression I couldn't quite read.

"I need you, Tori. All of you." I understood his meaning.

Something inside me compelled me to say, "I'm yours, Abraxas." It was the right thing to say. Like a spell had been cast, he shifted, his restraint gone. He pulled me up onto his lap, his fingers digging into my scalp. I pressed myself into him, crashing our lips together. He opened for me immediately, and I claimed his mouth with my tongue. He kissed me back with equal ferocity, as if I were the air he breathed. His hands slid down my back and clamped down on my ass, pushing me into his length. The teeny tiny lace piece certainly didn't hide how wet I was as I slid over him. He reached his hand down further, pushing aside the tiny slip of fabric, and brought his finger inside me.

"First that delicious mouth, and now this?" He added a second finger for emphasis, and I could feel myself melting. "You're so wet for me already." He latched his lips to my neck, and I felt him seat his broad head at my entrance, but again he waited. No amount of self-control could have stopped me now.

I pushed my hips down onto him, and gods, he felt better than I ever imagined. He stretched me, but even as ready as I was, I could only take half his length. "Good girl," he purred in my ear, "let me see that tight cunt of yours take my whole cock." He slid his lips down and clamped around my nipple. My inner walls pulsed, already stretched to the limit around him. But as he teased my nipple with his tongue, and ground his fingers into my ass, I opened more. After several small strokes, I felt him slide in and in and in, until my core met with his hips. "She how good you look taking me like this." A shiver down my spine. "Now ride me like you did in your fantasy." I wasn't in charge of this anymore, and gods I didn't care.

Chapter 39

Abraxas

Seeing Tori take my entire length was a sight more beautiful than anything I could recall. This princess kept surprising me. I had expected her to show up at my door tonight, but I hadn't expected her to drop to her knees and take me deep into her throat. Although I wasn't surprised by how gods-damned much I liked it.

I could see she was trying to take control of the situation, and she was so fucking beautiful I had let her, but this princess was *mine*.

Now she made the most perfect, breathy moans as she adjusted to me inside her. Every time I would pinch one of her sweet nipples I could feel her clamp down on me, and gods, that was everything. But then slowly she started following my command, raising and lowering herself, sliding me against the warmth of her.

Gods, she was already so aroused, and I couldn't keep my mouth off of her, latching my lips to her mouth, her neck, and those perfect hard nipples through the lace. I felt the straps of her garters dig into the supple flesh of her ass as I squeezed her and led her up and down, increasing the pace of her thrusts.

She was breathless now, the work of riding me, I knew her thighs were burning and could hear her heart pounding. I wanted to reward my little bird, so I moved one hand over her hip, slipping my thumb down between our bodies, tracing slow circles over her clit.

Oh, she liked that, her eyes rolling back, "Oh Gods...don't stop." I increased my speed and added more pressure.

"One day, I *will* fuck you just like this on my throne. Everyone will covet this cunt but know that you are mine and mine alone." She was close now, her cheeks flushed, her breath labored.

"Come for me, little bird." I felt her cunt clamp down on me in waves as she found her orgasm, her nails digging into my shoulders, "Abraxas!" she screamed my name, and hearing it cross her lips as she came almost brought me to my own climax. But I wasn't done with her. Not yet.

My good little bird kept riding me through her orgasm until she was completely spent.

I wrapped my arms around her, pulling her body to my chest, and she dropped her head to my shoulder, panting. I let myself enjoy feeling her, almost completely limp in my arms, my cock still buried deep inside her. I couldn't resist placing one soft kiss on top of her hair, before running my hands down her back and over that ridiculous ass. I lifted her and stood.

She wrapped her arms around my neck, and her legs around my waist, and before I had even taken two steps, she started grinding herself against me again. "Needy Princess."

"Abraxas, please, I need more." Her soft words caressed the sensitive point of my ear, and I slowly lowered her to the bed. I had never seen anything so bewitching as her laid out before me, her skin rosy from her orgasm, and her face hungry as she looked up at me. I slowly started pulsing in and out of her, and each thrust caused her breasts to bounce in time. She arched her back and pulled at the sheets to give herself more leverage as she tried to pull me even deeper.

I leaned forward, running soft kisses up her chest and neck, pulling her hips up to send myself even deeper inside her until I could feel myself hitting the very end of her. But it seemed it still wasn't enough.

She ran her nails down my back, which pulled a groan from me, as she whispered, "I need you deeper." And who was I to deny her.

I pulled back and flipped her over, but before I could guide her, she had raised her hips, putting her wet, swollen sex on display for me. Gods, it took everything I had to be gentle with her as I slowly guided myself back into her. She moaned into the bed, and I felt her clamp around me which removed any hesitation that remained. I gripped the tops of her thighs and pulled me to her, over and over, faster and faster.

"Oh fuck, Abraxas." She gripped the sheets, and pressed herself back into me, spurring me on. Watching myself pulling in and out of that delicious cunt, I knew there was nothing that would ever compare.

Her pants were more like whines now, and I knew neither of us would last much longer. Her legs started shaking again, and I pulled her to me even tighter, never letting up our pace, until I felt her crushing down on me as she cried my name over and over. I couldn't resist one resounding slap onto her ass as I released inside her, our orgasms chasing each other.

We lay panting, my body pressed over hers for as long as I dared. I slowly withdrew from her, but as I did, she rolled underneath to face me, and her face with alight with a smile that was more beautiful than every sunrise that had ever greeted me. She caught my face in her hands, and pulled me into a sweet, long kiss that had me lost to her.

I held her close, and then tucked her into my arms, her back and that ass tucked up against me. Her skin was still flushed from her orgasm, and she seemed to glow in the moonlight. I committed the image to memory, knowing I might not be lucky enough to see anything so beautiful ever again.

She sighed deeply and relaxed, before I felt her tense and try to wiggle out of my arms. "Perhaps I should—" I clamped my arms more tightly around her.

"Remember what I said, Tori." She shivered as I said her name, "Once you started this, I was not going to let you go." I wanted to tell her she was mine, that her body and soul were entwined with mine, but I reminded myself that we had time, and she still had much to discover about me, and herself. I didn't need to overwhelm her or scare her yet, so instead I placed a kiss at the point of her ear and whispered, "Goodnight, little bird."

Chapter 40

Tori

I never thought the Dragon King would be such a cuddler. I awoke in the morning, and he had left again. On his pillow I saw a small note that just read, *I'll be back soon.* I took that as an invitation to stay and wait for him. I rolled to get out of bed and found, once again, my legs weren't really cooperating.

They were sore and shook with even the small effort of moving, and my entire core was swollen, still covered in the fluids from the night before. The king hadn't allowed me to get up after last night to wash myself, so I could feel his dried seed on my thighs and the panties I still wore. Part of me was disgusted, but a deeper, feral part of me was pleased, thinking of me covered in his smell, the soreness reminding me of the mind-breaking sensation of him entering me last night.

I couldn't help a small grin from crossing my face, as I bit down on my finger, remembering all we had done. It had been a while since I had been with a partner who was so endowed, and gods, I had come so fast once I had finally gotten him inside of me. My core throbbed, but it sent shocks through the tender tissue. I needed a cold shower.

I managed to wobble out of bed. I looked out the huge, peaked windows to see the grey ocean pounding the rocky shore. The sky was clear today and the weather looked practically balmy for Xyr. To the side of the king's bed, a small door led to what I assumed was the washroom. I peeked in to see I was correct. It was very similar to the one in my room, with a bath and separate waterfall shower, but his shower was placed up against a huge floor-to-ceiling window that mimicked the ones in his room.

I stepped into the shower to look out. I supposed this high up in the castle and with no ships passing in the Shadowed Sea, one didn't have to worry about voyeurs. Although considering what he got up to in the night, maybe he wouldn't mind.

I saw a small table set somewhat out of place, and upon closer examination, a small note on top read, *Little Bird.* Underneath was a clean day dress. Simple, but made of exquisite fabric that floated like the clouds absent from the sky today in a dark grey to match my eyes. In typical Dragon Kingdom fashion, the dress itself was cut rather conservatively, with long billowing sleeves, tight at the wrists, and high boat neckline and a flowing skirt, but the dress was very sheer. A pair of lovely underwear and a matching corset-style bustier with white accents and a nude background were included as well.

It seemed my options once again were to slink back to my room, unwashed, or give in and embrace the king's gifts. The little voice in my head said to think of the look Abraxas would give me in this, and I was already stepping into the shower. It really was splendid to feel the water rushing over me while looking out at the majestic view. A girl could get used to this. *But she shouldn't.* I had started my plan well last night, but once Abraxas had opened his filthy mouth and hit me with the fire in his eyes, I was a goner. I scrubbed my skin harder, angry for so easily giving in to this man. This would certainly make things more difficult. I needed to get him to crave me, so I could ask for more. More books, more access around the palace, perhaps even permission to leave. I needed more resources to make my plan to escape, to help my brother.

I turned the water up to scalding temperatures, using the heat to drive away the helplessness rising in my chest. I didn't have a plan, not really. I didn't even know where my brother was being held. I assumed he was in the capital of Koron, but I couldn't be sure. *But Abraxas would know.* That was all the plan I had. Get that information from him. And if I kept giving in to his every whim in the bedroom, I didn't know if I would ever be able to extract it.

I took a steadying breath and looked out at the vast ocean as the burning water passed over me. The ocean here was always a deep grey, even in the sunlight, like today. The waves were treacherous and uncrossable, capped in white peaks that sliced across the rocks before them like swords. So different from the azure waters and calm tides of Niata. But as I stared out into the endless ocean, I could find that same calm, that same control I had at home.

No, the king was clearly still interested in me, at least for now. His words, *I'm not going to let you go.* They had seemed like playful banter at first, but now they seemed to mean more. I was sure that once he grew bored they wouldn't hold much weight, but for now, I could still play this game.

I stepped out of the shower and dried off. I dressed and saw how the blue-toned grey of my dress really did highlight my eyes, and the cut was flattering to my smaller chest and wider hips. I stepped back out into the room.

The king had not returned. I supposed I could get some snooping in. I saw now that there was another door between the main entrance and his bed as well. I tried it and it was locked. Perhaps it led off to some sort of meeting room, or somewhere for entertaining guests? Or maybe a study? How I wished I could see the books that it contained. But trying to break in when he was expected back didn't seem like a great idea.

I jumped as Ciara opened the door, and peaked her head in. "Your Highness, the king asks me to send his apologies, but he won't be able to return this morning. He asks that I escort you to your room." It seemed leaving me completely unattended in his private space wasn't his intention, so I stepped through the door to join Ciara and closed it behind me.

We walked in silence back to my room, and I craved the idle chatter she normally filled the air with.

When we had almost reached my room, I finally managed to speak, "Ciara, I apologize for the other day. I should not have—"

"It's alright, Your Highness," she said, but I barreled on.

"Pushed you. I was just feeling overwhelmed, but I should have never laid hands on you. It was not your fault, and it is unforgivable."

She looked at me with those large golden eyes, the biggest tell of her fae heritage. "It *is* alright, Your Highness. I too overstepped, I should not have..." she trailed off, perhaps hoping I had forgotten the hug she had bestowed on me. "By any means, there is nothing to forgive. I have had many encounters with fae much more brutal than yourself."

I suppose she was trying to make me feel better, but it really only made me feel worse to know she had been so mistreated. But I plastered on a smile, "You were only showing me kindness. You are one of the few who has since my arrival, and I truly appreciate that."

A true smile spread on her face, "Of course, Your Highness, you are my responsibility while you are a guest here." Guest indeed, but she seemed proud of her responsibility, so I smiled at her again.

"Should you have need of anything else, Your Highness,

please ask?" We had reached my door, and I moved to go inside, when a thought crossed my mind.

"Actually, Ciara, I need a contraceptive tea. Could you bring that from the apothecary?" I stuttered the words even though it was no secret what I had been doing with the king. But the smile dropped from her face.

"My Lady, the tea you drink every morning contains contraceptive herbs. I prepare it myself." She must have read the shock on my face, "Pardon, Your Highness, I thought you knew. If I should remove them—"

"No, no. Then everything is set. Thank you, Ciara."

She gave me a curt nod, and as I made to close my door, "Oh, the king wished me to tell you that you will be joining him for dinner at six this evening." Oh yes, that sounded like him—not a request.

"Is there anything else?" she asked meekly. I shook my head no and released her.

Pregnancy was rare among the fae, which is why children were considered so precious, and royal heirs even more so, the old bloodlines seeming to be ripe for infertility. This was one of the reasons so many half-fae existed, as humans seemed to be able to reproduce left and right, and a fae had a much easier time conceiving with a human than another fae. But even so, I had wanted to have the tea, as a precaution. But knowing that it had been given to me without my knowledge...An uneasiness settled in my stomach that threatened to shake all my thoughts loose.

Chapter 41

Tori

I wore the same gown he had given me this morning, knowing it would please him to see it. I had spent most of the afternoon sitting in front of my fire, willing my thoughts to settle, and pushing fears into the flames, incinerating them. Doing so had eaten up almost my entire afternoon and I missed lunch, so I was ravenous now that dinner had arrived. I floated down the long hall that led to the dining room, and a servant opened the door for me. I thought about what had been taking place here just a few nights ago.

Upon entering, I was surprised to find only the king seated at the head of the long table, with only one chair and setting out beside his own, placed at his right side. *It was to be just him and I?* That uneasiness crept back into my stomach, but I was able to shove it mostly away with logic this time. He'd had me riding his cock last night, I could handle being alone with him for a fully-clothed dinner. Unless of course, he intended to have me here as well... The thought curled that devious heat between my legs, but I swiped it away, focusing on the task at hand. This was an opportunity to have a real conversation with him, maybe even gain some information.

He stood as I approached, pulling out my chair for me. His eyes sparkled just the way I knew they would when he looked me over in my dress. The voice inside me sang at that.

"Don't you look lovely this evening? Our fashion suits you, little bird." I felt the heat rising in my cheeks and tried to hide it by ducking down into my chair. Before I could, he wrapped his arms around me and pulled me into a kiss. It was a soft kiss. Casual, as if this was something we did all the time: Ate dinner together, kissed like lovers, enjoyed each other's company. Even his small touch had my head spinning as he deposited me into my chair and returned to his.

My thoughts were scattering left and right, the waves of my mind roaring to life. How was he so able to distract me? I'd barely entered the room and he already had me on the defensive, working to calm my mind, and cool the spark that had been lit between my legs. *Damn him and his beautiful face, and his strong arms, and his throbbing...*

"Tell me what you are thinking, little bird." He took a bite of his meal and bore into me with those emerald eyes. He knew exactly what I was thinking about. "I heard you took a sleeping potion last night. I hope that nothing inappropriate is keeping you from restful sleep." His eyes gleamed like the trickster god of old, but he was also letting me know who was in charge. Of course, he knew I had taken one, I'm sure nothing happened in his castle without his knowledge.

I finally found my voice, "I've just been having bad dreams, and I wanted them to stop." Not a lie, not really.

The mischievousness in his eyes vanished, replaced by a serious look. He moved his hand as if he were going to reach for mine, but thought better of it and fluidly turned it into reaching for his wine goblet instead.

"With all that has happened, I am surprised everyone's nights are not plagued by nightmares." Interesting, considering he was likely the source of many people's nightmares. He pushed his lips together grimacing. "Oryx has developed potions that calm dreams, at least diminishing them. The sleeping potion can... well, I would prefer you not take it." He looked at me then, I thought I read true concern in his eyes. None of his usual iciness or snobbery.

I should have used that concern, allowed him some complacency to get closer to him. But my heart hammered. He couldn't possibly have known what I had done. But I was defensive, and I snapped, "If you are so concerned with the potions I take, why have I been given contraceptive tea my entire stay without my consent?"

Immediately that aristocratic look returned to his face as he drawled, "Every woman who stays in my castle is given contraceptive tea." This answer shocks me, my mind blank on reasoning. He read my face and continued, "I know you seem to enjoy ignoring this fact, but I am the king, and there are many who would hope to come to me and produce an heir. Not for love of my bloodline of course, but for their own power-hungry desires."

"Oh, and you must fuck every woman who stays in your castle?" I threw it at him like a dagger, but the only one cut by it was me.

He quirked an eyebrow at me, "Should I make it a habit to deny beautiful women who come to my door late at night seeking my *assistance?*" His smirk at his words only made my heart pound faster, blood rushing in my ears. I knew I was losing control of myself, but I couldn't stop. This unbelievable asshole.

I stood up from my chair, "Well, lucky for you, I have no desire to carry your heir, so you have nothing to worry about."

His eyes went pitch black, and I could feel the rage pouring off of him. He stood to his full height, the anger washing over me.

I guess that was the wrong thing to say. I did my best not to cower away from him, but kept my chin held high, despite every instinct in my body demanding I run—like prey.

He stalked over to me and grabbed the flesh of my upper arm, his grip so strong I felt it might leave bruises. He pushed me back so my ass was pressed against the edge of the table, and I could feel the heat rippling off his body. I heard the feet of the servants who had been in the room quickly shuffling out.

"That's not what it seemed like last night, when you opened that sweet cunt of yours to me so easily." My breath hitched, and my swirling anger coalesced into something obscene in my low belly, "When you let me fill you with my seed, then let it dry all over your thighs while you slept."

I shoved into him with my bad hand as hard as I could. It barely caused him to move at all. "You absolute *asshole*!" He released that low menacing chuckle that sent shockwaves through my whole body as he pressed his body into me, lowering his mouth to that spot below my jaw that had me throbbing.

"And I know you will do it again. You will let me spill my seed down your throat, on your skin, and into that warm cunt whenever I please. And you know why? Because you are mine, and every inch of you craves me more than you can understand, and you'll do anything to have me."

I tried shoving him off me again, but my injured arm didn't have the strength. I couldn't fight against him like my body knew how, and that pissed me off even more. I shoved my shoulder into him instead, ignoring the pain there. I went to bring my knee up to collide with him, but he pushed his leg between my thighs, the top of his thigh colliding with my core. The friction of it set me ablaze.

He had me effectively pinned against the table, and I couldn't fight him, so I threw the only thing I had at him, "Fuck. You."

"With pleasure, Princess. But you will submit to me first." He released me and I heard the tableware crash onto the floor behind me as he swept it away. I moved to strike him, my elbow coming up to meet his face. But he caught it instead and lifted me over the edge of the table. I crashed down on my back looking up at him. He lay one hand at my chest holding me down, as the other slid up my skirt, tracing that sensitive line along my inner thigh.

"Tell me you don't want this, and I will stop." His hand moved excruciatingly slow, every inch he moved toward the apex of my thighs drawing more desire from me. "Look at me and tell me you don't dream of my touch at night." He had finally reached my core, and he tugged my underwear to the side with commanding fingers. I longed to fight, to cut him with my words, but I was fae and I could not lie, not when the truth was so obvious as my hips bucked, begging for his touch. He chuckled as he pulled my legs up and my panties to my knees, resting my calves against his shoulders, and leaned forward to stretch me ever so slightly.

His hand returned to my core, but he teased me, only grazing my clit. I bucked my hips harder, my need overflowing, but he did not comply. "Tell me, little bird, tell me you would take my cock anywhere, anytime I demanded."

"Make me." His expression shifted from arrogance to pure lust, but that was the last I saw before he gripped my hips and spun me over, my feet now on the floor, bent over the table with my ass completely exposed.

"Such a bratty princess, perhaps it's time someone disciplined you for that." He kicked my feet further apart, but my legs were trapped by the underwear at my knees. Then I felt his hand collide with me in a resounding spank.

Oh gods, the flesh of my ass cheek stung where his hand had collided, blood flowing to it and throbbing. I tried to wiggle myself free, but it just resulted in another sharp slap, this one landing closer to my clit. "Every move earns you another," he said, and his hand landed on my ass again, the sound reverberating through the empty room.

Gods, my skin stung, and I could feel the welts he had left there. My face was burning with embarrassment. But the thought of his handprint left red and smarting on me caused my legs to shake. But I did not move. "Good girl." I was molten at his words, and it felt good, good to submit, good to let go. "Count for me."

"One."

Smack

"Two."

Smack

We continued, my skin growing more and more sensitive, his hand always finding a new place to strike. But even as the pain resounded, I could feel my core clench with desire, so by the time we had reached ten, I could feel my wetness trickling down my thigh. He finally laid his hand gently over my bullied skin, soothing the hurt, there. Then his other hand came up to wipe that wetness from my leg, and trace it back up, gently touching between my thighs.

"You are overflowing for me, little bird. Tell me what I want to hear, and I'll let you come." I felt him shift down, dropping to his knees. His hands stretched me apart, and I flushed again knowing I had no secrets from him now. I felt his tongue trace my inner thighs, up and up with antagonizing slowness. I moaned and shifted my hips, desperate for more pressure from him.

"Needy princess. You know what you have to do." I did need him. Every part of my body ached, like I was missing a part of myself. The teasing of his tongue was almost painful with how much it left me wanting.

"Abraxas, you can have me. Wherever, whenever you want." He finally slid his tongue to my core and pushed inside of me.

But I was beyond this, I needed more. "Abraxas, please, I need your cock, please."

He stood then, and I felt his hands trace over my skin and up my back. I heard him open his pants, but his other hand wrapped around my neck, and he pulled me up so my back was pressed against him. His lips grabbed the point of my ear, "I do so like hearing you beg, little bird. So, tell me what I want to hear, and I'll fuck you until you can't walk again." I knew what he meant, and I was so desperate for him, I didn't think twice.

"I'm yours, Abraxas, all yours."

He pushed me back down to the table, my breasts squashed against the hardwood, the sensation unbearable, "That's right. Mine." And then he thrust into me in a single motion.

I raked my nails over the table, and I knew I was leaving marks. He was not gentle, but that was exactly what I wanted. His hands locked around my hips, as he pulled me to him over and over again. Every sound I could imagine flew from my lips, and I could hear his own groans joining them. Every thrust sent the top of my thighs into the edge of the table, and rubbed my nipples agonizingly over the fabric that surrounded them. I could hear the remaining tableware clattering as the table rocked beneath us. His hand landed another slap on my ass, and my legs collapsed under me, the sensation too much. A purely male laugh left him, "Almost there, Tori, and then I'm going to fill up your warm cunt all over again." I barely heard him, as each stroke brought me closer and closer, his hips and skin crashing into me, his cock stroking that delicious place inside of me.

"Come, Tori, come all over my cock." I wouldn't, couldn't resist his command as every part of me released. I breached that place of starlight, and my skin shivered with each wave. I closed my eyes as my orgasm rode me, and the soft light of the room glowed golden through my eyelids. I felt him jerk, and his warmth filled me as he found his own release.

He traced his hands softly over my back and my tormented cheeks. He pulled himself free of me, and I felt the result of our joining go with him. Then he gently, so gently pulled my panties up from my knees, and covered me with my dress. I felt him place an arm behind my knees, and I collapsed into him. He lifted me with ease, and I laid my head against his warm, solid chest and inhaled the intoxicating smell of sweat, arousal, evergreens, and forest fires.

"I think I should have you for dinner every night." His eyes danced with mischief, and I felt my core tighten all over again. I realized that if I could just get my legs working, I would have him again, right here.

He chuckled and laid a soft kiss on my brow, "Soon, my little bird. But for now, I have something to show you." He carried me out of the dining hall, and down the hallway, and I let myself relax into him. I ignored how very dangerous it was that I had come to need him so much, so quickly.

Chapter 42

Tori

The sun was low in the sky, but Abraxas carried me to an awaiting carriage. He set me down inside like I might break at any moment. My legs were definitely not working. It seemed he had delivered on his promise. He knew it too, based on that look on his face.

"No reason to look so smug, Your Majesty."

"Oh, I can think of a few reasons."

I rolled my eyes, but knew I was smiling too. I let out a long, satisfied sigh.

"I suppose I could as well." I leaned forward and placed a gentle kiss on his lips. Seeing that look wiped off his face was the only reason I did, there were no other reasons. Now it was my inner voice's turn to roll their eyes at me.

He climbed in next to me, and we were off. I hardly noticed the ride, just enjoying the warmth of his body next to me. I realized I had dozed off when he gently shook me awake. I looked out the window and the sun settled over the cliffs outside the city. We stopped at the top of one that felt as if I had been there before. But that was impossible. Abraxas gently lifted me out again, carrying me towards the edge where it met the sea far below.

"Going to toss me off?"

I felt his chest rumble with laughter, "I thought about it a few times." He gently set me down and didn't release me until my legs were firmly planted. "I have something for you, I'll be right back." He headed back to the carriage, and I looked out at the sea. The low sun had set the mist ablaze and glowed a deep ochre. The wind whipped up from the waves and crashed over the top of the cliff. I let my arms stretch wide, the dress plastered against my skin— and I remembered.

I remembered the dreams I'd had in my recovery, of flying over these very oceans, the wind guiding me out and over the rocky islands in the distance. The wind blew harder, and I could almost imagine it lifting me off my feet.

"What are you thinking about?" The king had returned with a long, wrapped object in his hands.

"*On wings of freedom soaring high, Amidst the boundless, open sky, Where endless seas meet endless blue, The call of freedom rings anew.*" He paused and then smiled so that his whole face was alight, and it stole my breath away.

"I knew you would snoop." I threw a rude gesture at him, but he just held the wrapped object out to me. Carefully, I pulled at the strings holding it closed, and the cloth fell open, along with my mouth. Inside lay two of the most gorgeous swords I had ever seen. The steel had been treated so carefully that they almost shone blue, the single-edged blades curved with a beautiful organic shape. The hilts and pommels mirrored each other, and were woven out of fine dark steel, more like a rapier's blade than the shorter swords I was used to. The metalwork was exquisite, and clearly strong despite their fine size.

"Do you like them?" They were perfect, but as I reached to grab them, my left arm pulsed, and pain shot to my elbow. I pulled my hand back as if I had been bitten by a snake. The king's face sank into a frown.

"They are beautiful. But I won't be able to use them." My words hitched, my chest compressing. I had managed not to think about training, about the cohort. About what my injury would mean. My good hand flew to the scar on my left arm and understanding crossed Abraxas' face.

"Perhaps," he shifted, dropping the cloth holding the swords, and grabbing one in each hand. He gave them each an easy twirl, and my stomach roiled with jealousy. But then he brought the swords together, and with a small maneuver, I heard them slide and click together. He handed them back to me, but now they were one sword, the two single edges aligned to make a double-edged blade about the length of a broadsword, but still much lighter and finer. "But maybe it was beneficial you spent so many weeks training one-handed."

I took the sword with shaking fingers. But I held the grip strongly in my hand. It truly was a thing of beauty, still perfectly balanced even with the two swords knit together, the pommel of one extending above the other, to give the sword more length. I spun it around, going through the motions I had been practicing daily for weeks. I spun on my feet and faced the ocean again, the waters alight with the setting sun. Unfettered joy spread through me as I let the sword guide me, and then it hit me. I had seen this cliff before, through another's eyes. Through the eyes of young Abraxas, who had felt the same overwhelming joy.

I turned back to the king, "You had these made for me?" He nodded his head. "You would trust me with them?"

He wore a devious smile, "Well I'm going to have to do a thorough check to make sure you aren't hiding them anywhere when you come to visit me from now on." Arrogant ass.

"Why did you bring me here?"

He shrugged, "I thought this would be a sufficiently dramatic backdrop."

But I saw it then, the lie. This place was important to him. My sarcastic reply rose up to my lips, but I bit it back down. Instead, I approached him, rose up on my toes, and pressed my lips into his. I opened my mouth to him, but unlike all our other kisses, it wasn't a battle, but a soft embrace. I let myself linger there too long, before pulling back. I had come to need him in a dangerous way, but I knew he had come to need me even more. I could use that.

Chapter 43

Tori

I returned to training the following day. Avlyn arrived early and tossed some new practice swords at me before I had even fully opened the door. They immediately turned and headed down the hall. They were pissed and had every right. I ran after them.

"Avlyn, I'm sorry about everything." They didn't even look at me.

"Save it, Princess, we'll work it out in the arena."

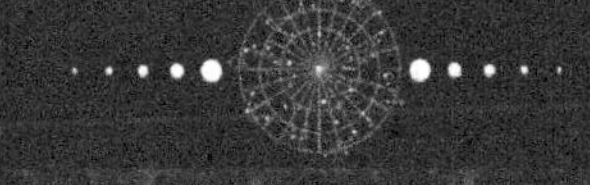

The swords they had given me were replicas of my new weapon, both in its combined and separate forms. I wrapped my right hand around the single sword. It wasn't heavy, but just the shift in my weight caused my left arm to throb. But I did my best to shove that away, as Avlyn already stood across from me, ready to duel.

They raised their sword, "Ready yourself," and then they struck. I was slow, much too slow, and barely managed to parry once before they struck me hard across the right arm.

I stumbled, but still, Avlyn was on me. I heard concerned mumbling from the crowd as I staggered to my feet, barely managing to block Avlyn. We had never dueled before, and I knew nothing about their style, but it didn't matter. A youngling could have beaten me at this point.

I tried to parry a strike, but my weakened muscles gave out before I could, and my body twisted, leaving me exposed. Avlyn mercilessly lunged again. The blow landed right across my scar, and a scream broke from me. I stumbled to my knees, clenching the injury.

"Commander, don't you think that's enough?" It was Kaleos' voice. I could feel the whole cohort shifting uneasily, but Avlyn pushed past him, sword raised.

"You almost died, you idiot. Don't you know what that would have done?" They swung at me again, and I braced, but I heard a crack as Kaleos struck Avlyn hard across the jaw from the side. They fell to their knees beside me, our faces only a few inches apart. "Don't you know what that would have done to him?" My heart stopped.

"Good thing you saved me."

They schooled their features to neutral, "Not sure I agree."

We locked eyes, neither of us backing down. "Why did you really have me duel him, Avlyn?"

"Why are you really fucking him, Princess?" I was taken aback.

"None of your fucking business."

"Oh, it very much is." But we both just stared at each other for a few more moments.

Finally, Avlyn broke, "Alright, all of you, back in lines.

Enough fun for one day. Oh, not you, Princess. You and Kaleos are on weapons maintenance today."

I heard Kaleos mumble, "Why me?"

"That's what you get for hitting a superior officer, Lieutenant. Now, don't make me tell you again.

WEAPONS MAINTENANCE WAS TEDIOUS. WE MOSTLY polished the practiced swords to prevent rust, but the small repetitive motions had my arm on fire, and despite my best efforts, tears leaked from my eyes, if only in frustration. Kaleos, gods bless him, mostly stayed silent as we worked.

That was until my rag slipped and I lurched my arm, sending pain radiating. I dropped the sword and clutched my scar. "I told the commander it was too soon to have you out here. We all saw you when you came out of the ocean. We all thought you were dead."

"Sorry to disappoint."

I heard Kaleos' sword smash to the ground. "Don't do that." I was shocked to find his normally handsome, happy face marred by anger. "Don't act like your life doesn't matter." I didn't know what to say, which he took as an invitation to continue.

"I remember when I first joined the army, it wasn't for the right reasons. I felt the same way, that maybe the best thing to do was go out in a blaze of glory. It made me a strong fighter, one of the best, because I didn't have any fear. What's to fear when you want to die anyway?" he sighed.

"But living like that isn't living, and it makes you weak in ways you can't realize until you are outside of it. I was lucky. Avlyn—the cohort—they helped me see, helped me see I was worth more than what I could sacrifice. I wish I could do that for you."

"You don't know me, Kaleos. I don't want to die." Not anymore. But the memories of the sleeping potion from the other night still curled its dark tendrils through me, a deadly promise.

"Don't I? I know that you handle a sword better than most soldiers I've ever trained with. I know that you tell hilarious stories if you don't get distracted. I know that I would never stand between you and a sweet treat." He grinned for a moment, but his face dropped to something more serious. "I know you would sacrifice yourself to save those you think need protecting, and I know that deep hurt in your eyes, Tori, because I had the exact same one for a long time." I could feel the tears rising up, and I turned away so he wouldn't see.

I asked him, "What happened, Kaleos?"

He sighed again. I wanted to let it drop, let the sadness and vulnerability pass me by like this conversation had never happened, but I felt my inner voice rise up, like he was wrapping his arms around me, and I felt safe. *You can do this. You can be brave.*

I reached out, and gently set my hand on Kaleos' back. It seemed the physical contact was what he needed.

"I grew up on the edge of the kingdom with my mother, a fae, and my human father. We didn't have much, but it was enough, and we were happy. I remember being happy." He paused, "Then one day, she was just gone. No note, nothing. I blamed myself for a long time. I thought maybe I wasn't good enough, I thought about what I could have done to make her stay. I trained, I became a soldier, I guess to prove I could be strong. But I was so fragile." I felt his breath hitch, and I wrapped my arms around him. Well, I tried. He was too bulky for me to really achieve it.

But he smiled then, "Like I said, I found the cohort, I found a family and I learned to live again. I even found this annoying fae sister who can't seem to keep herself out of trouble." That wide grin was back, but it was like he had punched me right in the chest. I couldn't hold his gaze.

"Kaleos, I–"

"Look, I know it's complicated. Maybe you don't even want to be here. But know that we want you to be here."

"I'm sorry. I'm sorry I worried you."

"Just don't do it again, alright?" he was still smiling. How could he do it? How could he forgive me so easily? How could he hold enough happiness for all of us, even inside that massive body?

"You know, I think you might be the bravest person I know."

He gave me another congenial laugh, "Not brave enough to face the king should anything ever happen to you again."

"What does he have to do with this?" Kaleos shot me a very knowing look, and I averted my eyes again.

"Just know I'm not getting friendly with you *just* to get in my future queen's good graces."

"That's not going to happen, Kaleos."

"Mm-hmm." I knew he was still staring at me, but luckily, the commander saved me from this line of conversation.

"I don't see much polishing going on over there!" Avlyn's shout smacked us both up the back of the head. We both quickly moved back to our work.

"I don't think Avlyn will be forgiving me any time soon."

"Give the commander some time. They've been overprotective of the king for as long as I've known them. Guess I can't blame them, the king did practically raise them ever since they were found here." I raised an eyebrow at Kaleos.

"Maybe it's not my place to say, but it's not a secret, so...well when Avlyn was a baby, they were found right here on this beach in a basket, washed up to shore. They never knew where they came from, but it seems the army took them in as their own."

I peered over at Avlyn, their tall form looming over the rest of the soldiers on the beach. It made me think of the memory of them sitting on Abraxas' shoulders, watching the troops train, and I remembered how much I didn't know.

But Kaleos and I resumed our work, an easy silence between us. I felt a piece of the armor I had held around my heart slip away, and I didn't even try to pick it back up.

Chapter 44

Tori

After my talk with Kaleos, I decided to start training the cohorts in hand-to-hand. They had some training in it, of course, but in the Pearl Kingdom, we had developed highly precise styles in movements that were unlike anything on the continent. I had kept that knowledge to myself, but it didn't feel right to do that anymore.

I ran small groups through the movements during breaks at first, Kaleos obviously being the first to join me. But quickly others joined in, and Avlyn eventually let me lead the sequences at the beginning of training, 'as a warmup'. Doing these movements without the weight of a sword was also much easier on my injury, and it helped me build my muscles back up with much less pain.

It seemed that since that first day, Avlyn and I had agreed to some sort of truce. But I found myself seeing them less and less. They had more excuses for missing meals. But even with this truce, they never let up on my weapons training, and I found myself crying on the beach more than I ever would have thought possible.

Even going back to one-handed, pain would still radiate through my arm with extended movements, or on bad days, just any movement. But my cohort never teased me, at least not about that. They never commented on the various hisses I emitted during training, or the tears that leaked constantly from my eyes. But I did find them being gentle with me, never pressuring me to duel, and Raula had even taken up massaging my bad shoulders and arm during our water breaks.

I'd convinced Abraxas to train with me in private, I told myself it was to help build up my strength and skills. *That was definitely the reason.* Abraxas had agreed readily, but maybe only because our training sessions often quickly devolved into a very different kind of fighting.

"You're off balance," Abraxas scolded me as he easily blocked my attempted strike.

"Yeah, I know that. It's the whole issue," I hissed back. We had been training for almost an hour, and I was a mess of sweat, and my arm ached terribly. But unlike on the beach, I refused to cry in front of Abraxas.

"Your arm won't ever have the range of motion you want, so you need to compensate with your other side, not leave an opening." He rushed at me again with all his speed, not holding back. In an instant, my sword went flying through the air, landing dramatically pointed down in the training room floor.

I turned my back to him, looking at my sword. A bad move in a fight, but I knew what he would do next.

The next moment I felt him pressed up against my back, his sword held across my throat, "I thought you knew better than to expose your back to the enemy?"

"Oh? But I thought this was your favorite side of me?" I rubbed my ass into him and felt him startle. It wasn't much, but it was just enough for me to free myself from his grasp and ram my elbow into his stomach. He groaned, and I swept his feet out from under him as he recovered.

He lay flat on the floor, and I slowly stepped over him, straddling his waist and pinning him down. He didn't resist, only gripped my hips with his hands, "Not a technique I'd recommend on the battlefield."

"But an effective one, wouldn't you agree?" I ground into him, and he met me with equal heat.

"Just promise me you won't use that against any criminals you find on your next patrol."

I'd been quite enjoying grinding into him, but I stopped dead. "I thought I was forbidden from that after the last time?"

"Tori," he sat up, so our faces were inches apart, "The best thing for you, for your arm, will be to continue with the cohort and that's not just training."

I didn't know what to say to that, so I said something that I hadn't thought about since I was in Niata, "It's not very princessly behavior, being out with the army on patrol."

Abraxas laughed at that, really laughed, "When has that ever stopped you before?"

Plenty of times. But now, that seemed so long ago, when I hadn't been allowed to do anything but train with the soldiers of Niata. A few times I had managed to convince a captain to take me out on patrol, but I had eventually been caught, and that had ended quickly. It had been one of the few times my father had left a lasting mark on me, breaking my wrist.

I rubbed it absentmindedly. It had healed long ago, but that didn't stop my body from feeling the phantom pain.

"Tori..." Abraxas looked at me with those soft eyes I couldn't stand, so I shoved him down to the dirt, despite how it made my arm twinge.

"Later, Your Majesty. We have a duel to finish."

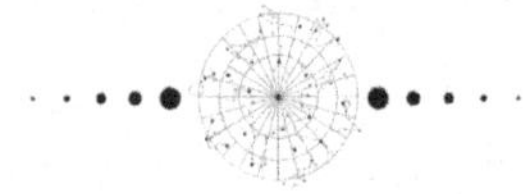

It seemed Ciara and I were also back on good terms, her warm chatter filling my mornings whenever she brought me breakfast. But today she was unusually silent.

I approached her slowly as she busied herself fluffing some pillows in my room, "Ciara, what's the matter?"

She continued fluffing for a few moments more, when she finally said, "Just some bad news from back home."

I walked over to her, placing a gentle hand on her back, as she had once done for me. She sighed, and I saw her face laced with tears, "Does it ever feel like no matter what you do, you can't escape your past?" More tears fell from her eyes. I was frozen. After our encounter before, I didn't want to hug her, didn't know if I could. But I felt that voice inside me swell, *he* was the only part of me that knew how to be soft. I imagined he lay his hand on my own, encouraging me.

"Ciara, I know all too well what you mean." I had never voiced this before, not even to Jun. We had come to an understanding to never speak of it. But I thought of Kaleos, of the cohort, and all their kindness. For a moment I even thought about Abraxas but shoved that away. But for Ciara, I could be kind.

"When I was younger—well, I was a fool, as we all are. I craved more than anything to be accepted by my father, for him to see me as worthy. But I see now, no matter what I do, I can't change how he feels." Tears leaked from my eyes now as well, I couldn't believe how much I'd cried in these last weeks. But I didn't shove it away, "But I couldn't see that then and I...well I tried to kill myself over it." Ciara's eyebrows shot up, but she didn't say anything, "I was lucky, my brother saved me, and he gave me the strength to keep going. But not a day goes by that I don't think of it, the helplessness trying to drag me under. And that was over a century ago."

"Your Highness, I'm sorry."

But this wasn't about me, "I'm saying this, well I guess because if even a spoiled princess can become completely lost in it, of course someone who has been through what you have has every right to be."

Ciara reached out and squeezed my arm now, "Tori, I've never thought of you like that." But I shook my head.

"I've seen how strong you are, Ciara. And you are good. I'll help you in any way that I can."

A new, dark look crossed her eyes. "I'm not good, Tori." She looked away from me then, and I had to admit this confused me, but she looked back with that warm smile replacing her sadness, "and you have already done enough. Thank you." She gave my arm one final squeeze, and then I saw that wickedness return to her grin, "Now tell me, how much longer am I going to have to keep waiting for you to sneak back to your room in the morning for me to bring you breakfast? I'd rather just end this whole thing and bring it straight to the king's room." She winked at me, and I screwed up my face which made her laugh.

"One of these days you'll give in, Your Highness." I didn't like how at that moment, her words felt very right. I had thought revealing the secret I had held so long would have left me anxious, but I felt myself feeling unusually light. I could hear Jun's voice in my head, *I'm proud of you, sister.*

Chapter 45

Tori

I spent the next week out with my cohort again, freely walking the streets of Xyr. We made our way through the city, and down the long main road, I could see the docks in the distance. A tiny part of me whispered this was my chance, but a small shopkeeper waved me over, asking for help in hanging a new lantern, and the thought drifted away.

We spent the morning as we always did, finding citizens who needed our assistance in one way or another, and delivering. But as our group was helping load barrels of dried meat into a wagon, a young soldier, Klys, ran down the street toward us.

"Kaleos! You're needed outside the city, urgently!" Klys shouted.

"What's all this?" Noki popped his head out from behind the wagon.

Klys bent over, his hands on his knees, panting from his sprint. But through his labored breathing, he said, "Reports of an attack...bandits from the Barrens...Lady Bogata's...closest cohort."

Kaleos snapped to attention, but not before his eyes had flicked to me. I was a liability, and we both knew that. But he seemed to decide it was worth the risk and commanded us into lines.

We marched at a breakneck pace out of the city and past the outer wall. It was still winter, and snow covered much of the land outside the city. Just outside the wall, a small stable run by the castle held a few horses waiting for us, and my heart dropped.

"I've never ridden before." Horses weren't common in Niata except for hard labor.

"Then you're with Raula," Kaleos yelled. I stood next to the orc woman and she practically tossed me up onto the saddle, then landed behind me, snapping the reigns.

Raula wrapped an arm around me as the horse took off at a gallop, which was unnervingly fast.

"Grip with your knees, don't just bounce in the saddle." I did as instructed and it did make it easier, until my legs were burning. But soon we crested one of the main hills surrounding the city, and our target lay in sight.

A great field, free of almost any snow, grew grass that was a deeper green and taller than any of its neighbors. Winter wheat, I had learned from Lady Bogata at some point during our many hours of idle chatter. I fluttered in the wind, but it was covered in clouds of smoke that billowed from the manor house in the distance.

"Fuck, these bandits were bold," Raula spoke behind me.

Kaleos rode up by our side. "How did they get this far into the kingdom without detection?" she asked.

"It doesn't matter," Kaleos replied, "All that matters is we get anyone still alive out safely. Stay in formation, be on the lookout, and don't hesitate to strike."

We rode up to the house but saw no one. The grounds were eerily quiet, and I worried we were too late. But the cohort quickly dismounted, and Kaleos kicked open the front double doors of the mansion.

Smoke billowed out, and Kaleos shouted orders, sending us into different parts of the manor, "You three, top floor, get anyone you find still alive, out."

I hurtled up the two flights of stairs to the top landing, Noki and Raula close behind. They ran to the right, and I took the left, where only one set of doors lay.

I threw open the doors, and smoke engulfed me. I kneeled down, closer to the ground, and saw her lying on the floor prone. Lady Bogata's soft auburn hair sprawled out across the floor, blood surrounding her.

I crawled to her, trying my best to avoid the smoke. I flipped her gently, and she moaned softly. Blood ran down from a huge gash on her face.

Her eyes fluttered, "Princess Tori? Am I dead?"

I suppose I was not the sight one expected to see when being rescued, "Not yet, My Lady. Let's go."

I grabbed Lady Bogata under her arms and tried to lift her. She groaned, and I saw the large gash on her forehead still wasn't healing. She stumbled and pulled on me, and my arm shot through with pain. I gritted my teeth.

"The others, are they safe?" She was barely audible over the crunch of wood as the house tried to collapse around us.

"They will be, come on." She shuffled her feet, and we made our way down the stairs, but with every step I nearly dropped her as my arm lurched. I bit my tongue so hard it bled, but I kept moving.

We made it down the stairs when I heard Kaleos. A moment later, he was on her other side, lifting her, and we managed to stumble down the rest of the way out of the house.

I saw the rest of our group outside, several helping servants and other household members, setting them down outside the danger of the burning house. We placed Lady Bogata with the others, and I knelt down to see the gash in her head still bleeding.

I looked her over quickly and saw an iron shackle clamped around her wrist. I grabbed a beat up sword from a horse nearby and used my fae strength to pry it open just enough for her to slip her hand out. Her wound immediately started to knit itself together. She blinked up at me in the harsh sun, and her face went ashen.

"Princess Tori, you can't be here."

"It's alright, Lady Bogata, you and your household are safe now." I held her shoulder. She was ice cold, going into shock.

"No, don't you see! They are still—"

An arrow flew past my face, barely missing both of us. My head snapped up, and I saw them. Dozens of men clad in thick furs rose up out of the wheat fields where they had hidden. They had us surrounded.

"Formation, now!" shouted Kaleos. The cohort lined up, shields locked together, swords drawn. But I still couldn't hold a shield. Gods, I was so useless— a weak link. I lined up behind them, the only thing I could do. "Stay with the wounded, Tori," Kaleos yelled. Yes, I could do that. I fell back, my sword at the ready.

The bandits closed in, and arrows flew, sending resounding knocks through the shields of the cohort as they hit.

"Hold!" Kaleos yelled. But the bandits immediately ran for us, they covered the distance with shocking speed, and in only a few breaths they were on us. Swords flashed from behind the shield wall. But they outnumbered us. Normally that wouldn't have been enough to break them up, but these men moved as a unit. They were trained with military precision, and quickly, the fighting devolved into direct combat.

I crouched with the wounded, awaiting my moment. Raula took on three men at once, and I found an opening. She positioned them, so their backs were to me, and I leapt out and struck one across the back. He didn't wear armor, and blood dripped to the ground. He spun, seeming unfazed, but he was unprotected, and this time I didn't hesitate to run him straight through his gut. He fell to his knees, clutching his stomach, but I watched in horror as even that wound started to knit itself back together. A fae? I didn't stop to ponder as I sent my sword through his heart, my arm aching with the force.

I turned to help Raula, but an arrow narrowly missed me again. I saw my assailant across the yard, notching another. His great bow was almost as tall as I was. If he landed a clear shot, I wouldn't be getting back up. He pulled the string back, ready to release.

I did not have a shield, but training with Abraxas had made me fast. The arrow flew and I swung my sword, striking it from the air. Another flew, and I slashed through it, each time closing the distance between us. I let my focus drive away my pain, until I was only a step away from my opponent. I swung my sword, knocking the bow from his hands, and used the momentum to spin around, sending my sword straight across his neck. A moment later, his head fell to the ground, a shocked expression still locked on his face.

But as I looked at him, his long hair pulled back and revealed long pointed ears. I looked at the rest of the bandits, and yes, most of them were tall, lean, and moved with a grace that a human could never match. A group of fae bandits? It was unheard of, what was going on?

"Princess Tori!" Lady Bogata screamed, and I turned, to see the largest of them all barreling at me. I swore he hadn't been there just a moment before. His face was mostly covered, but I saw a long white scar running over his left eye. I swung my sword to parry him, but I was off balance. He took advantage and knocked me to the ground, his free hand colliding with my injury so hard I thought my arm would split open again. I dropped my sword, and he kicked it away.

I fell to the ground, seizing, when his great arms wrapped around me. I struggled to free myself, to no avail.

A piercing whistle filled my ears, as he called to his men. "I've got her, fall back."

What? I doubled my efforts to escape, but he just laughed in my ear.

"Not so dangerous without your claws?" He laughed again, but then groaned and released me. I fell to my knees but spun to see a sword had pierced his side, Kaleos on the other end of it.

But he didn't hesitate long. He spun, the sword still lodged in his stomach, and pulled it free of Kaleos' grip. He kicked Kaleos hard across the face, and he crumpled to the ground.

"Filthy half-breed." He pulled the sword out, and I saw the wound quickly knit itself together. He turned the sword on Kaleos, so I launched myself at him. It was like trying to knock down a mountain, but gods be damned if I didn't try.

It distracted him from Kaleos, but not much else. "Fucking female, enough from you." He punched me so hard across the face that my vision went black, and I fell back down. Blood filled my mouth, but I heard from the distance, "Commander, reinforcements from the north. We have to move."

I felt the Commander grab me around my waist. "Head back to base. Take the half-breed as well, leave the rest."

I saw two men grab Kaleos' arms and drag him behind us. The commander covered my mouth with his hand, and I bit down until I tasted his blood. "Fucking bitch."

He grabbed my neck, squeezing it until I thought my bones would crack, and everything went black.

I woke up in the dark, to the smell of rot and damp. My wrists burned, and I yanked at them through the haze of my mind. Each motion caused the burning to surge, but the pain brought me back to consciousness.

My wrists were bound to a wall, extended outward like wings, with iron shackles. Every movement I made drove the iron into my skin, and I could hear the flesh sizzling. I got my feet underneath me, removing some of the strain, but the shackles were tight, and still my skin burned.

A moan sounded across from me, and I saw Kaleos, shackled much as I was. He was also bound in iron, but his flesh was pink from the iron, instead of burned like mine. We were chained in a small, dark room, but it didn't seem like a dungeon. The walls were smooth, and I could just make out carvings on the wall that held Kaleos. The relief showed a pair of dragons flying over our world. One spouted dragonfire, consuming all in its wake. But the other bestowed magic, and life grew uninhibited from its claws. Life and Death, the first gods. So perhaps we were in an old temple, not that it really mattered. The only light came from a crack in the wall far overhead, and through the tiny window on the door to the room.

"Kaleos! Kaleos, wake up." Speaking caused my jaw to click, still sore from where I had been punched, the iron slowing my healing. He groaned again, so at least I knew he was alive. For now.

A plan, I needed plan. I tried to focus on my breathing, but my arm and wrists were on fire, too much for me to calm down. This was all too similar to when I had been in Niata, trapped in my own dungeon. But I had fought then, and I would fight now. I had to get Kaleos out of here.

Then the door swung open, and several men stepped inside. They were led by the man I only knew as the commander. His long black hair was pulled back into a ponytail, and the white scar across his left eye seemed even more stark in the low light.

"Glad to see you are awake, gorgeous. Now the real fun can begin." He motioned for one of his cronies to approach me, and I saw him draw an iron knife from his belt, his only weapon. He approached me, and I let my voice shake, "Please...please don't hurt me..." The male's grin widened into something disgusting, and he drew closer, into my trap.

When he was just one step from me, I pushed into my wrists, the burning only driving me harder. I kicked the knife out of his hand and used the motion to lift my other leg all the way up over his shoulder and around his neck. I crushed his throat, and brought my other leg around, squeezing him between my thighs until I saw his eyes popping out of their sockets. He clawed my legs, but I held until his face was red and he grew weak.

"Let him go, Princess." It was the commander. He had a knife held to Kaleos' throat. "Drop him or the half-breed is dead." For a long moment I held his gaze, but then I released my legs, and the man between us fell to the floor, gasping. I lowered my feet back to the ground, the burning in my wrists was nothing compared to the rage in my heart.

"They said you would be a challenge, but I didn't think you could actually fight." The man I had held crawled over to the commander, but he looked down at him with contempt. "Get out of my sight before I finish what she started." The man lurched out of the cell, and the commander lowered his knife from Kaleos.

"Perhaps we should start again. I am Commander Luxos and I hope our time together can be quite short, Princess."

"The pleasure is all mine, Commander Luxos. Now perhaps you could remove me from these shackles so that I could introduce myself to you properly?"

He smirked at me, "I think not, gorgeous. But as I said, we

don't need to draw out our time together. Just show me your magic and we can be done."

I was shocked. I thought perhaps a ransom, but this... "I don't have any power. I feel like I keep repeating this."

"Come now, Princess. Don't be shy. The sooner you show me, the sooner this can all be over." I didn't much like the sound of that.

"Listen, Commander, it's obvious you were dropped on your head a few times as a youngling, so I'll repeat myself. I do not have any magic. You think I would still be stuck here like this if I did?"

"I think you're a smart girl. You know what this information is worth."

"Indeed, so who is paying you for it?"

His face dropped into a dark shadow, and unlike his companion, he didn't hesitate as he closed the distance between us and held the iron knife to my throat. "Last chance, Princess. You can show me what you're hiding, or I can cut it out." I spit on his face.

He stepped back, and slowly wiped the spit from his cheek. Then faster than I could see, he slammed his fist into my stomach, so I doubled over as the air was driven from my lungs. My wrists burned and my stomach heaved, but still, I managed a, "Fuck you." He pressed down on my arm, right at the seam of my injury. I screamed then, an uncontrolled wail as lightning shot through my whole body. I closed my eyes, and a golden light danced behind my lids, a cry for help.

"Stop...it..." It was Kaleos, barely conscious. *Shut up, you idiot!* But he got his feet under him, and stared down Luxos, "Get your hands off her." He snarled, the very image of his feral fae side, but it was no use. He was just as trapped as I was.

But Luxos released me, and my pain subsided. He walked to Kaleos and gripped his hair so tight the skin of his face pulled back.

"Unfortunately, I have been told not to damage you permanently. I have no such instructions for the mutt, however." He held the knife high, and before I could scream, slammed into Kaleos' stomach.

"*Kaleos*!" Luxos pulled the dagger out, and blood ran down Kaleos' thighs. Too much blood, it was far too much.

"The iron should slow even his pathetic healing. I don't think he has long, but he will suffer. I'll be waiting, gorgeous." He left the room, slamming the door. One guard remained, and he slid down the opposite wall to his seat, seeming content to ignore us. Kaleos groaned.

"I always seem to be getting hurt with you." Kaleos tried to grin, but his teeth were clenched.

"Shut up, you idiot! Conserve your energy." I was crying. I was always fucking crying and I was so tired of it.

Control, Tori, you need to control yourself. But I couldn't. My heart was erratic, along with my breath, and watching the life bleed out of Kaleos only made it worse. I looked to that ocean in my mind, and godsdamnit I tried, but it was a hurricane where I couldn't tell the difference between the ocean and the sky.

Then I remembered something Abraxas had told me, on our journey here. *Rage will set you free.* I let the helplessness I felt at watching Kaleos burn away, the hurricane of my mind turning into a firestorm. I wouldn't let those around me be hurt, not again. This was Luxos' fault, and he and his men would all pay.

I pressed into my shackles, the pain adding fuel to the fire. I wrenched at them, and either the wall would give, or my bones would, but I wouldn't stop until I found out.

"Tori, don't..." But then Kaleos' eyes went wide as the wall under my shackles cracked, dust falling as I ripped them free.

The guard didn't have time to stand before I was on him. I slammed my shackle into his face. I did it again and again and again until nothing was left of his head but a bloody pulp.

"I think you got him," Kaleos mumbled. His voice and pale face snapped me out of whatever trance I had been in. I ran over to him, and planted my feet against the wall, gripping his shackle. My fingers burned, but I barely felt it as I ripped him free. He collapsed to the floor. I ripped cloth from the pants of the very dead guard and used it to bind Kaleos as best I could. Then I grabbed his sword, holding it in one hand.

I gritted my teeth and slung my injured arm under Kaleos and did my best to lift him.

"Better just to leave me, Tori."

"I thought I already told you to shut up." The door hadn't been locked, and we inched along the hallway. I listened as best I could. We were clearly in the lower level of an ancient stone complex. Where? I had no idea. Light and the sound of voices peeked around the next corner. I gently set Kaleos down and leaned around the corner.

Four more guards sat at a table, dice and coins scattered about. I should have stayed and listened, tried to learn something, but I was far past that now. I charged and swung the too-heavy sword I carried straight through the first's neck. I spun as blood flew and jabbed straight into the heart of the next. The second two had flung themselves back, one falling off his chair and trapping himself. I went for him next but the fourth caught my sword with his own. I swung at him again and again, but he was a decent fighter and met my attacks.

Each strike moved my shackles, irritating the weeping burns on my wrists, but I moved using the speed and strength I had gained back these last few weeks. Soon he was falling behind, his defense slowing, until I managed to break through and slash across his thigh and blood flew against the stone wall. He fell and I knew I had struck true; he only had a moment to live.

But as I spun, pain hit me across my ribs. The last man had sliced me. I stumbled, and he swung again but I managed to block him as sparks flew. I knew our fighting was too loud, more would come soon. I let my rage surge and I moved fast— faster than I ever had. In three strikes, I'd caught the fae through his chest and his final breath left him.

I ran back to Kaleos, trying to hoist him up, but he couldn't stand on his own. He was mumbling something, his voice so soft, "Maybe one of these days I'll rescue you..."

"We are getting out of here," I promised him.

"Maybe I'll get that cute healer." Not only could he not walk, he was also delirious. My side still bled freely, the wound refusing to close with the iron still impeding my healing. My head spun, but we couldn't stop now.

I only had one option. Kaleos was bigger than me, but I had ripped us free from our dungeon. I could carry him. It would have been easiest to put him over my shoulder, but his wound didn't allow it. Instead, I scooped him up under his knees and back, ignoring the strain in my arm, and the way my vision tunneled as I lifted.

"Embarass...ing," Kaleos' voice was even weaker now. I slowly hobbled up the stairs, and I felt the air grow cooler, less stagnant. I listened again, hoping to hear any would be assailants.

But I was surprised to hear the clashing of swords, the moans and screams of a battlefield. Had a rescue come for us?

I nearly bumped into the back of twenty guards as I rounded a corner but managed to backtrack. I should have set Kaleos down and fought them. But my knees collapsed under me, and we both slid to the floor. Luckily, they were facing the other way, swords drawn, staring at a closed door. I could hear it louder, the clashing of swords, just beyond that portal.

"Captain, how many are we facing?" I could hear the man's voice shake.

"Just one, but, sir, he's not a man. He's a demon, he—" The

door shook violently, and the men fell silent. Their grips tightened on their swords.

"Stick to formation, we have the advantage, don't forget—"

The door was engulfed in flames that glowed an eerie, bright emerald green, as it exploded off the hinges. And from the heart of them flew Abraxas, his hair and face covered in blood. His eyes glowed that same deep green with fire and rage. I could feel the dark starting to claim me, but I couldn't take my eyes off him, even if he was too fast to see. Half the men were already dead, and it had only been two breaths. The rest scrambled to block or to flee, but the flames found them, and I could smell the charred flesh as even more fell under his blade. Only one man remained, and Abraxas grabbed him by the throat and slammed him into the wall. The crack of bones against stone would have been sickening if I hadn't been using every ounce of my energy to stay conscious.

"Where is she?" His voice was like thunder, deep and eternal. The man gasped, trying to free himself to no effect. Abraxas only squeezed harder, "Where...is...she?"

"Down...hall..." The man's neck snapped under Abraxas' hand, and he dropped him to the floor. He spun, but our eyes met, and suddenly all the fire was gone.

"I'm here, little bird."

"Abraxas, how did you find me?" I was also delirious.

"I told you; I always know where you are."

"Could have gotten here sooner then." He didn't laugh, just moved to pick me up. "No, Kaleos, he needs healing, I'm fine, Abraxas..." The dark was so close now.

Abraxas clutched me to his chest, "You're safe now, Tori. You are both safe." And I was gone.

Chapter 46

Abraxas

I'd let her get hurt again.

I cradled her in my arms as we rode back to Xyr. She slipped in and out of consciousness, as I held her tight against me. That she had achieved so much with iron wrapped around her wrists spoke to her strength and her actions had saved Kaleos' life. Of that, I had no doubt.

Unfortunately, between me and her, there had been no one left alive to interrogate. But with so many fae in the group, there was no way this was a simple group of raiders from the Barrens, despite what their clothes and weapons suggested. Something much more nefarious had happened, right under my nose. Avlyn was right, I had let these weeks of bliss make me sloppy, and it had almost cost me everything—again.

Tori stirred in my arms, a soft whisper escaping her lips, "Abraxas..."

"I'm here, little bird." I placed my cheek on the top of her head, but she shook, spinning her head around.

"Kaleos, is he alright?"

"Yes, you saved him." I nodded to the wagon beside us. The

rest of the troops had caught up to me as I had carried Kaleos and Tori out of that abandoned temple. Kaleos was unconscious but stable as we made our way back.

Tori relaxed into me, and I reveled in the feeling of her there, safe with me.

"The others, Lady Bogata?"

"All safe, and not much worse for wear. You are the one I am concerned about." I carefully lifted her wrist. The skin was healed where the shackles had burned her, but I could still see the raw skin. Her wounded side had closed almost immediately once they had been removed. She twisted her arm, observing the marks.

"Not so different from the marks you left on me when we first met." Shame filled me. She turned to see my face, her eyes laughing, but that smile faded. "Abraxas, I was just joking."

I didn't answer, I couldn't. Instead, I just tucked my riding cloak around her as the wind picked up. She was right, of course. I had done the same— treated her the same. I had been so desperate to have her, that I truly had been her captor. And right now, that same instinct, that same desire to lock her away begged me to keep her safe, keep her mine.

But I had already driven her to the edge once with my control and I knew, despite how much I wanted it, that I couldn't do that again. The realization felt like a ticking clock, counting down my moments with her.

"Probably another hour to Xyr yet. Rest, Tori, I'll watch over you." At least, for now.

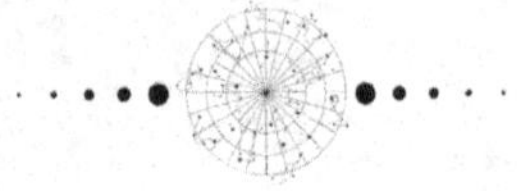

Oryx had fussed over Tori but deemed that she would likely be fine with a good night's rest. Kaleos, on the other hand, needed more attention. Tori had sat with him through most of it, holding his hand as Oryx cleaned his wound and dressed him.

I'd tried to give them space, despite the seething jealousy that filled my heart when Tori would hold his hand and stroke his hair gently. I found myself down at the beach, dueling more than I had in decades just to keep my mind occupied.

When Kaleos was near the end of his recovery, I approached the barrack where he was being kept, to hear them both laughing.

"You know, I'm happy to go harder on you in our duels if it means you get to spend more time here with *him*." Tori drew out the last word, all teasing.

"Tori, you have already cut my ego down to the size of a pixie's nut. I don't need any more damage, thank you very much."

They laughed again, and I thought about how I had never heard her laugh like that with me.

I rounded the corner and Kaleos grew pale, and despite myself, I enjoyed seeing it. Tori stood, suspicion growing in her eyes.

"It's time for your debrief, Lieutenant Kaleos. Princess, I'm afraid we will need privacy. "

"Why? I was there too."

"It's important to get separate stories, I'll come get yours when I'm done here." We hadn't discussed it yet, what she might have seen. It was actually the longest I had been without her since that night of Lupercalia.

She held my stare, but then to my surprise, gave me a nod. She squeezed Kaleos' hand one more time and left the room.

I sat down in the chair she had vacated. To Kaleos' credit, he held his expression neutral, but I could smell the fear rolling off of him.

"Your Majesty, I—"

"First, Lieutenant Kaleos, I would like to thank you." He froze. "Thank you for being there with her, defending her during the attack. I know you wouldn't be in the state you are if you hadn't done everything you could for her."

He nodded, "Of course, Your Majesty, anything for T—for the princess." He was being cautious with me, as he should. And that was about all the kindness I could muster for a male who still had Tori's scent all over him.

"Tell me what you remember from the temple."

"Honestly, not much. We were held underground, but after I was stabbed, I can't recall much. I remember Tor— Her Highness ripping herself free of the wall, and then me as well. She beat the guard to a pulp and then dragged me out, but that's the last thing that is clear."

I leaned back in my chair. *My little bird of prey.*

"But I know those weren't bandits, sir. The leader—they called him Commander Luxos. It was a military operation, no doubt about it. At the manor, they were after her. She was the goal all along."

I had suspected as much, but who was behind it all? I knew most of Hadeon's men, and Commander Luxos wasn't one of them. It wasn't impossible, but why be so underhanded when he could just come here straight to her?

"Did they want something from her specifically?"

"Yes, he asked to see her magic. That's why they stabbed me, to try to elicit a reaction."

"And?"

He paused then, for far longer than was appropriate for an officer, but said, "No. She was strong, no doubt about it, but I don't think it was magic."

I stood, but Kaleos spoke again, "How did they know she would be there, Your Majesty?"

"I don't know, but I will not rest until I find out." I strode out of the room.

Tori waited for me a few hallways down. She leaned against the wall, arms crossed, her steely eyes narrowed.

"No need to scowl, Princess. I left Kaleos just as I found him. Now, let's go to my room for your debrief."

She raised her eyebrows at me, "And here I thought you actually wanted to talk."

"Trust me, Princess, we have plenty to talk about."

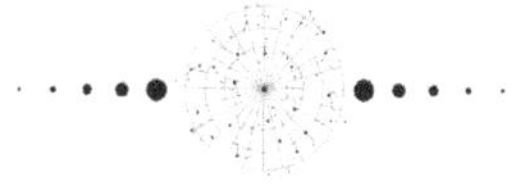

Tori sat across from me on my couch. She held her hands clasped together. I handed her a small glass of malt ambrosia, and she made a face when she took a sip.

"This is disgusting."

I laughed, "An acquired taste, certainly. Now, tell me what happened."

She swirled the liquid in the glass, then took another tiny sip, her face still shifting into that puckered look. She told me of her capture, of the demand to display her magic, of ripping the iron from the walls. She told me about killing the guards and making her way upstairs with Kaleos.

She sighed, "I don't know how many more times I can say this, but I don't possess magic. I've always been the fighter; Jun was the artist. I was the body, he was the mind, and we worked together." She swirled her drink again and looked at me. I readied myself to answer her questions, but they didn't come.

"What do you remember after that?"

"Not much, whatever had been driving me was wearing off. I was in a state of delirium. I thought I saw a battlefield, and flames... but that couldn't have been right." She paused, and I did not correct her. "But you were there, weren't you? You came for me?" She kept staring at her drink, unwilling to meet my eye.

"I told you; you are mine to protect, little bird." She screwed up her face then, as she always did when she was uncomfortable. I wanted to tell her then, what she meant to me. But we walked the knife's edge, and I was selfish. I was afraid of driving her away.

She finally looked up at me and set her drink down. She stood and approached me before she knelt, so our faces were level. She ran her hand over my cheek, the touch so gentle, so unlike our usual encounters.

"I heard there were no witnesses. You killed them all to get to me?"

Dangerous, this was so dangerous. "There is no force in this world that would keep me from you."

She said nothing but brought her lips to mine with unbearable gentleness. It wasn't like any of our other forays. She pressed herself into me as if she wished to melt into me and never be separated again. She ran her hands down my back softly, no nails or desperate touches. She traced her long fingers through my hair and opened her kiss to me gently like a dance, not a fight.

On the bed, she rocked our hips together slowly, building agonizing tension that I never wanted to be free of. I laced my fingers through hers, and held her tight to the bed, never releasing our kiss. I wanted to touch every single piece of her as that golden light threaded between our souls. It wasn't connected, I could still feel her resisting. But I had waited a lifetime for her, and if this was all I was to have, I would be grateful for the rest of my days.

"Abraxas," she looked deep into my eyes, worry on her face, "stay with me?"

"Until the sky burns, Tori."

Chapter 47

Tori

After that, I no longer resisted my need for him. I spent every night in the king's room. He would wake me with a kiss as he left for his morning meetings, and I would take breakfast there before heading out for training. I no longer suffered nightmares, my sleep calm and peaceful.

I spent my afternoons on patrol when I could. Kaleos had recovered well, no doubt due to the very attentive hands of Oryx. I'd invited the healer to join us for lunch, but he merely blushed and refused.

Some nights I attended galas and court events and realized I had become quite comfortable with the courtiers. My initial judgment of them had been horribly wrong. I'd found Lady Lovatia, who I had thought was just another gossip, to be the most connected woman in the kingdom. Her information about Koron and the Court of Flames had been invaluable to my plan for rescuing Jun.

The only thing holding me back now was that I hadn't found the information on breaking his enchantment. Nothing in the library had been useful, but Lady Lovatia knew an old scholar from the River Kingdom and that she would reach out discreetly. We would hear back soon, and then I would be ready.

The thought of leaving sent a pang through my heart, but I shoved it away. I had been doing that a lot recently, much to the protest of my inner voice. But I needed to ignore it. Jun was my goal. Everything else was just a temporary distraction. A very enjoyable one.

Tonight was another casual gala, and while I had tried to hold a conversation and learn more about the trade and economics of the kingdom, it seemed all I was really able to do was stare at Abraxas across the hall. Something about seeing him all dressed up and holding court... Well, it had me more bothered than usual.

It didn't help matters when he stood next to me as he joined our conversation and gently placed his hand on my lower back. He delicately traced his fingers over my skin, but he might as well have been branding me the way it set me alight. I couldn't take it anymore, so I gave him one quick meaningful glance before excusing myself and making my way down a vacant hall.

I only had to wait a few minutes before I felt him approach. Only a moment later he had me pressed up against the wall, my legs wrapping around his waist as we crashed our lips together. Neither of us bothered to be discreet as he slid himself into me, and I moaned into his ear.

Our fucking was fast and brutal, my head slamming into the wall more than once as he held me up, but still I could not get enough. I had never been like this before, so completely overcome with desire. I'd stopped trying to control it and gave in at every opportunity.

When we were both momentarily sated, he gently lowered me down and helped me adjust my dress. He kept me pinned to the wall with his body, and I reveled in the weight of it.

"I'm never going to get anything done in this kingdom again if you keep looking at me like that, little bird."

"Doesn't seem like you mind very much, Abraxas." I was still basking in his glow, high on the smell of him.

"In fact, I think I should come to all your meetings, how much more fun would they be if you had me under the table while you worked."

He growled then, and I felt his tongue trace over my neck, "Careful what you wish for, Princess." I could feel him already growing hard against me again.

"Take me there right now, Abraxas." He was carrying me before I could even react.

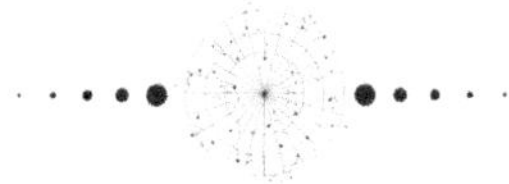

We reached the small room off his bedroom that I had assumed was an office. It was just large enough to hold a long table that was covered in maps and other documents. I tried to get a look at them but didn't have much time before he slammed me down on top of the table and crawled over me. I grabbed him with my knees and flipped him on his back.

I clawed at his shirt and pants, and he laughed at my urgency, "Needy princess." I slammed my mouth against his to shut him up when my eyes caught on something in the corner of the room. It was just a chair, but it stirred up my memories. I saw the king sitting there, one leg crossed over the other, reading me a bedtime story. I jerked away from our kiss and took in the rest of the room. The furniture was different, but I had no doubt this was the ceiling I had stared up at for days while my arm had first been healing.

"Where did you go?" The king looked at me with concern in his eyes.

"This is where I was when I was healing. You had me here, in your study? In your room?" I hadn't noticed when Oryx had taken me out of the room, I'd still been in too much pain. But now, it seemed so obvious. I looked at Abraxas, who still looked quite concerned.

"Of course. I had to watch over you." My heart was racing. I remembered my dreams. Of strong arms and soft kisses. Of a deep voice calling me home. But it couldn't have been him.

"But we hadn't even..." After my rescue, I knew it hadn't been the same.

I'd told myself I didn't care. That the softness of it didn't comfort me in the night, that my dreams hadn't changed from brutal fuckings to tender kisses. But this... he'd cared for me with so much tenderness long before I had ever surrendered to him.

No. He was the Dragon King. He was a monster, a tyrant. I pictured him bathed in blood and gore, the snapping of a soldier's neck, the beating of a severed heart. But underneath all that blood were his emerald eyes that held something so deep and precious—more valuable than any gem.

I thought of all I had seen, of Oryx talking about owing his mother's health to the king, of Avlyn's undying loyalty, of Ciara's rescue from Koron. Even of the soldiers' love and admiration for him. His people, who were cared for and happy.

My hands shook violently, and Abraxas clasped them in his. "Tori, what's wrong?"

"You're a monster. You're what mothers tell their children to fear in the night. A conqueror, a beast."

I looked down at him and I saw it. The hurt in his eyes. I almost missed it. No, I'd chosen to ignore it. For so long I'd wanted to hurt him and tried all the wrong ways. Here, I finally could, and it broke my heart.

"I am. And are you afraid, Tori?"

I was terrified. But not of him. It had never been him. I couldn't be weak; I couldn't let him see. *Control yourself.* That voice I hated echoed in my head. But I had never been able to control it, only push it away. So that's what I did, I pushed him away. And I ran.

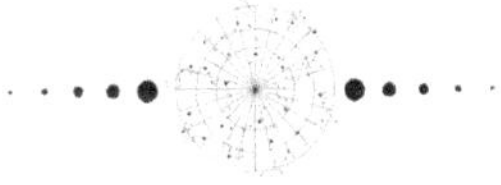

My feet led me back to the gala. I inhaled a glass of ambrosia, but my body craved something stronger while those deep, deadly shadows clawed at the edge of my mind. I grabbed another, looking for anything to drive them away. I gulped it down and spun looking for another when Lady Lovatia laced her arm with mine.

"Princess Tori, I have some exciting news."

"Lady Lovatia, I don't know if tonight is a good night to—"

"Nonsense, Lady Bogata just returned from the Capital. I'm sure she has news of your brother you would like to hear."

That crushing weight lay on my chest. This was too much, all of it was too much. Black threatened my vision again as Lovatia hauled me across the room.

Lady Bogata was chatting with many of the other ladies of court at the side of the dance floor, "Oh, Your Highness, not so often we catch you without the king these days?" She quirked an eyebrow at me, and I simply wanted to die on the spot. Everyone had known, everyone had seen but me. Kaleos, Ciara, Avlyn, even these fucking courtiers.

"Are you alright, Your Highness, you look quite pale?" Lady Lovatia's face showed true concern, but I pushed her away too.

"I'm alright, maybe just too much to drink, perhaps I should—"

Lady Bogata spoke over me, "We all heard, what you did against those raiders," she paused, it seemed she had omitted herself from this story, "We wanted you to know how grateful we are." She stared at me, and if I hadn't been using every ounce of my will to keep myself standing, I might have been able to see what she was telling me. "I travel to Koron often. I do enjoy your brother's performances; I would be happy to keep you updated on them." All the ladies were staring at me now. Not them too. I couldn't take this.

"I must be going." I fled, again. Out the doors and straight to my room. I should have just gone there straight away, but I was afraid Abraxas would have found me. No, not Abraxas, the king —my captor.

My mind wasn't a storm so much as a cyclone, the kind that had ripped apart villages leaving nothing but destruction in their wake. This wasn't like the temple. No rage filled me, only fear, that fear and despair that had almost pulled me over the edge so long ago. I couldn't go back there, but a path once trod is easy to follow and the sweet empty darkness called to me. Luckily, Ciara waited for me.

"Your Highness, can I—"

"Yes, I need a sleeping potion, a full dose."

She stepped back, "I'm sorry, Your Highness, but I have been forbidden from providing that to you."

"Alright, I'll take a half-dose, just bring it quickly."

"No, Tori." She stood to her full height, still much shorter than me, "I have been forbidden to bring you any. By the order of the king."

I finally found that rage. That cyclone was a firestorm again, and nothing would stop my destruction now. I left Ciara without another word and headed straight to him.

Chapter 48

Abraxas

I didn't have to wait long for her. I had thought we would have more time. I'd engulfed myself in her these past weeks with abandon, but it seemed that our time had run out. I had forced it already and had suffered the consequences. I would not allow that again.

She stormed through my door, a vision of rage and fire, hiding all that pain she carried every day. I knew it too well. I had used the same mask for centuries.

"How dare you? How dare you?" She slammed her palms into my chest. I couldn't resist playing this game with her one more time.

"My, Princess, whatever do you mean? You were the one who left me in quite a delicate situation."

"You know exactly what I mean! What sort of power play is this, that I can't have a sleeping potion?"

At that, my own anger swelled. I hadn't realized she'd asked again. I had hoped she was past this.

"I told you before, I won't have you using those."

"Why not, there is no risk now that I'm completely healed."

"That isn't the risk I was ever worried about."

She stared at me, unmoving for a long time. When she spoke again, it was barely a whisper, "You knew. You always knew. Did you see that when...when we exchanged memories?" We hadn't talked about that. Hadn't talked about so many things. And now it was too late.

"Yes, I saw the day you tried to take your own life." She was shaking, but it wasn't with rage. I reached out for her, but she slapped my hand away.

"You must think I'm pathetic. Some woeful excuse for a fae."

"Tori, I have thought you are many things, abrasive, reckless, demanding—" She twisted her face for just a moment, but it dropped away back into that deep sadness I couldn't stand. "Fearless, but also caring, devoted to your people, clever, and strong. So much stronger than I think you realize. But I have never once thought of you as pathetic."

"Stop it." Her eyes welled with tears, but she didn't try to hide them from me. "Please, just stop." She shifted her feet away, and I knew she was going to run again. I grabbed her uninjured arm,

"Come with me. I have something to show you." She tried to pull away, but I wouldn't let her, not yet. "I'm sorry, my little bird, but this one last time, you don't have a choice."

Chapter 49

Tori

We descended down the steep stairs that seemed to spiral into an endless pit. The walls grew damp with condensation. At first, I thought he was leading me to the dungeon, but these stairs were too deep and too narrow. We continued to descend until my legs shook and my arm began to ache at the shoulder from supporting it. I reached out my opposite hand, clinging to my forearm, trying to relieve the strain. He turned back to me and observed my discomfort.

"We are almost there."

What felt like *not-almost-there* stairs later, a faint light seemed to grow below us. It was an eerie pale blue, soft and harsh at the same time. We reached the bottom of the stairs, and instead of a doorway, a great gash in the wall led into the next room. On closer inspection, I saw that the wall was actually a giant slab of rock and the gash a great crack that allowed us to pass through.

On the other side, that eerie light grew, and I let my eyes adjust. We sat in a small cave where thin stalactites clung to the ceiling and stalagmites grew opposite them on the ground. I could hear the faint trickle of water from all around us, and it seemed to all flow into a shallow pool at the center of the space. The pool was about the size of a large table and only a few inches deep. But the water glowed that ethereal blue, lighting the cave that otherwise had no cracks to the outside.

Strangely, the cave was filled with vines and flowering plants that had no right to grow in a place without any sunlight. Over the water danced small whirls of light that I thought might be fireflies, but they dove in and out of the surface of the water with ease. Something about this place felt familiar, like an old friend.

"Wisp spirits," Abraxas stood close to me, as I leaned over the pool, "they are attracted to the wild magic here." I spun to face him.

"Wild magic? I thought it had all vanished."

A smile with no kindness crossed his face, "It is almost amusing how quickly people have forgotten what magic feels like, but it still exists all around us. You felt it at Lupercalia, didn't you? Something greater than ourselves. The embers of magic still linger in this land, hidden and dormant. It is not common for it to exist in such a concentrated form as this. In fact, I have only seen one other place like this in my life..." He trailed off, but I was thinking back to Lupercalia, the festival, how the death of the stag had caused a tidal wave of energy through the crowd.

"Death is the beginning," I whispered.

He looked at me with pride in his eyes, "Yes, death is a great catalyst for magic. One of the reasons so many great beasts were hunted down was for the release of magic at their death. One death could bring a bounty of life for an entire kingdom. But the cost is often far greater, for life and death go hand in hand."

I thought of the drought in the Pearl Kingdom, and the crop failures all across the continent. With no more beasts to slay, the magic of the world had dried up. But somehow, that explanation had never made much sense to me. Magic had existed since before there were fae and man to slaughter the beasts. Why was it gone now?

"If magic still exists, why can so few use it?"

"Magic is dying, make no doubt of that. When I was young, almost every fae could wield it to some degree, even some humans. But magic is an exchange of energy with the world, and it seems that our world no longer wants to trade."

"But it trades with you. I've seen you use it," he wouldn't look at me then. "You used it to save me in Niata."

He finally turned to me, "Yes, I can. And yes, I did. I've always had an affinity for the air, among other things," he raised his hand, and I marveled as a small flash of bright green fire hovered over his fingers.

"So, I didn't imagine it?"

"No. I conjured those mists that allowed us to invade Niata as well." Shame filled his voice.

"How have you hidden this from Hadeon?" I asked, barely a whisper.

"Oh, I haven't. He knows. He managed to kill most of the remaining magic users in the war, but there are a few of us in his control that he allows to live. Our magics are useful to him." His voice was laced with bitterness.

"He has imprisoned you as well." He toyed with the flames in his hand for a moment longer before it flickered out of existence.

"Not so directly as he has your brother, but the magic that I have now is but a shadow of the power I once had. It grows weaker every passing year, whereas his only grows stronger."

"I wouldn't have believed you would allow yourself to be controlled like that?"

He barked a dark laugh then, one that sent me back to that man I had met in Niata so long ago. "If you had asked me before all of this, I would have told you I would rather die than be in this position."

"Then why?"

"Because it allows me to be close to him, to work against him. I'm not so foolish as to believe I could destroy him outright, but with time..." He trailed off, and I realized something I had not truly considered.

"You hate him?"

"More than you can possibly know, little bird." I didn't want to press him anymore, he had already revealed so much to me, but I couldn't stop. I had never known how.

"Why have you saved me, over and over again? Risked yourself for me, gone up against him for me?" I already knew the answer but asked anyway.

He moved to me now, laying a hand gently on my injured arm, the other coming up to cup my jaw.

"I have brought you here before. When you fell from that cliff, you were so close to death I could see its hand reaching for you. I can't heal, but the magic of this place works in ways I can't understand. It called to me, and I knew I had to bring you here. I know the wild magic here healed you enough to keep you stable and let you fight your way back to me." My dreams, I truly had seen this place, seen the light, and seen him.

"I've told you, Tori, you are mine. When I first found you, I thought that meant I needed to keep you locked up like a precious gem, away with all my other riches. I have learned that you are mine, not as a bird in a cage, but one who is set free to soar on the wind, to bring more beauty to this world. You are mine and that includes all your pain and your joy, your hurt and your wonder. I cannot express the sorrow I feel knowing I have kept you locked away so long."

I wanted to shove him away. I wanted the words to stop as they carved themselves into my heart. But I didn't have to, because he did it for me.

"I brought you here so you could see that there is still hope out there in the world, for something better." He pulled a small notebook from his robes, "This is everything I could find on breaking the enslavement enchantments. It's not simple, but if you can get Jun, you should be able to. I still have some friends in the Court of Flames, they can help you." I ran my fingers over the notebook, the leather was supple from use.

"Why are you giving this to me?" I looked up and nothing but a deep, unending pain filled his eyes.

"You're free now, little bird. I've arranged transportation for you, and you have your plan. It will take you anywhere you want to go. Ciara is waiting, she will travel with you." He pulled me close and planted one last soft kiss on my lips. "Fly now, little bird, fly and don't look back."

Chapter 50

Tori

My feet carried me faster than I could comprehend, taking two or three stairs at a time. My lungs ached and my heart pounded as I crested the top of the stairs and sped for my room. I threw open the doors and immediately reached for the few possessions I had. I scrambled to my knees to pull the sword out from below my bed.

But as my hand landed on my sword I paused. I ran my fingers along the fine blade, and I saw Abraxas' face on the day he had given it to me, his beaming smile. I felt his hand slide over my jaw as it had so often these past few weeks, and tears streamed from my eyes.

I blinked them away, but the voice inside me was roaring and would not be ignored. I could practically see him standing in the room now, his hair pulled back from a worried face. I could practically feel Jun's hand on my shoulder, "In such a rush to leave, sister?"

"I'm coming to you, Jun, it won't be long now."

"Coming to me, or running away again?"

"Running away? Jun, we have to get home. I have to get out of here."

He let out a small laugh, *"I see you, Tori. Just as I always have. I saw you that day you tried to end it all, and I forgave you. I understood then what you were running from, because we ran together. But now? I won't forgive you this time."*

"Jun, what are you talking about?"

I could practically feel his hands on my face, see the look in his eye of disappointment. I could never lie to him; I don't know why I tried. Tears rose in my eyes again, *"I can't stay here Jun. I can't leave you with Hadeon."*

He laughed, *"Oh, I would very much like for you to come get me. But you don't have to do it alone."* His arms wrapped around me, *"You've always pushed it all away, all those feelings, all that sadness and rage—all your grief,"* I felt his eyes meet mine, *"all your love."* I could feel my heart cracking open, and no ocean or waves or depths could contain it now.

"It hurts, Jun. I'm so afraid, so afraid to end up back there, back on that edge you can't come back from."

"Tori, you don't have to be alone anymore. Look how much stronger you are, how far you've come since we were young. I've seen you be brave, be vulnerable. You've always taken care of me. You said it yourself then, that you would live for me. And for a time, that was enough. But not anymore, now it's time for you. And I'll be right here beside you, as I always have. Be brave, Tori." I saw his soft smile one last time, and then I was alone.

No, I wasn't alone. I had Jun, I had Ciara, I had Kaleos and the cohort. Hell, maybe I even had Avlyn. But above all, I had the man I needed to get back to right now.

I ran for my door and smacked directly into Ciara. She wore a sad smile, "Are you ready, Your Highness?"

"Change of plans, Ciara. Do you know where the king is?"

Her eyes twinkled, but her lips set into a hard line, "I heard him in his room, but perhaps you should wait—" I carefully pushed past her and sprinted. I arrived at those ebony doors in only a few heartbeats and pushed inside.

I was greeted by smoke and embers. The emerald fire engulfed his room. It spilled out over his furniture which had been toppled and torn to shreds. All his fine books had been strewn out over the space, as if hit by the gales of a storm. Many had caught the embers of the fire and were smoking obscenely. His curtains were still ablaze as they fluttered in harsh wind from his open balcony doors. I saw him there, hunched over the railing, his long silver hair blown wildly about by the wind. I approached him cautiously and laid a hand on his shoulder.

He snapped around and grabbed my wrist until the bones of my arm crunched together. His eyes were ablaze, as if that great viridian fire had been set inside of him, but the centers glowed a gold brighter than the sun. He looked at me like he didn't see me, and his grip tightened. I could feel it now, the great pressure of his magic, as he bared his teeth at me like some great beast. But I was not afraid, not anymore.

"Abraxas, it's me. Your little bird. I flew home, Abraxas." I lifted my weak arm, running my fingers over his cheek, until they laced in his hair. I pulled him to me, even as he held firm, running my lips over his, sliding his tongue against my own. But he shoved me away, and I saw that he still looked beyond me, that it wasn't me he was fighting. But I could fight him.

He charged at me, and I anticipated, moving out of his way at the last second. I let him fly past and tripped him. He sprawled on the floor, but quickly recovered to flip over. I slammed into him with my whole weight, pinning him to the ground. I managed to grab each of his wrists and stick them to the floor as he tried to claw at me and pinned his hips with my own. "Abraxas! Wake up! Snap out of this!" I'd gotten much stronger these past weeks, but it was still difficult to hold him, so I did the only move available to me and slammed my forehead into his face. Pain radiated across my face, but I felt him relax beneath me. I pulled back to see his nose bleeding and his eyes fluttering. He stopped fighting my grip and when his eyes finally fluttered open, they weren't glowing anymore.

"Tori?"

"I'm here, Abraxas."

"Why?" He was still dazed, his eloquence gone.

"You said I could go wherever I wanted."

He slowly sat up. "And this is where you wanted to be?" His eyes no longer contained those flames but something much more fragile, and this time, no part of me wanted to break it.

"Yes, I wanted to...come home." They were simple words, but I had feared them. And now I let them go and the fear was torn away by the wind. I knew that here by his side, was more home than I had ever been in Niata. I kissed him again, and this time he kissed me back. He wrapped his arms around me, and I pressed myself into him. His kiss was frantic, like he feared I might disappear at any moment, but it was gentle, unbearably gentle.

The moment seemed to stretch on and on, an eternity of time as I tried to imprint his touch into my memory. After a lifetime we parted, and he ran his hand up to my face. Then I saw that ridiculous grin spread across his face, and my heart had truly cracked open.

"How would you like to go on a quest, Tori?"

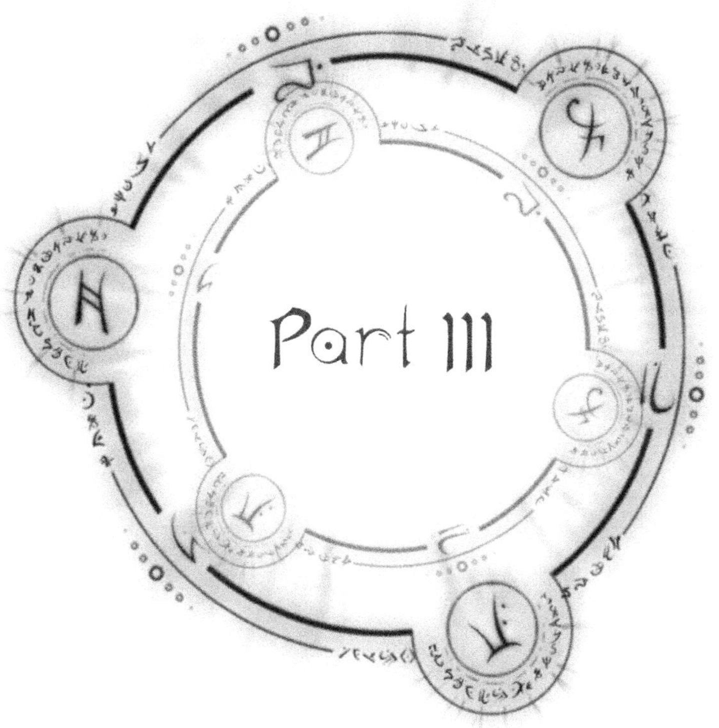

Part III

Chapter 51

Abraxas

I had brought Tori up to speed on everything we knew about Tenebrae forest, which to be honest, wasn't much. All the reports we had received still conflicted with each other, like the forest had a mind of its own. She asked if any of the healers were present.

"There are a few already stationed at the camp? Why?"

"Oryx had mentioned he grew up in this region. It might be useful to have someone who knows the terrain better since we don't seem to know much about it ourselves." She kept surveying the few maps we had.

"Why don't you go and convince him to join us?" I asked her.

She looked at me, confused, "Couldn't you just command him to join?"

"I could, but I find that being asked by a beautiful woman is a much more compelling reason." I loved that color still rose in her cheeks before she nodded and made her way out of the study.

Avlyn hated every minute of this. They were still distrustful of Tori and had not held that back.

"You can't trust her, Abraxas. She's proven that."

"Much has changed, Avlyn. Besides, can you really blame her?"

"I certainly can."

"You aren't guiltless in all this, Avlyn. Why did you have us duel on the beach that day?"

"I was hoping the two of you would just fuck and get it out of your system. I didn't think it would lead to all this." They gestured to me frantically. I knew Avlyn wasn't jealous, at least not in the traditional sense. They had picked up on my protectiveness after all these years together. After all this was over, I'd have to focus on getting them to direct that at someone else.

I laid my hand on their shoulder, which was actually higher than mine. I could still remember them as that little creature that we had found on the beach, the little terror running through the legs of soldiers during training. How many lifetimes ago had that been? But I still needed to remind myself sometimes they weren't that little fae anymore.

"I trust her, Avlyn."

They screwed up their face. I had to stop myself from chuckling. It was the same face Tori made. I'm sure they picked it up from her. They would hate that.

"Maybe you do. And maybe that's not the problem. Maybe what I don't trust is you around her. We've had this plan for so long, Abraxas, and ever since she's shown up, it's like it doesn't matter anymore. You've become erratic— reckless."

They weren't wrong. And they really weren't going to like what I said next.

"I'm going into the forest, and I'm taking her with me."

"No fucking way! I told you I wouldn't let you. None of our expeditions have come back, Abraxas, none!"

"That's why I have to go myself. You know we need this; all our other plans will have been for nothing without the diadem. There is no way around this now."

"See? This is what I mean! You're being ridiculous! There is another way, we just haven't found it yet. We just need more time."

I squeezed their shoulder, "Time isn't on our side anymore, Avlyn. It's time to act."

Avlyn pulled out of my grip. "I won't—I won't support this. I won't go with you."

Tori really was rubbing off on Avlyn far too much if they thought they could defy me. "Commander, this is an order."

"No!" They were backing away from me now and shaking. "I won't!"

"Are you refusing a direct order, Commander?" Avlyn was still shaking, and I saw their hand flick towards their sword for just a moment. But they raised themself to their full height and stood their ground.

"Yes." Their amber eyes bore into me, and a pang of sadness swept my heart. But it was paired with a swelling of pride. Perhaps Avlyn had finally outgrown this role.

"Then you are dismissed, Avlyn."

I saw the whites of their eyes, and their lips trembled as if about to speak.

I cut them off, "No going back now. Get out of here before I have you escorted out." The faces of the guards at the door showed clear division, unsure for a moment about what to do, but Avlyn spun and fled the room.

Tori and I prepared our horses for the journey together. Unsurprisingly, she was quite good with the beast, patting his snout kindly and sneaking him a few sugar cubes. She was being uncharacteristically quiet, so I could tell I was about to get a lecture.

"You shouldn't have sent Avlyn away." Here it was.

"They defied my direct order, it was non-negotiable."

Her lips pressed into a firm line, "It's not that simple, and you know it. They care for you; they are concerned for you."

I raised an eyebrow at her, "Oh, and now you are an expert on emotional availability?"

She hit me with those dagger eyes that I adored, "No, but..." she sighed. "At the very least it makes me feel like the wicked stepmother getting between you two."

"Avlyn is over five centuries old; I would think they can take care of themselves." She still held her face in that tight expression, so I couldn't stop from teasing her.

"So, I take you down to one magic grotto and now you are the mother of my children?"

She went redder than a beetroot. "Arrogant ass. Besides, can you imagine what our children would be like? I'm not ready for that unrelenting cyclone." She winked at me, but my mind had fled. For just a moment I let myself imagine and there she was. She was as beautiful as her mother and just as fierce, but with long silver hair that whipped around her face as she stood on the cliff above Xyr with me. Her smile was Tori's and it had my heart captured in just the same way.

Tori laid her hand upon my cheek, "Abraxas?"

"She will be perfect," I whispered, almost like a prayer. Softness I so rarely saw crept into her face.

"If she's half as mischievous as you, I really am in trouble." She placed a gentle kiss on my lips. Then she hit me with that smile that practically had me on my knees before she mounted up onto her horse. "Time to go, Abraxas."

We traveled for close to a week to reach the edge of the forest. Spring lingered on the wind, and the journey had been smooth. The snow had melted from most of the grass and hills around us, leaving only small patches that were shaded from the sun. Wildflowers had started to push through the earth, their colors dancing on the wind. Tori had done well on the journey so far, especially for someone who had never done this before.

"I had gone on patrols and small excursions back in Niata," I noted how she didn't say back home, "you know, driving off bandits and settling any disputes, but nothing like this." She was beaming. She seemed to be drinking in the scenery, and I often caught her stroking her horse's mane absentmindedly. She had quickly learned how to set up the tents and never complained about the dried rations, unlike the rest of her cohort.

At first, the cohort had been subdued, likely due to my presence. I remained withdrawn from them, as I always had. After giving them a few days of space, I saw them starting to come back together with Tori at the heart of it.

They joked and laughed as they worked and a few nights they had even had a few matches in the hand-to-hand combat that Tori had taught them. It seemed Oryx quickly was adopted as one of their own, although he was certainly less boisterous than the rest of them.

Long ago, I had accepted that I wouldn't be a part of this anymore, a king had to remain above and removed. But seeing Tori with them brought me almost as much joy as if it had been me.

She understood my reservations and allowed me my space.

But on the first night when she had set up a small pallet for herself inside one of the cohort tents, I'd dragged her away.

"You think I'm going to let them enjoy you all night?" I carried her to our tent, but she was hesitant.

"Not much privacy behind just a layer of canvas."

I ran my nose along her cheek and let the hand holding the back of her knees trace up and down her legs.

"I didn't think that was something that bothered you."

"This is different, they are...my friends. Besides, I know there is no way you could stay quiet." She smirked at me then and she wasn't wrong.

"Oh, I can think of a way, little bird." That heat in her eyes grew, and I fell asleep that night relishing the taste of her after she had ridden my face into oblivion.

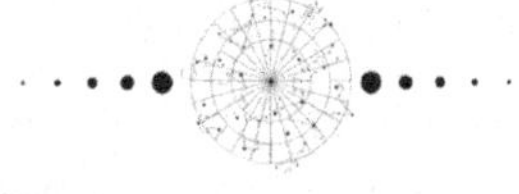

A SMALL CAMP SET UP BY THE PREVIOUS EXPEDITIONS WAS already in place. Canvas tents surrounded a central bonfire, with soldiers milling about. I could practically smell the body odor and rotting food from here. No matter how disciplined the army, a military camp was still a camp, and after weeks of existence, they started to fester. I looked at Tori to find her smiling, excitement radiating from her.

"Don't get too excited, Princess. We're upwind, you haven't smelled that place yet." Behind me the others made affirming noises, but her spirits weren't damped. She gently kicked her horse forward and led us down to the encampment.

We dropped our horses at the shanty that was being used as a stable. The rest of the cohort made haste to unload and integrate into the camp, but I led Tori toward the central command tent. I was greeted by Commander Talius who had been in charge.

"Any updated information on finding the ruins in the forest?" I asked.

"Unfortunately, no. We still send scouts and cartographers daily. Every time they come back with conflicting information. No one has stayed in the forest overnight and survived."

"I want to see it," Tori said with authority, and Talius didn't question it.

"I'll summon a soldier to accompany you."

"No need. I'll take one of my own." *Her own.* I couldn't help but chuckle.

"I'll escort the princess as well."

We made our way out of the camp, Tori finding Kaleos and Oryx along the way and signaling them to follow.

The camp had been set up a short distance from the edge of the forest. Initially, it had been along the forest's edge but had been moved back. I understood why.

While spring brought new life to the Dragon Kingdom, the forest seemed removed from that. At first glance one might have thought it a forest like any other, ancient beyond compare, but ordinary. But there was nothing ordinary here.

Just a few paces into the forest, even with the noonday sun high above us, no light penetrated the canopy. Total and suffocating darkness spread like a malignancy between the few trees that could be seen, and then nothing. No birds sang, and the wind that blew from the forest was frosty, despite the warm day. Occasional scuttling could be heard from inside, like a beast with too many legs crawling over the forest floor, but it was the unnerving silence that seemed to dominate all. Nothing survived there.

Tori shivered beside me, "Ever since the Eternal Kingdom fell, this place has been cursed. After the king and queen were murdered, stories say that the corrupted magic they possessed leaked into the surrounding forest, and it became eternally drenched in darkness."

"Doesn't sound so farfetched, seeing it now," said Kaleos, who stood behind Tori with a hand on Oryx's shoulder. The smaller, red-haired man shivered as well.

"Why is it so quiet?" Oryx asked. "The forest just to the west of here wasn't anything like this."

"It's stalking us," Tori whispered. "Waiting for us to walk into its wide-open jaws." As she spoke, another gust of frozen wind seemed to answer her.

She looked at me, "Good thing I've never been very good at knowing when to back down."

"Good thing we brought the harpoon," Kaleos chuckled.

Chapter 52

Abraxas

I'd finished the day preparing for our journey into the forest. I trusted that arrangements had been made, but I had to see everything with my own eyes before turning in. I returned to my tent to find Tori waiting for me there.

"Is everything to your satisfaction, my Domineering King?" She knew she could get away with anything if she said it while she smiled like that.

"Yes." Her face grew serious.

"Abraxas, I need you to tell me the truth. Why are we doing this? Why are you risking so much for this?" I was honestly surprised it had taken her this long to ask. But seeing the forest had made her realize the danger it held.

I pulled her to me, and we settled on the cot, her legs lying across my own.

"This is something only a few know—Avlyn and a few of my other most trusted commanders. And only Avlyn knows the whole truth." She squeezed my shoulder and encouraged me. "You asked why Hadeon fought Malech. The truth is, he took something from him, something powerful. That's what allows him to continue to pull magic from the earth with such strength. He has it guarded in his castle by unbreakable wards. No one can reach it, but with the diadem, we can. It was forged when magic flowed freely, and it can break any enchantment. It could easily remove the collar on your brother as well."

Her eyes lit up, but she settled, "Once I have Jun, I will free him, no matter what. But if we could break Hadeon's power, then we could kill him." *So bloodthirsty, my little bird.*

"Yes, and it would be easy. He has relied on his magic for far too long. He would be crippled without it."

"What does he have from the World Breaker?" she asked. But here I hesitated. I lied, "I have my theories. But it really doesn't matter. Whatever it is, we will destroy it."

She nodded, "What do you think is happening in the forest?"

"I do not know, but I am sure we will find out."

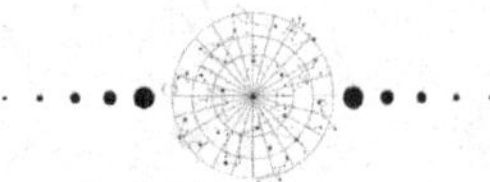

I STOOD AT THE EDGE OF THE FOREST WITH TORI BY MY SIDE. Our group spread behind us, two by two with supply carts bringing up the rear. The air was drenched in fear, but they stood strong as they were trained. Only Oryx shook, his lips set into a harsh line. Tori had paired him with Kaleos, and they stood just behind us, but I could still hear the man's teeth chattering.

But none of it distracted from the harsh wind that flew out of the forest, like a frozen breath waiting for us. I unsheathed my sword, and Tori did the same. I saw her wince, her injured arm still hurting her, but she stood strong and determined.

I raised my sword, and without a word, we entered those cursed woods. It was incredible, only a few steps inside the trees, and there was nothing but utter darkness. Two of the scouts for our party ran ahead now, torches held aloft. Even with them lit, we could barely see a few paces ahead. It was as if the forest tried to absorb any light that dared enter.

The trek was slow as we tried to navigate a path that would allow the supply wagons to follow. But this forest was old and dense, and we spent hours just lifting the cart over felled trees and ravines, not to mention leaving waypoints to mark our path out. I longed to leave it all behind, to journey on foot alone with just Tori at my side, but caution was necessary.

If anything lurked in wait for us, it would certainly hear us, as we made more noise than I thought possible. This also made it difficult to try and listen for any oncoming threats. We were ripe for an ambush.

But after hours of travel, nothing came for us. The cohort was exhausted, and I saw Tori clutching her arm as she often did when she had pushed herself too far. We reached a small clearing, and I motioned to stop, "We make camp here tonight."

Torches were set around the perimeter of the small space, and everyone went to work setting up tents. Quickly, camp came together, and I took the first watch while the rest ate. I looked out into that sea of darkness and saw absolutely nothing. But even with the sounds of camp, I could listen. The wind whipped around us, and I tried to calm it but found it resisted me.

It seems you have a different master. I was annoyed, but still, I listened. Sound came from every direction, but they weren't the sounds I expected from a forest. Instead, great creaks and groans met me, and a deep rumbling seemed to permeate the earth. But nothing sounded close enough to be of concern.

It was impossible to tell the time of day, but most of the party ate and quickly crashed into their pallets.

I felt Tori sit down beside me, "Something's out there, watching us." I could feel it too, just beyond my grasp. But she slid her hand into mine, lacing our fingers together, "We face it together."

She laid her head on my shoulder, and suddenly the forest didn't seem to matter at all. We remained there in silence as the sounds of the camp settled into the night. It seemed like everything was calm, until the quiet rumbling of the forest grew deafening.

Snaps and groans from the trees grew closer and surrounded us, but nothing moved within our ring of light. The ground beneath us shook violently, and I nearly toppled over Tori. I stood, sword drawn, but even then, I could barely hold myself as the ground moved like a wave under our feet.

Soldiers scampered from their tents, ready for a fight. But as soon as the noise and motion had started, it ceased, the forest falling into that eerie silence again.

"Everyone alright?" The soldiers called out in affirmation. What had that been? Tori had walked away from me to check on the others. I found her pulling Oryx out from under a collapsed tent. She helped him stand and checked for injuries when he whispered, "The waypoints."

I spun to where our last marker had been, just outside the camp. Sure enough, it was gone. Before anyone could stop me, I ran to where the next would have been. Nothing. I had set it myself, on a very distinct tree with a gaping hole in one side. But that was nowhere to be seen either. I ran back to the camp, Tori giving me a scowl and scolding me about running off alone.

I strode around the clearing, and I saw it. The trees were all different, just beyond that wall of light, as if the very earth beneath us had moved us somewhere new. Our markers were gone, and no navigational devices worked in these infernal woods. Without moving, we had become completely lost.

Chapter 53

Tori

It happened every night just as we settled in. The ground would shake and the trees quiver, and we would completely lose our bearings. We had tried to exit the forest and found very quickly that the path we thought would lead us straight out actually led us deeper in. But every day we journeyed, hoping to find sight of a lost waypoint or just a landmark that looked familiar. We found nothing.

Our camp was tense. The cohort barely slept despite the unending darkness. Food rations were starting to dwindle, and despite the growing chatter of animals around us, nothing could be caught to eat. Whispers of ghosts and phantoms traveled through the soldiers, despite Abraxas' attempts to quash it.

I lay in our tent, trying to sleep when Abraxas joined me. He must have just finished his watch and he looked haggard. I knew he hadn't slept in days, despite his insistence that everyone else did. He slumped down quietly on the edge of our pallet and hung his head in his hands. I rolled over and rubbed his back gently.

"I didn't mean to wake you," he murmured.

"You didn't."

He grunted; our mutual sleeplessness understood. I sat up and grabbed his hand from his cheek, kissing his fingers gently. "Lay with me?" He shook off his armor and clothes then wrapped me in his arms, cradling my back to his chest as he always preferred. But I wasn't feeling sleepy now, and a distraction was welcome.

I rubbed my ass back into him and purred as I felt him harden in response. "Oh, I thought you didn't like the idea of the camp hearing us?"

I spun to him, and pushed him down onto his back, "Then I guess you will have to be very quiet, Abraxas." I straddled him and ground my hips so that he could feel the wetness of me through his silk shorts.

"No promises." I lifted my hips and he quickly pulled himself free and placed his broad head at my entrance. I circled and pulsed, slowly taking all of him into me.

"Fuck, Tori, that wet cunt—" but I clamped a hand over his mouth.

"No, no, Abraxas. We must be quiet now." I felt him bite at my fingers, but just pushed down harder with my hand, while I rose all the way up to slam back down onto him. He dug his fingers into my hips with bruising strength, signaling his displeasure, but it only spurred me on further. I rode him harder and faster, his hands assisting me and his hips rose to meet my own. He pushed his head back, and his thrusts were more desperate, "Now it's your turn to come for me, My King." He shot me a look that was all menace, but I squeezed my inner walls around him, and he couldn't refuse me. I felt the warmth of him fill me as his hips jerked, and I removed my hand to place a tender kiss on his lips.

"Domineering Princess." He kissed me back, wrapping his arms around me. I rolled off him, and positioned myself back against his chest, draping his arm over me. "Good night,

Abraxas." He placed one kiss on the tip of my ear before I felt him finally fall asleep.

After I was sure he was asleep, I oh so carefully extracted myself from his arms, pulled on my leggings and cloak, and snuck out of our tent. I grabbed my sword near the entrance and belted it to my waist as I walked.

The camp was a sea of shadows, torches lighting up the canvas tents with an eerie glow that the forest seemed to try and consume. I made my way to the edge and found Kaleos on watch with Oryx sitting by his side. Perhaps they were having a moment, so I made to turn around when Kaleos waved me over.

I plunked down next to them, staring out into the forest. I could only see the shadows of the first set of trees before everything was swallowed by the perfect darkness. We all stared in silence for several minutes before Oryx spoke.

"It's funny, these trees are just the same as the ones I grew up with, but somehow they seem foreign."

"What do you mean?" Kaleos asked.

"I mean they are all the same species as the trees just west of here, but maybe they've been changed by the darkness? They look the same, but something feels different underneath."

Kaleos let out a laugh with no humor, "Oh, and what's that?" But I felt it too.

I didn't know the trees the way Oryx did, but I could tell they felt, "Angry."

Oryx nodded in agreement. Kaleos pressed his lips together, about to say something else, when the very distinct sound of a twig snapping drew all our attention. It had been loud, just outside our ring of light.

Kaleos and I both shot up, our swords drawn. Without turning his head, Kaleos spoke to Oryx, "Get back, now."

"What about you?"

"Go tell the night guard we need—" Then a creature taller

than any of our tents lurched out of the forest. It was wider than two carriages and covered in dark brown fur. Its front paws had long claws bigger than most daggers and its legs were thicker than tree trucks. It looked like an enormous version of the small, and somewhat cute, black bears we had in the Pearl Kingdom. This was not cute, but a vision pulled straight from hell, as its bulky neck led not to a pair of adorable round ears, but to a bone white skull protruding from the fur, with glowing red eyes that hovered in the empty sockets and long canine teeth that gleamed in the torchlight.

The creature rose up on its hind legs, and it scraped the tree branches above us it was so large. I barely heard Oryx whisper, "Nalle," behind me when a scream broke the strained stillness between us, and the beast attacked. I rolled to the side, just narrowly avoiding a deadly swipe from that powerful paw. Kaleos grabbed Oryx and did the same. The creature barreled between us, making its way into the camp. Tents flew as it ran through them, ropes and stakes dragging behind as screams from the soldiers trampled underfoot rang out.

The Nalle made straight for the center of camp, like it had a target. And that target was the king. I jumped to my feet and flew after it, screaming as I went. The tents were slowing it down, and I managed to catch up. I jumped, one foot landing on a barrel of supplies to give me more leverage as I flew into the air and brought my sword striking down into the creature's back. It screamed, the sound like howling wind mixed with a deafening roar and it rose up again. It swiped at me with its razor-sharp nails, but I held on to my sword, dangling like a tick off the creature's back, despite my left arm's protests.

Soldiers poured in, slicing at the creature's legs, doing their best to avoid its claws. But the creature smashed back down onto all fours, and its enormous jaw clamped down on the nearest man, and blood and guts flew everywhere as it shook him back and forth. His screams died out as a definitive crunch filled the air, and the Nalle dropped him before heading for another. I planted my feet on its back, retching my sword free, and moved to strike its neck when it reared again, and I was flung backward. I was caught by Kaleos, my left arm cramping. "The king?" I asked frantically. Kaleos pointed and I saw him fighting at the head of the beast, in a state of very unprotected undress.

He danced in front of the beast, engaging its fangs as if this were some kind of game, managing to land numerous strikes. But I saw those strikes heal even faster than they would have on the king, so the beast just kept coming. It snapped its jaw, trying to capture Abraxas as it had the other man, but he leapt away, landing another strong blow on the creature's skull, to no avail.

I heard Oryx behind me. "Get out of here!" Kaleos screamed, but Oryx just shook his head. "The skull! You need to destroy the skull." The creature had already taken numerous blows to the head with no lasting damage. How could we destroy it? My arm twinged again, and I thought of the rock that had almost taken it from me. I looked around for the wagon carrying the massive crossbow. It had toppled, but some soldiers were already righting it. Kaleos followed my line of sight. "No way we can get a good enough shot with that."

But then the creature snapped at a nearby soldier, whom Abraxas just managed to push out of the way. But the delay allowed the creature to swipe him across the chest, leaving four long gashes that bleed crimson. He fell to his knees, the wounds not closing, and I sprinted.

"You'll get one shot." Abraxas rose up, but he was slow, and the Nalle knew it. He battered him left and right, but I fell in and smashed the side of its skull with the pommel of my blade. It lurched but found its footing as I stepped in front of Abraxas. He still clutched his chest as blood ran down.

"No one makes him bleed but me!" I let my rage drive away

the fear and doubt as I faced down the creature. It lunged at me, its jaws opened wide enough to swallow me whole, and I raised my sword and screamed. I tried to dodge its teeth and slammed my sword into the roof of its mouth.

Pain exploded across me, but I couldn't identify from where. A great roar burst forth, and the Nalle rose up on its legs, its front paws clawing at the sword that was still lodged in its mouth. "Now!" I heard the whistle of the bolt as it flew through the air, and the blood-chilling crack of it passing through the creature's skull. Bone bits rained down on me, and the red glow of its eyes disappeared as its body hit the forest floor with a thud that shook the trees.

I spun, Abraxas still clutching his chest behind me. But the blood wasn't running as freely, even though his wounds were still open.

"I'll be alright, I've had worse." But his eyes grew so wide that I could see the whites around his iris. "Tori, your shoulder." Like his words had reminded me, I felt a lancing pain over my right shoulder. I looked and saw a great gash running from the top and down my back where I couldn't see. Before I could get a better look, Oryx was on me, pressing cloth to the wound.

"What's the point of me putting you back together if you are just going to get hurt again?" He pressed against the wound to stanch the bleeding, and I grunted in a very unappealing way. Abraxas looked at my wound. "It's not too deep, but injuries from the Great Beasts always take longer to heal. We should be cautious." I thought about the scars I still had on my leg from the Leviathan.

I hissed between my teeth as Oryx fussed over my wound, "I wouldn't mind not running into another one for the rest of my life."

A small smile cracked Abraxas' lips, "You do seem to attract them. I'm a bit surprised you decided to fight this one and not let it eat me as a snack."

But then the wind whipped up into a gale that would have put the typhoons of Niata to shame, and everyone was almost blown off their feet. The trees shook and leaves tore through the camp as our tents and supplies were blown everywhere. Abraxas pulled me to his still-bloody chest, and I barely heard him over the wind, "*Morka Tempeli.*"

The torches were nearly out from the gale, but I could just see leaves and embers twirling over the body of the Nalle, like a great tornado. Then the earth itself lurched, and roots from the nearby trees reached up out of the ground. They snagged over the limbs of everyone in the camp, trying to pull them under the earth and out into the forest. A root wrapped around my leg, but Abraxas sliced it with his sword, and the wind picked up.

"They're screaming." I barely heard Oryx, but he was right. The sound of the wind through the trees, it wasn't right. He grabbed my hand, and I could hear it carry words, in a language I didn't know, but that I felt. *Enemy.*

"We aren't your enemy!" I screamed, but the roots only pulled at us harder. I heard the blunt sound of swords chopping at the roots as more of the soldiers tried to escape. The wind blew even harder. *Enemy. Enemy. Cut.*

"Drop your swords!" Abraxas stared like I had gone insane. "*Do it!*" I rose to my feet and bellowed, "Drop your swords, that's an order."

I felt their hesitation, but I heard the metallic clank of swords hitting the ground. Roots pulled at my heels, and I saw men still being dragged down. But then the roots released, though the wind continued. "We are not your enemy!" I called again. The wind kept battering me, and while the roots retreated, I saw the trees at the edge of the clearing were moving, pressing into us.

Tents shuffled together as the trees crushed the camp. I heard wood snap as one of the torches toppled and lit a tent on fire.

The trees pressed faster. *Hurt. Hurt. Hurt.*

"Put out the fires, now!" I screamed. Abraxas rose next to me.

He locked eyes with me, his only hesitation before bellowing, "Fires out now!" Anyone who could rushed to a torch, smothering them. The tent took longer but Abraxas chucked a barrel of water at it. It finally went out and we were in pitch black. I could still feel the trees pushing in, hear them creaking as they crushed us. I felt Abraxas grab my hand tightly in the darkness. I still clutched Oryx on the other side.

But then the wind died down, and the crushing stopped. We all held our breath, and the wind tickled over my ear. *Scared.*

"I'm sorry. We didn't mean to scare you. To hurt you."

Hurt nalle.

"Yes, we were scared too. I'm sorry."

Why come?

"We are looking for something. Something that once belonged to the fae."

Mine now.

I felt Oryx's shoulders drop. Not good. We couldn't stand against a whole forest.

"Please..." How to explain?

Leave now.

It wasn't threatening, but it crushed my heart just the same. Small blue lights like fireflies rose from the ground, marking a path I was sure would lead us to safety.

"Please, we need—" Abraxas laid his hand on my shoulder. I didn't need to see him to know he was telling me to have patience.

"Ok, we will pack up."

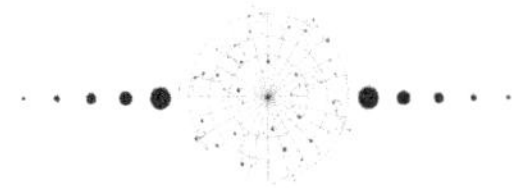

In the pitch black, we packed extremely slowly. Now that the torches were out, those of us who were full-fae found that we could see, if just a tiny amount. Everyone else was relegated to either packing next to the small amount of light emitted by the small blue path or working on folding tents in the dark.

I worked on loading what I could into the one wagon we still had that hadn't been smashed by the trees, when Oryx ran right into me.

"Sorry, I can't see anything."

"It's alright, I need you anyway." I pulled him aside, not that we really needed to hide in the dark, but hopefully we were out of earshot.

"You can talk to the trees?" I asked him.

"Well, so could you."

"No, I could because you could." I hadn't known the answer until I spoke it, but it was true.

He sighed, "When I was young, I always felt most at home in the forest. My mother always talked about how it was alive. As a youngling, I thought that was just a story, but as I got older, I felt it. I felt it like it was my oldest friend. I was always safe there, no matter what creatures lurked around me." He laughed, "Although the forest I grew up in wasn't as...verbose...as this one."

"We need to get to the ruins. Is there anything we can say?"

He was silent for a long time. "Forests aren't like you or me. The death of one tree, that's nothing in the forest. Just part of the cycle. The cycle of something that has existed for millennia. Now, many trees? That's different. This one was afraid of the swords. Fae must have been cutting lumber from its edges, taking the trees away." He sighed again.

"Perhaps I could talk to it." We both jumped about a foot in the air. Abraxas was so damn quiet when he wanted to be. He chuckled, "Sorry to startle you." He grabbed my hand, and I grabbed Oryx's. "Come with me, both of you."

Chapter 54

Abraxas

I led them away from the camp. Tori clutched my hand, and Oryx held her other. I could just see him shaking in the darkness, but he held his head high and followed quickly.

I stopped them when I could no longer hear the camp. Tori gave my hand a gentle squeeze, all the encouragement I needed.

"You have felt it, haven't you? Our world is no longer the same. Magic is dying." For a long time, nothing happened. So long I almost wondered if this was pointless. But then a soft gust ruffled the leaves around us, and just like before, I heard the voice of the forest.

Yes.

"You know why?" The trees around me shook as if in irritation.

Fae greedy. Tori and Oryx shifted uncomfortably next to me.

"Yes."

You greedy.

I laughed then, "Yes, I am."

Expected. Why come?

"Too few have hoarded magic too long. Almost all the Great

Conduits are gone. We must find a way to release it." The forest hung silent for a long time.

You do this?

I squeezed Tori's hand. "We will do this. We need to reach the ruins. Will you help us?"

You go. Fae stay.

"No. She comes with me."

Why?

"We are stronger together."

The wind picked up again, and I swore that it sounded like the forest was laughing at me.

Alright, brother.

A new set of lights rose from the ground, golden in color, leading away from the camp.

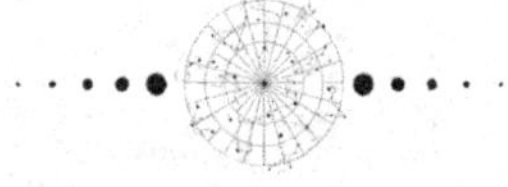

Tori and I made our way slowly down the path. We had sent Oryx back to camp to help the others leave. She was curiously quiet but I knew the storm was about to break.

"The forest seemed to like you."

"Maybe they just wanted to talk to someone closer in age."

She let out a soft hum, worrying her lip in the way I loved.

"What are the Great Conduits?"

"What we know as the Great Beasts were once known as the Great Conduits. Fae used magic in an exchange with the earth. But the conduits channeled the earth's power. Through them there was no exchange, but a partnership in the transfer of energy. That is why the Dragon Kingdom prospered for so long. Dragons were the greatest conduits."

"But now they are all gone."

"Yes." She turned to me, and I could barely make out her features in the soft, golden light. "That's why magic is gone, because there is nothing left to channel it."

"It's just my theory, but I believe so."

"But the Great Prophecy? It called to eliminate the dragons to save magic. It doesn't make any sense."

"Prophecies are tricky things. I don't think we are meant to understand them completely, so to take such drastic action because of one, it has had dire consequences." In the darkness of the forest, it was as if I could release my shame. A tear slipped from my eye, and I thought she wouldn't see it. But she carefully brought her lips to my cheek, and kissed it away.

"Some of the dragons, they were your friends?"

"Yes."

"He was your friend?" I didn't need to ask who she referred to.

"Yes."

"You lied to me, Abraxas." How could she see right through me, even in the pitch black? "You said you hadn't been alone, but that's not true. You've felt alone for a very long time."

"More than you know, little bird. But I don't feel alone, not anymore." Even in the darkness, her smile shone like the sun.

"Neither do I." She kissed me then, her lips caring but heated as she slipped her tongue into my mouth. I slid my hands down over her ass and she let out a moan that made me want to do nothing more than lay her down right here and fuck her into the dirt. But the lights that illuminated our trail flashed in obvious annoyance. We laughed and made our way down the path.

"Later, My King."

"Can't come soon enough."

Chapter 55

Tori

The ruins of the Eternal City greeted us slowly. At first, it was just large blocks covered in moss and swallowed up by the roots of nearby trees. But those blocks slowly changed into columns, and those columns to fragments of walls, each only moments away from crumbling into dust. The golden sprites still lit our path but spread out into the ruins of that once great fortress, their guidance now complete.

I saw what might have been the central tower, where a great tree emerged from its center, far taller than the fae-made structure had ever been. Its branches and roots had consumed the building, bursting through the walls, while also holding it prisoner. Bricks were suspended in the air on the precepts of destruction, only held firm by the tree's will. It seemed the forest really did own this place now.

Just beyond the edges, the forest once again devolved into darkness. The trees leaned in, caging this place, and us with it.

"So, what do we look for now?" I asked. Abraxas squeezed my hand and then released it.

"Well, I was hoping you would be able to sense its magic, or perhaps draw it out."

"Why me? You're the one with magic?"

"Yes, but you're the one who seems to have a habit of calling forth lost things." His eyes shone in the dancing light.

I remembered the Leviathan and the Nalle. I thought about talking with the forest and the way it had felt holding Oryx's hand. How I had felt them not as something separate from myself, but something that I let flow through me, like my own breath.

I focused on my breathing, letting the forest around me enter my lungs. Each time deeper and deeper, until it filled not only my lungs but my entire chest, my stomach, all the way to the ends of my toes. As I focused, my body slipped away and I reached out, feeling for anything that seemed to call to me. Minutes passed, and all I felt was the shift of the wind through the leaves.

But then something small scuttled across my mind, "There, in that tower."

We walked into the decaying building, careful not to disturb the ancient walls. It was much darker inside, and even my fae vision was limited. But I certainly felt something here, and I started shifting through the rubble, Abraxas doing the same.

Again, that presence shifted around in my mind, but this time it was accompanied by a very audible shuffling.

I felt Abraxas freeze, "Something's in here." He drew out his sword, when I saw a dark shape move in the corner of my eye. My heart hammered in my chest as the shadow slinked around the walls, crawling over our heads and disappearing out of one of the many cracks in the wall. I just about breathed a sigh of relief when something jumped at me, clutching onto my neck.

I felt its hairy legs clinging to me and saw the flash of at least four eyes. The sound of its pinchers crinkled in my ear so close it made my skin try to crawl off my body. Abraxas raised his sword, but the little creature jumped away again, landing on the wall. But it didn't run away.

It was about the size of both my hands, with all its eight legs outstretched. I could see its four huge eyes on the front of its furry head, four more disappearing down its back. Its pincers shifted about unnervingly, but it raised its front right leg, like it was waving to me.

Abraxas charged, but I raised my hand to stop him.

"Hello, little one." I waved back at him. He raised his other front leg and shuffled side to side. "It's nice to meet you." He flared his abdomen at me, displaying the bright red underneath the dark fur of his body.

"Don't tell me, you've found another creature to befriend?" Abraxas sheathed his sword.

"Don't be jealous, Abraxas." I held out my hands tentatively, and the spider jumped onto them. My heart stopped at his rapid motions, but he settled there, waving his legs and looking at me with those big round eyes. "You have to admit, he is cute."

I didn't need to see Abraxas to feel the eye roll, "You and your beasts. I just hope his mother isn't around."

"Was something chasing you?" The spider spun in a circle, which I supposed could have meant yes.

"Tori, we need to keep searching." Abraxas was leaving the tower now, and I shifted the little thing onto my shoulder, as much as him rustling my hair and that unnerving chittering he made had my nerves crawling.

"You can come with me." He spun in a circle and flared his abdomen again.

We searched the next few rooms to find absolutely nothing but some books that crumbled at even the slightest touch and old metal sconces that hadn't been completely corroded. We weren't going to get anywhere like this. I tried to focus my breathing again, but nothing came to me, especially with the creature on my shoulder spinning and chittering.

I sighed, "I don't suppose you know where it is?" He held my two eyes staring with all eight of his. I put my hand up to the top of my head, "We are looking for a crown. You haven't seen one, have you?" To my surprise, he jumped off my shoulder and walked away.

"Guess he didn't like my questions." But then he halted, and turned back to me, waving both his front arms. Abraxas and I exchanged glances, and then followed him.

He led us deeper into a fortress, then ducked behind a root and disappeared. When I looked, I was greeted by a dark abyss leading down into the dark. It must have been an old corridor that had been nearly consumed by the roots of the tree. I turned to Abraxas, "It could be a trap."

"Yes, but we can't turn back now. Aren't you the one who always dives in headfirst?" He was right. He flicked his fingers and that emerald fire danced over his palm. I felt the trees around us groan, but they didn't move.

"Let's go."

We descended into the tunnel, with no light except for the eerie green of Abraxas' flames. My little friend waited just inside, but then led us ahead as we entered. We descended further and further down, the chill in the air now paired with a sick humidity that clung to me. I kept walking until my feet started sticking to the floor. I held Abraxas arm to move his flames further down, and I saw then the entire tunnel was coated in...

"Spiderwebs," Abraxas whispered. Huge spiderwebs, enough for a whole nest. We both stopped, and our little guide turned around, waving his arms, motioning us to keep going.

"Oh, I'm sure you would like that," Abraxas mumbled. He turned around, but I held him. My heart raced as fear spiked through me. I placed my hand on his chest and let his slow heartbeat calm mine. I felt the warmth of him and let it guide my breathing, slow in and out. I closed my eyes and reached out again. Yes, there it was, something unnatural further down into the earth. The signature of it clung to my little spider.

"We have to keep going. Something is down there; this could be it."

"Tori, I don't think—" But I stepped forward and as I did, the web under my feet pulled like the string of a great instrument, and I felt it travel through the tunnel, resonating a path straight towards us.

Suddenly, we were surrounded. I could hear them shuffling as if they had just been lying in wait. I couldn't count them, as they stayed outside our small ring of light, but I had no doubt there were hundreds, and the few who came close enough to cast their shadow were much larger than our guide. Abraxas and I drew our swords back-to-back, and the flames in his had surged. The shadows came closer and closer, the web around us pulling tight with their weight.

But suddenly I heard a sharp chittering to my side, and our small spider had crawled up on the web and waved his arms frantically, making a noise much louder than I thought he could have emitted. He pulled at the web like a code, and slowly I felt his family recede, if only just a bit. They still moved, but it was quieter, further away.

Our guide jumped to the ceiling of the tunnel and flared his abdomen before he continued on. I followed with Abraxas close behind me.

As we made our way deeper, the web was harder to traverse but I did my best not to disturb it, ducking through small holes and openings. I could hear Abraxas cursing as various parts of his larger body kept getting stuck, but eventually, we made it to a larger opening.

As he entered, his flame illuminated hundreds of small holes in the web, each like a small tunnel leading away. Inside, I saw a few spiders about the size of our guide. The nursery.

My spider crawled into one of these holes, and I was worried he expected me to follow, but a few moments later he emerged, something shining on his back.

He had wrapped it around himself and carried it to me. The metal of the diadem caged him and was nearly as corroded as everything else I had seen here. I picked it up delicately, and still, it felt moments from dissolving. I flipped it over and nearly dropped it. A great red gem looked up at me, its heart glowing with a crimson light that was laced with dark shadows. This was it, the unnatural feeling. This was what we had come for.

Abraxas leaned over my shoulder, "Crystals are the order that forms in a world inclined to chaos. They can be powerful conduits themselves. This one has been corrupted—become something beyond this world. Despite how she was hated, Queen Soraya was a powerful magic user, perhaps the most powerful. I have never felt anything like this."

Yes, nearly two thousand years had passed, and still this gem held magic beyond comprehension. But there was no time to dwell on that now. Our little guide hopped back on my shoulder, and his hurried chittering told me it was time to go.

We made our way out as quickly as possible, and I never thought I would be so happy to see the pitch-blackness of the forest spreading over my head again. We followed our golden trail back towards the edge of the fortress, when somehow the darkness grew even deeper. The air dropped to a deathly cold, and my breath came out as clouds of ice.

My little companion tried to hide himself below the blanket of my hair, sending shivers down my spine as his legs stroked the skin there. But it was nothing compared to the fear that gripped my stomach as I saw them. Despite the darkness of the forest, these were even darker. Shadows that clung to the walls and the rocks, a pure void from which nothing could escape. They rushed at us, and leapt from their flat confines into the air, great billowing clouds of nothingness. I didn't even know if I could hit them, but I swung my sword, nonetheless. It felt like passing through the thick pudding served at solstice, except that everywhere my body touched, I froze, hoarfrost coating my skin. My joints locked up and I could barely move.

Abraxas saw this, and instead lashed out with his fire, creating a great wave of that deep green power. The magic of it thrummed through the air as swirling flames danced around his fingertips, his arms. A great wall erupted around us both as temporary safety.

More shadows lunged towards him, focusing their attack, and Abraxas unleashed another torrent. The flames erupted with intense heat, engulfing the creature in an otherworldly blaze. The shadow shrieked with piercing volume, then disintegrated into nothingness.

But there were more shadows, swirling and writhing, eager to take their chance. They lunged at Abraxas from all directions, their forms distorted and amorphous. Still frozen, I could feel the darkness pressing against us, even as they ignored me for the more powerful enemy.

Abraxas moved with swift agility, dodging and weaving through the attacks. His green fire blazed brighter, illuminating the forest with a preternatural glow. With each wave of his hand, tendrils of green flames shot out, his light cutting through each shadow.

It was beyond what he could do with a sword. He and the flame were one—a weapon that moved like a force of nature itself. But the shadows kept coming in an endless onslaught. Each one drew closer to Abraxas, his power fading. Each attack closed in on our small sanctuary.

As the flames approached us, I felt the frost holding me cracking, and I finally broke free. I ran towards Abraxas, but with a great wave of his power, he pushed me away.

"Run, Tori, get out of here!"

"Not a fucking chance. I won't leave you." Yes, it was stupid to stay when I was completely useless. But I had never let that stop me before. His wall of flames sputtered around us, and the shadows grew more frenzied, sensing the end was near. Abraxas never wavered, holding his ground even as his power drained from him.

My sword was useless, so I did the only thing I could think of and placed my hands on Abraxas' back, so at least he knew I was there, that I would be there no matter what. Somehow, knowing that, the fear that gripped me seemed to slip away.

My palms met his back and flames erupted down my arm. I screamed, and my small companion jumped from me as I was consumed by the emerald fire. I felt my skin sizzling as white-hot pain shot through me. But even through the pain, I could feel something more, something deeper.

My feet rooted to the ground, and despite the unending heat of the flames, something gentle and warm trickled up through my feet and my body. It ran through me to Abraxas, and suddenly his flames exploded.

Viridian fire pressed every shadow away, reaching to the canopy of the trees above and the walls of the fortress. For a moment, the whole scene was awash in light as the trees opened up to let the sun in, and every last shadow was burned away.

I slumped to the ground, the smell of my burned flesh stung my nostrils, and huge black scorches snaked across every part of me that I could see.

"*Tori*!" Abraxas wrapped his arms around me, clutching me to his chest. Immediately, the pain ebbed, as his very presence seemed like a soothing balm. I looked at my arms and saw the burns fading, new tan skin appearing beneath.

"I'm alright, I think. We have to go, Abraxas." I carefully placed my hand over the pocket I had placed the diadem in, and found my clothes were unharmed, the gem still resting inside.

With no hesitation, he swept me up and dashed away from the fortress. But slowly the trees grew back together over us, the darkness consuming everything once more. Abraxas ran faster, but I could hear them now, their eerie shrieking growing closer. I don't think we could pull off that miracle again.

He squeezed me tighter, "You're mine, Tori. And I'll keep you safe, no matter the cost." His feet stopped, but all I could stare at was his eyes, as the golden flecks at the center seemed to grow outwards, glowing like the sun.

All of a sudden, a small furry bundle landed on my chest, waving his little arms and chittering. They were everywhere, hundreds of them. Spiders of all sizes, from small like mine to as wide as three horses. They descended from the trees on spindles of silk or crawled around the trunks.

Whereas my sword had been ineffective, the spiders were able to snatch the shadows in their mandibles, pulling at their essence like some sick taffy. They stretched and pulled and wrapped them in their webs until they were immobilized.

My little spider waved his arms at me, pride shining in his eyes. "Thank you, little friend." Abraxas had regained himself and started running again. But as we left the fortress behind, a great shadow reared itself in our path. This one seemed more solid, and I saw it form into a shape that could almost be called human, its smoke-like form swelling out into great skirts, and shadows piercing up above its head like a dark pantomime of a crown.

She raised her hand, an accusatory point at us, at me, where the diadem lay. The forest around us swelled, wind picking up and lashing at her, but it had no more effect than a child pulling at his mother's skirts. A great gaping hole opened where her mouth might be, as a shriek that nearly pierced my ears emerged.

Thief!

Abraxas squeezed me close again, but then the shadow was gone, crushed beneath the body of something much larger. The spider was almost as large as the Nalle we had fought, its fangs longer than my arm. It sank them into the shadow's neck and curled its legs around her. Her shriek grew even higher, and I couldn't understand her words, but it didn't matter. Abraxas ran around the great battle between queens, and we didn't look back.

Chapter 56

Tori

We made it back to the site of camp, and I was relieved to see it empty. The cohort had followed Abraxas' orders not to wait for us.

Abraxas continued to run, but my burns weren't so severe now, so I forced him to drop me. He was panting, but together we kept sprinting along that blue lit path until we reached the edge of the forest.

When we burst from the trees, the shock of the evening sun blinded me. I blinked and rubbed my eyes until I could see beyond that endless white light and found every soldier we had lined up at the edge of the forest.

Their faces held a mixture of relief and shock, some held their weapons aloft. I was still trying to resolve the faces before me when a tall figure burst forward.

"You fucking idiots!" Avlyn threw their arms around me and Abraxas, crushing against my still aching skin, "You...absolutely... stupid...assholes...." They were sobbing. Tears streamed down their cheeks, dripping onto my hair and face. I was too stunned to do much, but I felt Abraxas wrap his arms around them, running his hand over their head.

"Where do you think you learned it from, Commander?" Avlyn laughed and sobbed, the sound coming out more of a cough. But Abraxas continued to embrace them, and despite their anguish, a smile spread on my face.

A few moments later, it seemed that Avlyn had composed themselves, and pulled away, "Don't you ever do anything like that again."

"Wouldn't dream of it, Avlyn." I couldn't help but smile at them.

They shook their head, "Let's get the hell out of this place, yeah?"

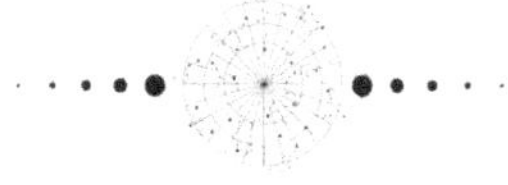

Our journey back to Xyr was subdued. I had finally pried it out of Kaleos and Oryx that what had felt like a few days in the forest had been closer to a month. Our journey to the Eternal City had seemed only a few hours, but three days had passed since the cohort had left the forest. Avlyn had arrived after our group had been gone for two weeks and had been running single-day scouting missions with no success.

That morning, a huge eruption of emerald fire had breached the forest, and they had been prepared to go back in. Luckily, we had come out before they could.

"So, what happened in there?" Kaleos had asked cautiously near the fire one night.

"I don't think you'd believe me if I told you."

He made to argue with me, when instead he released an extremely high-pitched screech as Spinner walked over his leg.

I had tried to send the little rascal back into the forest, but he refused, instead settling down on my shoulder as I helped pack up camp. He mostly kept near me, away from the others, except for Oryx. He had taken to bringing the poor male mice wrapped up in silk, like little gifts. Oryx laughed and patted him on the head, which caused him to perform one of his namesake spins and trot off. Oryx always managed to stash the dead mice somewhere discreet.

Now he curled up in my lap like some sort of eight-legged cat. Kaleos decided that was quite enough of our conversation and slunk off. I absentmindedly stroked Spinner's back and he chittered, "Don't mind him. It seems he has a bit of a phobia. Not your fault, but maybe you could stop walking over him?"

Spinner stretched a few legs lazily and settled back down, eyes closing. I felt Abraxas sit down next to me with barely a sound. He reached over and gave the spider a few strokes, which he leaned into greedily.

"Don't get too comfortable, little beast, I'm going to steal her away from you." Spinner gave an angry chitter, snapping his fangs at Abraxas. But with a small push from me, he stretched his legs again, and then sauntered off into the night. Abraxas chuckled, "Such a possessive little thing."

"I always did like the males in my life a bit possessive," I ran my hand over his thigh and leaned into him. He ran his fingers down my back gently, but then whisked me up into his arms.

"I can walk on my own, you know."

"Where is the fun in that, Princess?"

Chapter 57

Tori

Once we had reached Xyr, Abraxas had given the diadem—or what was left of it—to a few of his scholars most versed in ancient enchantments. Despite my need for it, it felt good to have it out of my hands, the wrongness seemed to linger on my skin.

After a very long shower, I finally felt like a fae again and settled in for a very long rest on an actual bed. Just as my head hit the pillow, Abraxas entered my room, no knock.

It was a bit strange to see him here, as we had spent almost all our time together in his room.

"You didn't come to bed."

"I thought..." Well, I don't know what I thought. I'd touched him since our fight in the forest, and I hadn't felt anything like that surge of power again, but I had still been cautious.

I moved and made room for him in the bed next to me. He wrapped his arms around me and held my head to his chest as he stroked my hair. A long silence stretched out between us, not uncomfortable, but held on the edge of what we both hesitated to discuss. But he broke the silence first.

"Tell me what happened in the forest."

I flexed my fingers, some of the skin there still paler than its neighbor due to the burns, "When I touched you, I felt your power jump to me, but I couldn't control it, so it ripped through me." His grip tightened on me, as if he could protect me from it. "I won't lie, it hurt like hell, but underneath that, I felt something gentle. Not from you, but from the earth itself. It flowed through me into you, and that's when your magic surged."

"You conducted the magic of this world. You are a conduit."

I sat up then, looking deep into him, and I knew there was no lie. "You said the Great Beasts were conduits. I'm just a fae, and one without any magic at all."

"You possess a deep connection with nature, a kinship with this world," he chuckled. "Every beast within one hundred leagues can't seem to keep their hands off you. Does it really surprise you so?"

"Jun was always the one. His singing, his presence. Perhaps I always knew it was more than just a natural gift. But the world stopped for him, never me."

Abraxas reached out, tracing my jaw gently then, "But you were always there beside him, weren't you? Who is to say it wasn't watching you both?"

"Always the spare, supporting someone else it seems."

He pulled me to him again, but I could feel his chest rumbling with laughter. "I don't think anyone would dare think you are anything other than extraordinary, Tori." His face darkened then. "You could learn to control this, to shape and command it. To pull almost unlimited power from the earth, far more than any other fae could."

"I thought that magic was fading, what would I tap into?"

"No, the earth has stopped allowing the fae to access it, but it's still there, deep below the surface. The conduits however..."

"How do you know all this? I suppose getting old has its

benefits." I'd wanted to see him give me that annoyed smile, but his face only grew darker.

"Yes, I've seen many things in my life, Tori, but these past decades have been unprecedented. So much has changed, so many things erratic and dangerous," he squeezed me now to the point of bruising, "Hadeon cannot know about this. I will burn this entire world to the ground before I let him have you." That emerald fire danced in his eyes, and my skin prickled. I had no doubt it was true, but I wouldn't let it come to that.

But I saw him there, that dark god who struck fear into the hearts of so many. An ancient fae who hailed from a time of unlimited magic and ruin.

"I wish I could have seen you at full power. You control fire and the air, you must have been extraordinary," I laid a soft kiss on his jaw as I said it.

His eyes stayed dark as he answered, "Be careful what you wish for, Princess, you just might receive it."

I knew he was more than that, more than an ancient force of darkness and magic. But there was one more thing I had to know, had to slot that one last piece in place.

I gently placed a hand on his chest, and I felt the smallest swelling of something light and golden.

"Abraxas, may I ask you something? Something painful?" He raised his brows at me but nodded his head, "Will you tell me what happened to your father?"

I felt his whole body shutter, and he released his grip on me. That icy mask I hadn't seen in so long, locked back into place.

"What is there to tell, everyone knows the story. Hadeon moved to destroy the World Breaker and my father stood in the way, unwilling to let go of the Dragon Kingdom's source of power. I stabbed him in the back, surrendered to Hadeon, and received this Kingdom as my prize." Anger rose in his eyes, "A coward's story."

"You are no coward, Abraxas. Tell me what really happened." I grabbed his face as he tried to pull away, "Tell me the truth."

His laugh sounded like a death knell. "What value does the truth have when none would listen to it."

"I'm listening, Abraxas. I trust you," I wove my fingers in between his, as he had for me not long ago, "and you can trust me."

For a long time, he was silent, but a sigh escaped his lips. "When my mother died, my father never recovered. I think that a son is always left wondering so many things about his father, but I never doubted how much he loved her. When he lost her..." He paused, I gave his hand a squeeze and he continued, "He no longer made choices as a king, but as a broken man. When the final fight came, I begged him to surrender. I knew that it wouldn't be a battle, but a slaughter. Hadeon didn't care who was in his way, he would destroy them all. Civilians, children, families, fae, and human alike. Our army could fight, but we couldn't defend them all when he specifically targeted them, and Xyr was in his path to victory."

"At first, my father agreed. He agreed to allow Hadeon's army into the city, so that he could continue on his quest for Malech. But he had lied, led Hadeon's army into a trap, and had our soldiers attack." Another long silence. "It was worse than if they had met in battle. My city burned before Malech even attacked." I remember my vision, of soldiers and bodies in the streets as Malech scorched Xyr.

I saw the tear that rolled from his eye, the ghosts still there that haunted him. "My kingdom was dying, and the man I loved was already long gone." I pressed a kiss to his cheek, the salt of that tear wetting my lips. I didn't need him to say more. I just needed him to know that I understood. He had held this pain alone for centuries and let it turn him into something frozen. But he didn't need to do that anymore.

I kissed his cheeks, gentle caresses to try and wipe away that pain. I kissed his lips, and felt him shift, his hand wrapping around the back of my neck and into my hair. He held tight to me as if he were afraid I would slip away, like I would melt into the mist that hung across the ocean. His touch became uncontrolled as he ripped at my clothes, his mouth bearing down on my neck and shoulders, his teeth scraping my flesh. But I could be that for him, I could pull all his pain away with my body, my mouth, my soul.

I wrapped my legs around his hips, and in an instant, he slid himself completely inside me. I let the pain guide me closer to him as I kissed his mouth once more, our bodies rocking together. I opened myself to him, wanting to take every bit of him. His thrusts became faster, more desperate. I lifted my hips to him, my body starting to build that beautiful tension.

"Tori..." I looked into his eyes, and they seemed so far away. I felt like I was losing him, that he was but a moment from slipping through my fingers.

"Make me come, Abraxas. Please, *My King*." I saw him then, the fire returning to him as he shifted his hand along my side and over the curve of my ass. He gripped my hips so that he was pushed up against that perfect spot inside me, and my head fell back. He continued to hit the very end of me as his mouth came down to clamp on my nipples. My orgasm tore through me, and I clung to him as if he were life itself.

"Tori—" The plea fled his lips, and I knew what he needed. I locked my eyes with his, "I'm yours, Abraxas, and you are mine." His lips and tongue danced with mine, and I lost myself in him, that familiar golden thread stretched between our hearts. His long fingers weaved in between my own, and I felt him pulse as he found his release.

We lay there, his weight pressed into me, and I wished I could stay there, smothered in him forever. I pushed his long hair aside and placed one last gentle kiss on his throat, which was laid bare for me.

"Careful, little bird. My neck has been much more sensitive ever since a certain someone almost decapitated me." He lifted his head, and that mischievous smile melted me.

"Eh, might have been an improvement on your looks, I'm still considering it." He nipped my lip in retort, but it turned into a long, soft kiss before he rolled me to him and we drifted off to sleep.

Chapter 58

Tori

A few days later, Abraxas brought me with him into his study, and Spinner demanded to accompany us. I hadn't seen him much since we'd returned to the palace, but Ciara had informed me that there had been no sightings of any mice or rats on our side of the castle since. It seemed that the cats who normally caught them had also gone missing. I would have to chat with him about staying in my wing, maybe giving my room over to him.

But once we entered the study, I was immediately overwhelmed by the gem, its dark tendrils reaching for me, all too similar to that deep sleep that some very small part of me still felt comforted by. I longed to run. But Abraxas placed his hand on my back, in line with my heart. I felt it slow back down.

A pair of scholars stood near the table along with Avlyn. One a half-fae woman with long golden hair, and deep brown eyes named Amara. The other, a human man far past the prime of life, with wild grey hair that stuck out in every direction named Fuscus.

On the table I saw the gem and swore it pulsed with an eerie heartbeat. Next to it sat an unbelievably extravagant necklace. Dark metal had been woven into intricate settings, holding seven blood-red rubies paired with countless black diamonds to create a dazzling piece that would have covered almost my entire chest. Well, six rubies and one empty place meant for an ancient, enchanted gem from a lost kingdom.

The woman spoke softly, "I have crafted this as you specified, Your Majesty. There are fortifying runes in the setting," she pursed her lips, "but I fear that will not be enough to contain this." She glanced over to the gem, beating on the table.

"I still have a few tricks up these ancient sleeves, Amara." He was beaming and gave me a quick wink.

The man spoke with a frantic, enthusiastic voice, "The gem holds incredible magic. In all our tests, just bringing it within an inch of the enchantment completely unravels it. No counter effect. Nothing. As if the enchantment were simply removed from the fabric of our reality." He sounded thoroughly impressed, and I saw Amara shoot him a soft, loving smile. "It's almost too simple, I can't understand it."

"The most powerful magics are often the most simple." Abraxas eyed the gem, but did not move to touch it. Spinner climbed out from under my hair, and both scholars started, but the man immediately leaned in, pulling a strange spectacle out from his pocket, and looking at Spinner closely.

"Fascinating, is this the beast that helped you find the gem?" I nodded my head, "May I?" He reached out his hand, and Spinner hopped right over to him. The man kept examining the spider, and I heard him whisper, "Fascinating," a few more times.

Amara cleared her throat and gave Fuscus that lovingly annoyed look I had seen Abraxas give me basically every day. I couldn't help my grin as he returned Spinner to me and turned back to the gem.

"Your Majesty, while the necklace may be able to hold this, it will be very obvious that this is no normal ruby. Even someone with very little magical knowledge will be able to sense it."

Abraxas' mischievous smile blossomed, but he said, "I will take care of it from here. Thank you for your assistance, Amara and Fuscus." They both bowed and took the dismissal. I saw Fuscus grab Amara's hand as they left, looking more like father and daughter than husband and wife. I was suddenly very glad that Abraxas would age at the same rate as myself.

"So, what's the plan, Abraxas?" Avlyn stepped forward, keeping away from my shoulder that held Spinner. Abraxas still had that grin on his face as he opened a drawer on the side of the room and pulled out a great vellum scroll. He rolled it out on the table to reveal an intricate glyph designed with runes and other markings I didn't recognize.

Avlyn ran their fingers over the border of the design, "A glamour? I thought this magic had been lost to you?" They weren't trying to wound Abraxas, but I saw the sadness reflected in both of their eyes.

"It was, but things have changed." His eyes shone with something it took me a moment to recognize—hope. "Tori, would you please assist me." I didn't know what I could do, as I knew so little about magic, but he waved his hand to the necklace.

I picked it up and held it, tilting it slightly so the hundreds of diamonds twinkled in the light from the window. "You had this made in only a few days? You must have quite the collection of gems to just have massive rubies like this ready."

I heard Avlyn laugh, "Oh, he has quite the collection, alright. I'm surprised he hasn't shown you."

"I wanted to make sure that Tori wanted me for my winning personality before I showed her my hoard. Many have been overcome by its sheer size." He winked at me again, and I laughed. I'd never heard him flirt with me like that before, and I loved it.

Avlyn, on the other hand, groaned, "What did I do in a past life to deserve this personal hell?"

But I set the necklace down in the glyph, and the room grew tense. After a few beats of silence, Abraxas said, "Tori, if you would set the gem."

My inside writhed like a pit of snakes, telling me not to touch that thing. I reached for it and flinched as pain numbed my fingers. But Spinner positioned himself on my shoulder again, and somehow, the pain subsided.

"Thank you, little friend." I placed the gem in the setting and used a simple tool to bend the metal to hold the gem in place. Despite Spinner's assistance, I was more than happy to let go of it.

"Good, now touch me just like you did in the forest." I heard Avlyn mumbling again at the innuendo, but I was too nervous to laugh.

"Abraxas, I don't know what I did, or how to control it. I don't know anything about magic at all really."

"Yes, but I do, and I will teach you."

I stepped behind him and placed my palms on his back. I closed my eyes. "Match my breathing, Tori. Good. Now let your thoughts go, focus only on the stone below your feet."

I imagined that ocean, the one I had known for so long. My breath synced with the soft waves, the sea foam lapping at my feet. The waves were warm, and slowly I sank in, but I was not afraid as I felt Abraxas as my anchor. Soon, the warmth consumed me but I still breathed. I felt it travel from me to him and a soft golden light filled the room. I opened my eyes. The glyph was glowing like a small sun, the warm light gently pressing down on the harsh red that rose from the jewel.

"Breathe, Tori." I closed my eyes again and focused, allowing myself to be empty, just a channel for that light. But then the light faded, and I felt Abraxas move. "It is done."

I looked around him at the necklace and felt...nothing. No oppressive energy, no strange shadows. The gem now looked like just another of the rubies, sparkling and innocent.

Avlyn stared. "How is this possible?" They looked at me with that raw adoration in their eyes, and I had to look away.

Abraxas placed his arm on my back again, "You've changed everything, Tori."

Chapter 59

Tori

Time sped by as we prepared for our assault on Hadeon. We spent days pouring over maps of Hadeon's castle that Abraxas' spies had brought in, figuring out how we would reach and destroy his enchantment.

But as much as I wished to spend every minute on our plan, life continued on, and we royals had to make our appearances.

Midsummer approached, and with it another celebration. Hadeon had invited himself again, but this time, I didn't break down. Instead, I knew this would be another opportunity to understand my enemy.

We'd received word he would arrive after the main celebration. I decided this meant that I could enjoy myself before that, if only just a little bit.

Ciara had been subdued, and I worried for her, but she gritted her teeth and got me ready with all the cheer she could muster. I wore a fantastic deep green gown trimmed with golden leaves. I noted how it matched the king's eyes almost perfectly, and I finally saw Ciara crack that wicked smile.

The summer solstice was celebrated in the fields outside the city, and much like Lupercalia, great bonfires had been lit. The warm evening air mixed with the soft embers and sent them skyward. The rolling green grass of the kingdom was at full strength and was welcoming beneath my feet. I couldn't help kicking off my shoes and running through it like a child, barely restraining myself from rolling myself down the nearest hill.

This festival was much more casual, and citizens milled everywhere. Music abounded, and already the party atmosphere was rampant.

Abraxas approached my side, "We won't have long out here tonight, and I need to greet several people before we leave." He held his hand out to me, but my eyes were caught on the dancing around the bonfires. Young girls in white were everywhere, beautiful flower crowns in their hair, all holding hands and dancing a simple but beautiful dance around the fire. A dark thought struck me.

"Will you play the role of the stag king tonight?" I felt his chest rumble with laughter as he placed an arm around my waist.

"What a jealous thing you have become. But no, I haven't done that in centuries. Midsummer is for the young, not ancient things like us." He pointed across the field, where I saw a young human boy adorned in body paint and a huge headdress of antlers laced with flowers and greens. He stood tall, but I could feel him quaking from here. I couldn't help my sigh of relief.

He pulled me closer, whispering in my ear, "The only sacrifice I'm interested in certainly isn't some green maiden, but I'll be sure to devour you just the same." I bumped my hip into him and shivered in delight. But my eyes were still on all those bodies dancing, the young people feeling that first experience of a hedonistic love that consumed everything. I did feel quite removed from them. How fast their lives were, and how very urgent everything felt.

"Go dance," Abraxas whispered to me. "Enjoy yourself, I'll

find you when I'm done." He didn't have to tell me twice. I smiled at him, then ran off towards the fire in my bare feet.

I joined the circle of dancers, moving with them, our hearts beating together. Sweat quickly built on my brow from the warm summer air in contrast to the cool grass between my toes. But then I felt it, that warm sensation, trickling up through me, running up my legs and body into my arms. I almost jerked away, unsure of what would happen, but I felt it flow into the circle of dancers and we all came alive. Our feet moved faster, but our energy grew. The flowers in the girls' hair shimmered and bloomed brighter and our skin glowed with a sweet warm light. I heard laughter from every direction, as euphoria raced through the crowd. And then I saw it.

One girl, beautiful with flowing locks of golden hair. She glowed brighter than all the rest. The vines on her head grew into spikes, a true crown for tonight's queen. I released the hands I held, but the magic stayed, winding its way amongst the crowd. But I made my way to the glowing girl, and gently pulled her from the circle. She wore a grin of pure, undiluted delight as she grabbed my hands and started spinning us in our own dance. Her white skirts flared and her bare feet skipped along with mine as I guided us towards tonight's king.

"I've never been so happy, and I don't know why!" She giggled, and kept dancing, "Do you think it could be me? Could I be the queen? What an honor!" She darted her eyes over to the boy who would be her consort tonight, and I saw color rise in her cheeks. "He's so handsome. No, it couldn't be me." Her eyes lowered.

"I wouldn't be so sure, mysterious forces are at play on nights like this." I grinned at her as her eyes widened. But before she could respond, I spun her, and her feet flew across the ground until she landed in the arms of the waiting stag king. I saw his eyes widen as well, as his arms wrapped around her. His cheeks matched hers as they glowed red, but after just a moment, the magic had caught him too, and they danced together.

"Playing matchmaker, I see," Abraxas said, returning to my side. "And that's not all, it seems." I hit him with my most innocent look, and he chuckled. "Time to head back to the castle, but I hope you saved a dance for me, my little enchantress."

The nobles had all gathered in the throne room, and it had been transformed into a beautiful garden. Greenery ran up the walls, and instead of the traditional torches, hundreds of tiny candles had been lit to fill the scene, twinkling like stars in the night.

Each of the nobles looked like exotic flowers, their clothes in every shade imaginable. The music was light and lovely, matching the atmosphere of the celebration still running wild outside our walls. I still had a few hours before Hadeon's expected arrival, and I wouldn't waste it.

I grabbed a glass of ambrosia and was going to make my way over to Lady Lovatia and her companions for a bit of gossip when a strong hand gripped around my waist.

"I will be taking that dance now, Princess." Abraxas grinned, in a manner so unlike his normal courtly appearance. I couldn't resist. I set my glass down and let him lead me out to the dance floor. We hadn't danced since Lupercalia, and we had never danced together at court.

It was ridiculous to feel nervous. It was obviously known we had a relationship, but somehow this felt different than hasty hallway dalliances. This felt more revealing. But he hit me with that smile I knew only I got to see, and I truly was enchanted.

He carefully grabbed my waist and injured arm and we were off. I had learned more of the dances now and was able to follow along more gracefully. He guided me around the floor, and through various spins and dips, and I found myself completely lost in him.

He spun me around again, and when I returned to him, instead of catching my hands, he let me fall into him, wrapping his arms around my back, and holding me close. The ambrosia and magic of the night made me bold, so I teased him, "Careful now, Your Majesty. Keep holding me like this and everyone will think there is truth to our engagement rumors."

His eyes twinkled, "Oh, so you think you could have me, do you?"

"Well, I could, couldn't I?" I pouted at him.

His face dropped to be much more serious, and he held my gaze, "Yes. Every part of me." My heart stuttered at his answer, but before I could even regain my breath, he brought his lips to mine and kissed me tenderly before his entire court.

My heart fully stopped then, thinking of what his words meant, what they revealed. He pulled back from the kiss, and I slid my hand up to his jaw, lost in the eternal meadows of his eyes, "Abraxas, I—"

But before I could form my thoughts, the doors of the ballroom flew open, and Emperor Hadeon strolled in.

My body seized, and felt Abraxas squeeze me closer for just a moment before striding over to the emperor, surreptitiously placing his body between me and our enemy.

"Your Eminence, I wasn't expecting you until this evening."

"Nor should you have, Abraxas, I wanted to make this visit a surprise." His eyes twinkled as they locked eyes with me. He wore elaborately decorated violet robes, as he always did, covered in gold embroidery of the flaming crown. On each of his arms clung a fae. On his left was a beautiful female with long, flowing golden brown hair, and fair skin. She wore a golden gown that, on closer inspection, was a beautiful combination of sheer and opaque in the appropriate places and clung to her body like oil. She was stunning, but her features were fierce, those of a hunter. This must have been Pallas, his long-time consort.

On his right, an equally beautiful male with tan skin and dark hair shorn short, only hanging long in the front, creating casually swept bangs. He wore a magenta jacket, and was covered in gold jewelry that complimented the golden eyeliner that accented his almond shaped eyes.

Bile rose in my throat, and I had to use all the strength I had not to heave all over the floor. I hadn't recognized him, his hair short and eyes dazed, but my brother stood there next to our mother's murderer, his head lying intimately on his shoulder. The twinkle in the emperor's eye had turned malicious as he saw the recognition in my gaze.

"I thought our dear princess here would like to see her brother; it has been such a while. Besides, we have some very good news." There must have been a very long pause, but I didn't notice it as time seemed to cease existing while I stared at my brother who wouldn't meet my gaze.

"What is your good news, Divine Emperor?" Abraxas's lips were tight, and I could feel him trying to calm me, keeping his body in front of mine to prevent me from pouncing.

"Tell her, my love." Hadeon swept a soft kiss over Jun's brow, and an acidic taste filled my mouth. Jun finally met my eyes for just a moment, before turning to the emperor and whispering in his ear.

"Well, of course, darling. You see, in the Court of Flames we don't really participate in marriage, such a naive and *human* tradition. But my lover, Jun here, has pledged himself to me for eternity, just as Pallas has." He nuzzled his nose into Pallas' hair and neck, but her face remained unmoved. But I didn't have time to decipher how she really felt about all this, as my mind had turned into a sea of lava, and all I could see was red.

I lunged, hands and nails outstretched, but Abraxas caught me across the chest. He pressed his mouth to my ear. "Calm yourself, now." But I could barely hear him and thrashed my hands out as if I could claw the emperor to death. "Still a hellcat, I see. Abraxas, I expected more from you on getting this little beast in line."

"She seems more than willing to submit for the right rewards, Hadeon." Abraxas tried to remain calm, keeping that cool aristocratic mask in place while he pulled my back to his chest, locking my arms to my side. He finally had me under control when Hadeon turned to my brother and ran a single golden nail down his cheek.

"Yes, I find that the right reward can lead to a great deal of compliance," he mused and stuck his tongue down my brother's throat.

Something inside me tried to rip out, burst through my skin, destroy everything that I was and burn it into something new. But Abraxas brought his hand up my throat and then to my jaw, turning me to look at him. He moved in close, and barely whispered in my ear, "Soon, my love."

My blood cooled, and I stilled my breath. Yes, it wouldn't do to ruin all of our plans and hard work. I pictured that ocean, deep and serene, and let that raging inferno inside me sink away until nothing but mist remained.

Hadeon released my brother, and I tried to put my own mask into place. It had been so long since I had worn it, I'd almost forgotten how.

"Please excuse my outburst, Your Eminence. Sometimes I still forget myself," I leaned into Abraxas then, head bowed, the model of obedience, "Please forgive me, My King."

We'd talked about this, the role I would have to play for

Hadeon. The little pet that I should have been. A submissive girl couldn't be a threat, could she? I cursed myself for forgetting before we had even begun. Fear stole into my heart. What if I had ruined our chances already?

Abraxas laced his hand around my throat, the pressure there very real, and my vision began to darken, "You'll receive your punishment later." Damn him, the smirk in his eyes told me he knew that had me throbbing, even if this was all an act.

"A fine idea, Abraxas, I had hoped to see our princess at the party tonight." Something deep and wicked filled Hadeon's eyes as he watched Abraxas for a reaction. But Abraxas didn't waver.

"So long as her brother isn't also there." Hadeon waved his hand, as if that was obvious. Abraxas released my neck, and I stepped behind him, face down. But I let my eyes drift to Jun, who now stood at Pallas' side. Her face was still stone, but I saw her pinky finger rub against Jun's for a moment. An accident? Perhaps.

Abraxas dismissed me with a wave of his hand and told me to go prepare for the party. I was heading out of the hall when Lady Bogata grabbed my arm, much more forcefully than I would have expected. It seemed she had returned with Hadeon from Koron. She dragged me away from the rest of the guests, "Before you go, Your Highness, I just wanted to let you know, your brother's singing is so beautiful, and I so enjoy it. But I was saddened on my previous visit, for I wasn't able to hear it. It seems he hasn't had the energy for it much recently."

She bore into me with her eyes that so mirrored the golden wheat fields that she oversaw. This time I understood her meaning, and my heart was clamped in a great vice. We were running out of time.

"Thank you, My Lady. I hope that on your next visit you will be able to enjoy the pleasures of Koron in a whole new light."

I exited the great hall, and my stomach churned. Hadeon's

guards in their golden armor surrounded a group of men and women dressed in nothing but rags, who were unloading supplies from Hadeon's caravan. Each had metal shackles on their ankles or neck. Slaves. Closer inspection showed me they were all human.

I set my jaw, teeth clenched, as I approached the guards. "What is the meaning of this, slaves are not allowed in this kingdom."

A guard looked me up and down from behind his helmet, "I don't answer to you, only to our Divine Emperor." I decided how best to run this cretin through with his own blade, when a trembling hand grabbed my elbow.

"Your Highness, please let's go." It was Ciara. She was shaking like a leaf, tears welling in her eyes. I wrapped my arms around her, and led her away, but not before shooting the guard one last look.

As we left, my resolve set. Whatever tonight would bring, I would face it.

Chapter 60

Tori

Ciara fussed around me. She was manic now. I placed a gentle hand on her arm, "It's alright, Ciara. Why don't you turn in for the night, get away from all this."

She paused, and I saw her picking at her nails the way she always did when she was agitated. "Some of those men with Hadeon. When I lived in Koron, they..." I squeezed her arm just as she had done to me some time ago. She didn't have to tell me.

"None of them will ever hurt you again, Ciara. I promise you." She looked at me with sadness in her eyes, but then it dropped, and she merely stood there, blank.

"Let me walk you to your room." I escorted her in eerie silence and made sure she was tucked away before returning to my own quarters.

Abraxas was there waiting for me. He wore a simple but finely made night robe, but he wore his crown atop his head which was such a ridiculous juxtaposition I almost laughed. But somehow, I couldn't find the humor in it tonight. He swept me into his arms, crushing me to his chest.

"You don't have to do this, Tori."

"No, I do. None of this will work if he suspects I'm not under your control."

"He will need to see you submit, fully." I understood what he meant, but I wasn't afraid.

His lips pulled tight, but he released me, and then handed me a package I hadn't seen. Inside was a tiny garment that at first was very confusing. It seemed to be composed of hundreds of small shimmering dark threads, each sparkled and shone as if they were infused with black diamonds. The 'dress' clasped behind my neck and covered none of my back, the loose strings hung over my breasts and created a very short skirt. They would move as I walked, revealing everything beneath.

"How long have you been waiting for me to wear this for you?" I smiled at Abraxas, but he did not return it. I laced my hand through his silver hair, "You said yourself, he needs to see this, he needs to believe. We can do this."

"This is not us tonight, Tori. This is an act. Know that." He grabbed my head the same way I held his, and I couldn't look away from his pained eyes. "Please know that if anything is too much, you know the word to say. I'll stop, no matter the cost."

"I know. We will play our parts. And I will be alright because I have you there with me." The smallest smile flicked at the corner of his mouth.

"And I always will be." He gave me the gentlest kiss but sealed it with a firm bite to my bottom lip. I hissed, and he gave me that deep chuckle that had me on fire. "I'll have to beg your forgiveness later, as I think I might enjoy this role with you a little too much." I smacked his chest lightly, but the nervousness in my stomach was coiling around something devious, and I enjoyed the sensation.

Chapter 61

Tori

The party was already in full swing when we arrived. The music blared and bodies in every state of undress could be seen everywhere. Abraxas led us through the crowd to the main stage, where a whole slew of bodies writhed. I didn't have time to parse them out before that horrible pressure filled the air, and I felt Hadeon approach us.

Pallas was draped on his arm, her dress a mimic of the one earlier tonight, but with even less fabric present. Hadeon stroked her arm, but she wore that same stone-cold expression I had seen before.

I didn't dare look at Hadeon, instead I continued to examine Pallas. She didn't wear a collar, or any other sort of jewelry I could see. So, she had no excuse. She finally reacted after I had been staring for quite some time, her eyes daggers that I felt were a mirror of my own.

The men led us away, breaking our eye contact. A moment later, Abraxas sat down in a huge chair, Hadeon sitting in its twin beside him. He pulled me onto his lap, and I curled up into him, the image of a subservient little doll. He traced his fingers down the bare skin of my back and thighs, and despite the proximity to Hadeon, I felt my lower muscles curl and wetness spread at my core, no cloth there to hold it back. The sounds coming from the stage only amplified it.

Hadeon positioned Pallas so she was seated on her knees on the floor in front of him. Her head rested on his knee, and he gently stroked her hair. The men chatted about recent news across the kingdom, but I let Abraxas keep track of that information. I let my mind wander, let myself focus on the sounds of the music and the room, and filled my nose with a mix of sweat and sex and ambrosia that lingered everywhere. The sounds from the stage reached a crescendo as this act came to an end. Out of the corner of my eye, I saw Hadeon's fingers clamp down on Pallas' head through her hair. My stomach jolted as he unlaced his trousers and pulled her between his knees. I turned my head away.

"No need to be shy, hellcat. It's all part of the show." Abraxas pressed his hand against the back of my head, pushing me into the crook of his neck, where I was comforted by the smell of him.

"She knows better than to look without permission, Hadeon."

"You've always been so possessive, Abraxas, I never understood it." His sentence ended with a very male groan, and I didn't need to see to know what was happening.

This was it. I couldn't hide in Abraxas' arms anymore. I shifted myself and attempted to lower myself to my knees to mimic Pallas. But Abraxas' fingers sunk into my hips, holding me to him. He was shaking. I looked into his eyes, and so much was trapped behind them. I didn't dare kiss him, so instead I said, "What do you desire, My King?" I placed my hand on his chest, right over his heart, and I hoped he understood.

He leaned into me, and whispered in my ear, "It seems you haven't been able to pay your Tithe, little bird." Heat swept from the back of my head where he still held me, straight down my spine. I shifted to straddle him, but before I could he whispered one last thing, "It's just you and me here, Tori." I pulled away from him, knees on either side of his legs, and ground my hips into him.

"Where's the fun in that, My King?" Only a thin piece of cloth separated us as I rubbed against him again, and I could feel my arousal making an utter mess of it. I swept my hands down his chest, opening up his robe, landing on the velvet hardness of him. I raised myself up, and he sunk the tips of his fingers into my hips with bruising strength as I placed his broad head at my entrance and slid down him.

For a few moments, it was just us. I could feel the rush of his pulse under my hands as I laid them on his shoulders, his breath synchronized with mine. But when I had taken him all, and my core rubbed against his hips, the sounds and sights of the rooms crashed back into me.

Whereas before the room had been loud, it seemed to have grown quieter, even though moaning and thumping could still be heard from every direction. Now I heard whispers, and I could practically feel the eyes landed on us. Abraxas ran his hands over the curve of my ass and lifted the short skirt of my dress up over my hips, and I knew I was on full display for everyone, spread open by Abraxas' cock.

I felt blood rise into my cheeks and rush through my ears, but Abraxas snagged my chin in his fingers, "Everyone wishes they could have that sweet cunt of yours, Princess. But they all know they can't. Show them who it belongs to." He guided my hips up and down, and our rhythm increased. He leaned himself back, the picture of arrogance as I fucked him, but his eyes never left mine. They held me, and kept me safe, and I moved. I rocked my hips, knowing it displayed us to the room, and a feral moan fled his lips. I copied it with my own as desire swept through me.

I continued to ride him, but he kept his hands on my hips. My clit ached for more stimulation, and I slid my own hand down. But he caught my wrist, and his other hand left a resounding spank on my ass cheek.

"Naughty princess. You know you need my permission to come."

"Please, My King. Please, let me come."

"When you've earned it, Princess." He grasped my hips firmly again, but to my surprise, lifted me off of him. He spun me around, so I faced outward into the room and slammed me back down upon his cock. His hands spread my legs wide. If I thought I was on display before, it was nothing compared to this. He thrust up into me as I continued to meet him, and his hands danced over my breasts, which bounced with each thrust. I could really see them all now, the eyes of so many of the court, locked on us.

Our word danced on my lips, as more and more pairs of eyes seemed to rake my body, that part of myself I had never before revealed. But that deeper part of me that had tried to keep dormant for so long, reveled in it. Before, I would have shoved it all down, buried the fear somewhere I couldn't see. But not now. I rode that fear and let it transform into something new. I did the same with my shame and burned it into pride. I let all my emotions flow through me and grow, each ratcheting up my arousal, bringing me closer and closer to falling over the edge.

"That's it, Princess. See how they worship you. But you are mine." He bit down on my neck in that delicate place, and I threw my head back as more and more moans passed my lips.

"Please, Abraxas." He finally relieved me, his fingers giving me that delicious pressure as he rose up into me again and again and again. I closed my eyes and golden stars danced behind my eyelids as I came, but I had a show to put on, so I didn't let myself go slack as I so greatly desired, but instead continued to ride him, continued to display myself, until finally he gripped my hips with his entire strength, slamming me down onto him as he released.

I allowed us a moment— just one moment, our hearts beating as one, before I pulled myself free of him and sank to my knees on the floor. I laid my head on his knee as he adjusted his robe. For another moment I was content, until Hadeon's laugh broke the spell.

"It seems you have trained her well, Abraxas." Ice-cold shame fractured any resolve I had built. I turned my head into Abraxas' leg, hiding any tears that might escape. "I don't know why I doubted you, old friend."

"You thought one little princess could undo me, Hadeon? Is that why you let me have her in the first place?" He stroked my hair gently as he spewed those frozen words.

"Don't sound so offended, Abraxas. You know I love our little games. I was just making sure you hadn't gone soft in your old age." Abraxas didn't respond. I finally managed to turn my head back to the room. I saw Pallas, still seated at Hadeon's feet. Her lips were swollen, and tears ran down her cheeks. But her eyes were that same stony stare I had seen before. Our gazes met, and for just a moment, I saw that gaze soften. But maybe I had imagined it.

"I forgot how good a party you throw. Perhaps I should come by unannounced more often."

"Actually, Hadeon, I think it's time for me to come visit you."

Chapter 62

Abraxas

I made sure to get Tori back to our room as quickly as I could without arousing suspicion. I immediately got her out of her dress and into a comfortable robe, placing her delicately by the fire. I'd made sure hot tea was ready for us, and added three cubes of sugar for her, wrapping her hands around the warm cup. After I was sure she was secure, I changed out of my robes that reeked of the party and came to kneel in front of her. She was sipping from the cup slowly, watching the fire, but she hadn't said anything to me since our performance.

I longed to wrap her up in my arms, but I knew that any touch right now might be overwhelming.

"Are you alright, Tori?"

She dragged her eyes down to me, but her expression remained blank. "I'm fine."

"Tori..." I growled at her in warning.

She finally turned her whole body to me. "I can't wait any longer, Abraxas. I need to go get Jun, now. I can't leave him with Hadeon."

"I know."

"We have to go as soon as possible; can we make it by next week?"

"Tori, there are still so many things we have to arrange, so much we need to—"

"I want him dead, Abraxas. I want to feel the life leave his body." I had never seen her so bloodthirsty, she quaked with it. "But first, I need Jun. I need him safe. Please, Abraxas." Her lips quivered and I couldn't stop myself from holding on to her then, even if it was just gently wrapping my hands on her thighs.

"Next week, I promise it." It was too soon. Not everything would be ready, it would endanger everything. I'd been making this plan for close to a century, making sure all the pieces were carefully laid, and pushing it early would risk its utter failure. But I couldn't deny her, I had never been able to.

She dove at me, her lips landing on mine, and she opened to me beautifully. "Thank you." She pushed me down onto the floor, her soft body pressing down on top of me. But I gently pushed her up.

"Tonight, just lay with me Tori?" I couldn't deny that every single male part of me had enjoyed our show tonight. But she was so much more than that. She had risen like the sun on what had felt like the eternal night of my soul, her light burning away that darkness that had for so long consumed me. I had never feared the vastness of the sky, but the sheer expanse of what she made me feel often overwhelmed me. She was mine, and I was entirely hers.

She led me to our bed, and gently wrapped my arms around her. I had almost drifted off when I heard her say in a small voice, "Why do you hate him, Abraxas? You never told me."

"I've had many centuries with him, there are too many examples to name."

"What aren't you telling me, Abraxas?" As always, she saw right through me.

"I have no secrets from you, little bird." *Liar*. But she didn't push me. She just nuzzled into my chest, and I held her until her breath held the steady rhythm of sleep.

Chapter 63

Tori

That week was agonizingly slow. We had so much to do and the hours passed quickly. But every moment seemed to pass so slowly, like fate itself was trying to hold me back. But I would not wait any longer. I had waited too long already, I knew that.

We set off to Koron with three full cohorts of soldiers. It seemed suspicious to me, but Abraxas assured me that he never traveled outside his kingdom with less. At his request, we had left my cohort back in Xyr. Abraxas had thought they might be a distraction, and he was right. I couldn't focus on our plan if I was worried about them. I had enough to worry about as it was.

Avlyn had not stayed behind, once again glued to Abraxas' side. But I was happy to have them, knowing someone else would watch over him.

We arrived, and I had expected fanfare or at least some kind of greeting. Instead, the streets of Koron were empty, doors and shutters locked up tight. I could feel the people behind them, scared almost to the point of panic.

Abraxas rode in front of our group, the image of the dark

Dragon King. He wore his formal armor, freshly polished, so the scale plates captured all the light around them. He wore his helmet, the great dragon's maw surrounding his face in fangs and brutality. Every one of the soldiers either sat straight-backed or marched, their footsteps and armor creating a cacophonous symphony.

I sat hooded and hunched, the image of the fear that surrounded me. And I was fearful, but I was afraid of failure more than anything else.

Koron reeked in a way that Xyr never had. The refuse of daily life was left to litter the streets, great piles of waste and broken spirits lay on every corner. Koron consisted of three great rings surrounded by high walls, each rising above the next. The outer ring, where the humans and lesser fae were allowed to live; the inner ring, where the fae nobles lived; and the center, where the Palace of Embers stood, the home of Hadeon's Court of Flames and the seat of all power in Adimos.

We reached the portal between the inner and outer ring, and it was blocked by a gate made of crossed beams thicker than a man's leg and bound together with metal. Abraxas merely looked at the guard who sat at the top of the wall, and I heard him shouting frantically down to the men behind it. A thunderous crunching filled the air, and slowly the gate began to rise. Behind, I could see the great chain being spooled by four men as they lifted the gate. We rode through, and the men lined up at attention as Abraxas passed.

"See that I am not kept waiting at the next gate." I shiver ran down my spine at the cold tone of his voice. The guards exchanged quick glances, and the one on the end took off sprinting down the road.

More people were visible in the inner ring, but still, the stench of fear remained. The streets were clean and lined with fine houses, but still, a darkness, unclean and putrid, seemed to cling to them. A few of the nobles, dressed in fine clothes and covered in jewels, would greet Abraxas, but most still kept to themselves. Many were followed or assisted by slaves, their metal collars cutting into white and tan and green flesh alike.

We finally arrived at the palace, and the gate was open, waiting for us. Our caravan filed into the courtyard of the keep, which was barren except for a few other carriages transporting nobility. Abraxas dismounted and strode up to the gates without a look back. Avlyn, also dressed in their dark armor, approached to help me dismount my horse. I was still a novice rider, and after such a long journey, I was happy to have them there to support my shaking legs.

"Steady now, Princess. We have a long way to go." They gripped my forearm, our soldierly gesture, for just a moment, before leading me into the palace.

Opulence wasn't enough to describe its interior. Koron was the capital of the empire, but it had been the capital of the Golden Kingdom long before that. Hadeon's father, who had been king, had been known for his extravagant taste. That had not been exaggerated.

The walls themselves were gilded with gold reaching dozens of feet in the air. Every fixture and chandelier was carved in great detail by hand. Thousands of candles and tapers lit the space, and flowers from every region were spaced in crystal vases along the walls. Nobles flitted about, their jewelry reflecting the light, and sparkling to near absurdity.

"Home, sweet home," Ciara said at my side. She stood tall, but I could see her lip quiver. I had asked her, practically begged her not to come. But she had insisted, "It is my duty, Your Highness."

I grasped her hand lightly in my own but did not speak. I felt her squeeze my fingers back, ever so slightly.

Abraxas was already gone, and we were quickly swept away

by two slaves who wouldn't raise their eyes off the ground. We were led to a room that was unnecessarily large for just Ciara and me, and they disappeared without a word. "I suppose it's time to get ready."

The fashion of the Court of Flames differed slightly from the Dragon Kingdom. The sheer dresses of home were not used here, but these dresses were no less revealing. Tonight, mine was a deep crimson, but it was cut so deep over the chest my navel was visible and a great slit ran nearly to my hip. I hadn't been able to bring the sword Abraxas had given me, but instead, one that had been crafted to specifically hide in the lining of my skirt. A small dagger was strapped to my hidden thigh. I felt vulnerable with so little, but it was the most we could safely conceal.

After I had dressed, Ciara tried to control my hair, as always, but in an odd silence. I didn't want to push her, knowing the strain of being back in this place. But as she failed with another pin, I heard her murmur, "You don't have to do this, Tori." I let my surprise show on my face. "You don't have to fight him."

Her hands started shaking so badly that the pin she held dropped to the floor, the metal sending a clang through the silent room. I grabbed her hands in mine and held them tight. "I promised you before, I won't let any harm come to you. No matter the outcome for me, you will be safe, Ciara."

Great tears streamed from her cheeks, "It's not me—Tori, you have seen him, but I grew up here. I have *lived* here. What he will do when he catches you..." Her shoulders heaved with sobs.

"When he catches me? Good to know I inspire such confidence." I smiled at her, trying to get her to mirror me, but she only sobbed harder. This was unlike her.

"Ciara, what is the matter? Has something happened already?"

"No, no...but, Tori—" The door to my room opened, and

Abraxas stepped through. Ciara spun, and hid her face from him, busying herself with my skirts.

Abraxas frowned, "Should I come back?"

Before I could speak, Ciara had cleared the tears and redness from her eyes. She turned back to the king and smiled. Maybe only I could see the pain laced in it.

"No need, Your Majesty, she is ready for you." She curtsied and then quickly exited to her attached room. I worried my lip, that great pit opening in my stomach that I hadn't felt in weeks. But Abraxas placed his hand on the small of my back and a gentle kiss on the curve of my shoulder, and my nerves calmed.

"Everything alright?" he asked as his lips grazed my skin.

"I hope so. We have no room for error tonight."

"Are you ready, little bird?" He looked at me with those soft eyes, those eyes I knew no one else got to see. I was ready, but I wanted one more moment to be selfish.

I wrapped my arms around his waist and pulled him into a soft embrace. I felt his arms wrap over my back, feeling the strength he had hidden beneath his layers of fine, dark clothes. I inhaled deeply, trying to capture the scent of him, of vast pine forests touched by winter and the wind, where forest fires raged, but now new life also blossomed. "I'm ready."

I pulled the black box containing the necklace out of my satchel. I had never let it leave my side. I saw the box was covered in a thin layer of spider silk and smiled. Spinner had been quite mad that I had made him stay behind. I opened the box and lifted the necklace while Abraxas carefully pulled my hair to the side. It was heavy, and it wasn't just the weight of the necklace. But I would carry it, no matter the cost.

His fingers lingered on the bare skin of my neck, and I felt his lips land there as well, shivers running down my spine. I spun around and grinned, "How do I look?" I stuck my hip out a bit, striking a ridiculous pose.

"As I suspected, no one will be looking at the necklace," His gaze lowered to the curve of my breasts, and I hit him playfully on the chest. "I have a present for you, little bird."

He pulled another velvet box out from inside his coat. He carefully opened it, and this time my jaw truly popped open. Inside was a crown—black gold and diamonds highlighted seven more rubies, the largest was the size of a robin's egg. Each was paired with a black metal spire that would pierce the air over my head. Seven spires that very much matched the seven black dragon's teeth on his own crown.

"Being a bit obvious, aren't you?"

His grin turned devious, "I have a reputation for possessiveness to maintain. You are mine, Princess. They should all know it." Heat curled in my belly at his words, and I know he felt it too. Despite our schedule, he couldn't resist one long, claiming kiss, which I returned in earnest. But he ended it much too soon and placed the crown on my head.

"As I suspected, ravishing." Even after all this, his words still had my cheeks turning red. He swept his arm behind my back, "Time to go, Princess."

Chapter 64

Tori

In Koron, court was held in a great ballroom that outdid the rest of the palace in its opulence. It was open to the air, and the setting sun was framed by great columns that rose up to the arched ceilings. The low sun reflected off of every gilded surface, making the whole room seem to glow. More columns lined the walls, allowing guests to mingle away from the main floor. Outside, a great balcony overlooked the gardens, and then onto the fertile fields of the Golden Kingdom. I could see nothing save for these fields of golden flowers, the light summer wind causing them to shimmer in the dying light.

A huge city like this, surrounded by plants that couldn't be eaten, while its people starved. I noted that the placement of the balcony and gardens also blocked the view of the lower ring. *Can't have the nobles viewing that suffering, now can we?*

Abraxas placed his hand on my lower back, the warmth there was my only comfort as we stepped into this viper's den. I kept my face schooled in cold neutrality, my back straight and chin high. I only deferred to Abraxas and the Emperor. Everyone else was below me.

Hadeon had gathered his entire court to honor Abraxas' visit. As we swept into the room, I felt the stares lock on us. Unlike when we had first entered court at Xyr, it wasn't curiosity that drove it, but a mixture of fear and reverence. While Abraxas' and my outfits were cut just the same as the nobles, theirs tended towards pastels and light colors. Abraxas' black and my crimson had us standing out like blood on clean linen. But that was the idea.

Shortly, some nobles approached us. After my introduction, most ignored me and spoke directly to Abraxas. I paid them no mind. A slave came by carrying a tray of ambrosia, and I took glasses for Abraxas and me. I made very blatant toasts with one noble after another, making sure they saw me drink from the glass before I found surreptitious times to dump the rest in a potted plant.

Eventually, Hadeon made his way to us.

"Abraxas, how long has it been since you've been to my court? And so kind of you to bring your little pet with you." He gave me that predator's smile, which I returned with a demur one of my own and a small curtsey. He frowned. "I must say, I was surprised you wanted to visit so soon, especially as I had just seen you."

"What can I say, Your Eminence? Perhaps I missed you." An emotion shot through Hadeon's eyes that I couldn't decipher, but Abraxas continued, "But I think I mostly liked the type of show my little princess likes to put on when you're around."

Hadeon's expression cleared, "Yes, I did quite like seeing her undone." Revulsion riled in my gut, but I hid it. "Perhaps I should have you and Pallas get better acquainted. Maybe Abraxas would be more partial to sharing you with her, especially as a spectator."

Abraxas played his part well, "Well, when you place such a tantalizing offer on the table, Hadeon, how can I resist?"

I saw surprise flash in Hadeon's eyes for just a moment, but then that grin returned. "Excellent." He waved his hand, and Pallas seemed to appear from nowhere, as if she had been waiting to be summoned. She was just as stone cold as I remembered, wrapped in a light blue gown that shimmered as if it had been sewn from ice. She was stunning, perhaps the most beautiful female I had ever seen. But her eyes were deep, and I knew they hid unimaginable things.

Hadeon spoke, "Pallas, my love, please escort the princess so the men can talk." Her expression didn't change, but she held her arm out for me to take. I took one last steadying breath, shoving the image of me sending the stem of my glass of ambrosia straight through Hadeon's eye away, and took her hand. But Abraxas tightened his grip on my waist.

"Now, Hadeon, my little princess has been so good of late, I promised she would get to see her brother. I haven't seen him tonight. Can you summon him?"

Hadeon stiffened, "Prince Jun desired privacy tonight, unfortunately." My heart caught in my throat. I needed to get to Jun, this whole plan wouldn't work without him. Was I already too late?

But Abraxas brushed me off, and Pallas pulled me away. My mind was spinning, trying to form a solution.

Pallas didn't seem interested in conversing with anyone, mostly just gliding around the hall. Most of the nobles seemed just inclined to avoid her.

"So, how long have you lived in Koron?" It was an inane question, but it was all I could think of in my distracted state. She bore her eyes into me, answer enough of what she thought of it. I swiped a glass from a passing tray, and she eyed it with disgust. I took a sip, but knew I had to be careful. I wouldn't be able to dump this glass with her watchful eye.

"What of the ambrosia harvest this year? I had heard much of the crop was lost throughout the land?" She didn't even blink and still said nothing. She led me around the edge of the room, behind the columns and out of sight.

The intense lack of conversation was grating on me.

"Where are we headed, My Lady? Actually, how should I refer to you? You aren't empress and you aren't royal, so what does that make you?" Finally, something stirred in her.

"Has anyone ever told you that you talk too much?" She said it quietly, but her grip on my arm tightened.

Good, I was getting somewhere. "Just trying to get to know you, Pallas." Oh, she didn't like that. She shoved me so my back was to a column. We were out of sight, and I wondered what she would do next. My nerves were fried, and I itched for a fight, even though that was a terrible idea. But she just continued to stare at me, her gaze tracing over my face and down my chest.

Pallas' gaze lingered on my neck, and I couldn't help as I squirmed. There was no way she could see through the glamour. Not unless she had magic of her own, which was impossible, wasn't it?

But her eyes snapped back up, and she latched her hand firmly around my wounded arm. A small whimper escaped me. She flinched, but then her eyes hardened again, and she leaned in, "Come with me."

I tried to look back to Abraxas, warn him, but I couldn't do so without making a scene as she dragged me out of the hall.

We headed down several halls, and by habit, I tried to memorize the route, but her hand was clamped down hard and pain shot through my whole side, breaking my focus. Eventually, she shoved me through a door and released me. I spun my feet into a wide stance and raised my hands, ready to fend off her next attack, but she just rolled her eyes at me.

"You have two minutes, that's it." She crossed her arms and stared at me. I finally took in my surroundings. We were in a bedroom, a fine one. I let my eyes leave her for just a moment and saw a bed along the wall.

"Jun!" I turned my back to Pallas and ran to him. It was a bad tactic, but I didn't care. He lay on the bed, sleeping or unconscious, I couldn't tell. I ran my hand over his forehead, and he was clammy and covered in sweat. "Jun, I'm here...Jun, wake up." It was too similar, all too similar to what he must have felt when he had found me nearly dead on the floor.

I turned to Pallas, "What's wrong with him?!" She stared at me, unmoving.

"One minute." She kept staring at me.

I turned back to Jun, and I knew Pallas' eyes were still on me. I would have to be discreet. I threw my arms around my brother, pressing my chest to his. I let fake sobs rack me.

"I'm sorry, Jun, I'm so sorry." It turns out I didn't need to fake it, as real tears streamed from my face. I held him close, and then through my sobs, I heard it. A small crack, like the shattering of glass, from where Jun's collar sat, just beneath my necklace. I didn't dare look, didn't dare move his shirt to see, but I pulled back, his face in my hands.

"Jun, wake up please." But he didn't. His face was still pale, and his breathing so dangerously soft. I wanted to shake him, scream at him, but I was pulled away.

"Time's up." I tried to pull away from her, to run back to him even as she sent pain radiating up my arm again. She yanked me harder, and I was forced to look at her, "We have to get back."

I knew it was pointless to argue, and she was right. If they noticed we had left, it would arouse suspicion. I realized then that she had put herself at risk to let me see him. I didn't know why, but that didn't matter. She had unknowingly kept our plan on track.

"Thank you, Pallas." She didn't say a word, just kept pulling me down the hall. When we re-entered the great hall, she released my arm and walked away, without a word. But it was time for the next phase of our plan, and I had no time to waste.

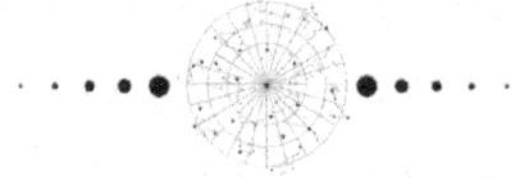

I was drunk, or at least I appeared that way. Lord Bolon had found me, and he was the perfect companion to down drink after drink with. I toasted with more and more of the nobles, and let my speech start to slur, stumbling as I walked. I went to get more drinks, and I crashed right into a servant, and his tray of drinks clattered all over the floor.

The hall went silent, all eyes on me. In an instant, Abraxas was there, his hand gripping my face harshly, nails cutting into my skin until they drew blood.

His voice was quiet, but I knew everyone could still hear, "What are you doing? You are an embarrassment." He shoved me, and I fell to the floor letting loose a whimper. I saw Hadeon and Avlyn from the corner of my eye. Hadeon looked disgusted as he stared down at me.

Abraxas turned his back on me, and waved to Avlyn, "Take her back to her room, immediately." Avlyn nodded and grabbed me roughly, but by my uninjured arm. They led me out of the hall, but not before I saw Hadeon wave two of his own guards after us. Just two. Easy.

I stumbled down the hall in Avlyn's grip, leaning into them for support. I heard the guard behind us murmur, "Sloppy slut." Oh, he had no idea. I stumbled again and used it to reach under my dress, grabbing my dagger.

We reached my door, and Avlyn pressed it open. We locked eyes for just one moment before we both spun. I hit one guard straight across his neck, in that tight seam between his armor and helmet. I struck true and hard, and almost took his head off. He tried to scream but couldn't with his vocal cords severed. He slumped down, bleeding all over me and I caught him, just as Avlyn did the same to theirs. We quickly dragged them into my room and closed thedoor.

"No going back now. Time to move." Avlyn threw me a linen from the bed, and I did my best to wipe the blood from my face and chest. It did basically nothing, but at least it wasn't dripping into my mouth anymore.

I used the dagger to cut the sword free of my dress and gave it one swing for good measure. I took the crown from my head, and set it gently on the bed, giving it one last lingering look.

Avlyn had managed to clean their armor much more effectively than I had my gown, and the dark color hid the rest. I made to leave the room when their hand came down gently on my shoulder.

"I have to head back now, but I'll see you on the other side, Princess. Good luck." I rested my hand on theirs for just a moment, steeling my resolve.

"See you soon."

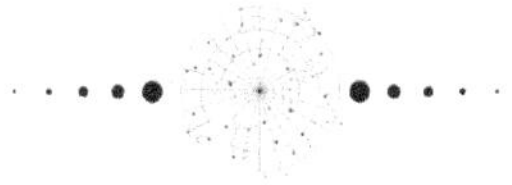

I MADE MY WAY DOWN THE ROUTE I HAD TRACED OVER AND over in Abraxas' study. I descended deeper and deeper into the bowels of the palace. As I neared my destination, I ran into more and more guards, but always no more than two at a time. With the element of surprise, I took them down easily. I shouldn't have bothered cleaning the blood off me earlier, as I was drenched in it now. But I kept moving.

The further I got, the more confident I felt. Yes, it was just as we planned, exactly as we planned.

Suddenly, unease snuck into my chest. It was too easy. My palms grew sweaty, but I tightened my grip on my sword. No going back.

The walls around me were no longer elegant, but roughly rendered from grey stone. The air reeked of rot, but it carried a static charge that set my teeth on edge. Close, I had to be close now. Once I got to the entrance to the laboratory, I would break the sealing enchantment with the gem, and any other protective measures that guarded Hadeon's greatest treasure. Then I would grab whatever this treasure was and run. Avlyn and the soldiers were positioning themselves now, ready for the moment Hadeon's power fled, and Abraxas would challenge him.

But I had to hurry. I moved faster. I was close now, close to the area of the castle no one could enter. But as I rounded a corner, all the torches went out. I skidded to a halt, and pressed myself against a wall, hoping I could defend from there, but it was too late.

"A pleasure to see you again, gorgeous." Out of the dark came a head of dark hair, with a long white scar over his left eye.

"I can't say I return the sentiment, Luxos, but at least I'll get to introduce myself properly this time." I raised my sword, ready to strike. He just sneered.

"I won't underestimate you this time, Princess." He snapped his fingers, and I heard the clatter of dozens of boots— a whole cohort. They had been waiting for me, and I couldn't fight that many, not alone.

I ran. "*After her*!" I heard Luxos shout. There was another way, deeper into the castle, I'd memorized every route. But it was longer, more twisted, and my lungs already burned.

But I did not stop. The clank of armor followed me, spurring me on. It felt like knives cut between my ribs, but still, I ran.

I was close now, so close. I rounded the corner, feet slapping against the floor as I tried to stay ahead of the guards, when everything went red. There she was, hanging above the door to the laboratory. My mother, nailed to the wall, her arms and legs outstretched.

She must have been preserved somehow, for her dead body still had flesh clinging to her bones, but huge chunks had come loose, hanging off it in grisly strips. Her bones were visible and beginning to turn black with rot. Her head lolled and the gash across her chest had only grown wider as the flesh was eaten away, thick black clots of congealed blood still stuck to her. Half of her face was gone, the skull visible beneath, but her black hair hung like a spider's web over her one remaining eye that had turned white.

My heart stopped, and my breath as well. That crushing sensation I had fought for so long smashed into my chest like a boulder launched from a trebuchet. My legs gave out and I collapsed to the floor. Everything I had suppressed these last months flooded back to me. Every memory and image I had drowned in the ocean of my mind rose to the surface, like the eldritch horrors of the deep. I saw it again, my mother's eyes going dull as blood pumped from her heart. Hadeon's laughter at my father's screams. Jun, wrapped in Hadeon's arms as he kissed him. Jun, lying lifeless on the bed upstairs. The faces of every man I had killed, all rose up from the depths, their clammy hand pulling me down into that ice cold water. I couldn't breathe, I was drowning—I was dying.

Get up! Run you idiot! But I couldn't move, and I hardly noticed as the very real hands of the soldiers clamped around me and everything went mercifully black.

Chapter 65

Tori

The sensations were all too familiar. My wrists burned with iron, and my shoulders ached from my dead weight hanging off of them. I got my feet under me, at least relieving my shoulders. My hands were chained together above my head, tied to a chain thicker than my thigh.

"Not getting out this time, gorgeous." I snapped my head up, and there was Luxos, leaning against the dungeon wall with his arms crossed. I screamed and ran at him. But the chain only allowed me a few steps before I snapped back. I bared my teeth at him.

Luxos raised himself off the wall, "They said you were a feral little thing. You owe me the life of quite a few of my men. I intend to exact my retribution in blood."

"I'd like to see you fucking try, coward. It wasn't me who ran away from those ruins." I'd struck a nerve, and he ground his teeth as he approached me. But before he could get close enough, Hadeon himself walked into the room.

"Luxos, what did I tell you about getting started without me?" Luxos backed down, stepping behind the emperor.

"Your Eminence, always a pleasure to see you."

"Oh, my hellcat, you do like to keep things interesting, don't you?" He raised his hand and lightning shot into me, but it wasn't as painful as it had been before. The gem was negating his power, but I had to keep that from him. I screamed, if a bit over dramatically.

"Now, why don't you tell me why you were slashing your way through my dungeons."

I had failed our plan, but there was still hope. Hadeon was here with me, and I had an advantage. I just needed to play this right.

"I was looking for Jun." He stepped forward and sunk his fist into my stomach. That actually hurt.

"Liar. Let's not play these games, I don't have the patience for it." He grabbed the necklace around my neck, pulling it down so I was trapped between it and my chains. I tried not to fight, I couldn't let him break it, but my bad shoulder and arm twitched with pain as it was pulled, and I flinched away. The clasp on the necklace broke, and Hadeon tossed it away.

My stomach plummeted. That was my last hope. He hit me again with lightning, and this time I felt its full force, and my scream was real. But it wasn't just for the pain. I had failed, and it had been my fault. When it had mattered most, I'd frozen like the pathetic thing I was. *Weak, so weak.*

"I know what you were looking for, Princess. Why do you think Luxos was ready for you?"

He had me there. I still hadn't recovered my breath, and darkness was starting to cloud my vision. I hadn't meant to say it out loud, but I did.

"How did you know? How did you know I would be there?" The emperor raised his hand and motioned to Luxos by the door. He retreated, but returned quickly, pulling a woman along by her arm.

Her soft brown curls swept back from small, pointed ears, and her golden eyes wouldn't meet mine.

"Ciara?" She didn't look at me, just kept her eyes on her feet.

"Yes, my own little Ciara. She's quite the spy, isn't she? So sweet, so soft. One would never suspect." He walked over to her, pinching her chin in his fingers, and I could see his nails cutting in, "Yes, almost as soft as her mother was. She has been feeding me quite the wealth of information these last few months."

It couldn't be, not the Ciara I knew, who was kind and gossiped with me and...shared my secrets. She had known about my hidden weapons, about our plans. And he was right, she had fooled me. I was twice the fool because it was the same disguise I sometimes used. Demure, soft, afraid.

I could barely stand to look at her. I had failed, but Ciara had made sure it would happen.

"Ciara, how could you? You know what he's capable of!" She still wouldn't look at me. Tears flooded my eyes. It was all ruined. Our plan, we wouldn't get this chance again, Hadeon would see to that. My heart ached. Did he have Abraxas already?

"You said I wouldn't have to see her," Ciara mumbled. Hadeon said nothing. "Where is my husband? You said I could have him, you said this would be enough." She looked at Hadeon with pleading eyes, and gods damn me, I understood.

He motioned with his hand again. Another guard dragged in the human man. I had seen him before. He had been one of the slaves with Hadeon at the midsummer ball, the night Ciara had been beside herself. I really was a fool, and now we all would pay the price.

He ran to Ciara then, and she embraced him as if she would fall off the world if he weren't there. Tears flooded both of their faces, and they collapsed to the ground a mess of sobs.

Hadeon let out an exasperated sigh, Ciara's sobs clearly

annoying him. He waved his hand again and I saw that purple lightning form at his fingertips.

"*No*!" I screamed, but it was too late. He sent the bolt straight through both of their hearts. Their bodies fell to the floor, still embracing.

"Foolish girl. Doesn't she know an exposed spy is a dead spy?" He stepped over their bodies and back towards me. I strained at the iron shackles, my flesh sizzling as tears escaped me.

"What, crying for your betrayer? It's no wonder you think Abraxas cares for you. But he and I have been playing this game a long time, my hellcat, and you are just another pawn to him."

Did he really think that? If so, maybe Abraxas was still safe, I could play my part, and at least he could walk away from this. I could be that foolish, reckless, weak girl one more time. It wasn't even an act.

"If he didn't care for me, then why would I have let him...he's forced me to do so many things." I sobbed, the very vision of a broken girl. Hadeon wore that same disgusted expression, and I waited for the bolt to enter my heart. But instead, he grabbed my hair and lifted my eyes to meet his violet ones, lightning dancing in them.

"You have been such a disappointment, hellcat. Pathetic like your parents, like your brother who couldn't even keep himself alive. I suppose you have that in common." Once, that might have broken me, to know he knew my greatest secret. But not now, it only steadied my resolve. I let the tears flow as he pulled my head back so hard my neck cracked. "And not even a drop of magic in you. Well, I suppose you can serve one final purpose for me." He smashed my head into the wall and my vision filled with stars.

Chapter 66

Tori

I awoke to a pounding in my head. I jerked, but a white-hot pain ran over my throat at the motion. "Ah-ah, Princess," Hadeon pressed his lips to my ear, "you wouldn't want to miss the show, would you?" I brought myself into focus, and I found that I was seated on Hadeon's lap, one of his hands laid lazily across my thighs, the other holding a dagger to my throat. We were in his throne room, and he had dozens of soldiers placed around us.

I saw Pallas and Jun seated to his left. Jun was slumped, but his eyes were half open and he was conscious. I saw Pallas stroking his arm gently. Everyone stared at the main doors, waiting. I tried to bring my hands up, to disarm him—to do anything, but they were locked at my side. I felt the tingle of lightning as I strained. "It's useless, Princess. You will have no choice but to sit here as I take everything away from him."

As the sick heat of his breath passed over my ear, the great double doors opened, and Abraxas walked through, Avlyn and their elite soldiers following closely behind.

"Ah, my loyal general. It seems your little pet here was

causing mischief. She killed quite a few of my men trying to get into the forbidden parts of the castle." He pressed the tip of the dagger into me, and my breath caught. Abraxas' eyes locked on me.

"My apologies, Your Eminence, she will be appropriately punished." His lips crushed together, as he kept his eyes trained on the dagger at my throat.

Hadeon let out a long hum, as if he were truly contemplating something. "It seems to me that you are the one who should be punished, my old friend. After all, she is your responsibility." He started tracing light circles on my thigh with his other hand, and I saw the rage grow behind Abraxas' eyes. *Oh, Abraxas, you fool. You're being too obvious.*

Through gritted teeth, he said, "If that is your wish, Your Eminence."

Hadeon continued to toy with me, now letting his hands slip through the slit in my dress, touching my bare skin. "Perhaps I could have you flogged, or maybe a few fingers removed. But those wounds would heal. Maybe I'll strip you of your kingdom, Abraxas? Something you can never recover." I couldn't see it, but I felt the wicked grin across his face.

"That hardly seems an appropriate punishment for the death of a few soldiers, who were bested by a girl, Hadeon."

"Yes, but I'm wondering what you would give me—how much I could take—if it guaranteed her safe return." His hand slipped further up my thigh. I felt it then, in him. He knew. Everything before had been a game, to break me. He knew I was Abraxas' weakness.

Abraxas shrugged, "She's my ward, Hadeon. My responsibility, surely, but I have no attachment to her." Hadeon flicked the knife again. This time Abraxas did not react. But it was too late.

"If that's the case, perhaps I'll keep her here with me. A few weeks with my men in the dungeons would serve to improve her attitude." He slid his nose into my hair and took an exaggerated sniff. "I do love the scent of her fear, I bet it tastes delicious as well."

Abraxas still held. But then Hadeon dragged his dagger down my chest, a small bead of blood flowing, tracing between my breasts. His other hand shifted so my dress splayed open, revealing everything underneath, and he moved his fingers to trace over the small piece of lace that covered me. I only kept from reacting by picturing my bare hands crushing Hadeon's skull into pulp.

"Tell me, my old friend, how much of you will I taste on her?" He pressed his fingers into me, and I imagined ripping his entrails out of him.

I felt it then, the beat of an ancient drum, deep and menacing, throughout the whole room. Agonizingly slowly, Abraxas stepped towards the stairs of the dais. I felt all the soldiers shift around me, tensing and readying their hands on their weapons, but they were laced with fear as the wave of Abraxas' power crested over them. Closer I could see that Abraxas was disarmed, but still, he walked forward, not paying them any mind. I could feel Hadeon's heart rate increase at my back. He tightened the dagger at my chest, the tip pinned over my heart.

"Listen, old friend," Abraxas whispered it like a dark prayer, "My army has already entered your lands, the largest land invasion in an age. You will be annihilated. There is nothing that will stand between me and your total destruction this time." Hadeon's breathing increased, he was as surprised as I was. This was never the plan, why had Abraxas...

"You traitorous wretch. I knew I should have killed you," Hadeon's voice shook.

Abraxas was close now, his smirk murderous. "But you didn't. Free the princess, and I'll let you run like the coward you are."

"You cannot best me, Abraxas." He rose to standing now, dagger still to my chest. "I will take everything from you."

For a moment, Abraxas stilled, then, "Get your fucking hands off my mate."

The room exploded. I felt Abraxas' power surge, and the dagger in Hadeon's hand flew free, into the neck of the nearest soldier. Hadeon flew back behind me, and I stumbled forward into Abraxas' arms.

"Run!" he yelled as he used his power to push back the tide of oncoming soldiers. *Like hell I would.* But I needed a weapon, I was defenseless, at least for now. I heard the crashing of swords all around me, as the Dragon Army clashed with Hadeon's soldiers. On the dais, Pallas had thrown herself over Jun, sheltering them behind the throne.

I dashed back to Avlyn, as Abraxas rounded on the emperor. "Sword!"

Avlyn swung their sword high, cutting down brutally through the arm of the nearest soldier. They collapsed, holding the bleeding stump, and Avlyn finished them by sending their sword through the back of their neck.

"It's my job to get you out of here, Princess," they yelled as they pulled the bloody sword from their opponent. I heard armor clashing as another man ran at me, but I dodged his blow at the last second, ducking down so he tripped over my body and flew onto Avlyn's now outstretched blade.

"I won't leave him!" I swore I saw them roll their eyes, as they engaged another opponent. But then, a great wave, like the shock of an explosion, ripped through the room, along with a blinding light. Everyone fell to their knees, and I turned back, squinting against the onslaught that blinded me, to see Abraxas and Hadeon surrounded by a ball of pure light, laced with purple lightning and emerald-green flames.

"Running out of time here, Avlyn." I crawled toward the

downed soldier's sword, the power of the magic still pressing me to the floor.

Avlyn kicked the sword towards me, and as my hand landed on the hilt, they swore, "I fucking told him."

Soldiers around me were starting to push up against the weight of the magic that swept through the room, and I pushed into my hands. My left arm buckled. *Not fucking now.* I pushed myself again, snapping to my feet, and lifted my sword just in time to block the blade of the closest soldier. We engaged, as I carefully turned us, my feet sweeping the floor to avoid tripping over any dead soldiers or rubble. I turned us so he was facing into the light that flooded from the dais, and when he squinted to recover, I lunged, sending my sword at the joint of his armor at the hip, slicing him open. Blood flooded, and he staggered, so I swept the sword again and removed the leg.

"Dramatic." Avlyn now had their back to me, and we circled, facing our opponents in tandem.

Our bodies moved as one, months of training coming down to this one moment. Blood spewed and swords sparked as we continued to down our opponents. But we were outnumbered, and the Dragon Army's soldiers were falling all around us. After taking down more men than I could count, Avlyn and I were wearing thin and making mistakes. One particularly large brute managed to slice Avlyn across the shoulder and then nicked their thigh. As they fell to their knee, I swung my sword back and over their head, blocking the next attack as they recovered. It left me open long enough for another warrior to land a blow on my bad arm, and pain radiated up through my shoulders and neck.

A great knock came at the double doors of the throne room, and more of Hadeon's soldiers flooded in. I couldn't see any friendly faces around us as the soldiers enveloped us.

"Shit, the north cohort must have gone down." More and more men in the deep gold of the Court of Flames spilled into the room. We were truly surrounded now, but the soldiers weren't engaging us, just forming a barrier to prevent escape. A trap.

"It's over, Abraxas!" Somewhere within the radiating ball of light, I heard Hadeon shout, "Surrender and the girl can go free." I felt the great pressure recede.

"No, he'll never let me go. Abraxas, *No!*"

But it continued, his magic fading. In an instant Hadeon was on him, lightning laced around his neck, choking him. He fell to his knees, and Hadeon slid him across the floor, facing the room—facing me. I ran to him, but Hadeon swept his hand, and I was shoved to the ground. I crawled, fighting that great force, desperate for him.

"Any last words, old friend, before I have her watch the light leave your eyes?"

"Tori," his eyes were so soft I nearly broke, "I waited over a thousand years for you and I had never truly lived until you burned me with that fire in you. These months together have given me enough joy for a lifetime, and if that's all I'm to have with you, then I can die a happy man."

Tears streamed from my eyes, my lips unable to form the words to beg him to stop, to beg him not to leave me. I reached for him, willing the space between the stars closer together so that I might touch him, feel him within my grasp one last time. I crawled up the dais, my hand so close to his jaw, and the electricity of magic ran through me. He hit me with that devastating smile that broke my heart. "Well, maybe not a man." And then my world shattered.

Chapter 67

Tori

I was thrown backward, my back colliding with the floor at the foot of the dais, cracking my spine horribly. The white light that had filled the hall during Abraxas and Hadeon's battle vanished and was replaced by a flame made of light the color of malachite. It cast shadows on the walls that spoke of ancient battles, strong winds, and a reborn god.

The room grew smaller, or no...it was no longer big enough to contain what lay within. A creature of nightmares, something from my dreams, unveiled itself above us all, descending from the shadows. It landed, its onyx claws scraping grooves longer than a man was tall into the stone floor. Those claws led into obsidian scales, each blacker than the night our world was born from, shining with an internal golden sheen. His long neck and back were covered in more onyx spikes, each following the next like the waves of the ocean. His great wings covered the ceiling of the entire room, and the torches cast shadows through them so they glowed red, and I could see the veins that ran through them— a spiderweb of life. His long neck led to a horned head, and his great maw fell open to reveal fangs longer than swords.

I stood and the dragon lowered his head to me. His nostrils emitted heat that rolled over my skin like that of the inside of a forge, dry and unforgiving. His eyes glowed golden like the sun, his internal flames filling them. But the edges were rimmed in green— green that spoke of open fields, ancient forests, and gemstones.

"Abraxas?" It seemed time had stopped, and I reached out my hand, laying it on the scaled snout of the creature before me. I ran my hand over the slit that was his nose, and he inhaled. And I saw his eyes shift, into that mischievous look I would have known in any life.

"It can't be." I heard Hadeon rise up behind me. His face was white, his elegant robes singed and torn, and his hands shook. Then the spell that had held time was broken, and the Dragon Abraxas lunged at the emperor. A wall of lightning erupted before him, but the dragon slammed into it, like two planets colliding. He swept me under him with the side of his claw, and I crouched underneath his massive belly.

The soldiers in the back of the room rushed at him, but he swept his tail from side to side, and they flew in every direction. I crawled under him to where Avlyn still lay, blood trickling down their leg, their face a deathly grey.

"Well, this is unexpected."

"Understatement of the age, Avlyn." I dragged them under the thrashing body of the dragon. He was so large he couldn't move from his spot in the center of the room without a wing or limb running into the wall. More soldiers poured in, and Abraxas continued to fling them about. His tail collided with the outer wall of the castle, and debris rained from the ceiling, wood planks and full stone bricks. He smashed again, and the wall came down, crushing numerous soldiers below.

"Jun!" I screamed, looking for my brother. As more dust rained down and I was deafened by the repeating crashes of claws meeting steel and magic, I saw him. Pallas still held him, but she had dragged him under an arched window in the corner of the room.

A flash of lightning leapt from the emperor's shield and flew through the beautiful flesh of Abraxas' wing. The cry he emitted shook another portion of the wall down, and then bright emerald-green flames erupted from him, engulfing the emperor. But Hadeon's magic protected him, and I remembered that he had already slain multiple dragons. Abraxas was not invincible.

The soldiers seemed to remember this as well and engaged more ferociously. The swords mostly bounced off his scales, but a few found purchase, prying them off and eliciting more roars from Abraxas. He gave one more devastating roar filled with flames, then lifted onto his hind legs, and crashed into the ceiling, his wings and claws tearing through. The night air whipped into the room, clearing the dust as Abraxas shielded Avlyn and me with his body and wings.

Then, one giant claw gently wrapped around me, and another around Avlyn, as he spread his wings and gave a mighty beat, sending dust and soldiers flying. As I lifted off the ground I screamed, "Abraxas! Jun! We need Jun, please!" His long neck turned to where he lay, and Pallas threw herself between them. I couldn't help but admire her audacity as she stared down a fully grown dragon, her arms outstretched to block my brother. But another flash of lightning struck us, and Abraxas simply gathered Pallas and Jun up with one sweep of his claw before we launched into the sky.

The force of the lift pressed me into the claws and wrapped my arms around one massive finger. *Or was it a toe?* The wind threatened to pull me free, but I felt him squeeze ever so slightly more. My hair whipped my face, sticking to my mouth, but I turned my head back and saw Koron shrinking in the distance, the Palace of Embers crumbling on one side. It truly resembled its namesake as we rose, the black walls lit with the glowing orange of torches and fires as we lifted to the stars.

The air grew ice cold, and goosebumps rose on my flesh, my breath coming faster and leaving me as sheets of ice. I tried to look around, to see Avlyn, to see my brother, but black stole into my vision, and the last thing I saw was the sheen of Abraxas' onyx claw.

Chapter 68

Tori

The first thing I noticed was that I was no longer cold. I was sweltering, in fact. The air clung to my skin and lungs like a damp rag, and I could feel it merging with the sweat already there. My face lay on soft grass, and the smell of damp and rot and life was everywhere. I slowly opened my eyes and was greeted by a light blue glow. I lay at the edge of a lake, lighter blue than the noonday sky. Will o' wisps danced all over its surface, like a colony of fireflies on a late summer night.

As I rose up, I felt the vines of the earth give way that had been enclosing my body, watched them crumble back into earth, their job completed. But this was not the grotto under Xyr's castle. The lake was massive, and I was just able to make out the other side. I looked to the sky to see pitch black, with only a few stalactites visible when a wisp would bounce up near them. So, a cave, but one larger than any room I had ever been in. I heard the sound of dripping water falling from the cave ceiling into the underground lake, accompanied by a great rumbling, as the cave seemed to breathe in and out.

No, not the cave. I turned to see him then. He was even

larger than I recalled, his black scales covered in vines that had grown around him. He had curled in on himself, almost like a cat, his head tucked in under the end of his sharp tail. I approached, and wisps danced over him, their blue light reflecting off the mirror of his scales as they bounced over his haunches, and along the spikes of his back.

I placed a hand on his neck, and he felt cool against the warmth of the cave. But that wasn't right. He should have been warm, burning. I ran my fingers over him, and he felt smooth and solid, as if he were carved from marble. But just the light movement of his breath told me that he still lived. I ran my hand up to his closed eye. "Abraxas, wake up. Please." Nothing changed.

Tears leaked from my eyes, and I didn't try to stop them. My breath came in short bursts, and I wailed. I let myself release it all, every pent-up memory and pain. I pounded my fist into him and screamed and cried and let the grief consume me.

"How dare you? How dare you lie to me? How dare you leave me?" I pounded my fist over and over, but it was like punching the side of a mountain. "How dare you? How dare you? How dare you?" My grief and rage swirled together, ice and fire mixing to consume everything that I was.

I slid down to my knees, defeated. As my breathing steadied and the tears dried up, I was greeted not by that wallowing pit of darkness, but by a small golden light. I reached out with my mind, and held it like a precious treasure, a small and fragile thing that I needed to protect at all costs.

"You knew, you absolute asshole. You knew I was your mate. I don't understand it, but you knew and didn't tell me." I stood and laid a soft kiss on his snout. "Come back to me, you arrogant domineering asshole. Please, my love, come back to me."

But still, he slept, as I lay against his cold scales. A few more dry sobs fled from me, but they barely had any heart to them.

"He hasn't moved at all, none of you have." I whirled,

reaching for a sword I didn't have. Near the edge of the lake, her beautiful blue gown, torn to shreds, was Pallas. She sat, her knees curled up to her chest, as she rested her chin, staring out into the water. "I thought you all might be dead, to be honest."

I moved my feet to a fighting stance and raised my hands, but then she turned her head to me, "They're over there if you want to see them." She motioned her hand, back to near where I had awoken. Now, on closer inspection, I saw that there lay two more bodies, covered in vines like Abraxas, the grass growing up around them like a blanket. I kept facing Pallas and moved my feet one over the other to reach the bodies, but she turned back to the lake, ignoring me.

Avlyn and Jun almost looked dead, but I saw their chests rise and fall, just like Abraxas. I saw that Avlyn had a higher concentration of vines over their thigh, where they had been wounded, and Jun's head seemed to be cradled. I reached down, they both felt warm, and their skin was bright, as if they were just taking a long nap. I ever so carefully pulled aside a vine over Avlyn's leg and saw that their wound was almost completely gone.

I ran my fingers over Jun's face. Vines had wound around his neck, and I saw they had strangled the collar around him. I reached in and at my touch, it dissolved until nothing but the broken violet gem remained. I picked it up and tossed it as far away as I could. The skin where the collar had been bubbled and oozed with sores.

"I'm sorry, Jun. I'm sorry I took so long. But you are free now. Please, please wake up." But just as before, there was nothing, and I was truly powerless here. "Please, Jun, you said I wouldn't be alone anymore. I can't. I can't lose you both." I watched as new vines grew, covering his wounded neck. I prayed it would be enough.

I trudged over to Pallas and sat down next to her. She didn't move at all, happy to ignore me. The minutes stretched by in silence until I couldn't take it anymore.

"Why did you stay while I was unconscious?"

"You see any place for me to fucking go?" Her swearing surprised me, coming out of that elegant mouth. "I haven't been awake much longer than you, but I haven't found a way out of here." She gestured wildly to the cave.

"And you didn't try to kill us?"

"Like I said, I thought you were dead anyway." It didn't feel like the truth.

"Why did you try to protect Jun?"

"Why did you?" she shot back at me with ice in her eyes.

"Ok, look. We are stuck in this cave together. I don't have a whole lot more information than you do right now, okay? We should at least try and help each other." She turned to look at Abraxas' sleeping form and made a huff that clearly said, *Yeah, sure.* Alright, she had no reason to trust me. Maybe I could be honest first.

"Look, I didn't know about...that," I gestured to the slumbering beast, "but we came to Koron to rescue Jun. I needed to get him out."

Her lips tighten, "And the army at the border, you didn't know about that either?"

I paused. "No, I didn't."

"Doesn't seem like you know anything." She tilted herself away from me, locking her eyes back on the lake. It stung me. She wasn't wrong. But I pushed through it.

"This lake is a well of sorts, a spring of wild magic. It's beautiful, isn't it?"

She slid her fingers forward, just letting the tips touch the surface of the water. "Yes, it reminds me of...Jun's singing." My heart stuttered. Jun had sung for her, really sung for her. Not that terrible and beautiful song the collar pulled from him, but the perfect and untamed song he used to sing for me. Pallas looked at me again, and I tried to see her, to see what he had seen.

But a moan sounded behind us, and we both snapped around as Avlyn slowly sat up. They rubbed their head and wiped the now desiccated leaves off their body.

"Fucking hot in here." They took in their surroundings, but their eyes locked on the dragon first. "So, it wasn't all just some really fucked up ambrosia dream." They scanned over to me and Pallas. "What is she doing here?" I felt Pallas tense beside me, but I shifted my body between them.

"She was protecting Jun. She is with us now." Both Pallas and Avlyn scoffed at that.

"Well, this day can't get any worse so... might as well." They walked over to Abraxas, and I left Pallas to join them.

"So, you really had no idea?" I asked.

"No. And something like this? The amount of magic it would take to transform..." They fell silent, and the moments stretched into minutes.

"What Avlyn?! Just say it!"

"He didn't have it anymore. That magic. He'd barely been able to control the wind these last few years. Something like this — it would have tapped directly into his life force. He might not... he might not be able to wake up."

No. No that couldn't be. I wouldn't let it. I placed my hands on him, just as I had in the forest. I waited for that warm feeling from the earth. But there was nothing.

I focused my breathing, and when that didn't work, I let rage fill me. But nothing changed, and he still felt cold as stone beneath my hands.

I looked at him, and I saw them. Shadows, slinking just beyond the vines wrapped around him. Soft, but hungry. They were waiting, the hand of death reaching out. I sank to my knees again.

"What do you know about magic, Avlyn? You could be wrong." I knew they weren't.

They twisted their fingers, and a small drop of water from the pool flew over, dancing over them like a crystal ball, "I know a few things."

"For fuck's sake, did I know anything? Any other great, important secrets that I should know while we are trapped here?"

"If it makes you feel better, Abraxas is the only one who knew about this," they said, molding the sphere of liquid into various shapes before discarding it back to the pool. "I've been good at keeping it a secret."

"I guess you got that from him." They thinned their lips and nodded.

"If you are done, maybe you could look for a way out of here." We both jumped as Pallas appeared right behind us.

Avlyn shrugged their shoulders, "I suppose that's better than just sitting around."

Pallas scowled, "Good, I'll stay and watch Jun." I made to argue, but Avlyn gently pulled me away.

"Let's focus on surviving for now, Princess. We can figure her out later."

Chapter 69

Tori

"Abraxas must have gotten us in here somehow." As if the sky responded to my words, the moon popped out from behind a dark cloud, and I could just make out a hole in the ceiling of the cave. It was likely over five hundred feet above us, and even I didn't think I could make that climb on the concave ceiling. "Let's keep looking."

We walked around the great lake. Plants grew everywhere, plants that reminded me of Niata. Tall trees with broad palms sticking out at odd angles from the top, covered in climbing vines blooming with purple and white flowers. Plants with huge, vibrant green leaves full of holes blocked our path but were easily moved out of the way. Each shake caused dozens of insects to scatter, and I couldn't help but shudder.

This place was teeming with life, and where there was life, there was always death. It seemed Avlyn had the same thought.

"Keep your guard up, anything could be in here," they whispered. We pushed on through the foliage, but my gown snagged on every twig and branch. I hissed in annoyance and ripped off the bottom of it. We eventually came to the wall of the cave, which was very solid.

"Do you feel that?" Avlyn asked. Yes, a small cool breeze cut through the damp heat of the cave air. We followed it.

We found a small opening, just big enough for me to walk through, Avlyn had to duck. The cool air gently folded over us as we stood in the opening.

"Thank the gods." Avlyn stretched their arms out and let the air dry the sweat pooling all over them.

"Seems like the best chance we have," I murmured. Avlyn lingered in that cool breeze a bit longer, but then lowered their arms, nodding.

We started making our way back to Pallas and Jun, but somehow our path felt very different. I was reminded of Tenebrae forest, and how the trees had tried to trap us, separate us. My heart raced. This place didn't feel malevolent, but nature didn't see a predator as evil. If we were the prey, we had already given it the advantage.

"We have to go, Avlyn." I broke into a run, but in my haste tripped over a massive tree root that I swear hadn't been there before.

"Always in such a hurry." A crackling voice startled a scream from me, and I rolled trying to draw my sword, which I still didn't have. Avlyn stepped over me, a small dagger drawn as they looked for our assailant.

"Now, now, is that any way to greet an old woman?" I followed the voice, looking for its source. It was as if the tree that had tripped me spoke. But then I saw her.

She was ancient. Age spots covered every piece of her skin, and combined with deep wrinkles, she greatly resembled the bark she leaned against. Her hair was thin, only a few strands still clung to her head, the skin there shiny and pulled tight over her skull. She was little more than a skeleton covered in skin as she sat cross-legged at the base of the tree. But her eyes— they glowed the same blue as the hot spring at the center of the grotto. When she smiled, her toothless gums showed through, nearly reaching from ear to pointed ear.

"I know you. I saw you in my dream," I said. Avlyn did not lower their defensive stance above.

"Yes, dear. And I know you, I have been watching you for some time now."

"Who are you?" Avlyn moved their dagger threateningly towards the crone.

"Oh, young one, who I am really doesn't matter. It hasn't mattered since I came to this cave nearly five hundred years ago."

Avlyn lowered their dagger, and I finally managed to stand up.

"Who are you?" Avlyn asked again.

The crone chuckled, and it sounded like dry leaves being broken apart, "You should be asking me what I know, not who I am. I thought you would want to save that Old God of yours."

Avlyn made to speak again, but I interrupted, "How? How do we save him?"

She laughed again, "Always in such a hurry. Sit down, both of you." Avlyn and I exchanged glances, but they sheathed their dagger. I plopped down onto the soft earth, the moisture of it soaking through the fabric of my torn gown.

"What do you know of the Old Gods, Tori Khato?"

"Well, I thought they were all gone, so obviously I don't know much." The crone didn't react, and Avlyn remained as still as a statue.

"And what do you know of Abraxas' father, Malech?"

"King Amaros was—" The crone's smile grew wicked as the realization came over me. Of course, if Abraxas was a dragon, then his father must have been too. King Amaros, who had refused to give up the Dragon Malech to Hadeon, because *he* was Malech.

"That doesn't make any sense...how could Malech have been..." Avlyn was shaking violently now, "I was there when he attacked the city. King Amaros would have never done such a thing."

"Oh, and how well did you know the man, Avlyn Unditem? How well did you know his rage and pain as he watched the history of the third age be written in the blood of his kin?"

I thought of Abraxas' story, of how he had lost his father to his own sadness. But it wasn't only his mate, Abraxas' mother, he had lost, but his entire people. I echoed Avlyn's own words back to them, "What would you be willing to do for those you loved?"

They pressed their lips together and didn't speak again. I turned back to the crone.

"So, the Corignus family, they were all...dragons?"

She smiled, as if I were finally on the right track, "Yes, before the first age when fae were first born into this world, the dragons knew that they would be their end. It was the first Great Prophecy, although the fae never knew it. One God changed himself, so that he could become fae, and thus the Corignus line was born, in the hopes of circumventing that destiny."

"But it didn't work, did it? The last Great Prophecy caused Hadeon to kill Malech, for the fae to kill all the dragons. Now only Abraxas is left and he..." Tears fell again, and my heart ached. What good did any of this information do me? It only made me feel more helpless.

"Why are you here?" I barely heard Avlyn over my own sobs.

The crone replied, "It was my penance, for my role in all this. If I had known what my Prophecy would have begotten, I would have ended myself before it was uttered."

Avlyn's head snapped up, "You were the Great Seer at Varnax? But that was—"

"A long time ago," the crone interrupted. "This place has allowed me to see what I needed, to correct destiny. I've been waiting here a long time to do so. People believe seeing the future gives you control of your fate, but they couldn't be more wrong. It only dooms you to it faster." She sighed, and I thought it might be her last breath.

"So, what? You told the world Malech was the World Breaker and instead of saving magic, it doomed it?" My words held more anger than perhaps this old woman deserved, but I didn't restrain them. But she only flashed me that wicked, toothless grin again.

"Oh, Tori. Malech was never the World Breaker. *You* are. And you are going to have to break this world open if you want to save the man you love." And with those words, I watched as she crumbled into nothing but dust.

Thank You For Reading

Thank you so much for reading my book. It's been such a journey not only for me personally, but I have loved watching Tori and Abraxas grow. They have so much more to get through, but I'm rooting for them.

I'm a self-published indie author, so if you enjoyed this book, please leave me a review. Reviews are what allow us indies to even try and compete with the big-name publishers. Any amount of time you spend on it is greatly appreciated.

I cannot wait to continue Tori and Abraxas' story, as well as the story of many others in the world of Adimos. We have so much more to discover about this world, and I hope you will join me for it.

Preview

Please enjoy this preview of Book Two of the Ember's of Magic Duology, *Rising from Flame and Starlight.*

Chapter 1

Abraxas

Six Months Ago

The mist I conjured had worked beautifully. Not that we had really needed the advantage against Niata. They had been caught completely unaware, the Long Peace making them compliant. *Fools.* But perhaps it was a blessing. It would allow us to hit their main defenses with minimal casualties.

I shouted at Commander Avlyn, but it was unnecessary. Avlyn had been running the army for decades, while I sat on the throne and strategized. Besides, I trusted them implicitly.

The last of the troops departed the boat, and I followed. I stepped off the gangplank to the rocky shore, and it was as if the world had tilted on its axis, the sky becoming the sea. The moment I touched the land of the Pearl Kingdom, a great force had wrapped itself around my heart, around my very soul. I could feel it sinking through me, like a golden tidal wave that removed everything that I was, and replaced it with something else. Someone else. *Her.*

I saw it then, flashes of her. A hand gripping the cliffs around the beach, pulling herself up. A scroll full of scribbles and doodles, a tutor looking on in disappointment. A pair of swords danced against an opponent, who was quickly disarmed. Human children, running around and through her skirts, and a soft laugh from her lips.

I clutched my chest and fell to my knees. My breath caught, and I coughed, trying to force air to my brain. "Abraxas, what's wrong?" Avlyn ran to me, a hand on my shoulder. I let them help me up, then pushed them off.

"Nothing. I need you to lead the army today."

Their face still held concern, but they rolled their eyes, "Wasn't that already the plan?"

"Yes, but I will rejoin you later." Their face showed confusion now, but they nodded and turned to return to the front of the ranks.

I didn't know where I was going, but my body did, as if she were a siren luring me in. I ran to her. My mind kept showing me more flashes. Younglings running through the rainforest, chasing after each other with sticks. Her sneaking through the kitchens at night, gathering up sweet rolls. A book opened before her, as the moon shone in through the window.

I passed through the main gates of the castle complex, which hadn't even been closed before my troops blew through them. I turned my back to a secluded alcove, getting my bearings. But my mind had caught up with me. *This can't be happening*. Centuries ago I had given up that I could have a mate. There were no dragons left, I would have felt them. No clutches of eggs were hidden anywhere, and even if there had been, no one to care for them. Any that would have been hidden away would have perished by now. And certainly, my mind wasn't showing me images of a dragon, but of what appeared to be a fae female.

But then, from the sea, a great volley of Emperor Hadeon's lightning projectiles fired at the castle, and with a crash that shook the very earth, struck one of the main towers of the castle. Another image came to me, but this one felt more vivid. Her being pulled away from the window, looking at the collapsed wall of the tower that I was now viewing from the outside. *There you are.*

I moved then. But the images were coming faster now, uncontrolled, as if the magic that connected us had been pent up for too long. Some were indecipherable, others manageable. Dancing feet sweeping across the floor. A dark room, where she hugged her knees and cried. A handsome half-fae male laughing, and then a moment later, that same man grinning as he gripped her breast and she rode him into oblivion.

My feet stopped as rage burned me from the inside out. It had been centuries since I'd allowed the beast inside me to awaken, but now he threatened to completely overpower me. I gripped the wall beside me, trying to regain control, my fingers piercing into the stone, when an unsuspecting cohort of Niatan soldiers appeared before me. Unfortunate for them.

Even I could barely keep up with my movements. In under a breath, half of them were already dead on the floor. The rest struggled to draw their swords and find defense ranks, but they were already far too late. Two more breaths and they were all gone.

Blood ran down the edge of my sword, dripping like the ticking of a clock. The beast inside me was satiated with blood, at least for the moment, but I had to keep moving. Another vision came, of a room overturned, and a voice whispering, *the tunnel in the kitchens.*

Avlyn surprised me, their hand on my shoulder again, "Your Highness, there hasn't been much resistance, we have favored capture over bloodshed." They looked over my shoulder at the very dead cohort at my feet, but kept a stony face, "We have located the prince. I'm sure the king and queen won't be far behind. We haven't yet found the princess. What are our next steps?"

"The kitchens, bring your cohort and meet me there." They let the confusion show on their face, but again, did not question me. They raised their hand and waved the cohort forward.

It was simple to find the kitchens, as if the building had seared itself into my mind. Half of the entryway had already collapsed, and we filed in. The building was quiet, as if holding its breath, waiting for the next move. We made our way to the back, when a cohort clad in silver mail charged us from a side hall.

I didn't have time for this, I needed to find her, now. I cut through the men in front of me, clearing a path when I felt her. That golden thread pulled taut and my head snapped up. She was the most beautiful creature I had ever seen. Her magenta robes were incredibly fine, embroidered with the white peacock of the royal family. They were covered in dust and disheveled, revealing the warm skin of her shoulder. I followed that perfect line up her long neck to slate eyes that blazed with rage. For a moment, she held my gaze, and I swear the entire world stood still. But then she ran away, and the beast inside me longed to give chase.

And then I was lost to him, my sword cleaving through every man in my way, my feet moving of their own accord. I could feel it, her fear as she ran, and how delicious it would taste on her skin. How satisfying it would feel to sink my talons and fangs into her, claiming her over and over again until the only sound from her lips was my own name. *She was mine.*

I whipped around the corner and saw her duck behind a hidden wall panel. I approached, ready to rip it straight off the wall, when that golden thread around my heart pulsed. It wasn't gentle either. It gripped so hard I fell to my knees again, my body frozen.

I tried to catch my breath, get my heart beating again, when I heard through the panel, "Princess Tori, what are you—"

My suspicions were confirmed, and it wasn't good news. She was the very princess I had been sent here to capture. My mate, whom I had waited centuries for, had given up hope for, was the very person my greatest adversary wished to sink his own claws into.

Avlyn and the cohort rounded the corner, "Your Majesty, why have you come back this way?"

"Commander, take the cohort and find the King and Queen. I'll finish up here."

It seemed that Avlyn couldn't hold themselves back anymore, "Abraxas, what's going on? This erratic behavior isn't like you. What about the princess?"

My teeth ground at the very mention of her, "I'll take care of her, you follow my orders, Commander."

They nodded, and led the rest out. I circled around the hallways, listening, when a loud crash came from behind a door. I listened, and I could hear her directing the human servants with her. But then the roof shook violently, and I threw open the door and reached out with my magic. It wasn't elegant, but I managed to grab her out from under the collapsing rubble at the last moment. She pushed herself up, and I couldn't resist her any longer, "There you are, Princess. I've been waiting for you." Waiting lifetimes, waiting even when I had given up all hope. My soul, which I had thought long gone, had just been in a deep slumber, dreaming of this moment when it would finally be completed.

But I saw her eyes fill with unmitigated hatred as she beheld me. That anger she held found a focal point, and I knew that if I gave her half a chance, she would destroy me. But the ceiling snapped again, and the whole building came down. I threw my magic out again like a net, trying to stop her from being crushed.

It half worked, and after the rubble had settled, she lay unconscious but she would survive.

I pulled the bricks and beams off of her, and gathered her up in my arms. Her breathing was steady, even if blood dripped from her head and she was bruised. She seemed so breakable like this, almost calm and serene. But as I held her, listening to the beautiful sound of her strong heart, I knew mine wouldn't survive it.

None of this made any sense. She was fae, and while I had pretended to be one for so long I had almost forgotten, that's not what I was. Fae didn't have mates, only dragons did, and she was no dragon. I pulled out my dagger and held it to her throat. She was breakable, weak, and if I let her live, that's what I would become as well. I could end this all here, just remember it as a cruel dream, fate laughing at me one more time.

Fate had taken my mother and father, along with every other dragon in this world. It has taken my people, and in the process, my soul. It had taken almost all of my magic, the only thing I still had to cling to remind me of what I once was, and with that, it had taken the sky from me. Now it dangled this last piece of hope in front of me, distracting me from the revenge I had allowed to shape me for these last centuries. I tensed my muscles, to pull that blade through her skin and feel her warm blood as the life left her. But I recalled that fire in her eyes, her fearlessness, and I knew I was only fooling myself.

"You will be my undoing, won't you Princess?"

Acknowledgments

First and foremost, I must thank my wonderful husband for all the support he has given me throughout this journey. Without you, I could never have done this. Thank you for letting me spread my creative wings, and for giving me the space to work on this story. You will always be my go to map-reviewer.

I also want to thank all my friends who willingly (or unwillingly) read my first drafts and helped me improve this story. Special shoutouts to Laura, Callie, Vanessa, and Jessica for being my first fans.

And finally, to the Writer's Nook Discord Group, I wouldn't have made it without all of you. Thank you for the sounding board, talking me through crazy ideas, beta reading, and all the memes.

About the Author

Ava has been writing stories since she was a child and has the handwritten notebooks filled with (terrible) stories to prove it. A shocking number contain morally grey love interests and badass women.

When she isn't writing, she can be found spending time with her husband and her two small children in the American Southwest, where she will talk your ear off about water conservation and sustainable living if you will let her.

Made in the USA
Las Vegas, NV
21 November 2023